Praise for *Bitt*

★★★★ 'This sparky debut puts the classic comic book origin story through the pop-cultural blender by gifting superpowers to a kid who just happens to be a massive sci-fi geek. For Smallville, substitute Tref-y-Celwyn, the mid-Welsh town where vowel-deficient teenage loner Stanly suddenly discovers a talent for flight and telekinesis. Accompanied by a potty-mouthed beagle (just go with it), Stanly up, ups and aways to London, where he throws his lot in with a bunch of Generation X-Men investigating a series of sinister child abductions. Zippy prose keeps the story barrelling along, the genre references come thick and fast (even the dog a Yoda impression does) and, in Stanly, Mohamed has created a hero you'll really root for. A flying start.'
—PAUL KIRKLEY, *SFX Magazine*

CHILDREN'S BOOK OF THE WEEK
'Never mind writing about superpowers, debut author Stefan Mohamed clearly has them himself - he's produced a highly original novel for young adults that is clever and funny, with characters you want to ask home afterwards.'
—ALEX O'CONNELL, *The Times*

'It's part superhero fantasy, part comedy, with an underlying love story and a creepy twist in the tail, all served up with panache, pace and punch.'
—SALLY MORRIS, *The Daily Mail*

Praise for *Ace of Spiders*

'Mohamed does everything right: the realistic tone, leavened by humour, is pitch perfect, as is the portrayal of Stanly as a precocious but vulnerable teenager. The plot careers from one dramatic set-piece to the next, with plenty of clever pop culture references along the way, before closing with a thrilling denouement. And Daryl the talking dog is an inspired creation.'
—ERIC BROWN, *The Guardian*

★★★★★ 'Doing what so many sequels fail to do, *Ace of Spiders* soars, with a thrilling plot, brilliant character development, and fantastically funny cultural references.'
—LUKE MARLOWE, *The Bookbag*

★★★★★ 'Old enemies mix with new enemies mix with Stanly's own shortcomings and frustrations to create an explosive mix of plot twists and revelations that had me gasping in shock, or running to hide behind the sofa.'
—JEN GALLAGHER, *Medieval Jenga*

'A rollicking good ride that I flew through and now desire more. This is impressive, entertaining, addictive stuff.'
—JACKIE LAW, *Neverimitate*

★★★★★ 'The long-awaited follow-up to Stefan Mohamed's brilliant *Bitter Sixteen* has arrived. And it's just as good as its predecessor.'
—*If These Books Could Talk*

STEFAN MOHAMED is an author, poet, occasional journalist and full-time geek. He lives in Bristol, where he does something in editorial. Find out things you never wanted to know about him at www.stefmo.co.uk

ALSO BY STEFAN MOHAMED

NOVELS
Bitter Sixteen (2015)
Ace of Spiders (2016)

NOVELLAS
Stuff (2014)
Operation Three Wise Men (2015)

STEFAN MOHAMED

STANLY'S
GHOST

LONDON

PUBLISHED BY SALT PUBLISHING 2017

2 4 6 8 10 9 7 5 3 1

Copyright © Stefan Mohamed 2017

Stefan Mohamed has asserted his right under the Copyright, Designs
and Patents Act 1988 to be identified as the author of this work.

*This book is sold subject to the condition that it shall not, by way of
trade or otherwise, be lent, resold, hired out, or otherwise circulated
without the publisher's prior consent in any form of binding or cover
other than that in which it is published and without a similar condition
including this condition being imposed on the subsequent publisher.*

This book is a work of fiction. Any references to historical events, real
people or real places are used fictitiously. Other names, characters, places
and events are products of the author's imagination, and any resemblance to
actual events or places or persons, living or dead, is entirely coincidental.

First published in Great Britain in 2017 by
Salt Publishing Ltd
International House, 24 Holborn Viaduct, London EC1A 2BN United Kingdom

www.saltpublishing.com

Salt Publishing Limited Reg. No. 5293401

A CIP catalogue record for this book is available from the British Library

ISBN 978 1 78463 076 8 (Paperback edition)
ISBN 978 1 78463 077 5 (Electronic edition)

Typeset in Neacademia by Salt Publishing

Printed and bound in Great Britain by Clays Ltd, St Ives plc

Salt Publishing Limited is committed to responsible forest management.
This book is made from Forest Stewardship Council™ certified paper.

To Agent Ben, for the frankly ludicrous levels of faith

????????????????????????????????????

'WHERE'S TARA?'

Kloe nuzzles into my neck. Her hair has dark blue streaks today. I point straight up with a sleepy smile and Kloe's eyes follow the gesture. She laughs when she sees her, our little girl, red and blonde against the summer sky, chasing clouds, raining giggles. I've always got one mental eye on her, just in case. I know she'd never fall, but even if she did, it'd be fine. I'd catch her.

Kloe walks two fingers across my bare chest and I shiver. The grass is slightly damp beneath us, cool and full of oxygen, the lake ripples contentedly, alive with the tiny sporadic splashes of playful fish, and the trees sway meditatively, tall enough to tickle the sky, the forest's low chant echoing between them. Whispering.

'What are we going to do today, then?' I stroke Kloe's head.

'I foresee more of this.'

'Cooool.'

Whispering again. I'm sure that it's the shiver of the trees, of leaves in the wind, but I'm also sure I can hear the suggestion of words. I can't make them out properly, though, so I ignore them. A yawn rolls out of me and Kloe catches it and yawns too. Above us, Tara's joyful laughter is like escaped memories, finally free . . .

Help us . . .

I

I shake my head. 'I'm hearing things. First sign of madness, isn't it? Or is that talking to yourself?'

'One or the other.' Kloe smiles. 'But you're a bit late for that, I'm afraid. You've been knitting with only one needle for a *long* time.'

I laugh and grab her and we roll over on the grass and everything's perfect.

Except it isn't. The wind has a steel edge and I can definitely hear voices, scratchy and blurry but growing more and more insistent. *Help us.*

Shadow . . .

The story-book sky has dimmed. I wasn't aware of it happening, it's just . . . grey now. Tara is still flying but her laughter is faint. I stand up and Kloe asks me what's wrong, but her voice has lost clarity. I look at her, she's there, I can touch her, but she doesn't feel right.

'I don't know.' My voice doesn't sound right either. The sky is granite, smothered by cold cloud, the trees still as charcoal pictures, the lake a sickly green murk.

Help us.

It came from behind me. I spin around but there is nothing there. I *know* the voice. The voices. All the same but all different. I reach for Kloe but she's not there. I call for her but she doesn't answer.

Shadow . . .

I look up and yell Tara's name. I can still make out her shape, just about, but the definition has gone. *Help us.* I try to fly to her but I can't, my wings have gone and so has the sun. Night snarls down, the stars bound and gagged and stashed away. *Shadow.* I scream for Tara but my voice doesn't come and she's not there anyway, I know she isn't, she's gone and my stomach is filling with pain, as though burning hot liquid is being poured in from somewhere. I double over. I feel like I'm losing bits of myself. *Help us . . . it hurts . . .*

A voice from another life murmurs *shimmers in the forest* and for a second I'm surrounded by beings made of pure, translucent blue. The agony is rising, snapping, boiling, seeping through pores and coiling black tentacles around my body, dragging me down. *Help us.* I'm lost in the dark, lost, drowning, thrashing around in living water, but no, it's dying around me . . . screaming . . . no air . . . I'm fighting to get to the surface but I can't, and through the blue and silver I can see a black shape and I want to scream but my mouth and throat are full of dying water—

Help us—
Shadow—

PART ONE

Chapter One

I OPENED MY eyes, in a manner of speaking. Actually, it was more like they were opened for me . . . although I couldn't feel it happening. I tried to move, but couldn't. Tried to speak. Couldn't. It was a familiar non-feeling, not that that made it any better.

Freeman? Is that you?

I became aware of my surroundings. A cramped public toilet, grimy walls sweating away the dregs of old posters, a general shiny stickiness to the floors and sinks. I tried to look down at myself, tried to raise my hands, but nothing was responding. I couldn't even blink. It was like I was a camera, being watched by somebody else.

The shimmers . . .

Things started flooding into my brain, which was a relief in one way because it meant that my brain was still working. In other, very important ways, it was the absolute opposite of relief. I was suddenly swamped with images: Kloe and Tara, alone in the woods. Eddie, broken beyond repair. Connor's furious face. Sharon's tears. Daryl's angry, bloodstained muzzle. Freeman disappearing back to a ravaged, devastated London, triumphant. Me, saving the scumbag's *life*. Overwhelmed by memory and feeling but with no mouth to scream, no eyes to cry . . .

What exactly the hell kind of fresh hell is this, then?

I thought Freeman's name with as much ferocity as a

non-specific ineffable presence could muster, but there was nothing. No indication that he was there or anywhere nearby, no suggestion of thoughts exerting their control over me. Just me, floating, disembodied, like a ghost . . .

Something made me turn towards the main door, just as it opened. A man was standing there. Tall, spindly, greasy-haired, leather jacket, gun. He gave no sign that he'd seen me. A toilet flushed and I turned again, against my will - if the concept of my will even meant anything now - to see a cubicle door open. If I'd been able to, I would have gasped.

It was me.

He was several years older, his hair longer, face a little more weathered, but he was definitely me. He stepped out and turned and I turned with him, and the tall stranger raised his gun and fired three times. I swung back, crying out silent-ly, watching bullets thump brutally into my own chest. The impact knocked him backwards and big dark poppies of blood spread across the dirty wall behind him. The wounded Stanly collapsed to the floor, gasping, clutching at his wounds, and I kept staring, unable to even consider doing anything else.

What am I seeing?

The gunman walked towards the other Stanly. Smiled.

Levelled his weapon . . .

Then Stanly looked up, with a look in his eyes that I knew well, even if I'd never exactly seen it myself.

The man's gun arm dropped to his side. He struggled, trying and failing to raise it, while the wounded Stanly got unsteadily to his feet. The older me closed his eyes, making a real effort to concentrate, to control his heavy, rasping breaths, then jerked painfully as three bullets exited his chest in a cloud of red spray and fell to the floor with a high, cheerful jingling noise. Through his torn T-shirt, I saw his wounds close, bloody, brutalised flesh becoming smooth, unblemished skin.

Stanly opened his eyes.

He smiled again.

The man with the gun had just enough time to make a disbelieving face before he flew backwards, as if he'd been yanked by an invisible rope. He smashed straight through the door and crashed to the ground outside on a bed of splintered wood, groaning. Stanly, giving no indication that he'd been even mildly injured, dusted himself off and walked past me.

What—

The thought didn't have time to complete itself, because suddenly I was somewhere else. Desperately, I tried to bring my racing, disconnected mind under control. I needed to think straight. I was not in the shimmer world anymore, submerged in the living lake. I supposed that this could have been a series of crazy dreams, theoretically, but shimmer dreams didn't feel like this. There I dreamt of serenity, of Kloe and Tara, peace and quiet and beautiful flight. Comforting, soft-focus lies. This was categorically not like that.

Plus, I couldn't really think in there. Not properly. And I certainly didn't experience grief, the gnawing animal pain currently lurking at the back of my cognition, waiting for its moment to break through and claim what rightfully belonged to it. Memories desperate to escape . . . and not in a joyful way . . .

Think, damn it.

I was trying, but at the same time I couldn't help but take in this new place, because it was fairly stunning, like a digitally spruced up watercolour painting of someone's idealised dream of the countryside: soft green hills and fields unrolling in every direction further than I could see, dotted with proud and majestic trees, a staggering view drenched in sun . . .

Then my view tilted downward . . .

Oh.

Monsters. Hundreds of them, all different. A centipede longer and fatter than a London bus. A shifting mass of black goo, limbs forming and un-forming with a grotesque slurping sound. Unholy combinations of bear, insect and asymmetrical shape. A huge armoured cockroach with tentacles sprouting from its back. *There are always tentacles.* A purple dragon, a five-legged rock man, several undulating black serpents with wickedly curved spines. Spiders.

There are always spiders too.

And at the centre of this ring of monsters, one small figure, in a fighting stance.

Another me.

WHAT—

A series of staccato flashes: a desert, with a younger me, barely fifteen, blasting a line of tanks into the sky with a thought and a giggle—

A hospital ward, a sea of vicious injuries, burns and blood and protruding bone, and an older bearded me, mid-forties perhaps, sitting by a low bed, eyes closed. He was healing the patient who lay there, horrific mottled black and red scars receding—

A city street at night and another me, thirty-odd, viciously beaten, bloodied, reaching out . . . to *another* me. A *younger* me. Something was happening, I couldn't see it but I could *feel* it, even in my non-anything state, *power*, glowing in the older me, rising in the younger me, as though one was inspiring it in the other, turning it on like a light switch—

WHAT THE WHAT—

Now flying, far above the ground, so high that the world was just an indistinct blur of colour. There was someone else flying a little way below me, arms outstretched, rolling and laughing. I caught a glimpse of his face a couple of times, not that I needed to. This Stanly was in his twenties and had bits of blonde in his dark hair, which was pretty odd.

Yeah, this was all standard operating procedure before, but blonde highlights? Yeah, they really tip things over the edge. However will—

SHUT. IT.

I waited for the inevitable attack, flying monsters or fighter planes or a giant robot version of my old headmaster or whatever trippy bollocks I was expected to endure next, but none came. I just floated in the air, watching my other self having fun, falling with style.

Great. I can remember Toy Story.

All is not lost.

I kept threatening to break down, or the non-corporeal equivalent of breaking down, because Eddie's face kept coming back to me, cut to shreds, lifeless, with Connor's voice saying *your fault your fault your fault* over and over again, even though he'd never actually said it, at least not to my face, but I forced it away. If and when the time came I could mourn Eddie, miss those who I'd left behind, punish myself for allowing Freeman his victory.

Right now, though, I had to work out what was . . .

Unless . . .

I would have slapped myself in the forehead if I'd had a hand. Or a forehead.

The shimmers live in another dimension.

Something tore me out of it.

And now I'm flashing through other dimensions.

The concept of things making sense didn't seem like something I could rely on at the moment, but that idea felt plausible. I hadn't really entertained the notion that there were other worlds, other universes apart from mine and the shimmers'. I'd not exactly had time to ponder it extensively, but I'd sort of assumed the shimmer world was a kind of underworld, something very definitely attached to mine. A sort of Hell, though with more skyscraping beasts, surreal upside-down forests and evil lakeside soliloquies and less fire and brimstone.

Not technically a soliloquy, it was more of a conversation.

Thanks for that. You're doing a bang up job today, brain. I should keep you on full time.

It made sense that there were more worlds. That was a thing, wasn't it? Many-worlds theory?

So I was seeing alternate versions of myself. Other Stanlys with powers.

The Stanly below started to dive, becoming a speck within seconds, and even though I had no stomach I felt an echo of that delicious lurch, the beautiful mania of remembering *I can fly, I'm ACTUALLY FLYING RIGHT NOW,* one of the best of all possible feelings . . . and with it I felt an anger, a *rage* that I wasn't in charge, that something, whether that was a sneaky unseen presence or just some bonkers consequence of extra-dimensional physics, was robbing me of my agency. I wanted to be *flying,* not just floating here like psychic mist babbling a hysterical director's commentary that only I could hear.

You're not really the director though, are you?

Seriously brain, don't make me come in there and—

Oh shut up.

HOW ABOUT YOU SHUT UP. I. Want. To.

FLY!

There was no pop. No flash. But that command, that *desire*, and the desperation behind it, had done something, because I was a person again. I was solid!

I was whole!

I was . . .

Plummeting through a freezing sky in hilariously inadequate hospital pyjamas, pounded by ferocious winds, limbs flailing.

Screaming my lungs out.

It was *amazing*.

All right. Let's punch it.

I took command. Felt my power, felt myself return to myself. Brought my descent under control, pulled up, flew.

Yes.

Yes!

YE—

NO!

I was gone again. Incorporeal, insubstantial, floating in yet another new place that I didn't recognise. This time it was a snowy city, all wonky neon and dilapidated buildings, mournful and neglected in the night.

This was starting to get pretty tiresome. *Listen,* I thought, trying to think loudly and authoritatively. *If there's someone doing this, show yourself. Please. Hello? Freeman? Is it you? Don't give me more reasons to kill you. Hello? Hello? HELLO? Shit.*

Another me walked past and I followed against my will. He was about my age, bundled up in a long grey coat and a silly red hat with furry ear flaps.

No. Ignore him.

Instead, I concentrated on *me*. My self-image. My legs, arms, face. I concentrated on my voice. On the feeling of being able to speak. The feeling of using limbs.

Maybe being anaesthetised in the shimmer lake had made me like this?

How long had I been there?

I pictured myself fighting, laughing, running, kissing, eating.

I imagined those feelings. Tried to translate the physicality into something mental, so my brain could really taste the memories.

Tried to break through, *force* myself into reality.

Tried so, so, *so* hard.

It didn't work.

AAAAARGH! Bloody let me out, you buggering shitweasel! Whoever you are, let me out or you're going to be really fucking sorry!

I could have laughed at the stupidity of that thought. For one thing, I had no idea whether someone was actually doing this to me. And for another, I didn't feel like I was going to be making anyone really fucking sorry about anything any time soon.

I managed to break out of this before.

By flying.

I tried picturing myself flying again, forgetting everything else. Just flight. *Flight.* I conjured the memories, bathed in them. Nothing. This was the prize jewel in the crown of frustration. I'd *managed* it before. I'd freed myself. And I knew the thought, the feeling that had done it, I knew it in the abstract, but I couldn't quite visualise it properly. Couldn't bring it to the forefront. It was like it was hovering *just* out of reach . . .

If someone is messing with me, you'd better hope I never find you.

If it wasn't a person doing this, though . . . maybe I was just collateral damage? Maybe the release of power when the shimmers had died – *if* they had died – had sent me screaming off, flying through parallel universes, an intangible ball of consciousness?

Maybe I'll settle down at some point?

Maybe I'll land somewhere and it'll be normal?

It happened once, it can happen again . . .

Although that might mean interacting with another version of myself. I wasn't sure I was ready for that. And might it cause a paradox and destroy the space-time continuum?

I really wish all my science knowledge didn't come from films.

The latest me had stopped on a deserted, snow-caked street, as though waiting for a bus he wasn't terribly bothered about catching.

Except he wasn't waiting for a bus. He was waiting for . . .

These guys.

Five men emerged from the shadows, all clad in black and variously armed with knives and guns. They all looked mean. Oh . . . and two of them were women.

This new Stanly stood, watching them come.

'I've been waiting for this,' said one of the women.

OK. Come on. Time for the big fight scene.

Stanly raised his hand. 'Don't fight me.'

The five assailants were immediately still, their expressions glazed, limbs floppy.

'Drop your weapons,' said Stanly.

They each dropped their weapons.

'Forget about me, and the House of Bird.'

Seriously? The House of Bird?!

C'MON . . .

'Go home. Be nice to your partners. Sleep soundly. Wake up as better people.'

All five nodded, turned and went their separate ways. Stanly watched them go, smiling to himself, then melted into the darkness.

Holy crap. Jedi mind tri—

Chapter Two

—ick.

I was somewhere else again . . . but immediately, something was different.

No, *lots* of things.

I felt warm.

I could blink.

I was . . .

Physical.

'I'm here,' I whispered. My voice made a sound. Real. A real voice. 'I'm *here!*' I yelled.

I'm—

Oh God—

A tsunami of nausea, as though every cell in my body had gone from sober to blackout drunk in less than a second. I dropped to my knees. My limbs felt like paper. I vomited and so did my brain, raw power spewing out of my head, and I heard the sound of a tree snapping in half and immediately threw up again, falling sideways onto the ground - *grass* - spasming violently, gasping, drawing my knees up to my chest.

Wh—

Wha—

What—

What t—

Seen this—

I've seen—

This—
Before—
CONTROL—

I'd seen empowered go through this, waking up from shimmer-induced slumber, unable to control their power. I'd been *responsible* for it. The pain in my body and head, the sickness, was bad enough, but there was other pain too, memories, emotions, flooding in. I'd been aware of them before when I'd been floating around: grief for Eddie, fear of what had become of my other friends, shame and fury about Freeman and what I'd allowed him to do, but the thoughts had been abstract. Now they were hitting me physically. This was too much. No way could I cope with this, come back from this, no . . .

No.

You WILL deal with this.

I squeezed my eyes shut and tried to think around myself, think a cocoon. Tried to bring my breathing under control, calm my racing pulse, stop the trembling.

Concentrate.

CONCENTRATE, YOU PATHETIC WASTE.

I opened my eyes again but everything swam. *Oh God, no.* I slammed them shut again.

Feel.

Smell.

Listen.

Where . . .

It was definitely grass beneath me, warm and springy. Fresh. Alive. Countryside? I could feel sun beaming down. No voices, no vehicles. That was lucky. At least I hadn't materialised in Piccadilly Circus, or in the middle of a war zone or something.

Come on, kid. Calm down.

I tried to remember what I'd done to help those wretched empowered and do it to myself, turn my own thoughts inward, bring myself in for a soft landing. After a little while I even risked opening my eyes again and this time I could actually see properly. I was lying in a flat, grassy clearing surrounded by trees, the uppermost branches and leaves haloed with sunlight, baby blue sky beyond. The grass smelled damp and lush. Springtime smells. I drank it in. Smell helped.

Smell.

Touch.

I gripped the grass and my whole body tingled. Amazing how much I'd learned to miss my other senses when I'd been without them for . . . how long? I had no idea. I'd barely had time to get used to them again when I'd reappeared in the sky above that one world. This whole thing, this weird trip, felt as though it might have been going on for twenty minutes . . . but God knew what it had done to my sense of time.

I managed to sit, then stand. My legs were weak, but not as weak as they thought they were, and I took a few exploratory steps, avoiding the sick I'd produced, which was not a healthy colour.

I'm hungry.

Maybe—

Wait—

Someone was coming through the trees and I didn't have time to think about hiding. I doubted I could have moved quickly enough anyway, in my current state. They'd definitely seen me now.

They . . . she.

A girl.

She was my age, give or take a year, olive-skinned, her brown-blonde hair pulled back into a dreadlocked thicket, and she wore big mud-caked boots and a functional brown and green outfit that looked like the sort of thing you'd wear while out hunting. This made sense, because she also carried an elegantly curved longbow and a quiver of arrows slung across her back.

Holy tights. I've gone back to Robin Hood times.

The girl stopped a safe distance away and eyed me with healthy suspicion, although gratifyingly she didn't immediately reach for an arrow.

'Um,' I said. 'Hi.' My voice was like stagnant water.

'Hello.' Her voice was mostly neutral with a slight edge of suspicion.

She speaks English. Cool.

'Um,' I said again.

Her eyes dropped briefly, taking in my dirty bare feet, hospital pyjamas and no doubt sickly complexion. 'Have you escaped from somewhere?'

'Kind of.' I realised what she was implying. 'Oh! You mean like a mental institution? No! I'm not an escaped mental patient.'

That got an unimpressed laugh. 'Well, you would say that, wouldn't you?'

'Yeah, fair point.'

OK, so she thought I might be a mental patient. Which means this could be my world. And it implies twentieth century at least, rather than Robin Hood times.

Why the bow and arrow, then?

The girl stared at me as though unconvinced that she could trust a single word that came out of my mouth. I didn't blame her. Then she glanced away and her eyes fell on the tree I'd broken. 'What . . .'

Oops.

'Sorry,' I said. 'I didn't mean to.'

She frowned. '*You* cut my tree down?'

Her tree?

'Not exactly.' I moved towards her but she took a few corresponding steps back and – *balls* – reached for an arrow. Even though I knew I could break it in half before it reached me, I froze and raised my hands. 'Woah! No need for that. Sorry, I'll stay right here. Look . . . don't worry. I'm harmless. Really.'

'That sounds like the sort of thing someone who wasn't harmless might say.' She positioned the arrow on the bow, although she didn't point it at me. 'And you just told me you *accidentally* cut down my tree.' Her frown deepened. 'Where's your axe? Hidden axe also implies you might not be harmless . . .'

'No axe.' I spread my hands further apart. 'Promise. I'm absolutely *not* an axe murderer.'

She laughed. 'You're not from around here, are you?'

'Kind of . . . not.'

'Then you don't know how ridiculous that is.'

'What?'

'The idea that I'd be at all worried about meeting an axe murderer. That would be far too interesting.' She put her head on one side. 'Are you all right? Do you need help?'

'Really . . . not all right,' I said. 'I . . . do you have a drink, by any chance?'

She nodded.

'Could I have a bit? I don't have any diseases.'

'Every time you say you aren't something, or that you don't

have something, it sounds like you actually are that. Or do have that.'

'Sorry.'

She put the arrow back in its quiver and placed her bow reverently on the ground, then reached into her pocket and withdrew an unmarked bottle full of clear liquid. She tossed it over.

'Water?' I said.

'Vodka.'

'Really?'

A sardonic tilt of the head. 'No.'

I opened the bottle, sniffed it to be sure and took a gulp. Water had never tasted so tasty. I drank as much as I thought was polite before throwing it back. 'Thanks.'

'You're welcome. So . . . you're not from around here.'

'No.'

'But you've lost your shoes.'

'Yes.'

'Where *are* you from?'

'I . . .' What the hell to say? 'Tref-y-Celwyn?'

'Where's that?'

'OK, never mind. London?'

She shook her head. 'Sorry.'

She spoke English like someone from England. A modern someone, too. And she seemed pretty intelligent. But she hadn't heard of London. Which meant that I was definitely, one hundred per cent, in a parallel universe.

Probably.

I sat down heavily, making her jump. 'Do you need me to call a doctor?' she asked. She sounded more concerned than suspicious now.

'I don't know. Maybe.' I put my head in my hands. The initial nausea had faded, leaving just a general upset stomach feeling, but I was starting to feel a very severe kind of mental vertigo. I imagined that it was a delayed reaction, as I hadn't exactly had the necessary tools to process dimension-hopping before. I almost wished I was intangible again.

'I could take you to one?'

'No thanks. I don't think I do need a doctor, actually . . . I need . . .' I decided to hedge my bets. 'My memory's a bit . . . gone. In places. Where am I?'

'You're near Dramawn.'

'Dramawn . . . that's a town?'

'Yes.'

'In which country?'

'Cwmren.'

'Cwmren.' It sounded like the Welsh word for Wales, but a bit different. 'OK. Um . . .'

'You're really strange,' said the girl, smiling as though she'd found some unattractive but scientifically fascinating plant life.

'Thanks.'

'And I probably shouldn't be talking to you.'

'Probably not.' I tried a smile of my own. It felt weak. 'My name's Stanly.'

'Senia,' she said, after a few seconds' hesitation.

Senia. Not an English name. 'Pleased to meet you.' I held out my hand. After a second she held out hers, but before we could shake I disappeared again.

Sigh.

More flashes. That desert again, except now I was looking at a statue, hundreds of feet tall . . .

A statue of *me*—

Sky. A jumbo jet, engines aflame, spiralling down, closely pursued by . . .

Guess who—

The valley of monsters, older me fighting off swarming beasts . . .

OK I GET THE PICTURE—

Green. Trees. Blue sky. And . . . I could feel. I could move.

I was me again.

I dropped to my knees and threw up yet again. Physically, that is, and with no accompanying release of power, which was probably a good thing. There wasn't a great deal left for me to throw up, admittedly, but what was there seemed to need to come up.

Composure regained, I stood up and looked around, wiping my mouth. I was back in the clearing where I'd met Senia . . . and there she was, walking towards me. She was dressed differently, but she still had that suspicious look on her face. More importantly, she was pointing her bow and arrow at me.

'I wondered if you'd reappear,' she said.

'I . . . disappeared?'

She nodded.

'Sorry,' I said. 'That was . . . I didn't do it on purpose.'

'My theory was right,' said Senia.

'Theory?'

'That you'd reappear today.'

'Today? You mean . . . what do you mean? How long have I been gone?'

'A day. Twenty-four hours exactly.'

What. The. Shit. I shook my head. 'I . . . I'm sorry. I really haven't got a clue what's going on. I'm as confused as you probably are . . .' I frowned. 'Hold on . . . why did you come back?'

Senia looked baffled. 'What do you mean?'

'I mean . . . I appeared out of nowhere, accidentally knocked down a tree, said a lot of weird nonsense, then disappeared. Weren't you freaked out?'

'"Freaked out"?' She said it as though she'd never heard the phrase, which I guessed was plausible.

'You know. Scared?'

'A bit. Hence . . .' She nodded at her weapon.

I laughed. 'What, did you think I was a demon or something?'

She gave me an impressively sarky look. 'What do I look like? Some sort of primitive?'

Ouch. Is it OK to say 'primitive' like that?

Maybe they don't have PC in this world.

'To be fair,' I said, *'you're* the one pointing the bow and arrow.'

Senia took a few seconds to think, then lowered her bow. 'Seemed sensible.'

'Probably. So . . . why did you come back?'

'Mysterious boy appears and vanishes minutes later?' Senia smiled properly for the first time since I'd met her. 'Then reappears at the same time the next day? It's like a story! Why *wouldn't* I come back?'

Ordinarily that might have made me laugh, but it just made me hear Freeman's voice in my head, sneering about stories. It reminded me how pathetic he'd made me feel. How he'd taken something I loved and . . .

Forget it. Forget him.

For now.

Also . . .

Hold on—

'Aaah!' I jumped to my feet and Senia recoiled in shock, one hand going instinctively towards her arrows.

'What?' she said. 'What's the matter?'

I'd felt something. It prickled the back of my neck, disturbing my blood, like a pebble tossed into a lake. A force, beneath everything else. Power.

It was going to happen again.

'I'm going to disappear,' I said. 'I can feel it coming.'

'Could you feel it before?'

'No, this is the first time . . . and I'm *not* going again. Screw this. I've had enough.' I gritted my teeth and gripped the ground with my bare feet, feeling the grass, the solidity beneath, thinking *no*. I concentrated on the trees and the sky around me. I was in charge and I wanted to stay here. *I'm in charge.*

I'm in charge of me.

I could feel it, though. Like a current, when you swim out further than you should have, that inexorable tug, pulling you where it wants you to go. I could feel no design underneath, no personality, no emotion. Just the tug.

Maybe it *was* natural, after all.

That scared me a lot more than the idea that someone had been doing it to me.

I felt myself begin to fade.

No. Not going. NOT GOI—

OK. Maybe going.

I was still physical, which was a relief, but I wasn't in Senia's world anymore. I was standing on the beach in the cave of shimmers, a tiny speck in their vast, scarlet citadel of alien rock. The lake, which should have been a deep, dream-like blue, glowing with unknowable life, was black sludge, and the cave was thick with a repulsive smell of rotting and wrongness. It made me gag.

So they are dead.

I was sorry. It was awful. I hoped there were more of them, somewhere.

But I hadn't killed them. I hadn't meant for them to come to any harm.

Just as they hadn't meant for any harm to come to my world.

So I owed them nothing, at least not for now.

I closed my eyes and thought *back*.

Back to the other world.

Back to the clearing.

I pictured the grass, the trees, the sky. I pictured Senia. I brought back the smell, the temperature, the taste of the air.

Recalled the conversation we'd been having.

Tried to find cracks between here and there, cracks into which I could slip psychic fingers, prise open a doorway . . .

Concentrated so hard that my temples began to pulse.

But nothing happened.

'*Damn it*,' I said. 'OK, whoever you are, how about—'

Chapter Three

'—you . . . show . . .' OK.

Cold.

Sharp underfoot.

Hold on . . .

I was standing on a mound of rubble which, on closer inspection, was all that remained of one half of a building. The other half was still standing, just about, although it looked dangerously close to collapsing. Hanging off the edge of one partially destroyed floor was a huge framed photograph that I recognised. A black and white image of London.

This was the Kulich Gallery.

I lifted a few centimetres off the rubble to avoid getting shards in my bare feet and floated down to the ground. Looking up at the gutted building made my stomach turn. It was simultaneously more imposing than it had ever been – the exposed brickwork, girders and wood looked like the teeth of some primeval beast – and weirdly forlorn. Where before there had been an electrified fence of some kind there were now big, solid barriers, more than twice as tall as I was, with coils of razor wire connecting smart-looking CCTV cameras. I couldn't see what lay beyond.

Is this home?

The building was obviously familiar, but after what I'd just been through I didn't want to assume that I was back in the right world. Maybe something similar had happened in a different one.

It feels *like home*.

I couldn't trust that, though. I rose up to peer over the barriers and saw two more layers of fences, some of which looked to be electrified, and plenty more viciously sharp razor wire. And beyond that . . .

I barely managed to stop myself before I hit the ground.

OK, deep breath.

Try again.

I floated shakily back up and looked again. Fences . . . razor wire . . . cameras . . . and then the river Thames, criss-crossed with bridges, some brand-new, some only halfway to completion . . .

And then the skyline.

A *new* skyline.

'This can't be home.' Saying it out loud felt safer than just thinking it. It meant that I believed it. Or that it sounded like I believed it, at least.

I'd seen plenty of devastation, but it had all been under cover of darkness, lit by otherworldly lightning and the glow of explosions. In a way, it hadn't seemed real. Now, in the light of day, it was like a boot in the gut. Many of the buildings were smashed husks, encased in protective webs of scaffolding and bridged by the arms of huge cranes, but some had already been fixed, to the point of being unrecognisable. Brand-new edifices of shining chrome and glass, like someone had plonked new buildings in there . . . even Big Ben had a new face. Similar, but different.

Different . . . like, why?

Either make it the same or . . .

I shook my head. More information needed. I zipped up and over the layers of fences and touched down on cracked concrete. It was, at a guess, February, and a raw breeze rustled its way under my pathetic hospital pyjamas. I looked down at them, ill-fitting around my legs and ending well above my ankles, and at my bare feet, which were pretty filthy at this point. 'Wow,' I said. 'What a state.' I giggled. It wasn't a healthy sound.

Right.

Come on.

Let's go.

I walked away from the gallery towards the street where we'd once parked my parents' car, with an Angel Group heavy locked in the boot. Last time I'd seen that car I'd been psychically hurling it at a huge slimy monster. It felt like mere hours ago . . . but it also didn't. I didn't really know *how* long ago it felt like. I didn't even really know how I felt generally. I was making a major effort to keep calm, to breathe normally, to think clearly, to be in the now. What was I doing *right now?* I was trying to find more information. For the moment, all that other stuff, other universes, other Stanlys, it all had to go in a brain box, locked away, along with Eddie and Kloe and Tara and Freeman and everyone, every*thing*, else.

There were no cars on this road, but as I walked I saw that vehicles were passing across the junction at the end. Some of them looked normal, old, dented, rusty, but some looked . . . new. Generally bigger and shinier, but more streamlined too. Some of the traffic lights were also different. Curved and grey, rather than boxy and black.

I don't like what I'm seeing.

A high mechanical whistling noise made me look up, just as something white zipped overhead, travelling incredibly fast. It looked familiar.

Drone?

I turned on the spot, looking around, checking the different corners of sky that I could see from here. Sure enough, there were more: sleek shapes, smaller than the ones I'd encountered in the past, zipping here and there, keeping a watchful eye.

I really don't like what I'm seeing.

I kept walking, emerging a few moments later on a street lined with businesses. Shops, cafés. Normal places. There were a lot of boarded-up buildings and several that were still basically ruins, propped up by scaffolding, but many were open. People were buying things. They were eating.

Where—

No—

WHEN—

NO—

I spun to my right, looking wildly around for someone to speak to. A middle-aged woman had just stepped out of a nearby shop and her eyes widened as she clocked me, her grip tightening on her shopping bags. I imagined I looked pretty terrifying, boggle-eyed and messy-haired in my hospital getup, stinking and shoeless.

'Excuse me!' I said. 'What's the date, please?'

The woman squinted at me. 'You what? It's Tuesday . . .'

'No, the *date*, please.'

Not the kind of question you want from a stranger looking like me. 'March,' she said, nervously. 'The fifteenth of March.'

Oh God.

Don't do this to me.

'No,' I said. And as the next words came out of my mouth I suddenly felt weirdly light. This *had* to be a dream, surely? Nobody in real life ever had to say the words I was saying, did they? This conversation I'd seen endlessly repeated in films and television series, this clichéd time-travel bollocks? Even this, telling myself that it had to be a dream, was so familiar. I was a dream me, or a fictional me wandering through a film version of my own life, some messed-up hyper-meta adaptation. Or whoever had taken me between universes was messing with me.

Surely.

'No,' I said again. 'I mean . . . what *year*.'

Haha.

Still in a story.

Always a story.

'Are you all right, love?' The woman, to her credit, was looking more sympathetic than scared now.

'Not even remotely. Please, what year is it?'

She said a year at me. I said it back at her. She said it again, but more slowly. I said it back at the same speed I'd said it before. I've never been the best at maths, but it still took an embarrassingly long time for me to work out how long it had been between the present as I understood it and the date I'd just been given.

I did realise, though, the penny dropping like a nuclear bomb, the mushroom cloud rising and spelling out the words MIND BLOWN in incandescent bubble writing, higher than the sky. Some time later I'd look back on this moment and think *wow, wish I could have seen my face.*

And her face when I vanished into thin air.

I fell to my knees on damp grass, body shaking, hyperventilating. Someone was speaking, using a girl's voice, who? I couldn't look up, just had to stare at the ground, ground, grounding

– *maybe if I hold on for a couple of hours I'll stop shaking* – gripping grass – *alliteration* – trying to think of any word but those two, don't think of those words, please, just look at the glass, the grass even – *oh God here it comes* – and now I retched, hard, like I was going to lose some organs. There didn't seem to be anything else that could come out at this point.

F—

No.

The voice, I realised, was Senia's. She was asking me what was wrong. What could she do. What was the matter. Her voice was far away, muffled, echoing . . .

Can't say.

Fi—

NO—

FIVE YEARS.

Oops.

Let myself think it.

I started to laugh. My body was fluctuating between feeling terribly heavy, *so* heavy, and utterly weightless, feathery, buoyant. I straightened up – *not flying right though haha* – and fell backwards in superduperultraslowmotion, down down down onto the grass—

No, not grass. Something hard. And wow. Noise. My hearing rushed back into my ears, bringing with it a cacophany of car horns, shouting, sirens. I sat up. I was on the bonnet of a car at the intersection where I'd been moments – *hours days FIVE YEARS* – ago. The road ahead was full of sleek police cars and black jeeps – *recognise those 'cept ooh they're a bit different* – and people in uniforms. Police uniforms. And . . . other uniforms. Smart, black. White As on the shoulders, like epaulettes. I swivelled and jumped off the bonnet of the car, landing unsteadily in the road – *ow my feet* – with the car's horn blaring at me, the driver gesticulating, shouting. A helicopter chugged overhead, flanked by a whole squad of white torpedo-like drones.

What is happening, please?

Voices. People with megaphones, shouting. Presumably at me. 'Stay where you are!' Guns cocked. Not everyone had guns, though. Some of the people in the black uniforms were just staring at me. Concentrating. I could feel power.

Empowered?

Empowered . . . police?

(*Stanly.*)

I spun. The voice was in my head . . . and I knew who it was. Lauren.

She was standing a little way away, her hair shorter, dark mahogany. Dyed. *Looks nice.*

What a thought to be having right now.

She was wearing one of those uniforms too, except the As on her shoulders were shiny and gold rather than white, and standing behind her was another woman, younger, twenty maybe, tall, black, her hair pulled back in a dark bob. She wore a similar uniform and seemed worryingly ready to attack . . .

Lauren wasn't, though. She was reaching out to me, smiling a reassuring smile.

(*It's all right.*)

Her voice in my head. Soothing. Like a warm sponge. Lilac scented. That's what calm felt like. Actual calm. Not weird numbness. Everything else, the voices, the noise, seemed to have melted away.

'Lauren . . .'

'It's OK,' she said. 'You're all right. You need to come with me.'

'Is this the right world?'

'Yes.'

'Prove it.'

She spoke, but in my head again. (*You're home. I promise. A lot of time has gone by, but this is your home.*)

'I said *prove it!*' I bellowed the last two words without meaning to and with them came a wave of raw power. The car I'd landed on jerked a foot backwards. Police stumbled. Fingers tightened on triggers. The other young woman moved towards me, but Lauren barred her way with one outstretched arm and she reluctantly hung back.

'Nobody fire!' Lauren yelled. Her voice was so commanding. I wasn't used to it. 'That is a direct order! Nobody does *anything* without my say-so!' She was talking to me at the same time, in my brain. It was confusing. (*Nailah told you about me. When we first met, I saved you from a soldier. Down an alley. Then you stayed with me. I cooked chicken. We practised with our powers. I played the piano. We travelled to meetings via the Tube. And once via the sewers. Then we carried out the attack, and . . . it went wrong. I got hooked up to the machines. You saved me.*)

No.

'No,' I said. 'NO—'

Grass. I fell gratefully down, flat on my arse. It was dry again now. I looked around. Senia was there at the edge of the clearing, running towards me. 'Stanly! Are you all right? Where did you go?'

She stopped a few feet away. I must have scared her before. Of course I scared her.

'Home.' The word sounded odd in my mouth. Like when you say a word loads of times and it loses all meaning, except I'd only said it once. 'What happened? From your point of view?'

'This is the fourth time you've appeared,' said Senia. 'The fourth day. Last time, yesterday, you were in shock . . .'

Yesterday? That was . . . like . . . ten minutes ago . . .

'Then I disappeared again?'

She nodded. 'And reappeared again today. Same time of day again. I was really worried.'

'Sorry,' I said. 'This is all . . . it's intense. Like . . .'

'It's all right,' she said. 'I can't imagine what it must be like . . .'

Haha.

Neither can I.

'Five years.' I'd already said the words multiple times. Thought them multiple times. But now, saying them out loud . . . that made them true.

I closed my eyes, clutched my head—

'There he is!'

My eyes flew open. I was back in the street, at the centre of the horrible chaos, police sirens and bright lights and helicopters and shouting, and Lauren was there, and that other woman, but before I could speak I felt something sharp in my neck and for about four seconds I felt incredibly stoned . . .

Then . . .

Then . . .

It seemed as though the flowers should have been wilting, but they stayed tall and bright, mocking the sombre room with their colours and perfume. The lady lying on the white bed, leaf-like hands flat on her blanketed stomach, something that could have been a smile painted weakly on her mouth with feather-light brush strokes, was too far away to notice them, but to the old man sitting next to her bed they were a chorus of insults. A rainbow-coloured choir of disobedient children, heartlessly intruding on this private, painful moment.

His hands shook and several of the flowers fell to the ground, severed at their stalks. His eyes flickered to the remaining flowers and they recoiled, shrivelling to dead brown skeletons.

The old man looked from the dead flowers to the lady on the bed and forced himself to respect her wishes.

Forced himself to let her go.

And, quietly, she died, comfortable and content and so far away.

The old man felt her pass, and wept. He wept for a long time, quietly and with dignity, the way elderly people do, and with every tear the dead flowers decayed further. By the time he had stopped crying they were barely more than dust.

He stood up and bent over the old lady. He whispered something in her ear, kissed her cheek, stroked her hair and turned unsteadily to the window. Then he closed his eyes and did to himself what she hadn't let him do to her. His skin flattened itself, absorbing its own wrinkles, re-distributing and removing them. Liver spots and other blemishes faded. He straightened up and muscles began to re-assert their dominance. Inside, his bones and organs changed, shrugging off decay and illness and decrepitude, and his sunken eyes began to shine again with youth. The process hurt. He could have stopped it from hurting but he chose not to.

The young man reached into his bag and removed a change of clothes. As he changed, he refused to look at the old lady in the bed. He had only ever seen her with old eyes. Now his eyes were young again and their memory of her would be as she had been. Young and smiling. Running. Alive.

The young man stepped out of the room just as a nuse arrived. He had seen her every day for weeks. 'Thank you for looking after her,' he said, with a smile. The quality of the smile was the only thing that might have suggested his real age.

The nurse's face creased in confusion. 'I'm sorry . . . who are you?'

'No-one. Goodbye.' The young man turned and walked away and the nurse stood shaking her head, certain that she must have seen him before.

PART TWO

Chapter Four

I FELT MYSELF begin to wake up, consciousness and unconsciousness still sloppily intertwined. I had a vague memory of cars . . . police . . . a clearing . . .

A cabin in the woods . . .

And . . .

Oh no.

I sat up, felt sick and lay straight back down again. I was on a hospital bed in a small private room, hooked up to various machines by long wires and sticky pads, surrounded by a general computer-ish hum and rhythmic bleeps and bloops that presumably represented my current physical state. Didn't sound too bad.

Must be faulty.

Sitting in a chair next to the bed was Lauren. She had short hair and wore black.

'Right,' I said, groggily, throat dry, voice cracking. 'Not a dream, then.'

'No,' she said. 'I'm sorry.'

Ignoring the nausea, I pulled myself into a sitting position and took a proper look around the room. Sickly green curtains drawn across the only window. One wall dominated by a wardrobe, the other by a huge painting of a serene tropical beach. For some reason, I felt as though there should have been dead flowers, an old man . . . *what? An old who?*

Dream?

Dream . . .

Like this isn't.

I glanced down at my arms. 'What's—'

'Don't worry,' said Lauren. 'We needed to monitor you, that's all. Make sure there were no adverse effects from the shimmers. Or from the tranquiliser.'

'Cheers for that, by the way.'

'We had to take you down quickly. I wasn't sure that powers would be enough.'

'And were there any adverse effects?'

'No.'

Good to know.

'We also removed the bullet we found in your shoulder,' said Lauren.

'Oh.' I glanced down at my shoulder. There was no sign that there had ever been a bullet in it. 'Actually forgot about that. Thanks.' I coughed. 'How long have I been unconscious?'

'Almost a day,' said Lauren. 'Seems as though you needed the sleep.' She smiled suddenly, as though she'd lost control of her face. 'Sorry, but . . . it's so strange. You don't look a day older.'

'Yeah.' There was a dispenser of water next to my bed and I poured a cup and sipped.

Lauren pursed her lips uncomfortably and her eyes fell to her lap. 'Sorry.'

I lay back again. My body felt so heavy, like a big bag of wet mash. 'So the world didn't end.'

'No.'

'What happened?'

'Shortly after you left us . . . maybe an hour . . . the monsters just faded away. Like they were never even there. It was eerie. They did some damage in the meantime . . . but it could have been worse.'

'Well,' I said. 'That's good.' *That is good. Sound like you mean it.* 'There was . . . I remember there was another big one. Did it . . .'

'It's been in and out of my nightmares ever since,' said Lauren. 'But we got it. It was sort of . . . stuck, halfway between, like the big green one. If it had been properly mobile . . . doesn't bear thinking about.'

I nodded. 'How is everyone?'

'Everyone?'

Don't make me go Gary Oldman on you. 'You know. Kloe, Tara, Sharon, Daryl. Skank. Connor. Everyone.'

'I don't know where Kloe is, I'm afraid,' said Lauren. 'I know she was OK, she survived, but that's all I know. Everyone made it.'

Apart from Eddie. Tears were queuing up for entry but I turned down their applications with extreme prejudice. 'What about Nailah? And my parents?'

'Nailah is fine too, yes. And as far as I know, so are your parents.'

How would she even know?

She's probably just trying to make me feel better.

It seemed as though a subject change might be appropriate. 'So you work for the Angel Group?'

'It's Angelcorp now.'

'Really.'

'Yes.'

'*Really?*'

'Really.'

'Terrible name.'

'It wasn't my idea.'

'Just awful.'

'Like I said, it wasn't . . .'

'Whose idea was it, then?' I asked. 'Freeman? He's in charge, I presume?'

She nodded.

I closed my eyes and gripped the sides of my limp, spongy mattress. *Don't psychically trash the room, demand to know where Freeman is, then fly to wherever he is and kill him.*

Yet.

'Stanly?'

Freeman's in charge.

Freeman won.

'I'm surprised,' I said.

'Surprised?'

'That I didn't come back to a full-on fascist police state. Sirens and searchlights and huge Big Brother-style posters of his face. Stormtroopers patrolling the streets, tasering dissidents. Although the drones gave me pause . . .'

Lauren looked confused. 'Well, the drones are necessary . . . but why would you expect a fascist police state?'

I opened my eyes. 'You what? Well, it's Freeman isn't it? We are talking about the same genocidal maniac, aren't we? Or is this just a hilarious misunderstanding?'

Also, the drones are 'necessary'? Wut wut WUT?

'Genocidal maniac?' Lauren frowned. 'He's not . . . I'm sorry, I really don't know what you mean.'

I was momentarily deafened by the clang of an awful penny dropping.

She doesn't know.

'Um,' I said. 'I . . . I think maybe my brain's a bit smushed.

44

From everything. Maybe it was a dream I had . . . sorry. Forget it. Babbling.'

Lauren still looked confused, but she nodded. 'All right . . . well. Yes, he's in charge. He took control of Angelcorp shortly after the monsters disappeared. Put procedures in place, processes, policies. Made speeches. Helped to soothe people's panic, the trauma . . .'

Trauma he was responsible for . . .

If she doesn't know . . . does anyone?

'What happened?' asked Lauren. 'Between you and him?'

'He hasn't told you?'

'It's classified,' said Lauren. 'And I got the impression that it was . . . difficult for him to talk about.'

Ha! Ha! My aching sides.

'To be honest,' I said, 'it's all a bit blurry. Cos of the shimmers, maybe? Or travelling back . . . scrambled brain . . . anyway, you were saying? After it was all over?'

She didn't believe my amnesia story, I could tell – possibly because it was painfully, laughably transparent – but she sighed and carried on. 'It was so strange . . . once we were sure that the monsters weren't coming back, that the atmospheric disturbances had stopped, obviously we had to rebuild. Not a small job. And people needed to heal . . . also not easy, with all this new knowledge, superpowers, monsters . . . things were on a knife edge. I thought there would be rioting, complete collapse . . . but there wasn't. Well. Some rioting. But . . . anyway. Freeman helped the captured empowered to recuperate, to integrate, and spearheaded the rebuilding campaign, in partnership with them.'

'*With* the empowered? They agreed to work for the Angel Group? After everything they did to them?' *I can't believe I'm hearing this.*

'More of them had volunteered than we thought,' said Lauren. 'To be hooked up to the machines, I mean. And the others . . . well, there were some who wanted no part of it. Some, it turned out, had been captured because they were dangerous. And . . .'

'What happened to them? The dangerous ones?'

Lauren fidgeted uncomfortably in her chair. 'They . . . they're safe. And people are safe from them.'

Jesus. That doesn't sound ominous.

'Without Freeman's leadership,' said Lauren, obviously keen to skip past this bit, 'and Angelcorp's knowledge and resources, London would still be in ruins. I mean, there's still lots to do. But it looks a lot better than you'd expect. The amount of rebuilding that's already been done should have taken ten, fifteen years. We've done it in less than six.'

Five and a half, if we're being nitpick-y. 'Good for you.'

'Angelcorp—'

'Can you just call them the Angel Group? For my benefit?'

'OK. Sorry. The Angel Group is part of the government now. Officially.'

'What? Like a political party?'

'Not exactly. It exists as a kind of . . . organisational framework. Law enforcement, transport, most of the big reconstruction projects, it's all co-ordinated by them. The government is in charge, of course, but Angelcorp is involved with practically every aspect of the decision-making process.'

'And people are happy with that?'

'People didn't have much choice,' said Lauren. 'The country was traumatised after the Collision. The *world* was.'

'The Collision?'

'The term we generally use. To describe what happened. You know. Two worlds colliding . . .'

'Oh.' *Bit generic.*

'Anyway, Angelc . . . the Angel Group stepped in and got on with it. Things are a lot better than we could have hoped for.'

'Fair enough.' *Or not. In fact, absolutely totally entirely ludicrously far from fair enough.*

'You have to bear in mind, Stanly, that they were pretty heavily involved with things behind the scenes before,' said Lauren. 'It's just that it's all out in the open now. And there's been surprisingly little resistance. Obviously not everybody's happy with it, but—'

I should bloody hope not. 'What about Morter Smith?' I said, suddenly remembering that joyful old pal o' mine. 'Did he survive?'

'He's still around, yes.'

'Working for Freeman?'

She nodded.

That made no sense, from several angles. Except . . . maybe it did. In fact, it probably filled in a major blank. Freeman must have used his powers on everyone. Made them forget. That was the only explanation, no way in hell would Morter Smith have agreed to work for him otherwise. 'Well,' I said. 'Nice to know murderous torturers and psychopaths get let off the hook if they can compromise with upper management.'

'What can I say,' said Lauren. 'I don't have much to do with Smith . . .'

'Lucky you.' I closed my eyes. Surely I was still dreaming? Still slumbering softly in that ethereal blue living lake? The shimmers had just got bored projecting my little forest paradise, tired of me flying with Tara, laughing with Kloe, singing under imaginary stars. They were having some twisted fun with me.

Surely . . .

'I'm so sorry you have to go through this,' said Lauren.

'What? Come back to a topsy-turvy nightmare version of my world that I have no place in? Pfft. All in a day's work.'

'It must seem overwhelming,' said Lauren. 'But when you've been here for a little while, seen how well things are going . . . there could be a place for you here. There *is*.'

'I need to see Kloe,' I said. 'I need to find her.'

'Stanly . . .'

'She'll have waited for me.'

'She—'

'She *will*. She will have waited.' I tried to fight the thought that was lurking. The knowledge. The *truth*.

That . . .

No.

Almost six years.

She'd be nearly twenty-four.

Of course she wouldn't have waited.

Wouldn't she?

'Please, Lauren,' I said. 'Before I do anything else, before this goes any further . . . I need to know where she is. Please.'

'OK. I'll see what I can do.' She got up and left the room and I lay there staring at the picture of the ocean, wishing myself there. Some dream ocean where nothing mattered, or maybe an ocean in a different universe, where none of the pain and confusion of this one could follow me. No people. No monsters. Just me and the sea.

No. Come on, kid. While she's gone, while we're having a break from earth-shattering revelations, let's absorb. Think. Review the story so far.

OK. I needed to at least vaguely rationalise all the crap that had been chucked at me. The fact that I felt like I could

48

do that was a minor miracle, or at the very least implied some severe emotional issues on my part.

Oh well. Waste not want not.

So I was back. I didn't know how, but *someone* was responsible. All that, however, the travelling, the other worlds, the other Stanlys, Senia's world, that was going on the back burner. There was nothing to be done about it for now. I needed to deal with what was right in front of me. Compartmentalise.

Hopefully I won't disappear again.

Or maybe hopefully I will.

One of my main concerns, at this point, was that I was probably in a lot of danger. Freeman wouldn't have been expecting this. He'd probably happily - *delightedly* - resigned himself to the idea that he'd never see me again. He wasn't going to be happy to find that I'd materialised unexpectedly in his new world, without the benefit of five and a half years of therapy and meditation to process my feelings towards him.

Or, y'know, mind control.

I had to assume that I was the only person who knew the extent of what he'd done. That put a fairly large target on my back.

So for now, I needed to keep it all to myself. Next to me, Daryl had known the most, and Freeman hadn't had him bumped off. That suggested that he'd messed with everybody's memories. Surely that was the only thing that would have stopped Connor from breaking the sonofabitch in half with his bare hands, stopped Daryl from tearing out his jugular a second time?

At least their ignorance meant that they were safe. I couldn't jeopardise that; what I knew was far too dangerous.

Although maybe it could work in my favour? If, as far as

everyone knew, there was no reason for Freeman to want to harm me, then perhaps he wouldn't? Killing me could draw suspicion . . .

So maybe I could make a deal with him.

If I don't decide to just murder the shit out of him, that is.

Jeez Louise. This is all a bit much.

Lauren came back after about twenty minutes and I could immediately tell that she didn't want to pass on what she'd found out. 'What?' I said.

'I made some calls.'

'And?'

'Kloe is fine. She lives in America.'

America. Wow.

'She's at Harvard.'

Harvard. Wow.

'She . . . she lives with . . .'

'A boyfriend.'

'I think so. A John—'

'I don't need to know his *name*, Lauren.' My guts felt like they were full of living shrapnel, gleefully churning everything up, slicing intestines and organs, mincing and dicing. 'Fucking hell. Why would I want to know his name?'

'Stanly, I'm—'

'Can you go away for a bit, please? Just . . . leave me alone.'

'OK. Call if you need anything.'

Call if I need anything.

LOL.

She left the room and I fell apart, because what else was I going to do.

Chapter Five

S OME TIME LATER, God knew how long, Lauren came
back with a tray of food. I'd cried myself dry – and hungry
– so I accepted it silently and ate.

'Do you mind if I stay?' she asked, gently replacing the
picture on the wall and pushing the wardrobe back into place.

I shook my head. The food was good, for hospital slop.

'Do you want to know about the others?' She closed the
curtains, retrieved her chair from the other side of the room
and sat down.

I nodded.

'Your parents are both alive. I checked just now. They live
in Tref-y . . . how do you pronounce it? Your old town?'

'Tref-y-Celwyn.' I was glad they were alive, so glad that it
made me warm. Whether or not I was going to seek them out
was another matter entirely.

Surely they'd want to know you're alive?

'And everyone else?'

'All in London,' said Lauren. 'We tried to recruit them but
they said no. Too painful, I think, after everything.'

Hmm.

'They're all active, though. Integration, rebuilding commu-
nities, getting things moving again, it's been complicated, as
you can imagine. Sharon and Connor are involved with several
big projects. Helping people recuperate, getting businesses
going, putting lives back together.'

Good for them.

'Tara still lives with her foster parents,' said Lauren. 'That's about all I know.'

Tara . . .

Shit on a Balrog.

'Sixteen,' I said. 'She's sixteen.'

Too weird.

Also, I'm going to need to have a word with those foster parents.

'What about Skank and Daryl?' God, I wanted to see Daryl so much. If anyone could help me through this, it was him. Lauren was doing her best, but behind her reasonable voice and business-like manner, there was a haunted emptiness. No matter how hard she tried to hide it, it was in her eyes, like she knew she'd been compromised. Like part of her had given up.

'110th Street was destroyed,' she said. 'Skank didn't rebuild it. Daryl lives with him, actually.' The thought of Daryl and Skank sharing a flat actually made me smile, which felt like a foreign concept, but one I could maybe learn to enjoy again, at some point in the far-flung future. *Yeah, round about the heat death of the universe.*

'And Nailah?'

'Also in the city. She runs a small independent newspaper. Mostly online, but they have a limited print run too. It's good stuff. Not exactly friendly to Angelcorp, but . . .'

'Cool.' I finished eating and put the tray on the table by my bed. 'By the way, where am I?'

'A private Angelcorp clinic. North London.'

'Is there a shower?'

'Yes.'

She showed me the shower and gave me my privacy. It

felt like I'd never showered before, and I spent a long time in there. It was, to state the blindingly obvious, cleansing. And when I cried again, my tears just became one with the water, which made it easier.

When I emerged there were clothes waiting for me: a pair of grey jeans, a white T-shirt, a black zip-up hoody and some skate shoes. There was also a toothbrush and toothpaste. I dried and dressed, grateful to be rid of hospital pyjamas – my disgusting five-year-old ones had thoughtfully been replaced with fresh new ones, but it still wasn't a look I was massively keen on.

I turned and caught sight of myself in the mirror and it gave me a jolt.

Who the hell is that guy?

Like . . . literally? Who?

Superhero, said one of the many voices in my head, in about the most contemptuous sneer my psyche could muster.

I gave my reflection an acid smile and brushed my teeth.

Lauren was waiting back in my little room. 'Thanks for the clothes,' I said. 'Did you pick them?'

'Yes.'

'Good picking.' She'd chosen clothes for me before, years ago.

Yeah, it's like poetry, sort of, they rhyme.

Shut UP.

What's wrong with your braiiiiin.

'Good.' Lauren looked nervous. 'Um . . . Stanly . . .'

'If that was you about to offer me a phone, and maybe a taxi, then yes please to all of the above.'

'Not exactly,' said Lauren. 'First, I really need to know how you came back.'

'Dunno. You don't have to worry about monsters, though. The shimmers are all dead.' I told her an abridged version of the story, leaving out most of the specifics of the other worlds. She was clearly fascinated, but I clearly wasn't up for an extensive post-mortem and she didn't push.

'So you can rest easy,' I said. 'No apocalyptic entourage. Were there any shimmers left behind here?'

'We've never found any. We assumed they all retreated to their own world.'

Wow. So they are *all gone.*

'I want you to know that I tried to get you out,' said Lauren. 'I agitated for years for us to work on a method of breaking back through to get you.'

'I imagine Freeman wasn't keen.'

'He said it was too dangerous.'

'He was right. But thanks anyway.'

Lauren nodded, suddenly uncomfortable again.

'Have you told him I'm back?'

'I haven't been able to get through,' she said. 'He's not in the country at the moment, I think he's in the States. But there's every possibility that he's found out anyway. He has eyes and ears everywhere.'

Well duh. I shrugged. 'OK. Well . . . can I go then?'

Lauren chewed her lip. 'I'm really not sure if I can, if I *should*, just let you out into the city . . .'

'I see where you're coming from, but I *don't* see how you can stop me leaving if I want to. I'm fairly powerful, as you probably remember.' *So is she.*

Yeah, but so am I.

'I could stop you,' said Lauren, mildly. 'Quite easily.'

'Are you going to?'

'I don't want to. But there are issues. You're not registered, for one thing.'

'Not *what*?' I gave her the full force of my most incredulous eyes. 'Empowered need to be *registered* now?'

'Of course,' said Lauren. 'We need to keep track of who has abilities. It's essential, if we want to maintain even a semblance of order.'

I didn't like it, but it did make sense. 'Well,' I said, 'I guess I'll pop down the post office at some point and pick up the relevant forms. For now, I'll just tell anyone who asks to give you a ring. Now, are you going to answer my question?'

'What question?'

'Are you going to stop me?'

'I don't want to.'

'That's not an answer.'

'I *could*, but—'

'Go on, then.' I moved towards the door.

(*SIT DOWN ON THE BED.*)

Her voice was in my head, as it had been before, but amplified to a massive extent. It went right through me, booming and deep, straight to my core, beyond, and before I could even consciously think about doing as she'd said – or disobeying – I was already sitting down on the bed. I frowned and stood up. 'What the hell? Was that—'

(*SIT DOWN.*)

Once again, I heard her voice everywhere. Not just in my ears but in my mind, my chest . . . and, most importantly, in my limbs. It was as though the request had bypassed Stanly and gone straight to Stanly's body. I frowned harder and tried to stand up, but Lauren thought-told me to stay sitting and I did so.

'All right,' I said. 'Cute trick.' It was something I knew, as well. Something I'd tried. Making soldiers sleep. Making people not notice me. This felt like a heavily levelled-up version, though, more like what I'd seen that other Stanly do. Stanly of the House of Bird.

I need this trick in my life.

'Sorry,' said Lauren. 'But as I said before . . . there's a lot that you've missed. There are more empowered now than there were before. They're living out in the open, able to use their powers. Which brings new challenges, new obstacles. New battlegrounds.'

She sounds like a trailer voiceover.

'Interesting.' I stood up. 'But now that I know what you're doing, I guess I just need to keep my wits about me. Not let my guard down.'

Lauren smiled at my cockiness. 'All right then. Sit down.'

She said it out loud but I still heard it in my head, and of course I obeyed. My frown became a scowl. 'OK, I didn't—'

'Stand up.'

I stood up. '*Enough.* I'm getting pretty f—'

'Don't swear.'

'—*fudging* tired of this.' I had to laugh at that one.

'Sorry,' she said. 'You just . . . need to be careful.'

'Clearly,' I said. 'If everyone can just mind control everyone now, it's got to be chaos out there.'

'It's not as easy as I made it look,' said Lauren. 'In fact, it's among the hardest psychic skills to learn, let alone master. Brains do not like to be told what to do by other brains, they reject it on a basic level. So it's a challenge. I've actually been quietly bypassing your defences for several minutes, I didn't just do it instantly on the spot.'

'Well, I suppose that's sort of good news. Mega creepy, though. Any tips?'

'It's much harder to do to a fellow empowered. Non-empowered are much more vulnerable.'

Freeman managed to get you though, didn't he? 'Right,' I said. 'Again, super creepy, but makes sense. *I'm* empowered, though. Pretty majorly. So . . .'

'It's also easier to do to someone you already have some sort of connection with. Personal, mental . . .'

OK. A hat-trick of creepy.

I wonder how many relationships have been totally ruined by this fun new pastime.

'Well,' I said, 'cheers. I'll bear all that in mind. Now can I go?'

'You can,' said Lauren. 'But there's one more important thing we should discuss before you go out.'

'Of course there is.'

'It's . . . a big thing.' She sat down.

Jesus.

What's she going to tell me?

Is someone pregnant?

Is there some sort of official league of superheroes?

Is Firefly *back on air?*

I perched on the edge of the bed, of my own accord this time. 'Go on.'

'The official story,' said Lauren. 'About what happened . . . that night. When the monsters came. It's different from . . .'

'From what actually happened?' *No way. I literally can't believe it except I completely can.*

She nodded. 'Very few people knew the real circumstances. It made sense to keep certain details . . . off the record.'

'What's the story, then?'

Lauren laid it out as quickly as she could. The Angel Group had been working with the empowered to stop the monsters coming through. It had been kept from the public for their own safety. There had been an accident, the specific details of which were classified. Monsters had come. Contingency measures had been put in place by various Angel Group personnel – and a few unnamed 'good Samaritans' – including Freeman, Morter Smith, Lucius and the dearly departed Pandora. Presto. New world order. My friends and I, to all intents and purposes, hadn't been involved.

'Lucius is still around, then?' I said. 'He wasn't Freeman's biggest fan, as I recall.'

'He's been one of his strongest advocates. He works for Angelcorp's US division.'

Wow. Way to totally betray your religious principles Lucius, you dick.

Unless he mind-controlled you as well, I guess.

'So what you're basically saying is that if I'm going to go out into the world, I have to keep shtum about what really happened,' I said. 'Not that I can remember everything . . . blurry, like I said . . . but I shouldn't waltz into pubs and restaurants or go on YouTube and announce myself as the saviour of humanity.'

'Basically,' said Lauren. 'Also, be aware that I will be keeping tabs on you.'

'Fine. Tab away.'

She reached into her pocket and handed me a very small, very shiny phone. 'This is yours. It has all the relevant numbers in it. Mine, Skank's, Sharon's.'

'Thanks.' I stared at the phone, feeling about as weird as I, or possibly anyone in the history of humankind, had ever felt. Weirdness in my life was a pretty fierce curve - *exponential?* - but this took the weird biscuit, blended it up in a weird blender with some weird milk and weird ice cream and made a weird milkshake, which was then force-fed to me through a weird funnel and—

OK, brain, you can be quiet now.

In fact, take the rest of the day off, if you want.

'The phone is your ID,' said Lauren. 'If anyone official asks, just show it to them. And there's some cash in the wallet, although people mostly pay for things with their phones too. Just so you know, I will be pushing for Angelcorp to look after you and help you get on your feet. As far as I'm concerned, they owe you. The world owes you.'

'Owes me.' I snorted. 'This whole thing is my fault.'

'No it's—'

'Forget it,' I said. 'Thanks for the phone. I'm going to call . . .' *Not Sharon. Can't speak to Sharon. Or Connor. Not yet.* 'Skank.'

'Of course.' Lauren stepped out and I successfully navigated the phone's overly oblique touch screen menu and found Skank's number.

Dialled.

Ring.

Ring.

'Yes?' Skank's voice.

A pathetic croak from me.

'Hello? Who is this?'

'Skank,' I said.

'Yes? To whom am I speaking?'

'Skank . . . it's me.'

'Who's . . .' He stopped abruptly. '*Stanly?*'

'Yeah.'

'But . . .'

'Yeah.'

'When . . . how . . .'

'I'll explain later. Promise. Is Daryl with you?'

'He's out at the moment . . .'

'Can I come and see you guys? I'll explain . . . but this is all a bit . . . kind of . . . peculiar. I need familiar faces.'

'Of course, of course.'

'Thanks. Text the address to this number, please. I'll be there soon. And Skank?'

'Yes?'

'Don't call anyone yet, please. Not Sharon, not Connor. Tell Daryl, if he gets back before I get there. But nobody else. I'm not ready yet.'

'Of course.'

'Thanks. See you in a bit.'

'Yes . . .'

I hung up and a few seconds later something appeared. A swirly text. It looked as though it was supposed to link directly with whatever map software was loaded onto the phone. Lauren poked her head around the door. 'You got through OK?'

'Yeah,' I said. 'He sent his address.' I handed her the phone and she did whatever needed to be done, although I imagined she probably knew the address already.

'It's quite a way from here,' she said. 'I'll get a car for you.'

Part of me wanted to go by myself, fly or something, but another part of me, a more sensible part, knew that was a stupid idea. 'OK.'

'Are you ready to go now?'
God knows.

London looked different. I'd already known that, of course. But it also felt different. Familiar buildings in various states of reconstruction, the Thames criss-crossed with sleekly anonymous new bridges to replace those that had been smashed . . . it was all as you might imagine it to be, although that didn't make it any easier to take in. Every now and then we'd pass a desiccated ruin, seemingly untouched but for some supportive scaffolding, and a chill would run up my spine as I imagined monstrous feet and fists caving in roofs.

Interestingly, the endless anonymous mirrored steel edifices that characterised central London seemed to be languishing at the bottom of Angelcorp's list of priorities. Many had had temporary steel webs erected around them, but it seemed more as a safety measure to ensure they didn't collapse – there were no work crews here. The busiest construction sites were around residential areas, shops, parks and transport links.

It was brighter than yesterday, warmer too, and our black executive car wound its way powerfully through the streets and over temporary roadways, following many, many diversions to avoid roads that had not yet been repaired. Our driver never once looked back and never said a word. The air conditioning was cool, the seats were some next-level leather, there was a TV and a fridge . . . the whole thing was too surreal to comprehend, which actually made it easier, in a way. I could just observe with a vaguely ironic feeling, smirking inwardly at how like totally bizarro everything was, yo. It meant that I didn't really have to process what was going on.

I probed a little bit, trying to work out how much Lauren knew. As far as she was concerned, Maguire *et al* had received some vague information that we'd all been far too willing to misinterpret, and some that was simply inaccurate, and the whole thing had basically been a horrible misunderstanding. Freeman was in no way culpable. No, no, officer, 'e's no villain, sir! He came up with the plan to *end* the Collision!

And I bravely volunteered to help. Yay for me.

I wondered if Freeman had immediately gone about the business of brainwashing my friends, or if they'd had time to consider striking back against him. It was all too creepy and infuriating for words, and hearing Lauren talk about my amazing sacrifice made me feel sick, so I decided to change the subject.

'How long did it take to get things working again? For people to come back?'

'Many never left. They didn't have anywhere to go. Those who did . . . it took a while. It was challenging. Central London took most of the damage, as you can see. There was obviously some fallout elsewhere in the city, isolated pockets, but . . . well, nothing big made it out of the centre, anyway. Not before you stopped it.'

'Right.'

'It wasn't just the physical damage, though,' said Lauren. 'It was psychological. I wasn't sure the place was *ever* going to be operating again. It still hasn't healed, obviously. And it took a lot of political manoeuvring to persuade any large businesses to touch the city with a bargepole. Pretty much all the really rich business people and property owners ran for it at the first sign of trouble, before the monsters even started to arrive, and many didn't come back. A large contingent relocated to

Birmingham, believe it or not. London is actually a more affordable place to live now. For, you know.'

'Normal people?'

Lauren nodded and laughed. 'Shame that it took an apocalypse for that to happen, but there you go.' She looked out of the window for a moment before continuing. 'But people feel an attachment to this city. A loyalty. It has so much history . . . and it's not like huge swathes of it haven't been destroyed and rebuilt in the past. This was slightly more . . . Biblical, I suppose. But I was still surprised.'

'By what?'

'People. I've always been pretty cynical about human nature, but people really pulled together to sort things out. Cleaned up. Helped each other. Everyone kept talking about the Blitz spirit . . . things aren't perfect, far from it. But it's better than anyone had any right to expect. And there have been wider changes. Throughout the UK . . . globally . . .'

Globally.

Woah.

'Might have to wait a bit before I start delving into the global side of things.' I watched a sleek new silver train glide over a bridge in the distance. Most of those I'd seen were the recognisably functional, cantankerous trains that I remembered, but this one looked like something from the future. 'What about the empowered? You said there were more.'

'Yes, lots more,' said Lauren. 'And not just those who were hooked up to the machines. New cases. The working theory is that all the otherworldly energy affected people's brains. Stimulated the process that leads to powers developing. Scientists are still trying to work it out.'

'What's the new policy, then? Or is it still lock 'em up

underground and hook them up to whatever machines you happen to need powering?' It was unfair, but at the same time I sort of didn't care.

'No,' said Lauren, patiently. 'Many were recruited. Most of them, in fact. That's partly why we managed to rebuild so fast. A combination of technology, money and superpowers. And sheer bloody-minded determination.'

Seems legit.

'Some chose to reject the power,' said Lauren. 'Unsurprisingly. After what happened, some felt that they were unnatural. Or just a horrible reminder of stuff they wanted to forget. So they opted not to use them.'

Also fairly legit.

I had more questions, but I decided to wait. Plenty of time. Although part of the reason I'd started talking was to drown out my own thoughts, muffle them with questions. I was still a long way from accepting the idea that Kloe was no longer mine.

She was never 'yours'.

Piss off. You know what I mean.

Or that Eddie wasn't going to be there for my return.

Obviously one hurt more than the other. Eddie's death was a death. Kloe was alive, at least. But the two things were inextricably tangled in my head. One immense, seething mass of pain.

Deal with it.

'There are things you're not telling me,' said Lauren.

'Oh?'

'Coming back, for example. You said something about flashing between universes.'

'Did I?'

'Stanly . . .'

'Can't explain stuff I don't know, Lauren.'

'But—'

'Plus, even if I did, why would I necessarily *want* to tell you? How do I know you won't just run and tell Angelcorp? Just because you've swallowed the Kool Aid doesn't mean I have to trust them too.'

'Thanks for that.' She looked away and I immediately felt bad. She didn't know what I knew. It wasn't fair.

'Sorry,' I said. 'I don't mean to be a dick. Just . . . I'm finding this all pretty hard.'

'I know.' She didn't look at me but her voice sounded softer. 'Things are complicated, Stanly. Sometimes compromise, sacrifices . . . they're necessary. Essential.'

'Hmm.'

'And you're right. I will have to report everything.'

'Well,' I said, even though I knew that had been a good cue to stop speaking. 'Your funeral. And my funeral. And everyone else's funeral, in every single universe.' I turned back to the window, staring out at what was to all intents and purposes a brand new city. 'How is Sally, by the way?'

'She . . . she's fine.' Lauren sounded taken aback. 'We're living together, actually. She's teaching.'

I smiled. Genuinely good news. 'Good. I'm glad. Be nice to actually meet her some time.' *She was kind of unconscious and freshly un-plugged from Smith's infernal machine before, after all.*

'Yes. I'd like that. I'm sure she would too.'

We didn't speak again until we pulled up outside Skank's house. Roughly half of the houses on the street looked like London originals and the rest were new. 'Thanks,' I said, awkwardly. 'I . . . do you want to come in too?'

She shook her head. 'No. I'll . . . no. Just call me when you're done. Or if I hear anything, I'll call you. And remember—'

'Stick to the rewritten version of history.' I nodded. 'Roger. See you later.'

I got out of the car and sniffed the air. Real air. Home air. Of sorts. I walked up Skank's path, butterflies in my stomach, like these were the last few seconds before going on stage – *haha going on stage like* Romeo and Juliet *which is actually something that happened in the same lifetime I'm currently living literally what the Christ* – and knocked on the door.

Skank answered almost immediately. He looked exactly the same and it made me want to cry my guts out and jump for joy. His beard still looked like someone had taken a pickaxe to a hedge and he wore a T-shirt showing a Borg reclining angstily on Freud's couch. And shorts and sandals, of course.

He was the same.

Thank God.

'Hi,' I said.

He just shook his head, exhaling slowly. 'Wow.'

'Yeah. Um. Are we huggers?'

'I don't know,' he said. 'My gut tells me yes.'

'Cool.'

We hugged and it was a bit awkward but also nice. Skank played a good strong hug game. 'Come in,' he said, leading me into the house and through to a pleasantly messy kitchen. 'Drink?'

'Coffee would be the best thing ever.'

'Yes.' He set about making coffee. 'Daryl isn't back yet. So he'll have quite a surprise.'

'Yeah. I guess it's not like you can text him or anything.'

That got a deep, dignified chuckle. 'No.' He looked at me. 'So. How's it going?'

I should have said 'same as always' and he should have responded with 'that bad, huh', but it didn't happen. 'Honestly?' I sighed. 'I haven't got a clue.'

'When did you get back?'

'Yesterday.'

'How?'

'Again, not a clue.'

Skank nodded slowly. 'Fair enough. Stanly . . . forgive me for being blunt. But I understood from what Daryl said . . . we haven't talked about it much . . . but I understood that were you to be released from the monster world, or wherever it was, then it would mean . . .'

'The end of the world again,' I said. 'Yeah, that's what I thought. But the shimmers are all dead. So that sorts that one out.'

'Dead? How?'

'No idea. They died while I was still in there.'

'Well,' said Skank. 'It's . . . very good to see you. And also good to know that you didn't bring a swarm of angry monsters with you.'

'Yeah. Always good to not do that. Just wish we hadn't been so keen to act on bad intel in the first place. The whole thing could have been avoided.'

Skank nodded. 'I can only apologise for my part in that.'

'It's not your fault,' I said. 'And at least . . . I guess . . . well, it sounds like Freeman has done a bang up job fixing things? Fixing our mess?'

Not a flicker. Just another nod. 'Yes,' said Skank. 'Commendable.'

Oh Skank. He got to you too. Trying to hide how much that confirmation cut, I tried a breezy smile. 'So. What have *you* been up to?'

The question was so hopelessly inadequate that Skank let out another chuckle. 'I have been . . . keeping busy.' He handed me a cup of coffee, sat back and started rolling a spliff. 'Trying to stay out of trouble. The shop was destroyed.'

I sipped the coffee. It tasted ridiculously good. 'Yeah, I heard. Sorry about that.'

'So was I. Lots of irreplaceable items lost. First editions, rare toys. Took me a while to come to terms with the fact that I'd never see my original rocket-launching Boba Fett again.'

'I feel your pain.'

'As far as tragic tales of the Collision go, it doesn't rate terribly highly,' said Skank. 'Luckily I still have a good chunk of my fortune, which has come in very useful. I've been helping Connor and Sharon out with their various projects . . . and I've been writing.'

'Really?'

'Yes. Science fiction, believe it or not. I've published three novels.'

'Wow! Nice one.'

'Thank you. They're not great literature. Potboilers, really. Throwback pulp stuff. But they were enjoyable to write, and they've sold adequately. The proceeds, such as they are, have all gone to charity endeavours in London. I also write for various websites. I'm entertainment editor for Nailah's paper, the *Sentry*.'

'Cool. And Connor and Sharon? How are they?'

'It took . . . time for them to recover,' said Skank. 'They're well now, though. We see each other regularly.'

'What about Tara?'

'I must confess that I haven't seen her for a while. None

of us have. She . . . went through rather a difficult patch at fifteen. She was angry with us, I think.'

Oh dear. I'd better go and see her ASAP.

Or should I?

'She'll probably be pretty angry with me,' I said.

Skank finished rolling his spliff and lit it. In my current state, the smell alone was enough to make me light-headed. 'With you?'

'I promised her and Kloe that I'd come back. And then I didn't.'

Skank looked uncomfortable. 'You made a sacrifice. She might not have understood that at the time. But now . . . I'm sure she does.'

'Guess we'll see.' I sat back in my chair and sipped my coffee. Skank seemed about to speak when I heard the front door open and I immediately stood up, my heart pounding.

Daryl didn't come into the kitchen immediately, but he started speaking anyway. 'You would not *believe* what just happened to me. Out minding my own business, the way I do, very demonstrably *not* shitting all over the pavement, and what do I get? A hail of abuse from some wheezing, jowly old baggage with a *cat* on a *lead*! To be fair to the cat, it looked mortified. But yeah, there she is, screeching away, *how dare I be out walking on my own! How dare I make my horrible messes on the pavement,* blah blah, disgusting creature, blah blah, oh yeah, what horrible messes are they then, love, cos I certainly can't see any, *why's that then,* oh yeah COS I KNOW HOW TO CONDUCT MYSELF IN PUBLIC UNLIKE SOME HUMAN SCUM—'

He entered the kitchen and the rest of the sentence died in his throat, cut off so abruptly it seemed as though there should have been a record scratch sound effect.

We stared at each other.

Daryl's jaw pretty much hit the floor.

I smiled pathetically. 'Hi.'

Chapter Six

'EVIL CLONE,' SAID Daryl.
  I shook my head.
'Evil android?'
'No.'
'Evil doppelgänger of any kind?'
'Not as far as I know.'
'Alien toxin-induced fever dream?'
'Possibly.'

Daryl nodded. 'OK.' Then he smiled wider than I'd ever seen anyone smile, human or animal. '*HOLY SHIT SNACKS!* He's back!'

I dropped to my knees and he ran over and I hugged him. He was solid and real and smelled just as he'd always smelled. Like home. A security blanket in dog form. I felt the threat of tears and forced them back, even though I knew they'd feel good.

'Christ, kid,' said the beagle. 'It's good to see you.'
'You too, Muttley.'

'I thought I smelled you, you know. Before I came in. I was *sure* I could. But I just figured I was imagining it. Cos I had to be imagining it. Cos there's no way you could be here.'

'That's nice, although the smelling thing you do is so weird.'

'You have *psychic powers*.'
'Fair point.'

After a while I drew back and looked at him properly. His

coat was a little shaggier and might have been lighter in places, but he was pretty much the same. 'You look good,' I said.

'Not as good as you, Lazarus Pitt the Younger.'

'Uh?'

'Wow,' said Daryl. 'Someone's lost their touch.'

'I got the Lazarus Pit bit. What was the other bit?'

'It was a historical reference to William Pitt the Younger,' said Daryl. 'You know history? Actual real-life history?'

Cough cough 'Robin Hood times' cough. 'I'm not familiar with this concept, no.'

'Evidently. Oh, and it was also a reference to the fact that you look younger than you should. Full disclosure, for something that came completely off the top of my head, a head that is currently spinning from your impossible reappearance, it was a *great* pun that worked on . . . oh, just so many levels.'

'I'm overjoyed for you.'

'Coffee, Daryl?' said Skank, as though what was happening was a pretty standard occurrence.

'God yes.' I sat back down and Daryl hopped up onto a stool. 'How?' he said.

I told them as much as I could. Daryl seemed as confused as me and Skank was beside himself with curiosity. Or as beside himself as Skank was capable of being about anything. 'I'd always wondered,' he said, shaking his head and stroking his beard. 'All different versions . . . possibly infinite . . .'

'Woah,' said Daryl. '*Infinite*? That's a bit much, isn't it? Not even Graham can count that high.'

'Who's Graham?' I said.

'Wow, I am on *fire* today. And you are practically moist with not being on fire.'

'What Stanly's describing fits with some multiple universe

theories I've read about,' said Skank. 'Some hypothesise that for every decision that is made, another universe is created. If you take all of the potential decisions being made every second by every person in the world, that means thousands, billions of potential universes being created every second.'

'All the worlds I saw seemed very different,' I said. 'Although to be fair it was all pretty brief and flashy . . . but if someone *was* deliberately taking me to specific worlds, I guess maybe they could have been skipping over all the worlds where everything's the same except I have a mole on my cheek, or Daryl doesn't smell really bad.'

'And there I thought I was pleased to see you,' said Daryl. 'Glad that's over with.'

'It's fascinating,' said Skank.

'It is,' said the dog. 'Also existentially terrifying to the *nth* degree. But honestly, I'm still reeling from the cool factor. You saw different versions of yourself with powers, fighting monsters and tanks! All this quantum physics malarkey is interesting, but why is nobody else shutting up and eating their awesome?'

'I don't notice you shutting up,' I said.

'Fine,' said Daryl. 'Don't join me on the joy train. I'll hop off at Killjoy Road and meet you back here at Oh No Let's Think Really Seriously About Everything Hill.'

'I don't remember you being this petulant and childish.'

'Your memory has obviously been affected by a five-year bathe in alien juice,' said Daryl. 'If you'll excuse the disgusting imagery.'

'Actually the whole thing was pretty pleasant, in a weird way,' I said. 'Meditative. Until I got back. Which has been pretty much the polar opposite of meditative.'

'I can imagine,' said Daryl. 'Well . . . actually I can't. At all.'

'It's OK, neither can I, to be honest.'

'So the Angel Group picked you up?'

I nodded.

'And they didn't want to chuck you in some super-person gulag?'

'Nope,' I said. 'Well, not yet, anyway.' I'd noticed he was using the old name. 'I see you're not down with the corporate re-branding either.'

'God, does it suck,' said Daryl. 'Sounds like a four-in-the-morning board meeting decision to me.'

'Lauren seems totally on board with what they're doing,' I said. 'I mean . . . I don't know. It does seem as though the rebuilding is going well. It's not exactly the totalitarian dys-topia I was expecting.'

'They *have* done a good job,' said Skank. 'They keep their methods and practices fairly transparent. Everyone knows the name Angelcorp. The trains run on time . . .'

'Sounds too good to be true.'

'Things could be a helluva lot worse, to be fair,' said Daryl. 'So . . . what actually went down? With you and Freeman, in the cave? Obviously I only got there right at the end. You know. In time to say goodbye.'

OK . . . interesting. 'I'm not really sure,' I said. 'The whole thing was so mind-scrambling . . . all the madness in London, and then the madness over in the shimmer world, and then . . . you know. Five years of dreaming. I guess he just explained how we could fix things. And I . . . did what I did.'

Daryl nodded. 'Yeah, figured. I'm sorry, kid. I wish I could have helped . . .'

'It doesn't matter,' I said. 'What *does* matter is Morter

Smith. He nearly tortured me to death, sort of, trying to find out where Tara was. And she's been living back in London for five years. He didn't try to track her down?'

Daryl shook his head. 'Nope. And last time I saw her . . . which, to be fair, was a while back . . . he still hadn't. Cross my heart.'

Mind control. Must be.

Fair play, Freeman. You've covered all your bases.

'How were they?' I said. 'Tara and Kloe? You know . . . after?'

The beagle shifted awkwardly on his stool. 'They . . . I mean, they were all right. Upset, obviously. I went out there myself. Found them, explained what had happened, as much as I could. They refused to believe it at first. I told them what you said.'

'Thank you.'

'Kloe went back to her parents, but Tara wanted to come back to London.'

'How much does she know?'

'Not much, really,' said Daryl. 'She definitely doesn't know that Smith is her father.'

So presumably she doesn't know that I thought I was her father.

Probably for the best.

'He's really never tracked her down?'

'Nope.'

I nodded. 'And it stays that way.'

'Seems like the best plan,' said Daryl. He sighed. 'I'm sorry I didn't do a better job of keeping in touch with them both. I tried, really. Tara wouldn't answer the door or the phone to any of us for so long, it just seemed like there was no point in trying. And Kloe . . . she wasn't . . . I think she just found the whole thing too difficult, you know?'

'Yeah.'

'Have you spoken to her yet?'

'I haven't,' I said, 'but Lauren's tracked her down. She's twenty-three. Living in America. With her boyfriend.' My voice cracked a bit. 'Good luck to her.'

'Are you not even going to tell her you're alive?'

'Maybe. Dunno what good it would do.'

'Mate,' said Daryl. 'That girl was absolutely *besotted* with you . . .'

'Look,' I said. 'Can we leave this alone for now? Still pretty raw.'

'Of course. Sorry.'

'Not your fault. Anyway. I think I'm going to call Connor and Sharon. See about going round there. You guys coming?'

Daryl nodded. 'Definitely.'

I took out my phone, looked at it for about an hour, then put it back in my pocket. 'Actually, could you call, please, Skank? I don't know if I can handle it yet.'

'Of course.' Skank went out into the hall and I stared at the table, wanting to say everything but not wanting to say anything. Daryl did a strange little whistling noise, which I presumed was his way of filling the awkward silence.

'Seen any good films while I was away?' I said.

'Yeah. Loads.'

'Good.'

'The Marvel Cinematic Universe has gone bonkers.'

'Cool.'

'They had to properly up their game once an actual attack of otherworldly monsters happened in real life. It's getting *weird*.'

'I bet.'

'Oh, also? Google "Chavengers" when you have a chance.'

'OK . . .'

Daryl glanced out into the hall to check that Skank was still on the phone. 'You do remember what happened, don't you?' he asked, in a low whisper.

All the hairs on the back of my neck stood on end. 'What do you mean?'

'I *mean*, it's for Skank's benefit, isn't it?' said Daryl. 'The amnesia act? You remember. Freeman caused the whole thing.'

Oh thank God. I nodded, unable to fight a huge grin of relief. 'How come *you* remember?'

'Turns out psychic brainwashing doesn't work so well on talking beagles,' said Daryl. 'Mine lasted less than a minute and then I immediately started remembering.'

'So he wiped everyone?'

'Everyone with any information about his part in what happened.'

'I guess that includes Oliver and Jacqueline Rogers.'

'Not sure,' said Daryl, 'but it makes sense. Kid . . . I'm so sorry.'

'For what?'

'That I haven't righteously killed the scumbag, obvz.'

'Not for lack of trying,' I said. 'You did sort of rip his throat out that time.'

'Yeah, but . . .' Daryl shook his head. 'I could have tried again. But once he'd made sure nobody could implicate him, he just . . . he let everyone get on with their lives. I felt like it was safer to keep it to myself.'

'For five and a half years?' I exhaled several balloons' worth of air. 'Jesus. How . . . I mean . . . wasn't that . . .'

'Not the funnest,' said Daryl. 'I've lain awake plenty of nights, meticulously planning detailed revenge scenarios. But I said I'd protect everyone. I promised you. This seemed like the best way to do that.'

I reached out and put my hand on his head. 'Thank you.'

'No worries, chief. Although it kind of begs the question . . . what do we do now?'

We didn't have any time to elaborate on that question because Skank had just come back in. He looked uncertain and guilty.

'What did they say?' asked Daryl.

'I spoke to Connor,' said Skank. 'He was . . . a bit bewildered.'

I wondered if I knew what was coming.

'And?' Daryl prompted.

'He . . . he's not sure about you coming around yet,' said Skank. 'I'm sorry.'

'Fair enough.' I sounded very calm.

'Um,' said Daryl, 'what the *shit?*'

'Stanly,' said Skank. 'You have to understand . . . it's been a while. They've tried to close the door on that whole time. Connor took Eddie's death hard . . .'

'He blames me.' *Great. Everyone remembers* my *part in what happened, at least.*

'Don't say that,' said Daryl. 'Of course he doesn't.'

'I don't think that's what it is.' Skank seemed to be choosing his words even more carefully than usual. 'And I'm not just saying that to make you feel better. Connor is—' He was interrupted by his phone ringing. 'Hello?' His eyes flickered towards me. 'Yes, he . . . really? But Connor . . . all right. All right. Yes. We'll be round soon. OK. Yes . . . yes. Bye.'

He hung up the phone. 'Sharon says we must all go round immediately.'

Daryl laughed. 'Good old Sharon.'

A warm bubble rose inside me and popped comfortingly. *Good old Sharon indeed.* 'Yeah,' I said. 'Great. Thanks, Skank.'

'Of course.'

Daryl jumped off his stool. 'Well,' he said. 'Let's go and have some kinda goddamn reunion.'

If things had felt unfamiliar north of the river, they felt even less familiar south. Untouched houses rubbed shoulders with scar-faced tower blocks, prefabricated shelters and half-rebuilt structures backing on to stacks of rubble, interlaced with substantially more green spaces than there had been before. So many gardens and vegetable patches, men and women carrying spades and brown sacks between large multi-level allotments and psychically hefting bricks and girders, in full view, as though it were nothing. There were also solar panels everywhere, glinting in the late afternoon sun.

As we walked, I noticed that Daryl wasn't at all worried about speaking loudly in public. He got a few strange looks, but nothing extreme. I suppose that after witnessing your city almost get wiped off the face of the Earth by giant monsters, a talking beagle probably didn't rate as high on the What-The-Fuck-O-Meter as it might have before.

I wonder how it affected people. Knowing that monsters are real.

I imagine they weren't all as chill as me.

Connor and Sharon had actually managed to upgrade to a nicer neighbourhood, taking advantage of the sharp post-Collision fall in rents. As Daryl had said, 'Subsidence and rising damp are pretty small potatoes compared to an army of Lovecraftian abominations descending on your property.'

As we neared their house, I felt anxiety rising, and took several deep breaths to keep it at bay. 'You OK?' asked Daryl.

'Not really.'

'I'm sure Sharon will have talked some sense into Connor.'

'It's not that.' It was partly that. The last time I'd spoken to Connor, we hadn't exactly been on good terms. I remembered the look on his face when we realised that Eddie was dead. When I failed to save him. The way he'd spoken to me when I'd threatened to bail on them.

Remembering my selfishness made me burn with shame.

'It's everything,' I said. 'It's been so long . . .'

'Gotta face the music and dance, kiddo.'

'Yeah.'

The front garden was immaculate, lush and bright with flowers and vegetables. I'd never known Connor or Sharon to be particularly green-fingered . . . I wondered if perhaps Sharon was green-brained. The thought of empowered people using their abilities to do something as mundane as growing vegetables . . . it was ridiculous.

Sort of fantastic, too.

Skank raised his hand to knock on the door, looking questioningly at me. 'Are you ready?'

'He's ready,' said Daryl.

Thank the flying spaghetti monster for that dog.

Skank knocked.

My heart climbed to the base of my throat in preparation.

Sweat prickled.

The door opened and there was Sharon. Her hand flew to her mouth and she made a strange noise, like a backwards sob.

I smiled my trying-too-hard smile, which was a close cousin of the smile I do when I know I'm in trouble but am hoping that everyone will just forget about it.

'Your hair's different,' I said. It was curly now. *Everyone's gone and bloody changed their hair.*

Except Skank.

And me.

And—

Hush, brain.

Sharon just stared at me, sunlight catching the tears in her eyes.

'It looks nice,' I said.

The hug she yanked me into was so fierce that it scared off any lingering doubt or dread, so I just closed my eyes and let the warmth rush over me. The whole time I was in her arms, everything in the world seemed fine.

'I can't believe it,' she whispered.

'Yeah,' I said, ineffectually.

After a while, Daryl coughed. 'Um. Shall we pop inside?'

Some might have thought that insensitive, but I was glad. It was starting to be a bit too intense. We laughed and drew apart and Sharon looked me up and down, smiling, her eyes glassy with joy and sadness and other things I wasn't sure about. I also couldn't quite tell whether she looked older or not. She certainly looked *different*, but . . .

'Well,' she said. 'Hello, young man.'

'Hiya.' I did my stupid smile again.

'In you come, then.' In we went. The place looked, smelled and felt like their house. I even recognised some of the pictures.

Sharon took us through to the kitchen and I locked eyes with Connor, who was standing by the counter looking like he didn't know what to do with himself. We regarded each other for several difficult moments. There was so much behind his eyes, so much between us. It was as overpowering as it had been with Sharon, but for utterly, painfully different reasons. I suddenly felt a bit sick. He was thirty now, if that, but he already had a few grey hairs and his face looked . . . I think 'careworn' is the word.

But I also noticed that he was wearing his fluffy werewolf slippers, which made me feel slightly better.

'Connor,' I said, trying a non-stupid smile.

'Stanly.'

I held out my hand but he rolled his eyes and pulled me into a hug. 'Bloody hell,' he said. 'You never stop surprising me.'

'I try my best.'

The hug ended and Sharon grabbed me for another one. To my surprise, we didn't immediately get on to another re-telling of my latest saga. Instead there was tea and Sharon produced two different types of cake and we ate and drank and talked about the most mundane things we could possibly have talked about, and at one point I looked around the room, from Skank, trying to brush crumbs out of his beard without anyone noticing, to Daryl, unashamedly licking his plate, to Connor, with his arm around Sharon, to Sharon herself, who kept half laughing and half crying, and even though the picture wasn't quite complete, and the world was insane and there were massively important things that nobody remembered, I felt utterly overwhelmed by one thought, which a few hours ago had seemed so far away as to be impossible.

I'm home.

Chapter Seven

EVENTUALLY THERE WAS a lull in the conversation and everybody started exchanging shifty glances. I pretended not to notice and cut a fourth slice of cake that I didn't really want, just so I'd have something to do, an excuse to avoid eye contact. But then Connor cleared his throat and my heart sank.

'So, Stanly—' he began.

'Connor,' said Sharon. Clearly, she knew what was afoot.

'What?'

'Maybe this should wait?'

Connor visibly restrained himself from snapping at that, which was not something I was used to seeing. 'I just have some questions,' he said. 'I'm sorry Stanly, I'm sure this is all pretty intense for you . . .'

'It's all right,' I said. 'Ask away.'

'It can wait,' said Sharon, 'if you want.'

'Honestly. It's fine.'

'There,' said Connor, only slightly belligerently. 'He says it's fine.' He put down his coffee cup. 'I was just . . . I guess I was wondering what your plan is.'

'My plan?'

'Yeah. Like, what you're planning on doing now.'

I glanced at Sharon. She looked unhappy. 'Um,' I said. 'Not really sure, to be honest. Haven't been back long.'

'I know. I'm just . . . I'm sort of . . .'

'Connor—' said Sharon.

'I guess I'm looking for some reassurance,' said Connor. Sharon's interruption seemed to have galvanised him; there was suddenly something very unpleasant in his voice. 'After what happened last time . . . are you going to be doing your . . . superhero thing again? Cos, basically, it didn't work out too well before. And to be honest with you, I don't really—'

'Connor,' said Daryl. 'You're being pretty confrontational. It's not really necessary.'

'Oh yeah?'

'Look,' said Daryl, clearly struggling to contain his own temper. 'What happened happened. Mistakes were made, by *lots of people*. And everyone's got to live with the consequences. *Including Stanly*. Now, we never thought we were going to see him again. And he's barely back five minutes and already you're implying that we're all at risk . . .'

'I'm not *implying* anything, but it's—'

'Bollocks,' snapped the beagle, losing his brief but valiant struggle. 'It's perfectly obvious that you think Stanly's going to put us all in danger, somehow, spontaneously, as though it follows him around, as though there weren't a hundred other factors at play before. And I'm getting the uncomfortable feeling that you'd rather wash your hands of him than have to deal with a shake-up in your —'

'Listen here,' said Connor, his voice rising. 'I never wanted anything to do with that fight, *Sharon* never wanted anything to do with it, *none* of us did, and he—'

'*He* did what he thought was right with the information—'

'You've got to be *kidding*, Daryl, don't pull that shit with—'

'Pull what shit? Eh, Connor? Which *shit* am I pulling, please do—'

'Daryl,' I said, before Connor could properly explode, 'you don't have to defend me. I appreciate it, but this . . . I didn't want this. I don't want to be fighting. Look, Connor, I don't know what I'm doing. I haven't got a clue. And I am sorry that you were . . . that I dragged you . . .' I lost my words momentarily and I could feel Daryl itching to leap back in, but I couldn't let him. I could feel his frustration, years of it, frustration every bit as legitimate as Connor's, and I couldn't allow the truth to slip out. If anything was going to put them all in danger, it was that.

'*But*,' I said, 'whatever you think of me, of how I've gone about things . . . whatever mistakes . . . I hope you at least know that I would do anything I could to protect you guys. To keep you out of danger.' *Hmm . . . the Prosecution would like to present Exhibit A, a cousin very much absent from this table.*

Thanks for that, brain. You're a real pal.

'Things don't always go according to plan, though, do they?' said Connor. 'For example, when we thought that Angelcorp were working to destroy the world, and we nearly ended up destroying it ourselves?'

'That's *enough*, Connor,' said Sharon. Her voice had taken on an unsettling harshness. It didn't sound right coming from her. 'Whatever happens, I trust that Stanly will do the right thing.'

'Well sorry,' said Connor, 'but I don't.' *Ouch.*

'You're bang out of order,' said Daryl.

'Oh am I?' said Connor. 'Well, forgive me if I don't hold a beagle's opinion in particularly high esteem.'

'I beg your f—'

'Connor,' said Skank, levelly. 'Daryl. Maybe you should both calm down.'

'I don't appreciate being told how to behave in my own house!' said Connor. 'And I am glad that Stanly is OK, I really am. But that doesn't change what happened. We made it through. We've built lives. And as far as I can see, if there's one thing, one person, who could upset that and send us all back to . . . sorry, Stanly, but I'm afraid that it's you.'

'You've got a fucking nerve,' said Daryl. 'Stanly's only *ever* tried to do the right thing, to help people, it's not his fault that—

'That what?' said Connor. 'That everything went so spectacularly, apocalyptically tits up that we—'

'I miss Eddie too.'

That shut everyone up. I got the feeling that his name wasn't mentioned very often. 'And I haven't had five and a half years to get over it,' I said. 'As far as I'm concerned, it happened yesterday.'

'Stanly,' said Sharon. 'Please . . .'

'I get that you're worried, Connor,' I said. 'And I understand why you don't trust me. But it would be nice if you tried to remember exactly *why* I haven't been here for five and a half years.'

Connor's face had gone red. It felt like a good moment to stop speaking, but sometimes your mouth just doesn't really fancy doing what it's told, does it? 'Or maybe you can't remember,' I said. 'I understand. Maybe the official story is better. Less complicated.' I stood up. 'Thanks for the cake and everything, Sharon. It's great to see you all. I'm going to go.'

'You don't have to,' said Sharon.

'I think I do,' I said. 'This feels like a pretty natural end to the afternoon. I'll see you soon.'

She nodded, blinking away tears. Connor didn't seem to be able to look at me.

'Bye,' I said to everyone, or to no-one, and left the room. Daryl followed me without a word, down the hall and out of the house, and I stood at the end of the garden path, looking at the unfamiliar skyline, playing a sort of game with myself. A 'how volcanically emotional can I feel on the inside while simultaneously not showing it at all on the outside' game. I was doing pretty well. I was going to have a job beating this particular high score.

'What an *ass*hole,' Daryl practically spat. 'What a stone-cold selfish motherf—'

'No,' I said. 'He's not . . . he just . . .' I couldn't think of anything to say.

Skank came out shortly afterwards. 'That was awkward,' he said. 'I'm sorry, Stanly. I honestly didn't think he'd be like that.'

'It's fine.'

'You can stay at our place,' said Daryl. 'Right, Skank?'

'Of course.'

'Thanks,' I said, 'but I think I'm going to call Lauren. Stuff to discuss.'

'Now?' asked Daryl. He sounded a bit hurt. 'Don't you want to come back to ours? You know, get a Chinese, watch some sort of violent sci-fi trash? We could have the bitching session to end all bitching sessions about Irish Troubles in there. And other stuff . . . there's loads to talk about . . .'

I knew what he wanted to talk about. Right now, though, I couldn't face it. 'At some point,' I said. 'But to be honest, I think I'd rather get on with . . . I don't know. Life admin, or whatever. If I sit and do nothing, I'm just going to stew.

And I've got a pretty big pot of stew to stew in. I'll call you guys later.'

'Are you sure?' said Skank.

'I am.' I managed a smile. 'Seriously.'

They weren't happy, but they accepted it and I headed off.

I didn't call Lauren, though. Speaking didn't really feel like a thing I was able to do.

Perhaps a walk in the park.

Do they still have taxis in the future?

The last time I'd seen Regent's Park, it had not been at its best. In fact, it had been a Hieronymous Bosch painting. Sky like you'd imagine the skies of Jupiter to be, alien storms spitting and swirling, spewing otherworldly lightning and misshapen creatures . . . and then in the park itself, the mother, mother-in-law and long-lost primordial grandmother of misshapen creatures. Bigger than giant. Tentacles and teeth, the whole nine eldritch yards. Tanks and guns blasting away, a few wannabe superheroes trying their best to help . . .

And then defeat from the jaws of victory. A plan well executed, a beast subdued . . . and just one *thwack* from one pesky tentacle . . .

I couldn't believe how different it looked now. It wasn't back to normal, not by any stretch of the imagination, there were still mounds of dirt and cordoned off areas, but the great blast crater from which that howling abomination had been trying to escape was almost gone. There was grass again. Trees. Benches. People were walking. *Laughing.* Like we'd actually won. This was why we'd fought, wasn't it? This was the reason?

This was why he wasn't here?

There was also a new lake and a great big tacky memorial fountain, guarded by stone cherubs and inscribed with the carved names of the dead. His was near the beginning, because of how the alphabet works. Eddie Bird. Not Edward. Eddie. It was Edward on his passport, on his birth certificate. But Eddie was who he was.

I stared at the name for a very long time, unable to quite bring myself to reach out and touch it, my stomach and chest taking turns to juggle with flaming knives that were too big to be juggled comfortably, so they kept scraping the sides.

He was there, at least. He was remembered.

I wondered where his grave was.

There was also a dedication, along with a line from some poem. When I saw who had written it, I felt sick. G. FREEMAN.

How dare he.

How bloody . . .

Hold on, 'G'?

Let the speculation commence . . .

After a good fifteen minutes of moody staring, I wandered off to a smaller adjacent play park and sat down on a swing, staring moodily at a group of kids horsing around. Within a few seconds, however, moodiness gave way to fascination.

Two were playing basketball with their minds, bouncing it around and through one another's legs, never once using their hands or feet, while the other two practised some pretty impressive gymnastics. One kept standing on his hands and then moving his hands to his sides so that he was suspended upside-down about half a foot from the ground, while the other kept running up the fence and back-flipping off, stopping herself before she hit the floor. Neither of them could levitate for very long or get much height, but that didn't matter to the younger kids sitting nearby, who laughed and cheered with each display of power. It seemed about as normal a scene as you could imagine. A city park in the early evening, kids enjoying the last gasp of sun . . .

Except these kids had superpowers.

I couldn't help but watch, transfixed. Obviously I'd already seen people using powers in the open, builders levitating materials . . . but this was so much more casual. Normalised. It was the first time I'd ever seen powers in this kind of situation beyond my own circle of friends, as though they were a part of the world, a fact of life. It was amazing. More than anything, I was surprised that adults were leaving them to it. I'd seen one or two distrustful looks from afar, which I guessed was inevitable, but there were no police to be seen. I couldn't even spy any CCTV cameras.

But then I heard the telltale whistle of a drone overhead and it all made sense. I didn't look up and was interested to see that none of the kids did either.

So superpowers aren't the only things that have been normalised.

I took out my swish new phone and rang Lauren. She answered quickly. 'Stanly? Are you all right?'

'I'm fine. I want to speak to him, please.'

'To . . .'

'Freeman.'

'I'm not sure I'll be able to get him. It might be better if you wait to see—'

'I'm not waiting for him. Put me through, please.' *Or I'll just turn up at his office and start making loud, violent demands.*

An exasperated exhalation. 'I'll try my best.'

'Thank you.'

I was on hold for well over a minute, the silence broken by the occasional click or buzz and underscored by the thump of my heart. I felt shaky and light-headed, as though I might fall off my swing, the hand that held the phone hot with sweat . . .

'Stanly?'

The bottom fell out of my stomach.

'I must admit, I wasn't expecting to speak with you again.'

He sounded . . . the same. Magnanimous. Almost avuncular. Or someone doing a pretty good impression of avuncular, at least.

'Hello? Stanly? Are you there?'

'You promised,' I managed to say.

'Yes?'

'You promised . . . to leave my friends alone.'

'I kept that promise.'

'I know. But you . . . no-one remembers.'

A pause. Then, 'No.'

I grimaced, gripping the phone so hard I thought it might shatter. 'I won't tell them. I won't tell anyone.'

'I'm relieved to hear it.'

'You hold up your end of the bargain, though. No harm. To *anyone*.'

'Does this mean that I shouldn't expect you to come crashing through my window, bringing a righteous hurricane of psychic vengeance with you?'

'Yes.' The hand that held the phone was trembling. I stared past the frolicking children, at the fountain, the awful tasteless monument that bore my cousin's name.

'For what it's worth,' said Freeman, as though he'd somehow read my mind over the phone, 'I'm s—'

'No,' I said, fighting not to sob at the monstrous injustice, the *audacity*. 'You're not. You are not *sorry*. Even if you *think* you are, you're not. You are a psychopath. There is no word in any dictionary that can sum up how much I despise you. So you do *not* apologise to me.'

'I understand. Well . . . then what do you want from me?'

'Nothing,' I said. 'Not right now. Just for you to renew the promise you made.'

'As I said, they won't be harmed.'

'You're god. Damn. *Right*.' Fear had turned into fury so suddenly that I'd barely noticed. 'Because if any of them *are* harmed, then there'll be nowhere for you to run. I think I made my case pretty effectively the last time we saw each other, but it's been five years for you so maybe time has diluted its impact. If you do hurt them, I will tear this world down, a city at a time, to find you. And if you somehow escape to another world, I'll follow you there. And I'll tear that one down too. And so on, until there are no worlds left for you to hide in. That's *my* promise.'

The very, very brief pause spoke volumes. 'I think we understand each other.'

'Good. Maybe I'll see you soon.'

'I'm not sure when I'll next be back in the country . . .'

'Take your time. Oh . . . actually. One more thing.'

'Yes?'

'What does the "G" stand for?'

'I beg your pardon?'

'Your name.'

'Oh. It's George.'

I snorted. *'George?* That's rubbish. Give me back to Lauren, please.'

Clicks and buzzes and my own heavy breathing. Then Lauren again. 'Stanly?'

'Hey. I think you should take me out for dinner on the company.'

Chapter Eight

'WHAT DID YOU say to him?' asked Lauren, for the third or fourth time.

'That's between us,' I said, for the fourth or fifth time.

Her frustrated sigh told me in no uncertain terms that she was making a major effort not to bounce me around with her mind while reading me the riot act. Maybe I deserved that, but this probably wasn't the place: a private booth in a posh restaurant seemingly made entirely from blue and white glass. And when I say private I mean *private* – we were the only ones on this floor and the staff apparently had to sign non-disclosure agreements because of the level of chat that went on.

'Does he have powers?' I asked. 'Freeman?'

Lauren looked surprised. 'No. At least, not as far as I know. And . . . I mean, I *would* know. Why?'

'I was just wondering. All the otherworldly energy, close contact with shimmers . . . seemed plausible. And I guess if the head of Angelcorp had powers, maybe that might help? With . . . integration, or whatever?' *Good cover. Shame Lauren's got a bit more nous than the eight-year-olds that might have worked on.*

'It would be very complicated,' said Lauren. 'There's still a lot of suspicion, even now, after all our efforts. There's widespread acceptance; you could even say the majority have come to terms with the presence of empowered in the streets, in their places of businesses . . . although schools have been a battle . . . but I think it might complicate the kinds of high-level deals Freeman has had to make with heads of state.'

Yeah. I bet it would. This was dangerous ground, so I grabbed a useful subject change with both hands. 'What was that about schools?'

'Initially there was quite a push for segregation,' said Lauren. 'It hasn't gone away. But Freeman has fought it every step of the way.'

'Fairish.' I drank some beer. 'So. What are *you* up to at the moment?'

Lauren took a meaningful sip of her water.

'All right,' I said. 'Top secret Angel Group business, obviously. Classified. Fill me in on some of the public record stuff, then. What happened after I left?' *Sounds like I went on a gap year.*

Our food arrived before she could respond. I'd been full to the brim with cake before, but just the smell of the eye-poppingly expensive spaghetti and meatballs I'd ordered was enough to make me hungry again, and we ate in semi-companionable silence for a few minutes before I managed to catch her eye.

'Oh fine,' she said. 'You asked for it.'

So it turns out that five and a bit years is quite a long time, especially when something as huge as the Collision happens at the beginning of it. By the time we'd finished our main course my brain was so full of information that I genuinely didn't think I could absorb any more. Angelcorp going public, emergency elections, historic treaties with overseas governments, skyrocketing numbers of empowered – many of the soldiers and police who had been in London during the Collision had ended up with powers, which was pretty convenient, depending on how you looked at it. There was even a drug treatment available for people who didn't want their abilities, which gave me pause, although Lauren assured me that it was only available following a strict vetting process, with interviews and consultations and so on. Apparently nobody had yet worked out how to give them to people.

'The thing that's made it all easier,' said Lauren, 'is that ultimately, people just want to get on with their lives. Forget about monsters and superpowers. We've worked really hard to take away the opportunities that people exploit to victimise and marginalise groups like the empowered. Having literal monsters for people to focus their fear and hatred on helped, admittedly . . .'

Just like Freeman planned. 'People don't think *we're* monsters?'

'Some do. Can't be helped, some people are going to be prejudiced no matter what. But believe it or not, generally, if you give people hope and opportunities, it brings out the best in them. Who'd have thought.' She laughed ruefully. 'You know, some people thought that all this, otherworldly insanity coming into the open, was going to be like the Singularity.'

I gave her my best blank face.

'That it was going to completely change things. Point of no return. Overthrow the established order, social, political, moral, technological. But it really hasn't, not on a day-to-day basis. People just want to carry on and live as normally as they can. Have jobs and families. Some of them just happen to be doing it with superpowers now, or with superpowered neighbours.'

'Any interesting new abilities?'

'Mostly variations on what we'd already seen.'

'Flyers?'

'Very few. None as good as you.'

'Wow. Go me.'

'It would actually be classed as a low-level offence to fly around the city, I'm afraid,' said Lauren. 'You should probably bear that in mind.'

You're joking. 'Low-level how?'

'The equivalent of a caution,' said Lauren, 'depending on the circumstances. I wasn't sure about adapting old judicial practices to empowered activity, but where we've managed to apply them they've worked surprisingly well. I think it's because it's familiar. People suddenly found they could levitate, move things with their minds. Crazy. But if you treat misuse of powers like drink driving or something, that's familiar. People can handle it. Obviously the justice system hasn't entirely caught up to all this new stuff yet, it's all been slightly ad hoc. We've got the finest legal minds in the world working with our best scientists to come up with new ideas . . . but the chaos I was expecting hasn't come to pass.'

Hmm. Yeah. Nice one, Angelcorp.

For making possibly the most awesome thing ever to happen to me illegal.

I drank some more beer. 'So what about mind control? Mental attacks? If there's no DNA evidence, how can you prove someone's committed a psychic crime?'

'It's . . . a challenge.' That sounded like something I very much needed to press, but some convenient unknown person chose that moment to phone Lauren and she excused herself.

I waited, prodding my dessert, full of food and knowledge and questions. When Lauren came back, she immediately asked where I was planning to stay, which took me a little by surprise.

'Um,' I said. 'Dunno. Daryl and Skank's?'

'Because we have a place for you. If you're interested.'

'A place?'

'A flat,' said Lauren. 'By the river. It's nice. And everything's sorted, ready for you to move in.'

'Why?'

'It was my suggestion,' she said. 'I felt it was the least we could do. We'll pay the rent, obviously.'

'What's the catch?'

'There's no catch. There may even be a job for you with us.'

'A *job*? With the Angel Group?'

I could tell she found it irritating when I used the old name, but she just nodded.

'As what?' I asked. 'Freeman's pet superhero?'

'Doubtful,' said Lauren. 'Superheroes haven't had a huge amount of success over the last few years.'

OK, I definitely 100 per cent need to follow up on that.

'It's kind of up to you,' she said. 'And to him, I suppose.'

Part of me hated the idea. Most of me, in fact. The vast majority of shareholders on the Board of Stanly wanted to tell Angelcorp to stuff it up their arse, that we'd be happy crashing on Daryl and Skank's floor, that we wanted *nothing* from them, or from their psychotic CEO.

But obviously I needed to play down my hatred of said CEO.

And a troublesome element did quite like the idea of a posh flat overlooking the river. Even for just one night.

Call me shallow.

'I'll have a look,' I said. 'If I like it, maybe I'll crash there for a bit.'

Lauren smiled. 'It's nice.'

'I believe you.'

Lauren picked up the bill and as we left the restaurant I touched her shoulder. 'Thanks,' I said. 'For sticking your neck out for me.'

She nodded. 'It's fine. I mean, it's not like you haven't helped me in the past.'

That brought back a whole tangle of unpleasant memories that I'd managed to suppress. All those comatose ghosts waking up. The pain I'd felt in that room, so thick I could have reached out and grabbed handfuls of it. I managed a smile. 'Well, I appreciate it.'

Dinner on the Angel Group. A flat on the Angel Group.

Brave new world indeed.

Also, "George"? Whose mortal enemy is called George?

So embarrassing.

The flat was in a huge, smart riverside building. I remembered this being a pretty prime spot for hideously expensive real estate and could only imagine what the rent was like. *I suppose rich people still need places to go be rich in this new superduperequal London.* We were greeted by a well-spoken man in an immaculate uniform, who greeted me as Mr Bird.

Too.

Weird.

As we rode the shiny elevator up, I kept wondering why I hadn't refused this on the spot. Why wasn't I hurrying back to be with Daryl and Skank? Why was I even thinking about accepting this kindness, if that's what it was, from people who had been my bitter enemies?

We got to the flat and Lauren handed me the key. 'Here you go.'

I unlocked the door and stepped inside, and my breath left me with indecent haste. It was *beautiful*. Shiny, just like everything else, and spacious, with furniture that managed to look simultaneously stylish and comfortable – usually I find it's either / or – and a dark blue and off-white colour scheme similar to my room back in Tref-y-Celwyn, which was either a nice coincidence or a sinister and cynical bit of decorating. The shelves were loaded with books and DVDs and there was a massive TV and a sound system so big and futuristic I was scared to go near it. Someone had even put posters up.

DVDs . . . would have thought they'd be obsolete.

I guess they thought I'd appreciate a familiar format.

Or maybe Blu-Ray died.

The bathroom looked good enough for an emperor to piss in. The bed was wide enough for four. It wasn't the flat I would ever have picked for myself, but the idea of living in it rent-free wasn't unappealing.

'There are essentials in the fridge,' said Lauren. 'And shops nearby. Or you can just order things. The Internet works the same, although it's faster. Your phone is linked to a bank account, which has money in it.'

'Thanks,' I said. 'Wow. This is . . . a bit surreal.'

'Do you like it?'

I shrugged, because I honestly didn't know how to answer that question. 'It'll do. I just can't believe you sorted it all so fast.'

'The building is ours,' said Lauren, 'and the flat was empty. I started making calls as soon as we had you sedated. Wanted it to be ready and welcoming. I know it's a bit posh . . .'

'It's good.' *Think of it as a favour from Lauren. Not from the Angel Group. And definitely not from Freeman.* 'Thank you.'

Lauren looked at her watch. 'Well. It's getting on. I'd better be off. Are you all right on your own?'

'I'll be fine.'

'I'll give you a call tomorrow.'

'OK.' We stood awkwardly for a minute and I tried a smile. It felt vaguely convincing. 'Cheers.'

'Don't mention it. Enjoy the flat.' She left and I stood in my new living room feeling excited and dispirited and confused and a whole host of other things that didn't mix. Then I made myself a cup of tea, as you do, brought it back through to the living room and opened the blinds. The view of the river and the city was the kind of view that I imagined people would pay thousands for, even now that a good proportion of the buildings had had pretty substantial chunks torn out of them.

This is my flat.

I looked around, touching things, removing and replacing DVDs, flicking through books.

This is not my flat.

I debated calling Skank and going around to hang with him and Daryl, but I didn't want to. I'd been away for so long, deprived of contact with anyone who wasn't a figment of my imagination, but it hadn't really felt like it . . .

Starting to now.

But even with all that time to make up, all that talk to be talked, all I wanted was to be alone.

Well this is the place.

If I was totally honest with myself, this was much more

my natural state than being surrounded by people. I'd spent most of my life hanging out alone, perfectly content with my own company. Even Daryl had been a comparatively recent addition to my circle of one.

Yep. Loner. No friends around. Definitely no girlfriend. And Eddie was AWOL. So . . . yeah. Business as usual.

I laughed grimly. *Yeah, keep repeating that and maybe you'll convince yourself.*

There was a computer in the bedroom. Maybe I could use it to track down Kloe. Contact her, tell her that I was back, that I was all right, that I didn't care whether there were now five years between us or twenty-five, that I didn't expect her to leave John Whoever-The-Hell and come back to me immediately, of course not, that I would happily wait for up to a day and a half.

These thoughts were momentarily satisfying but they quickly evaporated in bitter, acidic puffs. I wasn't going to call her. Definitely not yet, anyway.

Funny. I've fought giant monsters and evil masterminds. But none of them were as scary as the idea of phoning my girlfriend.

I realised too late that I'd thought *girlfriend.*

Ex-girlfriend, you mean.

I selected the comfiest looking armchair, sat down and flashed back to the last birthday I'd been conscious for. My eighteenth. A meal at Connor and Sharon's. Kloe was there. Eddie. Skank. No Daryl, but apart from that it had been pretty perfect. I remembered looking around the table, like I had earlier today, except I'd been thinking how sweet my life was.

But at the back of my mind had been that niggle. *Want to be out there. Want to be fighting. Want to be superheroing.*

That niggle, that poisonous dissatisfaction, had led directly here. No wonder Freeman had entrapped me so easily. I'd been waiting. Practically salivating.

And here you are.

Connor might not have known the whole story. But he wasn't necessarily wrong.

I sat for a very long time trying to work out which of today's multifarious headfucks was the biggest. Sleep came before conclusions.

The Irishman stood with his back to the big window, my spectacular view of London annoyingly obscured by an army of monsters smashing things in silent, crackling black and white slow motion. They looked so unconvincing that I wanted to laugh, but I felt I should listen to the Irishman. Everyone else was, sitting cross-legged on the carpet before him: little Tara in her red pyjamas, sharing popcorn with Daryl, Sharon leaning against Eddie, obviously tired, Skank and Nailah operating the big mixing desk, Lauren telling Freeman to stop texting, Freeman ignoring her.

'Can you all shut up?' I said, without moving my mouth.

They all shut up.

'This is a new one,' said the Irishman. 'It's called "Oh Great".'

His guitar looked so much bigger than him. He nodded his head, counting himself in, then began to play a standard blues riff. That one which is like *dum-DUM-dum-dum-dum.* 'I said oh great,' he sang, in a throaty Deep South growl. *Dum-DUM-dum-dum-dum.* 'Said Stanly's back.' *Dum-DUM-dum-dum-dum.* 'Back from the dead.' *Dum-DUM-dum-dum-dum.* 'Fancy that.'

Dum-DUM-dum-dum-dum. 'I said oh great.' *Dum-DUM-dum-dum-dum.* 'But I didn't really mean it.' *Dum-DUM-dum-dum-dum.*

'That didn't scan properly,' said Freeman.

'There's a rock and a hard place,' the Irishman continued. *Dum-DUM-dum-dum-dum.* 'And I'm between it.' *Dum-DUM-dum-dum-dum.*

'Between *them*,' said Freeman.

'I said oh great,' the Irishman sang. *Dum-DUM-dum-dum-dum.* 'Said Stanly's back.' *Dum-DUM-dum-dum-dum.* 'He'll bring doom down upon us all.' *Dum-DUM-dum-dum-dum.* 'And we'll all be in trouble.' *Dum-DUM-dum-dum-dum.*

'Well that didn't scan *or* rhyme,' said Freeman. 'Honestly.'

'Yeah,' said Daryl. 'I preferred his earlier, funnier stuff.'

'He means well,' said Sharon.

The Irishman was still singing and playing, but Skank and Nailah had muted him, so I got up and went through to the bedroom. It was the one from the small wooden house in the woods. The one where I'd left Kloe and Tara forever. Kloe was in there, looking sexy and bored and maybe older.

'Hey,' I said. 'I'm back.'

'Great, mate.'

I leaned in, grabbed her and kissed her like a hero should kiss the love interest, but I could tell she wasn't really into it and after a while I gave up and walked away. Everyone else had left and I stood in the living room alone.

'Tough luck, kid,' said Daryl. Maybe everyone hadn't quite left.

'Meh,' I said. 'Could be worse.'

He nodded. 'Yeah.'

The monsters had given up trashing the city and sloped

off somewhere. The city, for its part, just sat there, staring at me. I stared back. 'Yeah.'

I woke up and had no idea where I was. This chair, the walls, the furniture, the dark city view through the window . . . where was this? There was a pounding in my chest and I was sweating, and I toppled sideways off the chair and landed on the floor—

—which became grass under my knees. I was in the clearing, in Senia's world. Broad daylight. I was close to hyperventilating, that thumping still heavy and painful in my chest, surrounded by a hot, frightening tightness.

Breathe.
Breathe.
Breathe.

I caught a flash of movement and spun to look at it. Senia was hurrying towards me, looking concerned, but she stopped abruptly when I turned, clearly shocked by my manic movement. 'Are you all right?'

It was a little while before I could respond, but eventually the panic dissipated and I managed a nod. Senia handed me some water.

'Thanks.' I took a glug. 'How long has it been?'

'Same time, next day.'

'Really? It's only been a day?'

'Yes . . . how long has it been for you?'

'Um . . . two? Ish? I think?' I rubbed my head.

'You're not all right, are you?' I noticed that she was wearing red and yellow today, rather than her usual rural camouflage clobber.

'No.' I was fighting an overpowering urge to break down and sob – it didn't feel like the thing to do in front of a stranger. Even one I'd now apparently met several times over the course of several days, except actually only two days, sort of.

'You've been back in your world?'

I nodded, exhaling steadily to keep myself calm.

'How is it?'

'Well,' I said. 'Five and a half years have passed for everyone else, but it feels like a couple of days for me. One of my friends hates me, my arch nemesis – and I mean that very literally – is in charge of everything, he's literally brainwashed everyone so I'm basically the only one who remembers the horrendous crimes that he committed, and the evil corporation he runs has given me a posh flat to live in rent-free while they decide whether or not to give me a job. It's . . . challenging.'

Senia's eyes were wide. 'Five and a half *years*? You said five years just before you last disappeared, but I didn't think . . . wow.'

'Yep.' I looked at her and, improbably, a smile occurred. 'To be honest, even though I'm not entirely comfortable with the idea that I'm still randomly popping in and out of parallel universes, I'm relieved to see you.'

She smiled. 'I'm relieved to see you too. The last couple of times were . . . worrying.'

'Yeah, sorry about that. And sorry if I disappear again.'

'It's all right.'

'And I'm *extra* sorry if I come back tomorrow and I'm ten years older and missing an eye.'

Senia laughed. 'That's all right too.'

I drank some more water. 'So . . . enough about my ridiculous life. I don't know anything about you. How old are you?'

'Eighteen. You?'

'Same. Technically.'

'Technically?'

'Well I *was* eighteen, the last time I was running around and doing stuff like a normal . . . ish . . . person. But now five and a half years have gone past in my world . . . so technically . . .' I shrugged.

'You look about eighteen. Actually maybe younger.'

'Well, I definitely didn't get younger. So let's go with eighteen. Do you live near here?'

She nodded. 'With my dad.'

'What do you do?'

'I work on his farm. And I build things.'

'And hunt deer?'

She gave me a questioning look.

'The bow and arrow you had.'

'Oh.' She laughed. 'No, I don't hunt with that. I made it, though. Was on my way to test it out when I found you the other day.'

'You *made* it? Wow. It's awesome.'

'Thanks.'

'Have you been on the farm today then?'

'Day off today, actually.'

'Wow, and you came anyway? I'm flattered.'

'I've done other things too. I stayed in bed until ten o'clock for a start, which never happens. The rest of the time I've been fixing a car.'

'Really? Wow. Whose? Yours?'

'My dad's old one. He said that if I can get it running again by myself, I can have it.'

I smiled. 'Cool. I couldn't fix a car with a gun to my head. Lego's more my scene.'

'What's Lego?'

'Oh you poor thing. What *is* this cruel universe you live in?'

She laughed.

'Hey,' I said. 'Want to see something weird?'

'I don't know,' she said. 'Maybe?'

'It's good.' I looked at the bottle of water she'd brought and levitated it, swishing it lazily from side to side in front of her face.

Her eyes widened. '*What*.'

I turned the bottle upright, then fired it up into the air like a rocket. It reached an apex then fell back down, and I froze it in the air a foot from the floor. Senia laughed delightedly. 'That's . . . *what*? That's amazing!'

'It's how I knocked that tree down,' I said. 'Which, again, sorry. Release of power . . . side-effect of being solid again.'

'It's fine. Although I did really like that tree.'

'Yeah, you called it *your* tree, didn't you? Sorry.' *I used to have a tree, once upon a time.*

'I forgive you.' She smiled.

'Thanks. Hey, want to see something else that's weird?' I got to my feet—

—and stood up in the flat in London. It was night-time again.

Oh for God's sake. I sank to the floor and stayed there for several minutes, which became twenty, which became more. A new feeling had risen in my stomach, something that didn't immediately make sense. It was only when I'd turned off the lights, brushed my teeth and got into the huge, unfamiliar bed that I understood.

It was a feeling I hadn't had since I was a child, a time when I'd stayed the night at some other kid's house. I couldn't even remember the kid's name. It was one of only a handful of times that I'd gone for sleepovers, before I'd started to realise that I wasn't very good at having friends. My first night away from home, without my parents. Particularly without my mother. The feeling I'd had lying in a bed that didn't belong to me, alone in the dark, knowing I was far away from home but that there was nothing to be done about it. I'd cried then.

But I didn't now, even though I wanted to.

Be quiet.

Big boys don't cry.

Big boys don't cry.

Big boys don't cry . . .

Chapter Nine

I WOKE UP confused, with light streaming in. *Am I in a hotel? Kloe didn't book us a hotel, did she?*

I sat up. *Biiiiiig bed.* And very, very comfortable. Must be a hotel, surely? I looked around. No, this was a bedroom. Wardrobe . . . computer . . . posters . . . *Star Wars, Indiana Jones, Buffy, Tron . . .*

Not a hotel.

Yesterday came flooding back and I lay down again. Reality's myriad disappointments aside, I was still warm and felt no urgent need to emerge from this bed. It was the first proper bed I'd slept in for years, after all.

And I had literally no engagements.

Eventually the call of the toilet became too much so I went and washed and brushed my teeth. It was thirteen minutes past eleven. I made myself a coffee and some toast and ate it staring out of the window at the cloudy day.

What to do . . .

I felt as though I should call someone. Lauren? No. For now, a roof and a bed were about as much as I wanted from Angelcorp. *And money.*

Yeah, and that.

Who else? Skank and Daryl? Of course they were who I should be calling. Or Sharon. Yes, of course her. Or Tara.

Or Kloe.

Or Mum . . .

I didn't slap myself in the forehead, but it would have been appropriate. Mum. Obviously. Who the hell else was I going to call?

I think I definitely planned to call her. But for some reason I ended up sitting and thinking about something that Lauren had said yesterday. About superheroes.

And what was Daryl on about?

The Chavengers?

To the Batcomputer!

I quickly managed to find, of all things, an interview that Nailah had conducted with the Chavengers - because yeah, get this, they were a group of actual real-life superheroes. Four teenagers from a rough London estate who had survived the Collision and found themselves with powers. Reading the interview filled me with such joy that I inadvertently started levitating.

There were four of them, two guys and two girls. The guys were Captain England (telekinesis, Union Jack onesie) and the Incredible Funk (super-strength, bright green hoody and mask, purple jeans - geddit?). The girls were Iron Brew (LOL) and Thor Blimey (seriously) and they also had telekinesis, plus Thor Blimey had super-strength too. Their costumes didn't really match their namesakes, but I forgave them because the story was awesome. Four teenagers who had bonded over comic book movies - and a shared sense of injustice - and tried to make it as actual superheroes, protecting their estate and the surrounding area from assorted scumbags. They'd emerged about six months after the Collision and had apparently been significantly more successful at finding and defeating bad guys than I ever had.

'No-one who doesn't live here cares about what happens,'

said Thor Blimey in Nailah's interview. 'Not to people like us. And you spend your whole life feeling totally powerless while politicians and drug dealers screw up the place where you were born, the place you don't reckon you'll ever get away from. Then you get *actual superpowers*, so why wouldn't you try and clean the place up? Me and England and Funk were getting drunk one day and I said screw it, let's be superheroes. Funk came up with "Chavengers" on the spot. We pissed ourselves laughing and were like "fuck yeah".'

Legends, I thought.

Obviously it had been too good to last. Barely eighteen months into their career, there had been a shoot-out near their estate between armed police and a crew of drug dealers, some of whom also happened to be packing superpowers. The Chavengers had shown up to help and the Incredible Funk had been shot dead. It wasn't clear exactly which side had been responsible. They'd done enough to turn the tide, though – the police got the better of the drug dealers and arrested them.

Along with the surviving Chavengers.

Probably locked up in super-person jail now.

Freeman's Britain.

Having come perilously close to a purely good mood, I turned away from the computer and stared at the wall. I wondered if things might have turned out like that for me if I'd actually been good at being a superhero. Or maybe it was different for kids from council estates. The world didn't cater for them, did it?

Even before Connor's stinging words on the subject, I had pretty much convinced myself that the whole impulse to be a superhero had been flawed, if not downright stupid. It just didn't work in the real world. Stuff got messed up, people got hurt. Sometimes they died. But now I didn't know what to think. Did the Chavengers' story prove my point or contradict it? Had those kids been stupid? A gnarled, uncharitable part of me thought they were. Stupid irresponsible kids.

Stupid irresponsible kids doing exactly what you wanted to do.

But that had been when I was younger. When I thought that going out at night in a long black coat and hanging around dark alleys was the way to help people. As though evil was so obvious.

The thought of going out dressed all in black made me feel distinctly embarrassed now.

I spent another hour or so trawling the Internet, watching videos and reading articles. I'd remembered something Sharon had once said, about what the 'thinkpiece mafia' would do if powers ever came out into the open. She'd predicted chaos. And there had certainly been plenty of thinkpiecing: the philosophical implications, the scientific and technological implications, the effect on the 'ongoing culture wars', on gender relations and sociopolitical whatevers, what the monsters meant for the various world religions (mostly they seemed to have adapted pretty well). At first there had been a lot of worrying about Angelcorp and its ties with government, but those sorts of articles became fewer and further between, the closer you got to now. At this point, people seemed to have accepted it. And as someone dryly opined in the *New Statesman*:

"OK, there are drones in the sky and psychics in the streets and our government now plays obedient sidekick to a monolithic corporation with unlimited surveillance reach, whose democratic accountability is, shall we say, fuzzy. But . . . inequality is dropping. Sustainability is high on the agenda.

Meaningful moves are being made to correct the gender pay gap, restore the social safety net, rein in the excesses of big business and the financial sector – or at least funnel some of that bountiful cash in a more sociable direction – and even begin a half-civilised discussion about nuclear disarmament. And nobody I know has been eaten by a monster in nearly six years. It could be worse."

Um . . . OK . . .

There were some pretty entertaining videos floating around as well. Various YouTube edits that people had made, stitching together all the available phone footage from the Collision. *Looks fake.* A pilot for an aborted reality show called *Undercover Superhero*, basically *Big Brother* except one of the contestants was empowered and they had to see how long they could go without the others realising. *Looks horrible, glad it was cancelled, hope everyone involved is in prison.* A pretty awesome promo video for a post-Collision charity single by Radiohead in which Thom Yorke was levitated rhythmically around a room by a troupe of empowered. *Great video, great song, 10/10, would watch again.* An interview with *Eastenders'* first openly empowered actress, which I found weirdly moving. *What is wrong with me.*

One thing I could say for this bonkers future was that it was still very possible to waste an inordinate amount of time watching rubbish on the Internet.

Lauren rang later in the afternoon and I fobbed her off, saying I was tired. She asked if she could come by tomorrow, show me around the city. I said maybe. Part of me did want to get a feel for London again, beyond the brief taster I'd had yesterday . . .

But at the same time, I also didn't want to. What if people

were different? What if they acted strangely? What if they could immediately tell that I wasn't supposed to be there? I pictured myself getting into hilariously awkward scrapes, unaware of modern social etiquette, stumbling around like some ludicrous anachronism from a crap fish-out-of-water time-travel comedy.

I'm going to need a psychiatrist to deal with this bollocks.

I promised myself that I would go out at some point, but for now I was going to call my mother. I even came close to picking up the phone before I went to the shelf to look at the DVDs. There was so much choice that I felt like I might not be in the right mood for any of it, but then my eyes fell on a section of shelf containing five boxsets of the new version of *Doctor Who*. I'd never watched it but Skank spoke pretty highly of it. No harm in trying. I grabbed the first one, spent a further ten minutes trying to work the TV and the DVD player, and sat down to watch.

I liked it.

I was surprised to wake up in the flat the next morning. No involuntary teleportation. I got up and did bathroom things and was just cracking on with the second season of *Doctor Who* when Lauren appeared. She let herself in, which was kind of irritating.

'Hi,' I said, vaguely, keeping my attention focused on the season finale. 'Give me a minute, this is nearly finished.'

'OK. Mind if I make a cup of tea?'

'Help yourself.'

'Would you like one?'

'No thanks.'

She didn't move but I heard various materials in the

kitchen begin to arrange themselves in a tea-making formation. I watched the rest of the episode, switched it off and turned in my seat. 'Good view, isn't it?' said Lauren, walking to the window.

"Tis.'

'Would you like to go for a fly later?'

There was nothing I'd like more . . . but at the same time, the idea inspired an anxious stab in my stomach. *That's new.* 'Thought it was illegal.'

'Exceptions can be made, under special circumstances.'

'Ooh. Is that what I am? Special circumstances?'

'You're pretty much the definition of special circumstances.'

'Awesome.'

The kettle finished boiling and I heard a teabag fall into a cup, followed by the sound of pouring and stirring. Then a cup of tea floated across the room from the kitchen into Lauren's waiting hands. 'Smooth,' I said.

'Easy,' said Lauren. 'Should be simple for you. You don't need to look with your eyes, you can just use your mind. It's one of the new disciplines I've been trying. Sort of like sonar. Thinking outwards until your thoughts hit something, working from that. Useful.'

It did sound handy. 'Pretty good for stealthing about. Shame you can't go invisible.'

'I've tried it.'

'Seriously?'

She nodded. 'Manipulating minds so people don't see you. Not *literally* turning invisible. It's very difficult.'

Actually, to be fair, I'd tried that before as well. It had been very basic, thinking *I'm supposed to be here* over and over again so that nobody asked questions, and the fact that the air had been lousy with alien energy had helped. But still . . .

'How are your powers?' asked Lauren.

Funny question. 'Fine, as far as I know.'

'Up for some training?'

'Like the old days?'

She smiled sadly. 'I suppose.'

'I'm guessing things aren't like they were during the Collision. Psychic communication from one end of the city to the other, telling people to go to sleep.'

'Atmospheric conditions are different,' said Lauren. 'Less . . . conducive. I'm sure you could still tell someone to go to sleep, if you wanted.'

'Hmm.'

'Are you up for some training, then?'

'Why not.'

'Stand up and walk to the window.' She was doing her Jedi thing again. Entirely against my will, I did as she said. It was really, really annoying.

'I'm not a fan of that at all,' I said.

'Then learn to defend yourself.'

'Fine.' I pictured a brick wall around my brain and skull, a titanium barrier around that, an adamantium barrier around that, a dwarf star metal barrier around that and a force field around that. And then another force field around my body, just for luck. *Doctor Who* was forgotten. Mum, Kloe, Daryl, everyone, forgotten. *Oh yeah. It's on. Come at me. I'll show you who's*—

'Sit down,' said Lauren.

I immediately did as she said. 'Balls.'

'You're not going to get it immediately,' she laughed. 'Don't worry.'

'It's pissing me off, though.'

'So practise.'

'Is this really the best use of your time?' I said. 'Don't you have important Angel Group business to get on with?'

'You are important *Angelcorp* business.'

'I thought I was special circumstances.'

'You can be two things. I was in meetings for most of yesterday. About you.'

'Ooh. I'm . . . flattered? Maybe?'

'Maybe you should be.'

Just then, something occurred to me, something that I absolutely could not believe had taken this long to cross my mind. 'So if I'm so special,' I said, as though voicing a thought that I'd had ages ago rather than right now, 'presumably this flat must be bugged?' *Of course it is you idiot.* 'Hidden cameras and so on?' *Of course there are. You IDIOT.*

Lauren seemed taken aback. 'You really think that?'

OBVIOUSLY. IT COULDN'T BE MORE SCREAMINGLY OBVIOUS. I shrugged as though I wasn't hugely bothered. 'Isn't it?'

'No,' said Lauren. 'It isn't. I promise.'

'You promise.'

She looked me very deliberately in the eye. 'I. *Promise.*'

'Fair enough.' *Maybe she's right.*

Or at least, maybe she believes she's right.

We worked for another hour, Lauren trying to influence me while I tried to defend myself. We talked about her methods. What she was exploiting. Ways in. After a while, I started to realise that it wasn't a matter of erecting temporary defences, or blocking up the gaps. It was removing the gaps entirely.

I needed for there to be nothing to exploit. I needed to be a blank canvas.

'Are you reading my mind right now?' I said.

'I could,' said Lauren. 'But I would never, not without permission.'

'Thanks.'

'You're welcome. Sit down.'

That time, I managed to stop myself mid-sit. I looked stupid, wobbling in a half crouch, but I had definitely resisted. I stood up and Lauren smiled. 'Well done. Sit down.'

Again I managed to stop myself halfway and stand back up. Another five or six attempts, and I managed to stop before halfway. Another ten and Lauren's instructions to sit or walk across the room or stand on my head or sing the Welsh national anthem were starting to feel just like any other verbal order I didn't want to follow. I could still hear her voice in my head but it was muffled and didn't find its way to my limbs. There was an itch there, like that nagging feeling at the back of your mind when you know you *should* be doing something . . . but the best thing about that feeling is that you can ignore it.

'This is good,' said Lauren. 'Really impressive. I mean, I always knew your powers were exceptionally well-developed. But no-one else has caught on this quickly with these techniques.'

'Go me.' *Chosen one all up in the place.*

Chosen nothing, mate.

After a quick break for tea, Lauren said, 'OK. Let's try one more thing and then we'll pop out and see the city?'

I scrunched up my face. 'I don't know . . . still pretty tired. Might just stay in and then have a bit of a wander around tomorrow.'

She wasn't convinced. Hell, I wasn't convinced. But I wasn't going out, either. 'Tomorrow,' I said, firmly. 'And you can tell me all about your meetings.'

'All right. Now, I want you to make me do something against my will.'

There's something you don't hear every day. 'Like you were doing to me.'

She nodded. 'I'm not going to tell you how to do it. Just find a way.'

'You like your steep learning curves, don't you?'

'If you don't like them, you should stop being such a good student.'

I turned away and closed my eyes, trying to do what she'd described earlier, using my thoughts like sonar. I thought outwards in concentric rings and was amazed to find that it worked. The chair, Lauren, the hallway that led to the kitchen . . . I could . . . not exactly *see* them, but I knew what was there. They left impressions, outlines, ripples. I was aware of Lauren scratching behind her ear, shifting from foot to foot in anticipation.

I focused on her face.

Her eyes.

Windows into her mind.

I conjured up the instruction *do a cartwheel* in my own head and made it into water. Liquid suggestion, trickling from the ceiling, straight down into her eyes, infiltrating, through the cracks in her mind . . .

I turned around and said 'Do a cartwheel' with my mouth and my brain. Without changing her expression, she moved. In fact, she went through nearly half the motions that would have led to a cartwheel, managing to stop herself just as her two palms touched the floor. She jerked back and stood up, eyes wide with shock. 'Wow,' she said. 'That's . . . really impressive. Scarily impressive.'

'Sorry.'

'No,' she said. 'No, it's good. I mean . . . wow. I shouldn't even have moved. But it's probably because it's you. You definitely are a special case.'

I didn't know what to say to that, so I chose to look awkward and say nothing.

'That's enough training for today, I think.' Lauren exhaled. 'Tiring.'

'So how *do* you police this?' I said. 'Surely people can just . . . you know. Walk into a room, think someone dead. Or make people do things . . . you know. Bad things. How do you police it? How do you prosecute?'

'Steep learning curves.' She smiled. 'Like you said.'

'That's not an answer.'

'Don't worry. It's very, *very* difficult to just think someone dead.'

'Tried it often, have you?'

'On a daily basis. You should meet some of my co-workers. Right, I'm going to head off. I'll give you a call tomorrow?'

'Don't you have Saturdays off?'

'Some. Not tomorrow. You're sure you don't want to go out now? You're not going to see Tara?'

'I don't have her address.'

Lauren rolled her eyes and took out her phone. 'I'll text it to you right now.'

'Thanks. Think I'm just going to chill out today, though. Absorb the lessons, meditate a bit. Maybe go on the Internet and bone up on recent history.' *Aka get started on the season three boxset.*

'All right then.'

'Thanks for today,' I said. 'It was . . . instructive.'

'You're welcome,' said Lauren. She smiled. 'It's really good to see you.'

'You too,' I said, meaning it.

Once she'd gone, I spent nearly an hour combing the flat for bugs and cameras, looking in every conceivable spot, taking every single DVD out of its case, every single book off the shelf, looking behind every poster. Nothing. It didn't necessarily *prove* anything, Angelcorp were presumably much better at planting bugs than I was at looking for them . . .

But I did want to trust Lauren. So I made a promise to myself not to do or say anything incriminating while I was here, sat down and spent several minutes agonising over whether or not to go and see Tara this evening. Initially I hadn't been entirely sure why I was so reluctant, but it was obvious really. The same reason I hadn't called Kloe or my mother. I was scared. It was pathetic and I loathed myself for it, but that's what it was.

So what are you going to do about it?

What I did about it, in the end, was put the first disc of the next *Doctor Who* boxset into the DVD player and resume my position in my chair.

I mean *the* chair.

Chapter Ten

EDDIE THREW THE ball but it didn't reach me. 'You need to stop throwing it so hard,' I said, just as the last ball he'd thrown came back down. It had snow on it.

'I need to stop throwing it so hard,' said Eddie.

'You don't know your own strength.'

'I don't know my own strength.'

The playground was in the process of being dismantled and we were attempting to play volleyball, separated by some of the orange plastic netting the builders had left behind. In the distance, beyond the fence, the desert crackled and the red sun glowered behind the mountains' scorched peaks.

Daryl blew his whistle.

'Let me have a go,' I said, pointing to the huge pyramid of balls next to Eddie.

'You have a go,' said Eddie, tossing me a ball.

I tossed it. Hit it. Sent it over the net.

Up, up, up, up, up it went.

'Maybe I don't know *my* own strength,' I said.

'Maybe you don't know *your* own strength,' said Eddie.

Up, up, up.

And down.

Like a cannonball.

It hit Eddie, pummelling him into the ground with the force of a ten-ton truck. He lay, bent oddly, bleeding.

I just stood there.

Daryl blew his whistle.

I sat up in bed in the dark, screaming, with no idea where I was. I scrambled out of bed, stumbled towards what I thought was the door, feeling for a light switch, failing to find it. Details started to reassert themselves – the bathroom is this way, wherever I am, the bathroom is this way – and I managed to find the right room, fumbling again for a light switch, gripping the cord, pulling, squinting as light filled the room. Gasping and crying, I went to the sink and threw cold water on my face. The shock of the water jolted me backwards—

—into daylight and I lost my balance, overwhelmed by the brightness, the sudden temperature change, falling onto the grass, shutting my eyes tight.

Here again.

I could hear Senia's voice.

Here again.

She was saying my name.

Here again.

Wow. That dream was something.

Later on, I would tell Eddie about it. Freak him out.

I opened my eyes, cringing at the light, just about able to make out Senia's blurry shape.

No . . . I wouldn't tell Eddie. I wouldn't tell him anything. Ever.

She swam into focus and I opened my mouth to speak—

—but I was back in the bathroom, on the floor. I fought with myself, forcing my breathing to level out, forcing tears back in, forcing the gag reflex down. Somehow I managed to get up, battling through the headrush, and splashed more water on my face.

I looked up at the mirror. At myself.

No-one had heard me scream.

No-one would be coming.

I went to the kitchen to get a drink of water and check the time. Just before six. The thought of sleeping again filled me with dread. It wasn't so much the dream, it was the waking up. And it wasn't the possibility of waking up in a different place.

It was being convinced that Eddie was still alive and then realising once again that he wasn't.

I took a cup of tea and my duvet to the living room and watched the world get light, thinking. It was definitely me transporting myself between here and Senia's world. Not voluntarily . . . so what? A shock reflex? A panic reaction?

Next day, same time . . .

Had I become linked to her world in some way? Were we tied together?

As much as I liked seeing Senia, I didn't want this. Flashing back and forth, against my will. It was too disorientating. Even if some part of me maybe thought I was safer there – *that must be it, surely* – I couldn't continue like this. Apart from anything, it could get embarrassing. What if it happened while I was in the shower, or on the toilet or something?

Yeah. That's definitely the most worrying thing to be worrying about.

Speaking of things to worry about . . . what the hell was I going to *do*? What were my options? I had a horrible feeling that Lauren was going to offer me a job with the Angel Group, a job that would presumably come with strings – *best case scenario* – or could even end up being yet another horrific trap set by dear George.

It was an option, though, if not a great one.

What else could I do? I could get involved with Sharon and Connor's projects. Help the community. Help people with powers. Heal people, perhaps, like that other Stanly. That was quite an appealing option. Do some actual good with my powers, constructive good, good that didn't involve fighting. Maybe there truly was potential for a new and amazing world. Maybe rather than being distrustful, or trying to fight it, I should embrace it. Perhaps, ironically, I was *more* likely to have a proper place in this insane future than I had in the past.

Although I had a feeling that Connor wouldn't be too crazy about the idea of me inserting myself into their business, their life, their world. And it wasn't exactly my place to do that anyway . . .

What else? Open a detective agency? That was what people did when they split off from the regular cast, wasn't it? New status quo? Maybe Daryl could be my partner. We could get a small office, drink whisky, smoke cigarettes. Skank could have the 'also starring' role.

Except I don't really have any of the necessary skills to be a detective.

Let's call it an option anyway.

I could also just say bollocks to London and leave. And the more that option crystallised in my head, the more appealing it became. Why not go somewhere else? Walk the Earth – *like Caine in* Kung Fu, said Daryl's voice in my brain, a long time ago – helping people in need? Granted, it hadn't worked out brilliantly here so far, but surely if I just flew from place to place for long enough, I'd come across some wrongs that required righting?

'Cos that's what I needed to do. Whatever option I chose, I needed to be helping people. And not just to make amends for my spectacular balls-ups thusfar.

Because that's what the powers are for.

Satisfied, optimistic and motivated, I huddled in the duvet and proceeded to watch *Doctor Who* for nearly twelve hours. At some point in the afternoon I dozed off, waking to texts from Lauren, Sharon and Skank. Lauren managed to make her texts sound agitated, saying there was stuff that needed discussing, could she come round or could I meet her somewhere, blah blah blah. I gave her a 'maybe, got a non-specific something to do that doesn't actually exist' response, feeling slightly bad about it. Sharon wanted me to come for dinner. I told her something similar and felt worse about it. Skank was relaying his and Daryl's general concerns. I promised that I was fine and that I'd be in touch and felt a bit more worse.

You should really do something.

Such as?

Hmm . . .

Hundreds of feet up, the air was a huge cold hug, an empty ocean. I cartwheeled and back-flipped and looped loops, diving and soaring, shedding doubt and anxiety and everything else I didn't want. I managed nearly a minute of carefree fun before I heard the noise, half robot hornet buzz, half whistle. I glanced down. One drone. Two drones.

OK.

Let's see if you bastards can do ninety.

I accelerated fast just as one of the drones spoke. Well,

not spoke, exactly. A speaker started playing a pre-recorded message, a voice kind of like the one on the Tube that tells you to mind the gap, saying something about ceasing and desisting and waiting for an official someone. *Yeah, no thanks.* I flew, gaining speed, pumping power into my psychic engines, gaining height then diving, twisting around, peregrine falcon, *Millennium* Falcon, hearing them on my tail and enjoying the fact that they were very much struggling to keep up.

Oh yeah.

COME ON.

I realised that I was close to the Rogers' new address and abruptly entered a steep dive. As I rocketed towards the ground I glanced behind me and saw that two more drones had joined the pursuit. I could have destroyed them right then and there, broken them into pieces, but I knew I was pushing my luck as it was. I could outrun them. I could—

Phone's ringing.

Wonder who that is . . .

I thought it to my ear, maintaining speed. 'Hello?' I yelled.

'Stanly!' *Yep. Lauren. Shoulda put money on that.* 'You need to land right now!'

'Just out for a fly! Not hurting anyone!'

'You're not authorised! You need to stop!'

'Can you please just get rid of these stupid drones? I'll be landing in a minute anyway!'

'Stanly—'

'I won't do it again! I just . . . I needed a fly.'

'I understand, but you really can't be—'

'I *know*.' I could see the estate now. I flipped over so I was the right way up, standing in the air, steadily slowing my descent. I noticed that the drones were hanging back.

'I can cover you this time. But I can't keep doing it.'

'Thanks,' I said. 'I owe you.'

'Yes, speaking of that . . . there is something you could do for me.'

'What?'

'Come in to Angelcorp for a meeting. Monday morning.'

'A meeting? With who? About what?'

'There are just . . .' She sighed. 'I have some powerful people breathing down my neck. People who are agitated about you, your potential, your intentions. I've managed to hold them off so far, told them you're adjusting, but stunts like this aren't helpful. This will use up some very valuable goodwill.'

That drove a screw into my stomach and twisted it. She was just trying to help. 'Sorry. I'll come in. Is it with Freeman, the meeting?'

'No. He's still out of the country. You'll be meeting with Jane Walker.'

'Never heard of her. Is she nice?'

'Just . . . be on your best behaviour, please.'

Gulp. 'Fine. Pick me up in the morning?'

'OK. Thanks. Are you going to see Tara?'

As if you don't have me on drone cam right now. 'Yep, nearly there.'

'I hope it goes well.'

'Thanks.' I touched down, ignoring the stunned looks of two dog walkers. 'Have a nice evening. Going anywhere nice?'

'Dinner at home.'

'Great. Enjoy. Bye.' I hung up, thought the phone into my pocket and strolled up the street. The evening was pleasantly warm and the estate was pleasantly . . . pleasant. Although

129

unless the Rogers' old house had been completely destroyed by monsters, I wasn't entirely sure why they'd bothered moving. It looked pretty much the same: well-to-do in an entirely non-descript kind of way. Seemingly untouched by catastrophe.

I spotted their house and my heart started spasming.

You're here to see Tara.

Not for a confrontation with Mr and Mrs Rogers.

God I wanted one, though. I knew Freeman must have threatened them, that they must have hated themselves for going along with his scheme . . . but they'd still gone along with it. Made me believe I had a daughter.

What if they remember?

What if they don't?

I seemed to cover a lot of ground in a very short space of time, because suddenly I was at the door. I even seemed to be knocking.

Oh God.

What if Tara—

Tara didn't. Jacqueline did. At first she didn't seem to know who had appeared at her door, her brow furrowing. Then recognition. Her eyes turned into dinner plates and she took a step back, hand flying to her chest. '*Stanly?*'

'Hello Jacqueline.' I'd planned to be coldly cordial, call her Mrs Rogers, but her name just slipped out.

'I don't understand. How?'

'It's a long story,' I said. 'Can I come in?'

'Of course, of course!'

She led me through to the living room. The layout of the house was different, but the contents were the same. Same cheery tat. Same photographs . . . except no. There was Tara, older. Twelve-ish. Then older again. And older again. Fifteen, sixteen. Braids in her hair, more knowledge in her face, an edge of sarcasm, an attitude. She was pretty, too. Pretty like a daughter, except not. Like a younger sister, maybe?

Except not so young.

This is . . .

Truthfully I didn't know what it was, so I was incredibly glad when Oliver Rogers appeared and almost fell over. 'Stanly!'

'Hello, Oliver.'

'But . . . but . . . you don't look a day older!'

I smiled. 'Neither do you.' He did, though. They both did.

'Charming as ever,' said Jacqueline.

What the hell is this? Tea and cake with Mr and Mrs Lovely at 14 Absolutely No Baggage Whatsoever Drive, Denialville?

'How are you here?' said Oliver. 'We never found out what happened to you after all that terrible business. What *did* happen?'

'It's a very long story,' I said. 'Happy to tell it, but first . . . is Tara here?'

'She's out with friends,' said Jacqueline, with a beatific smile.

Ah. That's nice. 'OK then. Well . . .'

'Please sit down,' said Jacqueline, 'I'll make tea.'

I didn't want to, but I couldn't really say no. Jacqueline gave me a hug as though she'd suddenly come to terms with the fact that I was really here, then bustled off to make tea, and Oliver and I sat down. I made passable small talk with him until the tea arrived, then the three of us made more small talk. I made sure to be impeccably polite to cover up the fact that I was probing, trying to see what was really happening here, whether there was any fear, any guilt, any anger, whether their smiles were just masks they wore while they waited for me to drop the bombshell, demand to know why they had been complicit in Freeman's plan, why they'd lied to me, helped put Tara in danger so that Freeman could use her against me, how they had seen fit to lie to my face so many times . . .

But there was nothing. He'd wiped it all. As far as Oliver and Jacqueline Rogers were concerned, I was just the boy who had saved their adopted daughter from Smiley Joe. They were blissfully unaware of what had happened, what they'd done. I'd taken Tara to Wales that night, yes, but not because of anything they'd said. They knew nothing of the fake letter from my 'future self'.

More evidence erased . . . and more catharsis, more closure, stolen from me.

Eventually I made my excuses and left. Jacqueline said she'd let Tara know I'd come by, but I made sure to get a phone number too. I tried it a couple of times, but it went to answer phone. Her sixteen-year-old voice was like her eleven-year-old voice, except older.

I didn't leave a message.

Let her have her fun. Let her be with her friends.

Also, I don't seem to be walking in the direction of the flat. Complete opposite direction, in fact.

Hmm. Oh well. Might as well see where this is going, I guess.

Chapter Eleven

I ENDED UP heading south. There had been very little obvious damage near where Mr and Mrs Rogers lived, but between there and the centre I'd started to see more and more of it, more slumped and rotting buildings, windows covered by wooden boards. Further south, however, the devastation started letting up again – there was still quite a lot of construction work going on, but it seemed more like development than repair. The last time I'd wandered around these areas, they'd been fairly bedraggled. Now someone seemed to be giving them some care and attention.

All part of Freeman's master plan?

A lanky guy with straggly blonde hair dressed in a weird, mismatched tracksuit / leather jacket / Doc Marten ensemble offered me a *Big Issue* and I felt the weird lurk of déjà vu. Had I seen this guy before?

No.

I was just remembering, that was all. Remembering walking through south London, looking for trouble. Was that what I was doing now? I didn't think so. I was just . . . walking. It seemed as though it would have been fitting if it had been the same *Big Issue* seller, but it wasn't.

Because the world doesn't deal in meaningful coincidences.

Except for when it does.

'You all right, mate?' said the guy.

I realised that I'd zoned out. 'Sorry . . . yeah, I'll have

one. Thanks.' I gave him some money and as he fumbled in his bag for a magazine, the pouch that he wore around his waist unzipped itself and my change floated out and into my waiting hand.

I stared at it and then at him. 'You're empowered.'

He frowned. 'Yeah. And?'

'Nothing. Just . . .'

He straightened up, body language shifting instantly, tightening, tensing. Fighting mode. 'You got a problem? I'm just trying to—'

'No!' I said. 'Honestly. Sorry. I'm empowered too, look.' I grabbed the magazine with my mind, brought it into my hand, waved it. 'See?'

The guy relaxed, although the suspicion didn't entirely leave his face. 'OK. Just . . . you know. Some people don't like it.'

'I'm sorry,' I said. 'Didn't mean to . . . it was just a surprise. I'm not used to seeing it.'

He frowned as if I were simple. 'Eh?'

'I've been away . . .' I shook my head, put my change in my wallet and smiled awkwardly. 'Sorry. Cheers. See you.' And I carried on.

Smooth.

I kept walking for about twenty minutes, not really paying much attention to my surroundings, until I came across a quiet looking pub. Fairly rough looking as well, all peeling paint and battered furniture, but it was quiet. That was the important thing. There were five other patrons: two guys in rugby shirts playing pool, an elderly black man in a suit nursing a pint over a newspaper, two girls in their twenties giggling over wine. These latter two reminded me of the type of girls who frequented the pubs back home.

I went up to the bar. 'All right.'

The barman nodded. Between his brown jumper, strangely lopsided mop of white hair and almost spherical body shape, he looked like a Christmas pudding trying to pass as human.

'What ales do you have?' I said. It seemed like the right question to ask.

He indicated a single tap with an illustration of a golden horse rearing up on a hill.

'What's that?'

'Golden Horse.'

Surprise surprise. 'Cool, one of those please. Thanks.'

It didn't cost much more than pints had cost when I'd last bought one, which was a genuine shock. I took it to the corner, sat and sipped it – half decent, nothing to write home about – while I read the *Big Issue*. There was plenty of interesting stuff in there. A mosque built by empowered Muslims would be opening imminently. The Olympic Committee was considering the addition of superpower-enabled activities to the Games. Twentieth Century Fox was planning a multi-million dollar film based on the Collision. Michael Bay was their rumoured first choice for director.

Blimey, he's still getting work is he?

The door opened and I glanced up. A young man had walked in. He was somewhere in his twenties, pasty and chubby, and wore a leather coat that was far too long to seem anything but pretentious. He swaggered up to the bar just as the elderly guy stepped away with a fresh pint.

The bartender eyed the new arrival suspiciously. It seemed to be his default expression.

'Hmm,' said the young man. 'Whatchya got in the way of whisky?'

The bartender listlessly named a few brands.

'You don't have Bell's?'

The bartender shook his head.

The young man leaned back, shaking his head extravagantly. 'Wow. Well. What a dilemma.'

He glanced towards the pool table, just as one of the rugby-shirted guys miscued, sending the white ball flying clean off the table in a perfect arc that would have taken it right into the elderly guy's new pint . . . except it didn't. It stopped a few centimetres above, frozen in the air.

Everybody looked straight at the new arrival, who grinned cockily, raised his hand and drew the ball back through the air with his mind, placing it on the table. He bowed slightly. 'You're welcome.'

Nobody looked particularly gratified. The bartender frowned. 'Er, 'scuse me, mate. Reckon you could not do that in here?'

Hmm. This doesn't feel like it's going to go well.

The young man turned to the bartender. 'Pardon?'

'Can you not do that in here?'

'Do what?'

'Use those . . . you know.'

'I know? What do I know? Use what?' With each word his tone grew more belligerent, the volume louder. The elderly guy looked very uncomfortable and the two girls were making a very obvious effort to stare into their drinks.

'Hey,' said one of the pool players. 'No need for that tone, mate. We just like to keep things, y'know. Normal in here.'

Ouch. Pretty poor choice of words.

The young man turned towards the pool players. 'Normal?' As he spoke, he snatched both of the men's cues away from them with his mind and started twirling them around, too close, too fast.

'Oi,' said the bartender. 'You stop that, right now. If you want to piss around with your magic powers, you can go and do it in Jinx Bar or one of those places.'

'But I *want* to *drink* in *here*.' The pool cues spun faster.

'*Stop that*, or I'm going to—'

'You're going to do *what*?' the young man yelled. 'I just came in here for a quiet drink, I stopped *him* from lobbing a pool ball in *his* pint, and suddenly you think it's all right to treat me like a freak?'

'You can get out right now!' said the bartender. 'You hear me? Right now, or I'm calling the police!'

'And what are you going to tell them? That I was standing in your pub while being empowered? That's a *crime* now, is it?' The young man snapped both of the pool cues in half and the two players jumped.

'That's it,' said one, moving towards the young man, but he was immediately stopped in his tracks. Holding out his hand for effect, the young man raised a finger and the other guy rose a few centimetres off the floor.

'Stop it!' yelled one of the girls. 'Leave him alone!'

'Leave *him* alone?' the empowered guy said. 'I'm the one being victimised here!' He turned back to the bartender. 'What if I was Asian? Or a gay guy, or something? Would you tell me to leave then? Tell me to stop being gay in your pub?'

'It's not even the same bloody—'

'Shut up!' said the young man. 'I'm sick of it. *Sick of it*!'

Stanly, this is probably your cue. No pun intended.

I stood up, feeling my way towards him with my mind. He wasn't very powerful, not compared to me. I could wipe the floor with him – *literally* – without breaking a psychic sweat.

That wasn't the plan, though.

'Hey,' I said.

He turned towards me and I took the opportunity to break the connection he'd made with the pool player. The guy retreated to the other side of the table, watching with the other patrons.

'Yeah, what?' said the young man. He was trying too hard to sound sneering, it was obvious that he was worried.

'I think you should leave,' I said, as calmly as possible. *Don't lose your temper. Stay cool.*

'Oh yeah? Or you'll do what?'

'Much worse things than you can do to me.'

The young man frowned. 'You're like me.'

'No,' I said. 'I'm not.'

'You're not empowered?'

'I am. But I'm not like you. I didn't come in here looking for a fight.'

'I didn't—'

'Yeah,' I said, 'you did. You knew before you came in that they don't like empowered types in here. And you came in hoping someone would pick a fight with you, so you could be the big badass with the superpowers.'

'You can't talk to—'

'Bullied at school, were you?' I said. 'No friends? Girls didn't like you? And now you've got yourself some powers and, what, the world owes you something? It's all right for *you* to be the bully now? Nah mate. Not happening.'

He spluttered righteously but I interrupted again. 'Also,' I said, 'your "what if I was gay" analogy was possibly the stupidest thing I've ever heard – and some of the people I went to school with would have had trouble outwitting livestock. Gay people don't have *telekinesis*, you tit.'

'You f—'

'Now *piss off*,' I said. 'Before I show you some *real* superpowers.'

He wanted to fight me. He wanted to throw things. But I think he could feel my power, the same way I'd felt his. He knew mine was greater. He knew I could re-shape his arse quite painfully, if necessary. And I felt as though I was doing a pretty good job of looking like someone who was not in the mood to be messed with.

Even though I am actually kind of in the mood to be messed with.

Without looking at anyone else, he turned and stormed out. I took a deep breath and carried my empty pint glass up to the bar. 'Sorry about that,' I said. 'What a cretin.'

The bartender didn't seem to know how to respond.

'Do you want me to leave?' I said.

He shook his head. 'No . . . why did you apologise?'

Truthfully, I wasn't sure. 'Dunno,' I said. 'Can I have another Golden Horse, please?'

'Yeah. On the house.'

'It's OK, you don't have to—'

'I know.'

'OK. Thanks.' I half expected the other patrons to come up and say something, thank me, but they all kept their distance. I didn't mind. I was glad, actually. It would have been embarrassing. 'So,' I said. 'Does that sort of thing happen often?'

'No.' The bartender gave me my fresh pint, reached under

the bar and pulled out a nearly empty bottle of Bell's. He poured himself a measure and I manfully resisted the urge to smirk. 'Every now and then,' he said, 'you get some cocky ones in. But . . .' He sipped his whisky. His hands were shaking. 'I ain't got anything against you lot. You know. Happy for anyone to drink in here. Just don't like people flashing it about, you know? Makes some people uncomfortable. On edge, you know? If you ain't got 'em, it's like someone's got a weapon they can pull at any time, and you ain't.'

I nodded. I felt as though the guy wanted to speak more, open up. I was keen to hear what he had to say. 'Must be intimidating.'

'Yeah,' he said. 'And it's hard to prove, as well. Obviously they've got ways of finding out, and I could get cameras in here, but I don't want to. Enough cameras in this city as it is, plus those bloody flying things.' He sighed. 'It's all . . . I dunno.'

'I guess everyone's just expected to get used to it.'

'Yeah. And . . . yeah, it's been a few years. But . . . you see people coming in, doing six people's jobs without lifting a finger, and that's fine, I suppose, it's how things always . . . except . . . but then you have them coming in, acting all . . . it's . . .' He trailed off and drank some more whisky.

'Difficult,' I said.

He looked at me over the top of his glass and I saw the walls go up, or the blinds go down, or whatever metaphor was best to describe the total retraction of his desire to open up. Maybe I'd imagined it in the first place. He finished off the whisky and put the glass down. 'Anyway,' he said. 'Cheers. For getting rid of him.'

'No problem.' I sat and drank my pint in silence. After a

while the elderly guy came up to the bar and sat next to me.

'I think I owe you a pint,' he said, as though he'd just come to a pretty satisfactory conclusion after a protracted process of mulling things over. His accent was Jamaican.

'You don't. Really.'

'Actually,' he said, 'I think I owe you *two* pints.'

'Two? Why?'

'One for the one that didn't get spilled. And one for seeing off that little shit.'

I frowned. 'But . . . to be fair, *he* was the one who stopped your pint from getting spilled.'

The old man stared at me. 'I know. But I ain't going to be buying *him* a pint, now, am I?'

'I suppose not.'

'Thing is, I don't like to owe people,' the man continued. 'So if I buy *you* one, as far as the universe is concerned, it all works out.' His expression and voice were totally deadpan and I stared at him, trying to work out whether he was being serious or not. Finally he cracked, letting loose a jet of hoarse laughter. It sounded like a car being started for the first time in years. I liked it, and I laughed too. 'Well done, anyway,' he said. 'Plenty wouldn't have said anything, would have let him get on with it.'

'I don't like bullies.' It seemed a slightly ineffectual thing to say.

The old man nodded and that was about the extent of our conversation. He bought me two pints and I drank them. Then I insisted on buying him one, and then he insisted on buying me *another* one – 'I told you, I don't like owing' – and by this point I was more than a bit drunk and actually quite happy not to be talking. I wasn't even thinking, particularly, which was also nice. So we just sat there getting quietly, companionably pissed, and eventually I stumbled back through my front door and collapsed into bed, making a mental note to be impressed with myself the next day for finding my way back here.

As far as I knew, I didn't dream.

Chapter Twelve

GOING TO BED drunk had two major effects on waking up: one negative, one positive. On the negative side of things, I was hungover, dry-mouthed, with a bubbling sick feeling in my stomach. On the positive side of things, I woke up in bed in the flat, not curled up in the grass in another world.

Hmm. So if I just drink lots, all the time, I can avoid unintentionally panic-teleporting myself to a parallel universe.

Somehow, that didn't necessarily seem like a workable long-term solution.

Oh well.

I got up, showered and cooked myself a fry-up, feeling the roughness slowly subside. By my third cup of tea I almost felt ready to do something. But what? Practise with my powers? I definitely had a way to go where discipline was concerned – the fact that I kept accidentally transporting myself to Senia's world meant that I had nowhere near as much control as I thought I had. Which could have consequences.

Maybe Lauren can teach me some stuff. How to be calm. Keep the brain under control.

So much to do, so little time.

Or loads of time actually, to be fair.

I was still mulling things over when Sharon rang. I smiled, because I suddenly really wanted to talk to her. 'Hiya,' I said.

'Hi.'

'How's it going?'

There was a pause before she answered. 'You say that so casually.'

'Sorry.'

'No! No, it's good. It's great. Just . . . strange. I thought we'd never speak again.'

I floated through to the living room and sat down. 'Yeah.'

'How are you doing?'

'Good thanks. Sorry I haven't been in contact. Kind of . . . I don't know. Getting used to things. Stuff.' I felt as though she was letting me spin this out, wallow in my own patheticness. 'And I'm sorry things got awkward the other day, too.'

'So am I.' *Yay, she talks.* 'It's . . . it's complicated. Connor doesn't mean to come across the way he does. He just finds it all so difficult. And you remind him so much of Eddie.'

Hearing my cousin's name made my chest tighten painfully. 'You don't need to explain.'

She sighed. 'I hope you'll come back soon. I hope you'll come back a lot. He just needs to get used to you.'

The thought didn't fill me with excitement, which was very sad. 'Yeah.'

'So you have a posh flat now.'

'Yeah. Fully paid for by our good friends at Angelcorp.'

'"Good friends".'

'I was being sarcastic.'

'I know.' She didn't sound like she knew. 'Are you doing anything for them?'

'I'm having a meeting with them tomorrow. More as a favour to Lauren than anything . . . although I am kind of interested to hear what they have to say. I do get the feeling there'll be a proposition of some kind.'

'Are you going to say yes?'

'I have no idea. Maybe. Depends. It could be a good opportunity.' *Why are you talking yourself into this? There's been no offer. And why the hell would you ever accept it, if there was?* 'I can learn more about them from the inside than I can from the outside. I can see whether they really are on the level. And I can hopefully do some good into the bargain.'

'Hmm.'

'You're not convinced.'

'I don't . . . maybe. I just want you to be careful. You have a chance to be safe, to have a life, and that world . . . it's so dangerous. It's not what we thought it was. You don't need to feel like you have something to prove.'

This was news to me. 'I don't feel like I have anything to prove. I just want to put my powers to good use.'

'Angelcorp isn't the only place where you can do that,' said Sharon. 'There's us. What we do.' It was painfully obvious that she was hurt because I hadn't shown much of an interest in her and Connor's activities so far. I would have hoped that it was painfully obvious to her why that was.

'I know,' I said. 'What sort of things are you working on at the moment?'

'Helping young people, for one thing,' said Sharon. 'Young people with powers. Not just young people, of course . . . but confused people with no support network. Like we were, once. There are lots of official programmes, of course, but people still fall through the cracks. Not everybody trusts the authorities. I do counselling, in groups and one-on-one. Teach control, show people how to put their powers to good use if they want to. Or just how to stop themselves from waking up in the night with all of their furniture smashed.'

'I'd like to help,' I said, truthfully. 'I would. I will come and see it all, soon. Promise. I'm just . . . taking things slow.'

'Oh Stanly.' She sounded like she was going to cry. I really hoped she wasn't. 'I missed you so much.'

I wanted to say the same thing, but it wasn't like that for me. I hadn't had time to miss anyone. 'Yeah,' I said. 'Me too.' *Thank God this is a phone conversation. She'd see right through me. With her eyes, let alone her brain.*

We talked for a while longer, small talk, normality, but eventually I said that I had to go. 'I'll come by soon,' I said. 'If that's all right.'

'Dinner at our house?'

'OK. That'd be nice. Take care.'

'And you. Love you, you silly boy.'

'You too. Bye.'

'Nervous?' Lauren asked.

'I still kind of feel like I shouldn't be doing this.' We were in a black car, pulling into an underground parking garage beneath the Shard. The building was now coated in mirrored black glass and a number of new constructions had been built adjacent to it, connected to the main structure by round glass tunnels in various states of completion. Against a backdrop of forlorn, half gutted skyscrapers, spoiled princes and princesses whose pretty party clothes had been callously ripped away, this new Shard 2.0 radiated menacing authority. 'Camp Freeman,' I said. *Aka the Death Star.*

'This is Everest Tower,' said Lauren.

'Everest what?'

'Everest Tower. Angelcorp's London headquarters.'

'Um, I think you mean *the Shard*.'

'It was renamed Everest Tower.'

'Jesus. What is it with Freeman and his boner for re-naming things? Before long the human race is going to have to refer to itself collectively as Freemankind. Bet you a tenner. Do you still have tenners? Or do we pay in Freemans now?'

'Glad to see your sense of humour's intact.'

'If it wasn't, I'd probably have had myself sectioned by now.'

We got out of the car and Lauren pressed a guest pass into my hand and led me across the garage to a lift. Our driver, a blank-faced mid-hulk Hulk in a tight-fitting black suit, came with us. I wondered if he was empowered.

Be really handy if I could just tell, like Daryl can.

Probably be an essential skill, actually, in this day and age.

The first lift ride took less than ten seconds, depositing us in the building's huge lobby. I recognised it, as from my perspective I'd only been here about two days ago, but it also looked different – somehow they'd manage to redecorate and re-design a boring, anonymous corporate room and make it look just as boring, anonymous and corporate as before, except in a different way.

The main difference, in fact, was the frankly unnecessary level of security. Multiple X-ray scans, a thorough pat-down and an uncomfortable extended staring contest with a very intense-looking dude in a smart grey outfit, who I assumed was some sort of empowered security guard. I smiled breezily at him while he tried to saw me in half with the power of his mind or whatever he was doing, then it was on to another lift and up.

'I can't believe I'm here,' I said, glancing around the elevator, wondering when the gas was going to be released.

'Believe me, I know what you mean.'

'It'd be good to know a bit more. About those meetings you were on about. The me meetings.'

'Better for Ms Walker to tell you about it,' said Lauren. 'She was chairing said meetings, after all.'

'Fairish.'

We emerged from the lift and walked down a corridor that smelled of hot photocopies, to a door bearing a bronze plate with J. WALKER embossed on it. Lauren knocked and a woman's voice invited us in.

The office was spacious, brightly lit and full of potted plants. Sitting behind a massive, impeccably neat desk was a woman in her late forties (possibly), her platinum blonde hair pulled back in a severe bun. She wore a dark blue trouser suit and so much eye shadow that she looked vaguely supernatural.

And speaking of supernatural . . .

Standing guard behind her was a girl who could have been anything from my age to thirty. She was ghostly pale, with shiny waist-length black hair and frozen blue eyes, and wore a red skirt and a white hoody. She had a similar blank, vaguely otherworldly quality to Leon, the human anime character and psychic sword-wielding lapdog to Lucius . . . but while I'd always felt that Leon was a threat, a danger to keep an eye on and deal with if necessary, she was *scary*. Leon's blankness, ultimately, seemed like an affectation, like he was too bored – or felt too superior – to offer you anything other than the most basic facial expression in his repertoire. This girl was just . . . blank. Dead. There was nothing in those eyes.

Shudder.

'Lauren,' said the older woman, standing up and smiling.

'Ms Walker.'

'And Stanly.' Ms Walker leaned across the desk, hand outstretched. 'Jane Walker.'

'Hi.' I shook her hand. 'Pleased to meet you.'

'Likewise. Do sit down.' We sat. 'Tea? Coffee?'

'No thank you,' said Lauren. I shook my head. I could see that Lauren was uncomfortable with the scary girl's presence. Weirdly, nobody introduced her.

'How are you settling in?' asked Walker.

'Fine, thanks.'

'The flat is to your liking?'

'It is. Cheers.'

'Good.' Her smile was fifty per cent charming and fifty per cent worrying. 'The least we can do is make sure that you're comfortable.'

'Much appreciated.'

'We do what we can. You have us at something of a disadvantage, we're all rather scrambling to catch up.'

'You're not the only ones,' I said. 'The whole thing caught me by surprise too. I was fully expecting to spend the rest of my life asleep in another world.'

'Yes. Well . . .' Walker leaned forwards. 'There are a few things we should clear up before continuing. First and foremost, very few people know the real circumstances of what happened that night. Less than a handful of people at Angelcorp, and beyond these walls . . .'

'Tight circle,' I said. 'I'm aware.' *Does she even know what really happened?*

'So you understand the importance of discretion,' said Walker. 'We're walking a tightrope between order and chaos, it's a very delicate balancing act.'

'You don't want me rocking the boat.' *Or spoiling your metaphors.*

'Not to put too fine a point on it.'

'Well, don't worry,' I said. 'I know I've been a bit . . . noisy. Adjusting. But I've calmed down.'

'That's good to know.' Walker smiled. 'It's an exciting time. In fact, I think I can say without hyperbole that we are truly on the cusp of a new era.'

I gave her my sunniest smile in return. 'Tell me more.'

'Our CEO implicitly understands that the best way to maintain order, to ensure that chaos does not reign, is to allow people to live their lives productively and comfortably. The machinery of government and Angelcorp are working, in tandem, to that end. Making this country, and hopefully the world, better.'

'Fair enough.' *I wonder how many foreign leaders Freeman's had to hypnotise in the meantime.*

'Excellent,' said Walker. 'Now. I appreciate that your history with our organisation is . . . complex. Mistakes have been made. There has been conflict. But I'm sure that we're both reasonable parties and that we can see past the past – if you'll pardon the pun – and move forward co-operatively.'

Was that even a pun? 'I hope so,' I said. 'Although if you're talking about signing me up, you'll forgive me if I'm . . . skeptical.'

Something might have flashed in her eyes, and the ratio of charming to worrying in her smile tipped slightly in favour of worrying, but she nodded sympathetically. 'I completely understand. I just hope that you're open to being persuaded.'

'I'm not *not* open. What's the offer? What's on the table?'

'It depends,' said Walker. 'We're happy to take you on, on

a freelance basis, at whatever rate you negotiate. Or, and this is our preferred option, you would become a fully paid-up member of Angelcorp, with all the perks that come with such a position.'

Jesus on a pogo stick. I'm not ready for this. 'OK,' I said, maintaining total nonchalance. 'For the sake of argument, let's say I signed up properly. I'd be an employee?'

'Yes. With an extremely generous starting salary, health benefits, an appropriate level of access and the potential for a *very* rapid rise through the ranks.'

Fnarg. Mlaaaab. Bunt.

This is surely not happening.

I am not being offered this by my arch nemeses.

Also, the scary girl literally hasn't blinked for about five minutes.

'Interesting,' I said. 'Um . . . and Mr Freeman is aware of this offer?'

'You needn't concern yourself with that,' said Walker. 'I have the power to negotiate on the CEO's behalf – and on my own behalf.'

'OK . . . so . . . what would you want from me?'

'The specifics of your role would be fleshed out in due course,' said Walker. 'Suffice it to say, for now, that Angelcorp wants you on board. You are one of the strongest empowered on record. That's including those who have registered in the US, in Europe, in the Middle East. You have incredible potential, and we'd hate to see it go to waste.'

I nodded. 'Rightio. Well . . . cool. Guess I have a lot to think about.'

'You could become someone very, very important, Stanly,' said Walker. 'Not that you're not already important, of course.'

She smiled sharkily. 'And while I'm sure that some of our policies might seem to conflict with your . . . how can I say this without sounding condescending . . .'

'Please.' I gave her my best corporate bargaining smile. I had no idea what it looked like. 'Condescend away.'

'I've read your file,' said Walker. 'And I've spoken to Lauren, Mr Freeman and others. I'm aware that you have an admirably . . . idealistic view of the world. Part of what led you up against us in the first place. I bear you no ill will for that. Nor does anyone else at Angelcorp.'

'Not even Morter Smith?'

'Morter Smith does what he's told,' said Walker. 'What I mean is that you may feel that your idealistic views are incompatible with what we do.'

'It crossed my mind.'

'And I completely understand. But think about it. These abilities add a whole new dimension to human behaviour. There are so many potentially positive applications . . . and equally, so many potentially negative ones. They simply must be regulated. And we are the best placed, the best informed, to do that regulating, more so than any other organisation in the world. We're trying to do our best *for* the world under very challenging circumstances. I hope you can see that.'

'I can.' And I could, in a way. 'It's just going to take some getting used to.'

'Of course,' said Walker. 'And we're more than happy to give you as much support as you need to adjust to these new realities. Every step of the way. You are, after all, an invaluable resource. Sorry, what a terribly clinical and impersonal way of putting it . . .'

'I get your meaning,' I said. 'Don't worry.'

'Thank you. Stanly . . . Lauren and Rosie here are the two most gifted empowered that I, personally, have ever encountered. We have hundreds in our employ, and many of them are impressively powerful too. But you are unique. You can understand why we want you on our side.'

Because I'd be a pretty scary enemy?

No. Because people like this can never have enough power. Even if it's just other people's power that they're using.

Also . . . Rosie, eh?

'Because I can help you to do as much good as possible?' I said.

'Exactly.' Walker smiled widely. 'I think you understand more than some have given you credit for.'

'I imagine some people weren't keen on bringing me in.'

'To be blunt, no. Some don't know awesome potential when they see it.'

And some probably bear me a wicked grudge.

I nodded. 'Well. This has all been really interesting . . . but I'm afraid I have another meeting. And I'd like to take some time to think it all over. If that's OK?'

Walker nodded. 'Of course.' We all stood up and she and I shook hands again. 'Thank you very much for coming.' She sounded like she genuinely meant it.

'Thank *you*,' I said. 'Be seeing you.'

'Take care.'

In the lift on the way back to the lobby, Lauren looked at me. 'So. How do you think that went?'

'No idea. You?'

'I thought it went quite well.'

'She's interesting,' I said. 'Bit Pandora-ish. Like if Pandora had an aunt who was possibly evil.'

'I never met Pandora.'

'Oh yeah.'

'I know her by reputation, though,' said Lauren. 'I think it's probably an apt comparison. Walker is . . . not to be trifled with. But she's good at what she does. Ferociously intelligent.'

'A Freeman ally from way back, I presume.'

Lauren nodded. 'She headed up the New York office for years. One of the first things Freeman did was install her over here and send Lucius over there.'

Bezzie mates with Freeman, eh? So unless he was in the habit of wiping his allies too, there was a strong possibility that she knew the full story. Perhaps she'd even been involved in the conspiracy. One more reason not to trust her as far as I could throw her.

With my hands, at least.

'Who's the girl?' I said. 'Rosie?'

'I don't know. Some say she's Walker's daughter or niece, maybe even a much younger sister, but nobody really knows and her file isn't accessible. I've only met her a couple of times. Dangerous and terrifying, that's all I can really tell you.'

'Great.'

'Will you consider the offer, then?' asked Lauren. 'Seriously?'

'I will.'

Oh dear God, I think I might mean that.

'So they've pretty much offered you the company,' said Daryl.

'Seems that way.'

'And you're tempted?'

My face squirmed. 'I don't know. Sort of. I mean, if they

are on the level . . . it could be an opportunity to do some good.'

Daryl put his head on one side. 'You really think that?'

I nodded. Then I shook my head. 'Maybe? I don't know. At least if I can get in behind the scenes, I can investigate a bit. Find out if there's anything else going on. And there are definitely things I'm not happy with. The whole registration thing . . . unauthorised use of powers being classified as a crime . . .'

'I know how it seems,' said Skank, 'but what's the alternative? Just to play devil's advocate. Not everybody can be trusted not to abuse their newfound advantages. People's brains have effectively been weaponised.'

'Hmm,' I said. 'I guess . . . I don't know. Not a clue. But what do you guys think? About me signing up? As an experiment.'

'For what it's worth,' said Skank, 'I think it could be a fascinating opportunity. And I think you can be trusted not to let power, a nice flat and a hefty salary go to your head.'

'Thanks.'

'You're welcome. Although I can't say Connor will share that trust.'

'Well,' I said. 'If I really want to avoid pissing Connor off, I should probably head back to the shimmer world and go to sleep forever. Except, oh, I can't, cos they're all dead.'

Skank looked a little uncomfortable at that. 'Yes . . . well. Excuse me, final preparations. Pop through in a few minutes, it should be ready.' He got up and left the room. He was cooking Jamaican-style curried goat.

'What do *you* think?' I asked.

'I think you've been avoiding me since you got back,' said Daryl.

'I haven't. I swear. I just . . . I've been adjusting. Absorbing. You know me. Sometimes I need to be alone.'

'I know,' said Daryl. 'Sorry, I do understand, but . . . we need to talk about it all. Freeman. What went down. What we're going to do about it.'

'You're going to hate me for saying this,' I said. 'But for now . . . I don't think there's anything we *can* do. We've got no proof. Of anything. And as long as Freeman thinks I'm the only one with any knowledge, that minimises the danger. I know it must have been impossibly hard for you, these last five years, but you were right. Staying silent was the best way to keep everyone safe. For now, that *has* to be our priority. We can't lose another one.'

Daryl nodded. 'OK. So . . . what, the sonofabitch just gets away with it?'

'For now,' I said. 'Hopefully not forever. In the meantime, though, what do you think? About me joining up?'

'Honestly? I dunno, chief. I don't like the idea of you getting close to them. And not knowing what Freeman might be up to, it's dodgy. But I agree, it does have potential. At least we can safely say that the company isn't out to destroy the world. We were pretty much morons to believe that they were. Not exactly good business strategy. Would play merry hell with stock options.'

'So you're not against it.'

'In theory . . . no.'

'That's good,' I said, 'because I want you to join up with me.'

Daryl blinked, then delivered the most Blackadder-esque 'What' of his career.

'Join up with me. Be my . . . I don't know, my partner. You

have a history with them. I'll say that I'm happy to agree to their offer, on the condition that they take you on too. I feel like I've got some bargaining room. Might as well use it.'

Daryl whistled. 'I don't know, kiddo . . .'

'Think about it. You can keep me on the straight and narrow, the way you always sort of have, kind of, a bit. You'll get paid.' I leaned forwards. 'And come on – tell me the idea of us being partners, kicking down doors, investigating bad guys and busting heads doesn't sound like the coolest thing ever invented?'

'It does,' said Daryl. 'It sounds badass. But I don't trust them.'

'Neither do I. It's perfect.'

The beagle sat silently for a moment, mulling it over. 'Think about it,' I said. 'Take a couple of days.'

'I've thought about it,' said Daryl. 'Bollocks, I've got nothing else on at the moment. What's the worst that could happen? Apart from loads of really horrendous stuff?'

'Bendigedig.' I held out my hand and shook him by the paw. 'Let's go eat some goat.'

As soon as I left, I called Lauren and pitched her the idea. She was skeptical, to say the least, citing his 'problematic' history with the company, the fact that he was a loose cannon, the fact that she didn't know what the current policy was on hiring animals, vocal chords notwithstanding, and about a hundred other things. I accepted these, but stood my ground. He could sniff out empowered people. He was useful in a combat situation. He would also make me feel more comfortable and help to ease the transition. I made it pretty clear that it was a deal-breaker.

'It's never simple with you, is it?' said Lauren.

'Rarely.'

'I'll get back to you.'

'Cool. Bye.' I hung up and considered my options. The gravitational pull of the flat was undeniable. I was already associating the chair with comfort, safety, solitude . . .

But I still hadn't heard from Tara. And even though I knew I should respect her space, I had to see her. I needed to know she was OK.

I needed to know if she was angry with me.

Jacqueline answered the phone. 'Hello?'

'Hi, Jacqueline. It's Stanly. How are you?'

'Oh fine, thank you, Stanly, how are you?'

'Pretty good, all things considered. Is Tara there?'

'Tara's not feeling well, she's in bed. Terrible fever.'

'Ah. Poor thing. OK . . . well, could you tell her I rang?'

'Of course.'

'Thanks, bye.'

'Bye.' I hung up and stared at the phone, frowning. Something in her voice . . . I wasn't sure what it was. Jacqueline's default tone was pleasant, but she'd sounded so placid, so . . . mechanical.

In fact, she sounded exactly like she'd sounded on Saturday when I'd asked her what Tara was doing. When she'd told me she was out with friends.

I wasn't sure why it didn't sit right. I was probably being stupid. Paranoid. But even if I was, I still needed to see Tara. Best-case scenario, I could bring her a hot lemon drink and a sick bucket and we could talk about our feelings.

And the worst . . .

First things first, kid. Like, how the heck do buses work now?

Chapter Thirteen

MY SNAZZY PHONE found and paid for buses, as it turned out, and I even managed to not look like a complete spanner operating it. I had to take three: two that were as tatty as those I'd ridden back before the Collision, and one that was all shiny and sleek and new. Future bus. As I travelled, I watched people. They were just like normal human beings. More hands-free devices than I remembered, admittedly, and lots of unfamiliar names, designs and faces on T-shirts, but mostly just . . . normal. No sign of any powers. Maybe it was a faux pas to use them on public transport.

It almost felt like reality.

'Stanly!' said Jacqueline. 'I wasn't expecting you!'

'Sorry,' I said. 'I was passing. Can I come in?'

'Of course.'

'I know you said she's a bit under the weather,' I said, as she ushered me in, 'but could I see Tara, please? I think she'd want to see me, even if she does look feverish and gross!'

'She's out with friends.' Jacqueline smiled. The same smile as Saturday. The same tone as well, the same inflection, the same emphasis on the word 'friends'. This was not normal.

I frowned. 'But when I spoke to you before, you said she wasn't well.'

Jacqueline's brow furrowed. 'I . . . I don't think . . .' She paused. It was like I was seeing through her, catching a glimpse of confusion beneath, but then she recovered and did that smile again. 'She's out with friends.'

'Jacqueline,' I said. 'When did you last see Tara?'

'Oh, just today. She's out—'

'With friends.' Panic was starting to bubble in my stomach. 'OK. Which friends, do you know?'

That furrowed brow again, a splutter of confusion in her eyes . . . then the smile returned. 'She's out with friends.'

'OK.' I tried a smile of my own. 'That's fine. Is Oliver in?'

'No,' said Jacqueline. 'He plays cards on Monday evenings. Can I get you a tea or a coffee?'

'Sure,' I said. 'Coffee would be great. Mind if I just pop to the bathroom?'

'Of course.' She went through to the kitchen and I hurried upstairs. Rather than go to the bathroom, though, I went to find Tara's room.

The first thing that hit me was the bad smell. The second was the fact that Tara was very much not there. The third was how different it was from her old room. All the posters and pictures were different, some bands and actors I knew and some I didn't. No photos, I noticed, none of Tara with friends, or with her foster parents. Different bed. The room didn't look like anyone had been in it for a while, and this was confirmed when I found the source of the smell – some old plates under the bed, the leftover food they held in an advanced state of mouldering.

Don't panic.

Feeling more than a little uncomfortable, I checked some drawers. It definitely looked like there were clothes missing. And . . . *oh God. No no no I am not looking at Tara's underwear—*

PULL YOURSELF TOGETHER, YOU MORON, *TARA'S UNDERWEAR IS NOT YOUR CONCERN; THE FACT THAT SHE'S NOT HERE AND JACQUELINE HAS CLEARLY BEEN BRAINWASHED IS.*

I scanned the bulletin board, looking at various flyers for nights that surely, even now, she was too young to attend. Nothing leapt out, but I used my phone (with difficulty) to take a few pictures anyway. Then I headed back downstairs, stopping by the bathroom on the way and flushing the toilet. Keeping up appearances and all that.

Jacqueline was waiting in the living room with my coffee, smiling as though nothing were amiss. I copied the smile. 'Thanks, Jacqueline. I'll be in to drink it in a sec, I just have to make a call if that's OK?'

'Of course!'

I went out to the front porch, closed the door behind me and was about to call Lauren when something stopped me. I'd been thinking I'd get her to connect me to Freeman and demand to know where Tara was, because obviously he must have kidnapped her. After all, he had already interfered with Oliver and Jacqueline's brains once. And he was my enemy.

But . . . no. It didn't make sense. Surely Tara had served her purpose, as far as Freeman was concerned? He had used her against me and won. She didn't have powers. What further use could he have for her? It made sense that he'd have wiped Oliver and Jacqueline's memories, two less loose ends . . . but why take Tara? Why now? Why antagonise me?

More to the point, I was pretty sure that mouldy food in her room had been there longer than I'd been back in the world. That made it even less likely that Freeman was responsible.

OK then. We can probably wipe G. Freemeister off the suspects list.

That left the second – or, thinking about it, perhaps the first – most obvious possibility: Morter Smith. Her father. The man who had, in a manner of speaking, covered me in spiders, shot me, electrocuted me and chainsawed my hand off. Granted, he'd used a shimmer controlled by a messed-up-in-the-head empowered to make me *think* that was what was happening, rather than actually doing it, but it had been fairly convincing. More to the point, it had all been about Tara.

But again . . . did it fit? Everyone was sure that Smith hadn't gone near her since the Collision. *And* he was working for Freeman now. The only explanation for both of those things was that he'd been brainwashed. Presumably at this point he didn't even know she was his daughter.

So . . . what? Someone else?

Goddamnit.

OK. New plan.

I went back in, all smiles, accepted my coffee and made small talk, like I had on Saturday. This time, however, I tried a different mental tactic. I'd only been feeling for Jacqueline's thoughts then, acting like a receiver, but now I was being proactive, trying to actively go into her mind, see if I could feel anything out of the ordinary. I felt horrible, going in without her permission, but surely it was justified in this instance? I could have let her know something was amiss, but I was reluctant. What if it screwed up her mind somehow?

Jesus Christ, I have no idea what I'm doing.

It was tricky doing this while maintaining a normal conversation but somehow I managed it, and pretty much immediately I felt that something was wrong. There were . . . patterns that shouldn't have been there, odd masses of foreign colour, thoughts that . . . it was like they *smelled* wrong, except I was smelling with my brain rather than my nose. Beyond that, I couldn't interpret what I was feeling. All I knew was that there was wrongness afoot and I was fairly sure that a cursory scan of Oliver's mind would find something similar.

As soon as seemed polite, I made my excuses. 'Sorry, Jacqueline, got to run. Meeting someone.'

'Oh, all right dear,' said Jacqueline, giving me that smile again. It was creepy . . . but more than anything, it made me sad. And *angry*. No matter what lay in our respective pasts, whatever damage she and her husband had done, this wasn't right.

I reached out and took her hands, squeezed them, smiled. 'It'll be OK.'

'What will?'

'Nothing,' I said. 'Just . . . I'll see you soon. Take care.'

I left the house, swiping a photograph of Tara on the way out. It looked like one of the most recent ones, her in a navy-blue school sweatshirt that reminded me dizzily of the one I'd worn in my final, truncated year of school. Outside, I took a second to compose myself, eyes closed, breathing deeply.

Then I rang Lauren.

'Sorry, Stanly,' she said, 'they haven't made a decision yet—'

'You need to go to Oliver and Jacqueline Rogers' house,' I said. 'You need to read their minds. Someone has been messing with them. Implanting some sort of programmed response, altering their memories. You can check for stuff like that, can't you?'

'I can. How do you know this?'

'Trust me. I know.'

'But why would anyone—'

'Tara's missing,' I said. 'And someone wants to cover it up. When you go round there and ask about her, Jacqueline says she's not in, that she's "out with friends". She says the exact same thing every time, word for word. Same tone. She even does the same smile. But if you phone, then she says Tara's ill in bed. I reckon the phone response is there to keep her school off the scent, in case they ring.'

'You're *sure* Tara's missing?'

'Yes. I know her parents. I know how well they look after her. Her room hasn't been touched for days, there were mouldy plates . . . it's not like them. At all. And clothes were missing.'

'Maybe she's run away,' said Lauren. 'Maybe . . .'

'No,' I said. 'It's not that. She's been taken and someone's tried to cover it up.'

'Who?'

'My first thought was Morter Smith.'

'Smith? Why on earth—'

'She's his daughter.'

'She's *what?*'

'His daughter.' I frowned. Something in my gut told me it wasn't Smith, but I definitely wanted to talk to him anyway. 'Can you organise a meeting?'

'You and Smith? I'm not sure that's a good idea . . .'

'I just need to ask him some questions. You can be there, you and whoever else, it's fine. Put a toughened glass window between us if you want, I promise I won't go postal on him. I just have to see if he has anything to do with this. *Please*, Lauren.'

'I'm not even sure where he is. Freeman often sends him off on hush-hush assignments. Even his home address is classified.'

'Please can you try?'

'All right, I'll do what I can.'

'Thank you.'

'What are you going to do now?'

'I'm going to look for Tara.'

In reality, looking for Tara entailed sitting on a bench, scrutinising the pictures I'd taken of her bulletin board for about half an hour, wishing I'd spent longer checking for clues. I was almost at the end of my tether when something tucked away in the corner started ringing a very, very faint bell: a flyer, almost completely covered by another one, for a DJ night happening at Jinx Bar.

Jinx Bar. Where had I heard . . .

At that pub. The bartender. He'd told that douchebag in the coat to go to Jinx Bar.

I rang Skank and he confirmed that it was a favoured haunt of both empowered and 'their fans'. 'I'm going to head there now,' I said.

'OK. I'd come and meet you but I'm just on my way out. Shall I dispatch our canine agent?'

'Yep, send in the beagle.'

From the outside, Jinx Bar looked like some sort of squat in the rough part of Neo-Tokyo: what few windows it had were either blacked out or boarded up and JINX was spelled out in drips of red and purple plastic that would presumably light up when it got dark. I had a feeling that the windows were meant to look broken. It was well before club hours so there were no signs of life, and I sat on a wall impatiently kicking my legs up and down, waiting.

'Man alive. I am definitely not used to seeing you yet.'

I turned to see Daryl padding up the street. 'Aww,' I said. 'That's sweet.'

'I am sweet.'

'You did see me earlier today, though.'

'I know.' He hopped up onto the wall next to me, his agility reminding me more of a cat than a dog. 'This the place?'

'It is.'

'And you think there might be some Tara-related clues afoot.'

'I do.'

Daryl took a sniff of the air. 'Hmm. Maybe . . . hard to tell from this far.' He jumped off the wall and I followed him across the road. A drone whistled overhead.

'How do people put up with those things?' I said.

'With what?'

'The drones, obviously.'

'Oh. Well. Think I just gave you your answer. They've pretty much been a fixture since the Collision, people barely notice them now.'

'That's messed up.'

'I guess it is.' We walked towards the entrance, Daryl sniffing carefully between words. 'Nailah actually wrote a really good piece about it a while ago. You should look it up. "The New Abnormal", it was called.' He stopped, sniffed. 'Hmm. I'm definitely getting some essence of Tara. She's been here.'

'Recently?'

'In the last week. Possibly the last few days even . . . it's a bit tricky to tell. Not an exact science.'

'Right.' I gave the door an exploratory knock. Nothing, as expected. We walked around the edge of the building, Daryl still sniffing away, and found a side door and a back entrance, but none yielded anything. I glanced around to see if anyone was watching.

'Hold on,' said Daryl.

'What?'

'That was you checking if the coast was clear for you to fly, or blast a door off its hinges or something, wasn't it?'

'Maybe . . .'

'You're thinking you're going to break in and look for clues.'

'Possibly . . .'

'How about this?' said Daryl. 'I would guess that Tara has either upped sticks by herself, of her own accord, or gone with someone who doesn't wish her harm. Why would her clothes be gone?'

'I'm not particularly keen to chill out based on that hunch.'

'I know,' said Daryl. 'But hear me out. Stuff like this has happened before.'

'To her?'

'No, but to other . . . troubled youths. Hypnotising their parents with their new abilities, or getting friends to do it, running off, partying . . . not saying it's good, by any means. But it's a thing. It's been in the news.'

I looked unhappily at the locked door.

'Stanly,' said Daryl. 'Your position with Angelcorp is pretty tenuous right now. I agree with you that the best course of action is to avoid trouble. You don't want to give them, or Freeman, *any* excuse to come down on you.'

Ugh, stop being right. 'So?'

'So this place will be open in a few hours. Let's go and have a sit, a think, then come back and do some non-illegal investigative whatevers. Sound good?'

'But what if you're wrong? What if she's in real trouble? Any time that we waste . . .'

'At least wait to hear from Lauren.'

I didn't want to wait. I wanted to be looking now. This was the only thing I had that even resembled a lead.

'Look,' said Daryl, patiently. 'Last time I saw Tara, she was a pretty pissed-off lass. Angry at the world. Angry at us.'

'At me.'

'*Anyway*,' said the dog, 'I wouldn't have put it past her to run away then. I wouldn't put it past her now.'

'But the brainwashing . . .'

'Maybe she has an empowered boyfriend or something,' said Daryl. 'Again, not saying it's not bad, but it's not necessarily *mega* bad.'

Oh God, no. Tara can't have boyfriends. She's a child. 'You reckon?'

'If she's been here,' said Daryl, 'she's been mixing with empowered. Definitely.' He fixed me with an unusually solemn gaze. 'Stanly, in your heart of hearts, do you really think that she's in danger, like life-threatening danger, right now? That there's literally no way you can wait? If you really feel that way, if you *genuinely* think you need to go stampeding in there, breaking into private property, risking arrest, beating a confession out of the first poor shmuck you come across . . . then I'd still ask you to chill out and wait.'

I managed a laugh. I really didn't like the idea of hanging about. But what he said made sense. 'Fine. Where shall we go?'

'I actually had a rather excellent idea on that front,' said Daryl. 'We're near Balham, aren't we?'

'Think so?'

'Well I might know someone in Balham. Someone who might even be able to help us out.' The dog winked.

I stared at him for a moment. 'So? Who is it?'

'Oh. Nailah. Her office is in Balham.'

'Why wouldn't you just immediately say that?'

'I thought we'd just go, and it would be a surprise.'

'A *surprise?*'

'Yeah.'

'What, like in a film? You just wink at me, and then we smash cut to us being at Nailah's office?'

'Well . . .'

'That's where you thought the cut would be, didn't you? After you did that wink?'

'Screw you.'

Chapter Fourteen

NAILAH'S OFFICE WAS in a dilapidated brown building near Balham station. I pressed the buzzer and waited, feeling a bit more casual than earlier – bantering with Daryl was pretty good medicine for stress. 'You definitely reckon she'll be here?'

'She's always here.'

A moment later a fuzzy male voice came over the intercom. *'Sentry.'*

'Hi,' I said. 'Is Nailah about?'

'Who's asking?'

'A kid and a beagle, tell her.'

'You what?'

'A kid and a beagle. She'll understand.'

'What? Look mate, I don't have time to piss around. Who are you?'

'Seriously, say a kid and—'

'Tell her Stanly and Daryl are here,' said Daryl, cutting across me. He gave me a Look. 'Did you get out of the annoying side of bed this morning, or did you put extra annoying milk on your Annoying Flakes?'

'Just having a bit of a joke with the guy. What can I say?'

'You can say less. Less would be good.'

I blew a raspberry.

'Y'know,' said Daryl, 'I think I prefer stressy vengeful Stanly.'

Another voice came over the intercom before I could respond. A voice I recognised. 'So. Either someone up here is messing with me, or someone down there is.'

'Hi Nailah,' I said.

She whistled. It sounded weirdly scratchy through the speaker. 'Well. Skank told me you were back, but I thought he was succumbing to some form of early onset geek dementia. I said I'd have to see it for myself.'

'Buzz us in and all will be revealed. Sort of.'

Nailah buzzed us in and we headed down a cold, echoing corridor and past a presumably dead lift, its half-open doors criss-crossed with red tape. Everything was brown and smelled of old, and while most of the other small businesses based in the building looked tatty and forlorn from the outside, when we reached Nailah's digs on the top floor it was immediately obvious that she had spent a bit more money. The door was heavier and newer than anything else in the building, with multiple locks, a metal plate with THE SENTRY HEAD OFFICE embossed on it and even a CCTV camera mounted on a swivelling ball above.

'Blimey,' said Daryl. 'She's had the builders in since I was last here.'

I knocked and a rectangular peephole slid open. 'Hi,' I said to the suspicious eye beyond. 'Stanly and Daryl to see Nailah. Please.'

The peephole closed and the door swung open. 'Well,' said Nailah. 'I do declare. The boy who lived.'

''Sup dude. You look literally the same. Apart from the glasses.'

'All my scars, weight and hairstyle fluctuations are on the inside.' We hugged and Nailah nodded at Daryl. 'Snoopy.'

'Ms Editor.'

'Come on in,' said Nailah. 'Welcome to the battle bridge.'

If not for the computers' paper-thin screens and wireless touch-pad keyboards, it could have been the headquarters of some kind of alternative 'zine from the Seventies. Framed front pages on the walls, clippings everywhere, half-smoked cigarettes in ashtrays. There were two other people sitting at cluttered desks typing furiously: a skinny brown-skinned guy with THIS WEEK'S DAILY MAIL HATE FIGURE written on his T-shirt and a round beehive-haired girl wearing thick red glasses and luminous kitten-pattern leggings.

'Amrik and Becca,' said Nailah. 'Stanly and Daryl.'

Becca grinned as us, although her typing didn't miss a beat. 'Hey.'

Amrik granted us a very brief nod. 'All right.'

'Nice to meet you,' I said.

'Yo,' said Daryl.

The typing stopped and both Amrik and Becca furnished us with their undivided attention. Becca's eyes widened, while Amrik's narrowed. 'Did the dog just talk?' he asked.

'He did,' said Daryl.

'That's the one?' asked Becca. 'The one you were on about?'

'He is,' said Nailah.

'I honestly still kinda thought you were taking the piss,' said Amrik.

'Nope.'

Amrik grinned. 'Awesome.'

'Oh my God,' said Becca. 'Tumblr is going to *explode*.'

Nailah chuckled. 'Best sidekick ever, yo.'

'Side*what?*' said Daryl.

'*Anyway*,' I said. 'Nailah, keen for a chat?'

'Side*who?*' said Daryl.

'Chat?' said Nailah, hand flying to her chest. 'Why, do you mean to tell me that this is a *business* call? I'm hurt. I thought we were going to catch up and have smoothies.'

'Should have thought of that. I know you journos are all about the sweet, sweet bribes.'

'Yep, one plastic cup of blended-up fruit mulch and E numbers and my front page is anyone's.' She led us through a door with NAILAH ADEYEMI – EDITOR written on it, into an adjoining office.

I blinked. 'Wow. So you took the crazy serial killer wall concept and just crazied it to its logical conclusion.'

There was barely an inch of wallpaper showing beneath the coating of newspaper and magazine clippings, photographs, charts, Post-it notes, front covers (although these had been ripped and glued rather than neatly framed) and other miscellaneous scraps of paper and card. Even the bookshelves, into which were crammed vastly more books than the shelves had been designed to hold, had things pinned to every spare patch of wood.

It's like my old bedroom, only fifty times more mental.

Nailah grinned. 'I prefer the term Room Full of Crazy.'

'Not enough handwritten mathematical equations and Bible quotes,' said Daryl.

'I'd like to see you crazy up a better one.' Nailah sat down at her desk, whose clutteredness made the clutter in the other room seem pretty well organised. 'Take a seat.' She motioned towards a bed in the corner. I made sure that the door was closed behind us, then sat on the bed. Daryl took the floor.

'So,' I said. 'Do you . . . live here?'

'Pretty much,' said Nailah. 'Couldn't exactly afford to rent this office *and* a flat of my own. Still paying for the security gear, and probably will be until long past death.'

'How's the paper doing?'

'Good. From certain angles. If ya squint *real* hard. My social life would say no. But *pfft*. Who needs such distractions?' She smiled. 'Everyone said I couldn't have picked a worse time in the history of print to launch a new print publication, but against all the odds, readership is growing and we're not quite bankrupt yet. The co-op model is working pretty nicely, and people respect our editorial integrity and the fact that we refused the various post-Collision creative grants that Angelcorp were offering. You should see what's happened to the publications that *did* accept them. Vanilla as shit.'

'Bet that suits Angelcorp.'

'To be fair to our new overlords – and it physically pains me to say that – they leave us alone. Those who took the funding, less so. And the mainstream media is as zealous a centurion of the Overton Window as it ever was.'

I smiled sympathetically, even though I didn't really know what that last bit meant.

Nailah shrugged. 'Anyway. *That's* boring. Please tell me how you came to be back in the world, not a day older.'

I told her as quickly – and safely – as possible. 'OK,' she said. 'Seriously. You *have* to let me profile you. You did agree to it, once upon a time, remember?'

'I know,' I said. 'And yeah. Sometime. Although I couldn't help noticing that you got your super-person interview already.'

'Full disclosure, I got a few. To which do you refer?'

'Chavengers. Wicked piece. Although really shit how that all ended.'

174

'Shit indeed.' She shook her head grimly.

'I couldn't find any info about what happened afterwards. To the others.'

'Yeah,' she said. 'When the powers that be want some info contained, it stays contained.'

I narrowed my eyes. 'You know, don't you?'

'Course.' Nailah grinned. 'Well. I know that Thor Blimey, aka Danielle Dewornu, is now rapidly rising through the ranks of Angelcorp's superpowered police force. Which I actually kinda wish I didn't know.'

'Are you serious?'

'Look at this face.'

'You *are* serious.' *Must be where all formerly idealistic super-people end up.* 'And the other two?'

'The other two,' said Nailah, 'are *not* doing that. In fact, the other two are at large.'

'How come? I thought they were all arrested?'

'They were. I've never been able to find out exactly what happened, but somehow they escaped custody before they could be brought to trial.' She smiled. 'Good for them.'

I nodded.

Ask about Tara.

She blatantly doesn't know anything about Tara.

But . . .

'I feel you itching to ask me something,' said Nailah. 'I did wonder if there was some sort of motive afoot.'

'*You* want to talk to *me* about ulterior motives? I might refer you back to that time you came to me with info about this empowered girl named Lauren and withheld certain key details . . .'

'OK, OK, touché and all my guilt and sorrow for all time.'

She grinned apologetically. 'Seriously. I'm sorry. It's kept me awake more than once.'

'Forget it.'

'I won't, but thanks. So. What's up?'

I told her what had happened, or what I thought had happened. 'I vaguely know Jinx Bar by reputation,' said Daryl. 'Thought you might know a bit more.'

Nailah nodded. 'Empowered bar. Well. Empowered plus lots of groupies. Power shippers, y'know.' I felt Daryl give me a Meaningful Look, which I pointedly ignored. 'It's a pretty dodgy spot,' Nailah continued, 'and there are a few others like it, also dodgy. But Angelcorp doesn't want the empowered getting all uppity and feeling maligned and victimised and potentially rising up and taking over the world. So as long as they're not tearing buildings down, they're treated like super special people, and they can just get on with their dodginess, and nobody cares. Meanwhile, we can't get a non-superpowered maintenance guy to come and fix our elevator, or the air conditioning, because *they're* all off doing the jobs that the superpowered maintenance people *aren't* doing because *they're* doing the big prestige projects up town . . .'

'I sense beef,' said Daryl.

'Oh, I gots beef,' said Nailah. 'I gots, like, a month of Sunday dinners' worth of beef. You can read all about it in my latest editorial.'

'I will,' I said. 'But maybe we could come back to Tara?'

'Sorry,' said Nailah. 'I'm . . . let's just say I don't get much sleep these days. Ever. So yeah, sounds to me like your girl either developed herself some special abilities, or she's involved with people who have 'em.'

'She doesn't have powers,' I said. 'Does she, Daryl?'

'Oh, yeah, she does,' said the dog. 'Forgot to tell you, sorry.' He levelled me with a wrecking-ball stare. 'Of course I would have neglected to mention that *absolutely essential information*.'

'All right, love, calm down.'

'I'm sure she's not empowered,' said Daryl. 'I'm more inclined to go with the empowered friend angle. Or boyfriend. Or, y'know. Girlfriend. Bad boy, bad girl, something. She's at an impressionable age.'

'Speaking as someone who was once a sixteen-year-old girl,' said Nailah, 'it's so plausible that we might as well just make it our conclusion now.'

'But . . .' I shook my head. 'I don't get it. Why would Tara go along with that? Why would she fall for some dickhead bad boy with powers?'

Now it was Daryl and Nailah's turn to exchange Meaningful Looks. 'What's that look for?' I said.

'Stanly,' said Daryl. 'Let me tell you a story, about a little girl. One night she went out into the world and got kidnapped by a monster, and taken back to its scary lair. She would have died as well, except she was rescued by a handsome older boy with superpowers. Well. Maybe not *handsome*. Sort of cute in a slightly emo, geeky kinda way. Anyway, this older boy then rescued her a few more times, before vanishing forever, shortly before she entered the wilderness years of puberty. She then—'

'All right,' I said, feeling myself go red. 'I get your point.'

'Again,' said Nailah, '*terrifyingly* plausible.'

'Fine,' I said. 'Fine. So you think Jinx Bar is a good bet?'

'I'd say so.'

'Cool . . .' I frowned.

She raised an eyebrow. 'Something else on your mind?'

'Angelcorp,' I said, thinking about my meeting that morning. It felt like a very long time ago. 'You mentioned beef. Care to elaborate?'

Nailah shrugged. 'A liberal, benevolent-ish, socially responsible, transparent-when-it-suits-them, environmentally-friendly corporate dictatorship is still a corporate dictatorship.'

'That should definitely be their slogan,' said Daryl.

'I'll pitch it to Lauren,' I said.

'Haven't seen much of her lately,' said Nailah.

'I have,' I said. 'She seems pretty on message.'

'You kind of have to be, in her position.' Nailah sighed. 'Look, I know it's not black and white. This is a new, complex, scary world. People gotta do what they gotta do. But if you want *my* opinion of Angelcorp? Or whether I think you should trust them, or accept anything they may be offering you? Then N-O spells "dear God, boy, stay the hell away".'

Wow. Astute. She must be a journalist or something. I nodded. 'Thanks.' Then something occurred to me and I frowned again. 'Um . . . would you include mobile phones among the things not to accept from them?'

Nailah's eyes narrowed. '*Tell me* you didn't bring an Angelcorp phone into my office.'

'I might perhaps have maybe possibly—'

'Jesus!' She jumped up. 'Give it to me! Now!'

I took out my swanky phone and Nailah was in mid-snatch when it started to ring. It was Lauren. I yanked it back. 'I have to take this. I *have* to.'

'Don't you dare,' said Nailah. 'Not in here. You have no idea what—'

'Fine, fine, show me out! Is the corridor out there OK?'

'*Ugh!*' Nailah bustled me out of her room and through

the main office, practically shoving me into the corridor and telling me in no uncertain terms what would happen if I tried to bring the phone back in. Then she slammed the door.

I answered. 'Lauren?'

'Hi,' said Lauren. 'I've just been to talk to the Rogers.'

'And?'

'You were right. Someone's been interfering with their brains. Fairly simple stuff, which makes it easier for the brain to accept. Pre-programmed responses to certain questions. Stanly, I should get them to a clinic.'

'A clinic? Why, are they . . .'

'It's all right, this sort of interference doesn't damage the brain – but if you try to remove it without knowing what you're doing, that can cause problems.'

'OK,' I said. 'How long will it take before you can find out what happened?'

'It depends. Several days, at least.'

'Great.' I sighed. 'Can you hold off on reporting this? Just for now?'

'Stanly, this is a crime. Tampering with minds . . .'

'Lauren, *please*. I need to find Tara myself.'

'The clinic will have to make it official, they have a legal obligation.'

'Can you stall them? Tell them it's . . . I don't know, a sensitive case or something?'

'No,' said Lauren. 'I can't. I'm sorry.'

'Fine. I . . .' *Lightbulb*. 'OK, how about this? I want to investigate their case. Officially.'

'What do you mean?'

'If Angelcorp want me on board, I want this to be my first case.'

179

'They haven't even decided if they're going to accept you, let alone what your duties might be . . .'

'Is it a possibility, though?'

A seriously exasperated sigh. 'For God's *sake*, Stanly, you can't just expect to immediately go off investigating whatever you want. Even if there *was* the slightest chance that Walker would allow you to take on something like this, there's inductions and paperwork and—'

'I'll talk to Freeman, then.'

'*What?*'

'I'll talk to Freeman. I'm sure he'll happily let me loose on it. After all, I did help him save the world.'

'Stanly—'

'I have to go now, Lauren. Let me know if you hear anything else about the Rogers, or if Walker et al make a decision about me and Daryl. Oh, or if you manage to sort out a meeting with Smith.'

Another sigh. 'You are a *severe* pain in my arse.'

'Lauren! That's not like you to say "arse".'

'Oh, shut up.'

'Also,' I said, 'I might have to lose the phone you gave me.'

'What? What do you mean, lose it? Stanly—'

'Sorry! Thanks! Bye.' I hung up and knocked on Nailah's office door again. The peephole opened. 'I'm done now,' I said.

'Turn the phone off.'

'Give me a pen first.'

A brief pause, then she pushed a pen through the peephole. I quickly wrote all my essential numbers on my hand before switching the phone off. 'Phone's off.'

'Put it on the floor.'

I did so.

The door opened and Nailah emerged with a hammer and proceeded to smash my phone into an impressive number of pieces.

'I think you killed it,' said Daryl.

'Damn right I did.' Nailah looked at me disbelievingly. 'How in the hell . . . I mean *why* would you . . .'

'Hey, I'd just got back from five years in alien deep freeze. I wasn't about to look a gift phone in the mouth.'

'Get in here.' She swept up the pieces, deposited them in a glass of water and took us back through to her office. I resumed my position on the bed and Nailah threw herself into her chair and reached for a packet of cigarettes. 'How do you think they keep track of everyone?' she asked, lighting one. '*Especially* empowered?'

'I thought you smoked an e-cigarette thing.'

'You try doing my job and smoking one of those things. Not happening.' She blew out smoke. 'One of Angelcorp's first big gifts to the UK was establishing a very high tech – and, more pertinently, *free* – mobile phone network. They even brought out their own range of dirt-cheap, responsibly-manufactured smartphones, for people who otherwise wouldn't be able to afford one. And because it's basically impossible to get through life now without a phone, everyone has one. I mean *everyone*. Empowered registration details, all personal info in fact, is kept on phones. And, most importantly, all subscribers to the A7 network may from time to time receive certain upgrades and software packages from our friends at Angelcorp. Y'know, for *security* reasons.'

'And . . . what, people just . . .'

'Yeah. Free unlimited phone use? In exchange for a very poorly defined invasion of one's civil liberties? Yes please! Sign me up!'

'So . . . phones can track *power* use?'

'New ones do,' said Nailah. 'All power use within a certain proximity. Along with God knows what else. I think it's safe to assume "everything". Hence me not wanting one anywhere near any of my computers.'

'Guess at least it makes people less likely to steal them,' I said.

Nailah laughed darkly. 'That's one dull-ass silver lining. It's not just phones that track power use, though, so do CCTV cameras *and* our friendly neighbourhood drones. Oh, and most trains and buses. It was all there in the Post-Collision Domestic Security, Surveillance and Public Safety Bill, pushed quietly through a late-night session of parliament while George Freeman live-streamed an inspiring speech on Angelcorp's website to a million or so viewers.' She smoked bitterly for a moment. 'You want to know the worst thing? They *know*. People know all about it and they trundle happily along. Non-empowereds feel safer, empowereds I guess are just glad they're not in super-prison. Even crusading moral justice-y types are all like "well, so long as I agree with Angelcorp's general approach to things, I'm happy for them to have all the anti-democratic powers in the world".' She shook her head. 'Damn liberals. Thing is, when some not-so-benevolent overlords come along, which they inevitably will, those same people will probably start complaining immediately. And I bet you they won't even see the irony.'

Lauren could have mentioned this. I looked at Daryl. 'Did you know? About the phones?'

'Not in detail. But yeah. Sorry kid, there was so much . . .'

'Don't worry,' I said. 'I mean . . . I guess . . . it kind of makes sense? I was thinking it must be a nightmare if you're trying to get some dirt on an empowered criminal, anything that would help . . .'

'And those with nothing to hide have nothing to fear,' said Nailah. 'Maybe you *should* go and work for Angelcorp.'

'Woah there, sport! Calm down.'

'Sorry. I just feel pretty strongly about this stuff.'

'No shit,' murmured Daryl.

'I sympathise,' I said. 'I do. But, Jesus, how am I supposed to have an opinion on post-apocalyptic policy making? I haven't got the faintest idea what to think about anything.' *Need a subject change ASAP.* 'I just want to find Tara.'

'Well,' said Nailah, thankfully happy to go with the subject change, 'one thing I would say on that front – your chatty sidekick . . .'

'Side*huh*?' said Daryl.

'He may bring you some unwanted attention at Jinx Bar.'

'What do you mean?' I asked.

Nailah smiled. 'Daryl, you haven't seen a web comic called *A Boy And His Dog*, have you?'

'No . . .'

'OK. Sorry I never showed it to you . . . to be honest, I thought you might find it upsetting.' She leaned over to her computer, called up a browser and typed something in. A website appeared, done up like the front page of a comic. I blinked. The titular boy was an anime-style character who looked suspiciously like me, floating a few feet off the ground, watched admiringly by a dog that looked vaguely like Daryl, in front of a stylised London skyline.

I looked down at the beagle. His jaw had dropped. 'What in the holy hump of hell is this?' he said. 'Who . . .'

'Dunno,' said Nailah. 'Never managed to track the artist

down. Not even sure she's definitely a she, just going by the signature. It's been around for a couple of years.'

'It's about *us?*' I said.

'Yep,' said Nailah. 'Very first story is set during the Collision. Stanley – with an 'e' – and his noble dog pal rescue a girl and her little brother. The rest of it is the boy and the dog wandering from place to place, world to world, fighting bad guys, monsters and the like.'

'Hold on . . . a girl . . .' I practically fell into a flashback portal. I could *see* her. 'Remember, Daryl? At the Kulich? The girl with the crowbar?'

'Lucifer's balls,' said Daryl.

'It must be her,' I said.

Nailah was looking at me enquiringly and I explained. 'We *did* save her. Well . . . we didn't exactly do much, actually, just took her and her brother inside, showed them where to hide.'

'I would imagine she's probably our artist,' said Nailah. 'Awesome! Mystery maybe solved. I've been dying to know who came up with this.' She grinned at my dumbstruck expression. 'Man, you should *see* your face. Priceless.'

'Well, it's *weird.*'

'I bet.' She re-lit her cigarette. 'Look. Obviously the official story is the official story. But there are mutterings. In certain circles, mostly empowered, people talk about the possibility of a different version of events. Like maybe there was someone who helped, or perhaps did more than just help. Someone who's been wiped from the record. Been that way ever since the Collision. This comic just added fuel to that fire.'

'I can't believe I didn't know about this,' said Daryl. 'You're an *urban legend*, kid!'

184

I shook my head. 'Nope. I'm not. But Nailah's right, you'll attract attention if you come with me. I'll go alone.'

'No you—'

'Yes I will. You can wait nearby. I'll meet you when I've got all the info I need. And if I get into trouble, I'll think a little whistle and you can come storming in. Anything else that might help me, Nailah?'

'Just be careful,' said Nailah. 'Some serious weirdos hang out in Jinx Bar. I'll keep my ear to the ground anyway. If I hear anything, I'll get hold of you.'

'How?' I said. 'Just thinking about my total lack of a phone.'

She rolled her eyes, rummaged in a drawer and took out a battered phone. 'Here, take one of my spares.' She quickly input a couple of numbers.

'Cheers.'

'No worries. Just make sure you keep your promise, re: that interview. And maybe you can do me some other favour some time.'

'Will do.' I put my other hastily scrawled numbers into the phone and pocketed it. 'Well. I'm going to go and get something to eat. Then I'm going to go and get my detective on. Keen, dog?'

'I don't remember signing up to be a detective,' said Daryl. 'But fine.'

'Think of it as a rehearsal for our potential forthcoming employment.'

Nailah chuckled. 'Stanly Bird, boy detective, dog at his side. I can't quite get my head around it. I'm going to have to start calling you Veronica.'

'Making me Backup?' said Daryl.

'You knows it.'

'OK,' I said. 'I feel like there's a reference I'm not getting. Which might be the scariest thing to have happened since the monster apocalypse.'

'It's happened a couple of times,' said Daryl. 'You're slipping. And FYI it's a reference to *Veronica Mars*.'

'Oh. Never watched it.'

Nailah fist-bumped Daryl's paw. 'I pity him.'

'I never don't pity him.'

'I hate you both,' I said. 'Anyway. Shall we get going?'

'Yeah, I need to hoof it as well,' said Nailah. 'There's a new mosque opening in Croydon and they're doing a welcome event this evening. Press duty calls.'

'Is that the one built by empowered?' I said, as we headed out into the main office. We waved goodbye to Amrik and Becca, who waved silently back, their fascinated eyes fixed on Daryl.

'It is,' said Nailah. 'Well, not entirely by empowered, but spearheaded by an Imam who found himself with powers after the Collision. He encouraged a bunch of other empowered Muslims who were scared to admit they had powers to . . . come out, for want of a better phrase.'

'Weird,' I said.

'Why?'

'Just can't really imagine religious types being cool about powers, that's all.'

'Religious types *en masse?*' Nailah raised a familiar devastating eyebrow.

'Well, yeah,' I said. 'Can you imagine, like, mental Christian Evangelist preachers welcoming empowered into their flock? Wouldn't they think we were Satan spawn or something?'

'Thing about "mental" religious types,' said Nailah, 'is that they're kind of like "mental" *not*-religious types.'

'Yeah?'

'In that they're not necessarily representative of the vast majority,' said Nailah. 'Religious leaders have been some of the strongest advocates of sticking together and welcoming confused empowered, building community bridges and so on. Obviously some hard-line believers doubled down, like you'd expect – "this is what you get, permissive society, rain of monsters, blah blah blah". Although they still seem angrier about gays than super-people. But they're definitely in the minority. It's almost as though religious folks *aren't* all brain-dead Dark Age misfits.'

I felt myself going red. 'I didn't say that . . .'

Nailah grinned. 'Don't worry, kiddo. You've still got lots to learn.'

'Well, that's about all we've got time for today, folks!' said Daryl. 'You've been watching *Tolerance Hour* with your host Nailah Adeyemi! Now here's Daryl the wise-cracking beagle with the weather.'

Chapter Fifteen

NIGHT DESCENDED AND the empowered came out to play. Jinx's neon lettering lit up strip-club scarlet and black-eye purple, and red velvet ropes were extended to herd the queue of people towards the bouncer. I zipped my hoody to my chin and glanced up at the moon, hanging cold and flat above the upturned teeth of skyline. It seemed to be trying to imply that this wasn't the best idea I'd ever had.

They were a peculiar lot, the Jinxers. Weirdly co-ordinated, for one thing. The general theme seemed to be black or white clothing, with all the colour concentrated in accessories (lurid green bow ties, flashing violet earrings, luminous yellow belt buckles and cufflinks), make-up (vampiric red eye shadow was popular) and hair – a guy and girl with identical magenta mohawks particularly caught my eye. With my unkempt dark brown mop, red hoody, jeans and conspicuous lack of make-up, I felt like a bit of a crasher.

What if they don't let me in?

I don't even have any ID.

Balls in a bap.

I thought I looked eighteen, but that was looking through my own eyes rather than the eyes of someone who was paid *not* to give people the benefit of the doubt. So I just tried to look nonchalant, as though I wasn't particularly bothered whether I got in or not, hands in my pockets, breath rising in front of me in crystalline clouds.

When I reached the bouncer he looked me up and down without saying anything. I opted to stay silent as well. It was only when he'd spent a few too many seconds staring into my eyes that I realised he was reading me. Part of me wanted to object, but I guessed that it was standard procedure. He was checking for powers, maybe even checking my age.

'In you go.' He waved me past, not even bothering to pat me down.

'Cheers.' I gave him a nod and headed past, down a narrow grey corridor and through a submarine-style airlock door.

OK.

This is a thing.

The club was open plan, with two levels: the ground floor was big and wide and lit by coloured spheres hanging from the ceiling on long wires, a sickly kaleidoscope of purples, greens, oranges and reds, with a spiral staircase leading to the next level. Shelves and shelves of bottles were stacked ludicrously high behind a long glass bar and some techy, moody drum'n' bass was being played by a shaven-headed girl in a pod-like DJ booth.

The first word that came into my head as I absorbed everything was . . . *naff*. Like what someone from the mid-Nineties would imagine the future looked like.

This is where empowered people like to hang out?

My God . . . everyone must think we're complete wankers.

I sauntered up to the bar, reaching into my pocket for Tara's picture. There were two bartenders, a tall blank-faced guy and a short cheery girl with fairy wings and a Dora the Explorer haircut. Unfortunately I ended up getting served by the blank dude.

'What can I get you?' he asked.

'Have you seen this girl?' I held up the picture.

He didn't even look at it. 'No, mate. What can I get you?'

'Please,' I said. 'She's missing. Have you seen her?'

'I said no.'

'You didn't even look at the picture.'

Without speaking or changing his expression, the bartender turned away to serve someone else. I burned briefly with anger and considered making a scene, but it didn't seem prudent so I waited for the girl, catching her attention with a smile.

She leaned over the bar. 'Hiya.'

'Hi. Pint of that, please?' I pointed to a lager.

'No problem.'

I held up the picture. 'You haven't seen this girl by any chance, have you?'

She actually looked up from pulling the pint, which was progress. Her face betrayed nothing. 'No,' she said, with a shake of her head. 'Sorry.'

I didn't *think* she was lying, but it was hard to tell. I couldn't even work out whether she was empowered or not. I knew I should just try and read her mind . . . except I also knew I shouldn't do that.

This is hard.

'Not to worry.' I smiled. 'Thought it was worth a try.'

'Sorry.' She handed over the pint with a smile, charging me nearly twice what I'd paid in the pub last night, and I retreated to a corner and nursed it, trying to work out what to do while also not looking too suspicious. A group of four empowered were playing doubles on the pool table, lifting the cues with their minds and joking with one another – I wondered how anyone could be sure that nobody was cheating – and a little way away, two more were playing a different game at a table, levitating a silver ball in the air between them. They seemed to be trying to overpower each other, each working to psychically move the ball closer to their opponent.

Thumb war, the next generation.

Even the DJ was using her mind, floating records – *wow, they still like vinyl in the future* – out of her bag, manipulating the cross-fader and the basses and the trebles, air-scratching with her hands and translating the movements to the decks themselves via her brain.

I guess Lauren was right.

People basically just want to do what they usually do. Except with powers.

The weirdest thing was that nobody seemed remotely bothered or impressed by any of it. Nobody was even watching the DJ and the pool players were aggressively casual. Were people already bored of superpowers? Already jaded? Or was it just that this place was so insufferably cool that to look impressed was to find yourself an outcast? And speaking of outcasts, I was pretty sure that people kept casting disdainful looks my way.

Wow. And all I'm doing is sitting here in a hoody. Imagine if I actually looked like I was enjoying myself. They'd probably Scanners the shit out of me.

As I sat there, I realised I was getting an odd feeling in my stomach. But it wasn't new odd. It was *old* odd.

I felt like I was back at school.

Bollocks to this place. And to every single one of these super-powered hipster twats. This is what I fought for? Now I know how war veterans feel.

The behaviour of the non-empowereds was also ringing a

very specific, aggravating bell. I didn't even need to be psychic to tell which ones they were, they stood out like sore thumbs. They wore the same sort of getup as the empowered, but whereas the empowered genuinely looked like they couldn't even imagine what giving a shit about something might feel like, the non-empowered looked like they were trying far too hard. Their insouciance stank of insecurity, while those with powers stank of superiority. I understood now why Nailah had called them groupies.

Again, bollocks to this place.

Why would Tara hang out here?

I felt as though wandering around showing people her photo might not do the job. For now, maybe I could see if anyone mentioned her.

Hey . . . how about . . .

I focused my thoughts on the people playing pool, concentrating on them, on their mouths, moving inaudibly against the blanket of music. At the same time, I forced my ears to drain the rest of the noise away. No music, no talking, no clang and clatter of tables and chairs. I filtered out the vibrations I wasn't interested in, focusing purely on the ones I wanted.

'Yeah,' said one player. The voice was slightly muffled, as though through water, but clear enough to hear. 'He's been unbearable lately.'

'He's still pretty upset,' said another.

'Yeah, but still, not an excuse . . .'

I smiled to myself. *Skills.*

I think it, it happens.

So – lightbulb – what if I just think away my feelings?

It wasn't an un-appealing prospect. Go into my brain, poke

around, find bits I didn't like – Eddie-related pain, Kloe-related pain, monster-related guilt, general anxiety and paranoia – and delete them, like malfunctioning plot threads in a story. I could even get rid of my knowledge of what Freeman had done, enjoy blissful ignorance like everyone else.

Simple.

Also TERRIBLE. A terrible and highly unhealthy thought process. Bad lightbulb. Smash lightbulb. And FOCUS.

The range of my new hearing thing – *super hearing woop woop +500 EXP level up* – wasn't brilliant – OK *maybe not quite level up* – so I had a casual wander around the place, listening. No mention of Tara or anything incriminating – or remotely interesting, if I'm honest – on the lower floor. Upstairs was more crowded, with another DJ playing some sort of sparse wallpaper-y techno, which the Jinxers seemed to be more into than the drum'n'bass downstairs, insofar as they were into anything. There were even a few people dancing and I spent a moment watching the couple with the matching mohawks that I'd seen before. One or other of them was empowered, the girl levitating a couple of feet off the ground as they danced, twirling around, holding the boy by the hand and pulling off some fairly nifty moves. Whether he was levitating her or she was doing it herself, it looked cool. I couldn't resist a grin.

Then I thought about Tara and her theoretical evil super-powered boyfriend doing such a thing and the grin dissolved. I resumed my search, moving through the people and listening for clues.

This is getting me effing nowhere.

I was on the point of saying *screw it* and just going from table to table with my photograph when someone tapped me on the shoulder. 'Hey.'

I turned and blinked, assaulted by a pungent waft of deodorant that smelled like it should have been applied with a gas mask on. The guy who'd spoken was older than me, thirtyish, scrawny and pointy-faced, with thinning blonde hair and a bright blue ring in each ear. He wore black trousers and a white shirt but I couldn't help thinking that he looked very much like a wannabe Jinxer rather than a proper one.

'Yeah?' I said.

'You're looking for her,' he said. 'Tara.'

I frowned. 'How do you . . . do you know where she is?'

'Come with me. Too many people listening.' He led me back downstairs, across the room and through a side door marked STAFF ONLY into an empty corridor. We carried on walking and about halfway down the corridor he opened a door to his left and held it for me as I went in.

This new room was small and sparsely furnished with a table, chairs and fridge. I turned to the guy just as he turned a key in the lock. 'Hold on,' I said. 'What . . . I . . .'

What was I saying . . .

My vision was going blurry and I kept forgetting what I wanted to say. I was vaguely aware of the guy walking towards me, so slow, so calm. I suddenly wanted very much to drop to my knees, so I dropped to my knees.

No . . . don't want to . . .

'You shouldn't have come here,' the guy said.

Come where? Where am I . . . why am I . . .

No . . . he's trying to make me forget . . .

I thought of heavy oak doors, metal barriers, electric fences and gun turrets, force fields, great mountain ranges, trying to erect them around my mind, build them up, up, up between us. Split us off, push . . . him . . . *back* . . . YES. He staggered backwards a few steps, his face twitching as he tried to maintain concentration, surprise registering in his eyes, like he hadn't expected me to be empowered. Surprised . . . I was surprised . . . no . . . *he* was. I was here for . . .

'Tara,' I managed to say.

'She's fine,' the guy said, his voice thick with concentration. 'I promise. I'll do you a favour and let you remember that. Everything else, you're going to forget.'

She's fine . . .

But . . . forget . . . forget what . . .

'You won't come here again.'

I won't come here again . . .

My head was full of water.

Things were drowning.

Thoughts were drowning . . .

I was . . .

No. No. N—

Yes. The man's voice in my ears, in my head: 'You won't remember me. You won't try to find Tara again. She doesn't need you.'

Tara? Who's Tara . . .

No

NO!

He's in my head.

No-one gets in my head.

Not anymore.

I thought a flash of lightning and he stumbled, letting out a gasp of pain . . . along with a thought. A stray thought . . . no, more like a bundle of feelings, mostly pain, but the pain was linked to his body, which linked to his identity . . . to his name.

Tim Hart.

I grabbed it, pulled it into my mind, locked it away, tried to stand, but it was hard. It was hard because I didn't really want to. I didn't want to . . . didn't know why I should . . .

But this guy . . . Tim . . . he knew . . .

Knew?

Who . . . was he?

Who was . . .

No. He's still . . .

Still inside . . .

My brain was rock. Solid rock. Impermeable. No cracks. No gaps. Nothing.

There has never *been a gap in my mind.*

The man's eyes flickered, spasms rippling across his face. He was having trouble, whoever he was.

Whoever?

Tim.

Tim Hart.

Tim Hart Tim Hart Tim Hart.

I got to my feet, breathing heavily. I could see his thoughts, winding around and around themselves, nasty long wriggling squirming worms made of colour, words, sentences. Orders. *Forget me. Forget this place. Forget Tara. Forget yourself.* I saw them and I brought down a blade made of *no*, cutting them down, dismembering them into their component letters, which scattered across the carpet like spilled alphabet soup, meaningless.

I am Stanly.

Stanly Bird.

I know why I'm here.

And I know your name now, pal.

He tried again but his commands just bounced off me, popping like abstract bubbles. I gagged him with a thought, gripped his arms and slammed them to his sides, held him still, never once moving any of my own limbs. I built a wall around him, a wall of metal and rock and heat and cold and forgetfulness, and walked towards him, maintaining eye contact, maintaining the link, because now, ha ha, *now I have you.* He was struggling, eyes bright and furious. Keeping him subdued was a challenge, his thoughts kept threatening to bypass mine, find their way back into my brain . . .

Nope.

No vacancies.

I looked into his mind, hoping to find what I wanted, but all I could see was churning colour, blurry shapes of emotion. Anger and confusion and the resolve not to let me see anything useful. He was angry with himself for giving me his name, it had been sloppy . . . but then again, our names would naturally be near the surface, wouldn't they? Among the most obvious thoughts, the quickest to hand.

He was still angry, though.

I wasn't going to just extract the information I needed.

But . . .

I could see his defences. He built them from fire, kept them white hot but indistinct, obscuring everything, stopping himself from being vulnerable.

I visualised a tidal wave crashing down on them and he relaxed a little.

'Tim,' I said, with my voice and my mind. 'Where. Is. *Tara.*'

'I don't know,' he said, through the rising steam of his extinguished defences. He sounded exhausted. 'We . . . we're

197

made to forget everything . . . I was just told that someone was snooping around, that I should make you forget . . .'

OK. *So this guy isn't Tara's much older empowered boyfriend.*

Lucky for him.

'Told by *who*? Who told you?'

'I . . . I don't know. We use thoughts, codes . . . I was telling the truth when I said that she's all right . . .'

'*You* don't know that,' I said. 'Someone might have just given you that lie to feed to me. If you believe it, it makes it more convincing.' I slammed him up against the door and moved towards him so that we were almost nose-to-nose. 'You'd better tell me something useful,' I hissed. 'Or God help me I will do *terrible* things to your mind. I don't even know how it's done, so there'll be no finesse. Imagine a chimpanzee with a tray of torture implements and a man, *you*, strapped to a chair. *Understand?*'

'I don't . . . I can't . . .'

'What business are you into? All this, dodginess, mind wiping, you must be up to something pretty important. What is it and *why is Tara involved?*'

'I don't know!' said Tim. 'I don't, like I said, everything except essential info . . . wiped . . . brought back when necessary . . .'

I shouldn't have done it. It was not OK. But it was obvious at this point that Tara was caught up in something dangerous, potentially extremely so. And this guy had just tried to wipe my memory to stop me from finding her. I was not happy.

So I lunged, diving into his brain with mine, channelling as much ferocity as I could, as though my mind was a whirling mass of spinning blades that chopped straight through, mince-meating his barriers, rushing in with such un-tutored brutality that he actually cried out in pain.

Oh God, what am I doing . . .

You're finding Tara, that's what you're doing.

I couldn't find anything related to her, not even her face, which suggested he didn't actually know who he was supposed to keep from me, but somehow, amongst the twisted confusion of memories and feelings and truth and lies, the chaos of cognition, I managed to discern a particular strand, something important that was somehow tied to our conversation. Something he really wanted to keep hidden. A name.

'Steven . . .'

'No!' he gasped, with a violent psychic lash that lifted me clean off the ground and sent me flying across the room. *Damn it.* I stopped myself inches from the wall, freezing in mid-air. He was already coming at me, whipping out mental ropes to grab chairs and batter me with them, but I thought a protective cloud around myself and the chairs smashed harmlessly against it.

Get a grip.

Hold him in place.

Not done yet.

'Steven,' I said.

'Don't you d—' he managed to choke.

'SHH.' He obeyed. *Steven,* I thought, and it was as though I was remembering something, as though I'd taken extra information from him without even realising and was only now understanding it. *Steven Hart.* His nephew. Somehow, whatever this business was, it connected to him – although right now, without all the necessary information in his mind, even Tim wasn't totally sure how. But connect it did.

OK. Um . . .

'Do you have any meetings lined up?' I said. 'With the people involved in this thing?'

He nodded, barely. I'd clearly weakened him with my intrusion. Trying not to think about that, I pressed on. 'When and where?'

'Here. Upstairs bar. Wednesday. Half past nine.' I was pretty sure he was saying it out loud. He might have been thinking it.

'Good. Who with?'

'Won't . . . know until I . . . get there . . .'

'OK. Right. You're going to go to that meeting. And in the meantime, as far as you're concerned, you did what you needed to do. You wiped my mind and I left without a care in the world.' As I spoke, I thought the words, made them into commands, fed them into his mind. It seemed to come incredibly easily. I guess we were connected now.

After I forced myself into his mind, yeah.

'The last few minutes,' I said, 'this fight, me going into your mind . . . you're going to forget about it. *Forget it all.* Then you're going to carry on, however you were planning to carry on.' I looked into his mind again, gently this time. On the very surface I could see myself, floating in a psychic sea, lashed by waves of fury, and I plucked myself out, leaving just the water. Then I drained that and turned his thoughts backwards, forming them into the hands of an analogue timepiece, watching them whir, two, three, five minutes.

I left him there and headed back through the club and out the front, maintaining a placid expression, as though my mind had just been wiped. As I passed the queue, which was even longer than before, I heard a voice. 'Bird.'

I stopped dead, my head snapping around. It was a young black woman, tall, dark hair down to her shoulders, dressed rather stunningly in what seemed to be a white all-in-one. She was leaning over the bar's velvet rope, regarding me inscrutably. I frowned. 'Um . . . hello?'

'You don't remember me, do you?' Her accent was part very London, part very somewhere else.

I stared at her. 'I . . .'

Flash. Me, appearing in the street. Helicopters, police cars . . . Lauren . . .

And . . .

'You were there,' I said. 'When I . . . came back.'

She nodded. 'My name's Danielle.'

No way. 'Danielle . . . Dewornu?'

Now it was her turn to frown. 'How did you know that?'

'I may have read about . . . an ex alter-ego of yours.'

The frown deepened. 'You don't know anything about that.'

'Oh,' I said. 'OK . . .' *What is this conversation . . .*

'Anyway,' she said. 'I just wanted to make sure you weren't causing any trouble in there.'

'Oh? Why?'

'Because then I'd have to deal with you. Which would ruin my night.' She looked severely pissed-off now. 'Whatever you've read, you know nothing about me. But I know about you. Be careful. We don't need your kind of chaos in London. Not now.'

My kind of chaos? 'What's that supposed to mean?'

'Reckon you know what it means. Just watch yourself.'

'OK.' I nodded. 'Cool. Will do. You . . . have a nice night now.' I turned and sloped off to meet Daryl, who luckily wasn't in sight of the queue.

'Bloody hell,' said the beagle. He looked ready to burst. 'You were ages! I was worried! What—'

'I have a lead,' I said. 'A name. Steven Hart. His nephew . . .'

'Whose nephew? Steven Hart's nephew?'

'No, guy in there. Somehow, he's connected to something.'

'Wow. That's delightfully vague. Who's connected? The guy or the nephew?'

'The guy. Tim.' I told him as much as I could, blurring over my precise methodology. I still felt odd, like I was in shock.

'OK,' said Daryl. 'So . . .'

'So,' I said, taking out my new old phone, 'I am texting Nailah with the names Steven and Tim Hart. Seeing if she can find anything useful.' I finished the text, sent it, pocketed the phone. 'And now . . .'

'Now,' said Daryl, 'we go *home*. You need sleep. You're so pale Edward Cullen would look like the poster boy for factor ten billion fake tan stood next to you. I'll come over in the morning and we'll work out what to do next. Sound good?'

'OK.' It did sound good, especially the part where I'd be alone. For one thing, I couldn't get Hart's voice out of my head, the way he'd cried out when I invaded his mind. If I was alone I could sit, clear my head, shower. Meditate.

Maybe throw up a bit.

'Hello?'

'Did I kill anyone?'

'Stanly? What . . . it's the middle of the night, are you all right?'

'I need to know if I killed anyone.'

'What do you mean? When? Has something happened?'

'Before. During . . . in all the fighting. Obviously people died, and I'm at least . . . I'm not . . .'

'Stanly—'

'But directly. The soldiers I fought. Did I kill any?'

'It's not—'

'*Please*, Lauren. I need to know.'

'As far as I know, you didn't kill anyone. Plenty of broken limbs. Some concussion. Nothing that couldn't be fixed. Stanly? Hello? Stanly, are you there?'

'Is that true?'

'To the best of my knowledge, yes. I would know if you had. And so would you, don't you think?'

'I don't know. I . . . I hurt people though.'

'It was—'

'How many did die? In total? Everyone?'

'Stanly, I really don't think—'

'Tell me, Lauren.'

'One thousand, one hundred and twenty-two.'

'Wow.'

'Do you need me to—'

'Thanks. Sorry to wake you. Speak to you tomorrow.'

'Stanly—'

'Goodnight.'

The town was called Tref-y-Celwyn. It was a small, unassuming place, tucked away in the hills like a secret. A higgledy-piggledy up-and-down town, with a clock tower at its centre and a river snaking through it.

And it was burning.

First, he had closed off every exit road, blocking them with lorries, buses, tractors and any other vehicles that he could find, wishing them into place, conducting them like a child playing with toys. Then he had set them on fire and waited for the chaos to begin, for people to run out into the streets, calling to each other to find out what was happening, crying out.

Then they had seen him, hovering in the air above them, his face a mask of terrible joy, his long coat billowing in the wind, arms outstretched in triumph, and the real screaming had begun.

Now the clock tower exploded, flying apart and scattering broken, fiery time on the street below.

Now every window on every street shattered, with a high sweet ringing that echoed between the hills.

Now he spoke, his voice amplified a hundred-fold, telling them what would happen next.

Now they fell to their knees.

Far away, watching from the top of the forest, sat another boy. They shared the same face. They might have been the same person, once upon a time. The boy who stood in the sky above the town, however, was a child at play, albeit a troubled one. The boy who watched might not have been a boy at all, so old and unfathomable was the look in his eyes.

He watched the town burn.

He watched the people run.

He watched the boy laugh.

He did nothing.

And when the boy grew bored and decided to fly to the next town, where the school was, the boy who was not a boy followed, always keeping his distance, never interfering.

Chapter Sixteen

I THINK I was screaming before I woke up. I definitely was when I opened my eyes. I had fallen asleep in the living room and as wakefulness ambushed me, my mind retaliated with an involuntary release of power. It knocked DVDs from the shelves, sent my chair and table flying, smashed the window – *what every window on every street shattering what* – and I felt myself drop to the floor, no, to the—

—grass. I landed hard on grass and clamped my hands over my mouth to stem the screaming. I closed my eyes. No. No. No. Stop.

Another bad dream.

STOP.

I wasn't fierce with myself. I wasn't angry. I forced myself *not* to be. It made calmness easier to find. I was where I was. I was on the grass. I was in Senia's world. I was not in the sky above Tref-y-Celwyn, raining down fire and giggling in delight. Neither was I watching myself do that.

I was here. I hadn't *meant* to come here . . .

But I was here.

I opened my eyes. Making myself feel calm seemed to have worked. I was still, my breathing becoming softer, more regular. I could smell the dampness of the grass, the *life* in the air. It was mild, the sky slightly overcast.

I was *here*.

And then I looked to my right and saw Senia lying on the grass a little way away, staring at me, face pale, eyes wide with shock. She looked as though she'd been thrown to the ground.

'Oh no.' I jumped to my feet. 'Are you all right?'

'I . . . I think so.' She pulled herself up into a sitting position. 'Ouch.'

'I'm so sorry.' I started to move gingerly towards her, extending my hand. I felt like she might recoil, but she didn't. She took my hand, let me help her up. 'I didn't even realise you were there.'

'I came early,' she said. 'Things are busy at the farm, I wasn't going to be able to be here for long. Saw you appear, and then there was this . . . like an invisible wave?' She rubbed her head and managed a smile, for which I was monumentally grateful. 'Those powers of yours are . . . powerful.'

'I'm *so* sorry, I didn't . . .'

'It's fine, really.' It was hard to tell if she was just being nice. I still didn't really know her well enough to read.

'I was having a nightmare,' I said. 'Panicked.'

'Must have been a bad one.'

'Pretty bad.' OK, *maybe managed to get away with accidentally blasting her, let's not now freak her out with details of messed-up dreams.* 'So,' I said, keeping my tone level, my breathing under control, filling my head and my body with thoughts like *stability* and *locked* and *anchored*, willing them to flow through my blood like antibodies. 'Um . . . yeah. Maybe next time you come . . . if you come . . . you might want to keep a safe distance. Until I manage to stabilise myself.' I was trying not to think of the tree I'd ruined the first time I'd come.

I could have killed her . . .

'Good idea,' said Senia. 'And I *will* come back.'

'You don't . . .'

'Shut up.' She smiled. 'So. What's new in your crazy world?'

'I . . . am looking for a friend. I think she's mixed up in something dangerous.'

'Dangerous? How?'

'I'm honestly not sure.'

'Are you close to finding her?'

'Again . . . not sure. I just . . . I did some not good stuff yesterday, trying to find her. And . . . um . . .'

'You're worried you'll do more?'

I nodded. 'And I mean . . . part of me thinks I should stop at nothing. I've lost some important people. One forever. I can't lose this one.'

'You must know, though,' said Senia. 'When you've done something you shouldn't have. Or when you're about to.'

Currently waiting on a job offer from Morally Grey Incorporated. So . . . not totally sure about that one. 'Hmm.'

'So if you think you shouldn't, don't.' Senia shrugged. 'Seems pretty simple to me.'

Simple. Chance would be a fine thing. I laughed. 'Honestly, I can barely remember what simple feels like.'

'Honestly?' said Senia. 'I'm *bored* of simple. Swap you?'

'With pleasure.'

'Great. Um, would you like to—'

And I was back in my living room, face-to-face with Lauren, who cried out and blasted me with a thought. It propelled me violently into the kitchen, as though the living room had de-pressurised, and I hit the counter in a clatter of plates and kettle and cutlery and leftover food, rolled off and sprawled on the floor, all the wind expelled harshly from my body. Wow. Serious ouch.

And . . . ironic ouch?

'Oh my God, Stanly! I'm so sorry!' Lauren rushed over and knelt down next to me, joined seconds later by Daryl. 'Are you all right?'

'Yeah.' I managed to sit up. 'Don't worry. Just . . . all my important bits . . . are broken.'

'Jesus, kid,' said Daryl. 'What the hell happened?'

'It's fine. It's fine.' I frowned at my two unexpected visitors. 'What's going on? What are you doing here?'

'Security called me,' said Lauren. 'They said there was commotion, smashing. And after talking to you last night, I was worried . . . anyway, I came straight round and found Daryl outside your door. He said he was supposed to meet you here but there was no answer, so I let us in and the window was broken and you were gone . . .'

'Yeah,' I said. 'Sorry about that. The broken window was me. How long . . . when did security contact you?'

'About forty minutes ago.'

Forty minutes . . . I definitely hadn't been in Senia's world that long.

What the frig . . .

'Where did you go?' asked Lauren.

I couldn't think of a good excuse, so I decided *sod it* and told them both everything. The panic attacks. The dislocation. The fact that it was always the same time in Senia's world, but a day later. The fact that I was sure I was doing it myself.

They listened, Lauren's face growing more grave with each new detail. When I'd finished, she closed her eyes and shook her head.

'I'm so sorry,' she said.

Eh? 'For what?'

'I should have known you weren't OK. You should be in a hospital, undergoing treatment. You need *therapy*, for God's sake, after everything you've been through, not to be left to your own devices, pressured into joining Angelcorp when it's so complicated . . .'

'Um,' I said. 'I'm fine. Honestly.' *Um, you're honestly not. Yeah, but she doesn't need to know that.*

Um, she definitely already does *know that.*

Well, yeah, but shut up.

'And there's no pressure,' I said. *Well. There kind of was.* 'Um . . . do you think Angelcorp will pay to fix my window?'

Daryl sniggered and Lauren rolled her eyes. 'Of course, you idiot.'

'Great. Well . . .'

'I really think I should take you to the clinic,' said Lauren. 'We can check you over properly.'

'I'm fine,' I said. *And absolutely anti-keen for getting wired up to any Angelcorp related machinery, ta.* 'Really. And Daryl and I . . . we were going to go and see the city. You know. Maybe catch a film. I think a day of normal London stuff will do me good.'

Lauren glanced at Daryl, who confirmed what I said with a wag of his tail. 'Are you sure? What about Tara? You said . . .'

'Can't really do anything until her parents are better, can we?' I said. 'Any word from the higher-ups, re: my proposal?'

'I should have an answer soon.'

'Great. Just let me know.'

'How? You "lost" your phone.'

'Oh yeah. Thanks for telling me about the next-gen snooping tech, by the way.'

Lauren went red. 'Sorry. Honestly, I felt like you were overloaded with information, and it would just . . . it would be . . .'

That was convincing.

'Plus,' she said, 'I told you I would be keeping tabs. And you said "tab away".'

'Seriously?'

'Sorry. You did ask how we could possibly police . . .'

'I know,' I said. 'It's fine. I mean, it's not fine. It's dodgy. But we can discuss it some other time. Anyway, this is my new phone.'

I showed her. She didn't look impressed. 'Where'd you get that?'

'From a . . . person.' I called her quickly then hung up. As I did so, I noticed a text from Nailah. *Please be something useful.* 'There, now you have the number.'

'You know that if you work for us you'll need an Angelcorp phone?'

'Yeah, we'll see about that.'

'It's your ID.'

'Think I'd rather just have a card.'

'It's how you pay for stuff too.'

That stopped me, because I'd suddenly remembered that I'd used up the last of my cash getting back from Jinx Bar last night. 'Um . . .'

With a roll of her eyes, Lauren took out a handful of notes. 'You'll be the death of me.'

'Thanks!' I accepted them with my most ingratiating grin. 'Bye!'

'Smooth operator,' said Daryl. 'Sorry, did I say smooth? I meant to say that she definitely one hundred per cent knew that you were lying about what we were doing today.'

'Well, she *is* a mind reader.' I ate the rest of my sausage roll and spoke with my mouth full, mostly because I knew it annoyed him. 'Shall we get going?' Nailah had found a name – Mary Hart, Steven's mother – and an address, although she had prefaced it with a long-winded disclaimer saying that she was very much out of the scooping private individuals business and this was a one-off and blah blah blah.

'Don't talk with your mouth full, you filthy human.'

'Sorry.'

'And this parallel universe thing . . . might not be a bad idea to get yourself looked at. It's a pretty insane condition to have.'

I shrugged. 'Might do. Honestly, it's fairly far down my list of priorities.'

The dog sighed. 'You'll be the death of me.'

'Y'know, it's weird, people keep saying that.'

Mary Hart lived in the East End, on a warren of an estate where every living thing, from the humans to the dogs to the cats, looked at us suspiciously. We eventually found the right street, a row of houses seemingly competing to see which could look the most forlorn. 'Jeez,' said Daryl. 'Talk about Depreston. Which house?'

'The one with the policeman coming out of it,' I said. 'Act like a dog.' I mimed writing a text, trying not to look suspicious, and Daryl started sniffing around the floor. I sneaked a look at the policeman as he walked away from the house. He was a big guy with brown curly hair and a face that looked as though it had been frozen mid-sniff of some gone-off milk. Weirdly, I couldn't see a car anywhere, even though you could obviously drive and park here. He quickly disappeared down a narrow avenue between houses.

I looked down at Daryl. 'What do you reckon?'

'Law enforcement officer. Caucasian male. Profoundly, borderline upsettingly ugly.'

'Thanks for that.'

'Sorry. Does seem weird, visiting alone. Don't they always need to be in pairs?'

I moved tentatively closer to the house, still not totally sure what I was going to do, and jumped as the front door opened again. A woman emerged, late twenties, blonde, washed out and harassed looking, with a small and very excited boy hanging off her arm.

Mary and Steven, I presume.

'Where are we going, Mummy?' the little boy said.

'Just out.' Her tone was a tad snippy, but the boy didn't look bothered. He just seemed delighted by the very concept of being outside. I wondered if his mother needed to clear her head after the policeman's visit.

'Now what?' Daryl muttered.

'Now . . . we follow.'

And follow we did. We followed them to a nearby shop, where Mary bought Steven a milkshake. Then we followed them to a park, where Steven played on the swings for about half an hour and Mary sat watching him, clearly preoccupied. I tried throwing a stick for Daryl and hoped that nobody saw the dirty look he gave me, because it was clearly not the expression of a normal dog.

After a while they left the park and we followed them again, always keeping our distance. They stopped at another shop, where Mary bought some stuff. Then they returned home.

'Stanly,' said Daryl.

'What?' We were sitting on the kerb a little way away from Mary's house.

'This is getting us nowhere.'

'I'm aware of that.'

'I think we should call it a day on this one. Tim Wotsit is having his meeting tomorrow night. Not long.'

'And in the meantime, God knows what's happening with Tara.'

'Stanly,' said Daryl, again. 'I understand that you want to look out for her. I do. But . . . mate, the girl's sixteen. When you were sixteen, you ran away from home and got involved with a bunch of superpowered weirdos. Time's a flat circle, kiddo. You can't—'

'Where's that from?'

'What?'

'That "flat circle" line. It's been occurring to me a lot, recently. Well . . . not recently. Five and a half years ago, technically . . .' I put my head in my hands. 'Jesus. What is my life? What the hell is . . . everything? I don't even know what I'm doing. Following some poor woman around, spying . . .'

'Look,' said Daryl, 'it's totally natural to feel completely overwhelmed by all the craziness you've had to deal with. You'd be pretty weird if you weren't. Come on, let's just go and chill somewhere and hope that nothing else—'

My phone rang and I floated it to my ear and answered without touching or looking at it. 'Hello?'

'Stanly? It's Lauren. Walker said yes to your proposal. She wants you and Daryl to come in tomorrow afternoon for inductions and so on.'

'Right. Cool. Great.'

'Are you all right?'

'Peachy. Cheers. See you tomorrow.'

'I'll send cars for you both. Midday.'

'Great. Bye then.' I hung up.

'They didn't accept, did they?' asked Daryl.

'They did.'

'Flaming heck.' The dog sat down heavily. 'With bugger-me sauce. I honestly didn't think they would.'

'Well, they have.'

'Errm . . . well. Shiiit.'

'Innit.'

'Uh . . . shall we go and see Sharon?'

That sounded like a severely good idea. 'OK.' I stood up.

'Good,' said Daryl. 'Oh, and it's from *True Detective*. The "flat circle" line.'

'Oh. I never even watched that. How do I know that line?'

'Well, I think it might be Nietzsche originally. Maybe you know it from him.'

'Oh yeah. Good old Nietzsche.'

'Yeah, top geezer.' Daryl wagged his tail. 'Come along, my little ubermensch. Let's make like Zarathustra and thus speak.'

'I understood that reference.'

The gods of luck were clearly smiling down upon me because Connor was not in when we popped by. Sharon was very much in and very much delighted to see us and we sat in their garden with tea and snacks, enjoying a surprise appearance by the sun. I explained about Tara and she seemed to share my concern, but she also seemed pretty sympathetic to

Daryl's idea that the girl had some empowered squeeze and was teenage rebellion-ing it up.

Why does nobody else think she might be in mortal danger?

I guess cos everyone else isn't a massive drama queen?

'But the Rogers were *brainwashed*,' I said.

'Which is awful,' said Sharon. 'And if Tara did it, then . . . I'm sure she already feels guilty, and will feel worse. But I remember being sixteen. Pretty sure you can too.'

'Vaguely.'

'I did some bad things,' said Sharon. 'I still feel guilty about them. I hung out with bad people, stropping along, hating the world. It's a phase. It passes.'

'But she might get hurt.'

'She might,' said Sharon. 'She probably will. She has been already. We all have. Look at you, for goodness' sake. Look at what you've been through. You're remarkably sane and well balanced, considering.'

Yeah, as far as you know.

'If you're really that concerned,' said Sharon, 'why don't you ask Lauren to look into it properly? Get the police on the case?'

'I don't trust Angelcorp. I don't want them involved.'

Daryl's head snapped around as though he'd been punched. 'What's the matter with you?' I asked.

'Sorry,' he said. 'I just got whacked in the face by a huge flying clod of irony, probably because we're going to Angelcorp tomorrow to start a new job.'

'*What?*' said Sharon.

'Um,' I said. 'Yeah . . . about that . . .'

We explained. Or at least, we tried. Sharon wasn't happy. Profoundly *un*happy, in fact. And while she didn't come out and say it, I knew a lot of it was down to me choosing Angelcorp when I hadn't even come to see what she and Connor were up to.

'Sharon,' said Daryl, seeing that I was increasingly at a loss to defend my decision, 'you know how I feel about them. I've eaten business lunches in the belly of that beast. But I think there's potential here. Stanly and I can look over one another's shoulders. Badness isn't inevitable.'

'It's possible, though,' said Sharon. 'It's dangerous. You said you wanted nothing to do with them, Daryl. Like all of us, you said that after everything . . .'

'I know what I said.'

'This is why Connor was angry the other day,' said Sharon. '*This* is why—'

'It's kind of not, though, is it?' said Daryl, keeping his tone totally level and reasonable. 'Part of it, maybe, but mostly he's just angry with Stanly, angry about Eddie, and unable to process his feelings properly. Even now, after all this time.'

'He's *worried* about Stanly,' said Sharon. 'About all of us.'

'Worried about Stanly? Don't make me . . .'

'Guys,' I said. 'Please. Can we not? Can we just . . .' No. *Not crying. Don't want to cry. Absolutely one hundred per cent do NOT WANT TO CRY.*

'Stanly . . .' said Sharon.

'Sorry,' I said. 'Um . . . yeah. So.' I forced a massive smile. 'Pretty stupid, eh? Me working for the Angel Group. With a talking beagle! It's . . .'

'Are you all right, kid?' asked Daryl.

I laughed. It almost sounded genuine, if you'd never heard me - or any other human being, for that matter - laugh before. 'I'm . . . bendigedig. And probably . . . yeah, just exhausted.

217

You know. Should probably get going, actually. Be good to have a bit of a chill, get prepped for tomorrow.' *Get away before Connor gets back, you mean.*

I stood up.

'You don't have to go,' said Sharon, 'really. I'm sorry. I . . . it's not my place to judge. I just . . .'

'It's fine,' I said. 'No sweat. No harm. No . . .' I stopped talking, because I could feel myself slipping away. My grip on where I was, the feel of the grass, the smell of the air, it felt tenuous.

I hadn't wanted to cry before. I'd wanted to disappear.

I took a deep breath, composing myself, trying to think myself *here* even though I kind of wanted to . . .

No.

Stay.

STAY.

Sharon was standing up now, reaching out to me. 'What's wrong, Stanly? You look . . . you *feel* . . .'

'Woah!' I recoiled so violently that she jumped. I tried to laugh. It sounded awful. 'No sneaky mind reading there! Not . . . not cool . . .' I shook my head. *Get a GRIP, kid. You're scaring me.*

I'm scaring YOU?

'Thanks for the snacks,' I muttered. 'Got to go.' I turned and hurried out, through the house, out of the front door, down the path. Daryl ran after me, calling my name, but I didn't stop until I was a good distance up the road. I leaned against a bus shelter and closed my eyes, taking deep breaths. I couldn't look at the sky, the pavement, the houses, they were all phasing, flexing, threatening to pixellate and bleed away . . .

'Kid,' said Daryl. 'Stanly.'

'I'm fine.'

'You are *not*, by any stretch of the imagination, fine. It was starting to happen, wasn't it? You were going to disappear.'

I might have nodded.

'You need to get checked out,' said Daryl. 'You *need to*—'

'I'm *fine*.' The wall of the bus shelter I was leaning against bent sharply inward as I spoke, creaking unpleasantly, suggesting that maybe I wasn't fine.

'Call Lauren,' said Daryl. 'Tell her you're not up to going in tomorrow. She can make excuses for you. You're not ready to be back in that world. You need—'

'I've been OK, though,' I said. 'I mean . . . not OK OK, but I haven't . . . this is . . .'

'These things can be delayed,' said Daryl. 'They can sneak up on you.'

Sneak up on you . . .

Like sneaky mind readers . . . trying to make you forget . . .

Tara . . .

I made myself stand up. Made myself open my eyes properly and look at the sky, at the houses. Thought so fiercely it felt as though I might burn myself: *You are more than this.*

You are BETTER than this.

'I'm all right,' I said. 'I'm going in to Angelcorp tomorrow. If you don't want to come, I understand.'

'Stanly . . .'

'I'm going home. See you tomorrow.' I strode off, even though I still wanted to vomit myself into another universe. This time Daryl didn't follow.

Later on I sat in the flat, staring out of my already immaculately repaired window, thinking. I still had absolutely no idea how Mary and Steven Hart could possibly connect to Tara

. . . but at the same time, I *knew* there had to be something. Something that would lead me to her. All I could see was her eleven-year-old face in that cabin in the woods, all I could hear was her voice, giggling, taking the piss out of me. And as I sat there, I thought about what Sharon had said. About hurt. Everybody got hurt. Everybody dealt with it.

Some hurt is worse than other hurt, though.

And not everyone deals with it.

Look at Alex.

I wondered what he was doing. Had he survived the Collision? Had he been eaten by monsters?

Hmm. Maybe I'll have time to care about that later.

I wanted to think that I'd *know* if Tara was in real danger. If she literally needed me to come crashing through the window right then and there, whip her out from the jaws of death, spirit her away to safety, I would have known. There had been too many times in the past when I'd known stuff, known without knowing. In my gut, I felt as though she was all right, at least for now. It was OK that I wasn't combing the streets, smashing down doors, demanding answers.

It wasn't really OK, though.

Just like it wasn't OK that I'd invaded Tim Hart's brain and his sister's life.

Or that I was going into Angelcorp tomorrow to see exactly how much of what remained of my soul they wanted. That I was even considering letting Freeman's crimes go unpunished.

But I had to tell myself it was.

I wish you were here, Eddie.

I miss you.

And I'm sorry.

Chapter Seventeen

T HE NEXT MORNING, after congratulating myself
for being in the right universe, I immediately headed out
and took a train to the East End. Trying not to think about
how guilty I felt, how not OK this was, how *creepy*, I hovered
around Mary Hart's estate, waiting. What for? I had no idea.
But eventually she left the house, alone, and like the terrible
weirdo I was, I followed.

Onto a bus. Off a bus. Onto another bus. It turned out that
she was picking Steven up from a morning at play school. He
was in high spirits and as I followed them both back through
the busy city, Steven burbling away, Mary listening attentively,
I felt worse and worse about what I was doing. Even if this
did lead to Tara, my methodology was . . . flawed. At best.

It's for Tara.

It's for her.

Mary and Steven stopped at a crossing and I hung back, seriously considering abandoning this whole thing and checking
myself in to a mental institution. On the opposite side of the
road, a group of teenaged boys who should probably have been
in school were messing around with a football as they waited
to cross. One of them, in the act of jokingly pretending to
push his friend in front of a car, lost control of the ball and it
sailed across the traffic, straight towards Mary, who happened
to be looking the other way . . .

About a foot from her head, it stopped. Frozen in the air.

I looked down at Steven, who was giggling and pointing with his free hand.

'Look Mummy!' he cried. 'Look what I did!'

Mary looked at the suspended ball, then at her son, whose face was a bright mask of delight. 'You . . .' She couldn't get the words out. Her skin was suddenly several shades paler, her eyes as wide with shock as the boy's were with delight.

'Hey!'

The mother jumped at the voice and the ball dropped to the ground and rolled away into the traffic. Steven smiled after it. The new voice belonged to a policeman, a big guy . . . the same one from yesterday.

OK, so I'm not the only one following her.

Mary immediately started to panic. 'Oh!' she said. 'I—'

'Excuse me, Mrs Crane,' said the policeman, more confrontationally than I thought was necessary. *Crane, eh?* 'I presume your son is registered?'

'Registered? N-no! He . . . he's never . . .'

'You *are* aware that it is an offence for empowered to go unregistered?'

'But he's never done it before!' The poor woman was on the verge of tears. 'He's . . . he wasn't even born when all that stuff happened! He—'

'Calm down, Mrs Crane.' The policeman took out some sort of electronic notepad.

'I told you yesterday, it's *not* Mrs Crane, it's *Miss* Hart—'

'You are married, yes?'

'I was. My husband is *dead*.'

The policeman's lip curled. 'Well, whatever your circumstances, your son just—'

'Hey,' I said. 'It wasn't him.'

The policeman looked at me, eyes narrowing, lip curling even further. 'You what?'

'It was me. I stopped the ball.'

'You took your time speaking up.' The policeman didn't come towards me. He seemed to want to keep the woman and her kid boxed in between us. 'I don't think I believe you,' he said.

I shrugged again and raised a finger. The policeman's notepad rose out of his hand and he went red and snatched it back. 'Oi! Less of that! Doesn't prove anything anyway, just proves you're empowered. I heard the kid, he said he did it—'

'But he *didn't* do it!' said Mary. Steven whimpered.

'I didn't realise that a small child's imagination carried that much weight with the police,' I said.

The policeman stepped around Mary, towards me. 'You *what?*'

'She said he's never done it before,' I said. 'I just told you I did. Seems a pretty open and shut case as far as I can see. Plus, you're scaring the boy. There's no need to be such a . . . to be like that.'

Please don't provoke me because I really probably shouldn't assault a cop when I'm going to start my new job in like one hour.

The policeman was uncomfortably close now. He was much taller at this proximity. 'You're telling *me* how to do *my* job?'

'No.' Keeping my voice under control was a fairly mammoth task. 'I'm just saying that all the available evidence seems to point at me, not at him. And your attitude—'

'My *attitude?*' The policeman's lip quivered. He was clearly even angrier than he was letting on. 'I don't take advice about my *attitude* from nosy little shits like you.'

'Let me guess,' I said. 'You don't like people with powers.'
Oh God, Stanly, just shut up and apologise and hop it.

'*What?*'

'You don't like people with powers, so you'll happily harass a little kid and his mother—'

'All right,' said the policeman. 'I've had enough of you. I presume that *you're* registered?'

Oh bugger. 'Yeah.' My tone suggested that what I'd said didn't necessarily reflect the truth, the whole truth and nothing but the truth.

'Now I *definitely* don't believe you.'

'Please,' said Mary, 'can I just go? I need to get Steven—'

'Wait. There.' The policeman scowled at her. 'Now, you. Show me your phone.'

'Don't have one. *But* if you'd like to call my supervisor . . .'

'Your *supervisor?*'

'At Angelcorp.'

The policeman looked even less happy than before, except now there was an edge of misery bleeding in. Witnessing it was like eating a particularly rich cake. 'Angelcorp.'

'Yep. Call her if you don't believe me.'

'You're f . . . *bloody* right I'm calling your supervisor.' I gave him Lauren's name and number and he tapped it into his notebook thing, which seemed to be hooked up to an earpiece. *Handy.* It rang and we all waited.

'Hello?' said the policeman. 'Lauren Stone? This is Police Constable Morgan with the London Metropolitan Police. I have a Stanly Bird here . . . well, he's been causing trouble. You do know him? He does work for you?' He looked at me and I could see bitter disappointment in his eyes. *Ooh, come on. Let's have an éclair on top of that cake.* 'He's been interfering in police business. Obstructing my . . . well I'm sorry, but he has . . .' He gave a brief and somewhat creative account of what had happened, with the emphasis firmly on my bad behaviour. 'It's not . . . yes. Yes, I understand. Well . . . fine. Yes, fine. Thank you.' He hung up and looked at me. 'You're lucky.'

I ignored him and turned to Mary Hart and her son. The little boy was clutching at his mother's leg and she was watching the altercation, eyes wide and bright with fear. 'You all right?' I asked.

She nodded.

'That's enough,' said Morgan. 'I need to ask her a few more questions.'

'I kind of think you might be done harassing her,' I said.

'You *what?*'

'You know *what.*'

Morgan's eyes burned with genuine malevolence. 'Get out of here.'

'With pleasure.'

'And you'd better hope I don't see you again.'

'I hope I'm never in the same *postcode* as you again,' I said. 'Laters.'

It took less than thirty seconds for Lauren to call me. 'Before you say anything,' I said, 'that guy was chatting absolute b . . . balderdash.'

'Oh, was he?'

'Yeah!' I told her what had happened. Well, sort of. I told her that I had stopped the ball and that he had blamed the child.

'Well,' she said. 'OK. Doesn't sound like he was very professional . . .'

'He was being an arsehole! Bothering them for no reason . . .'

'Not for no reason. There is a *very* definite reason that we have registration procedures in place.'

'Fine, fine, I'm sorry.'

'No you're not.' Her sigh was loud and long and, I thought, a bit OTT. 'You can't keep doing things like this, Stanly.'

'I *said* I'm sorry.'

'You're starting here *this afternoon*, you can't be using me and Angelcorp as a get-out-of-jail-free card . . .'

'That wasn't the plan! I just can't stand power-tripping wankers, no matter what uniform they wear.'

What about creeps who follow unsuspecting single mothers around?

Fair point, well made.

'I understand,' said Lauren. 'I do. But still. You need to control your temper. And be careful about using your powers like that.'

I was starting to lose my temper, which was ironic considering what Lauren had just said, but I overpowered it, wedgied it and hung it on a changing room hook. 'Sorry,' I said. 'Seriously. I'm just . . . he really pissed me off. A lot. Sorry. I'll be more careful. Anyway, I'm going to go. Don't worry about sending the car, I'll head to the Shard myself. Still on for inductions and everything?'

'I think you might need to do some anger management courses first.'

'I am a picture of blissful calm.'

'Oh, shut up.'

'Stanly,' said Jane Walker. 'Daryl. Welcome to Angelcorp.'

We were standing in one of the large warehouses adjacent to the Shard, surrounded by training apparatus. Standing behind Walker and Lauren were ten tall, expressionless men and women in black combat gear. I tried a friendly smile, hoping that I hadn't broken any of their legs in the past.

'Thanks,' I said, looking at the rather flash ID card she'd given me in lieu of a phone. Daryl had been given one that was attached to a collar - unbelievably, he hadn't immediately gone feral on receipt of said indignity.

'I must admit,' said Walker, 'I'm sorry you've chosen not to take advantage of the full employment package.'

'Just for now. We're not ruling it out.'

'I'm very glad to hear it. First things first - a little test of your combat readiness, to see what training you might require.'

'Combat?' said Daryl. 'I haven't even been shown where my locker is.'

Walker smiled indulgently. 'Obviously we like to avoid combat where possible. But sometimes it's necessary, and as we're still working out exactly what roles you will be playing, we need to see how ready you are.'

'Well, I'm ready.' I sounded like I meant it. I *did* mean it. I had slept for a bit last night and woken up in the right place - on my current scale of being OK, that was a solid eight.

'Me too,' said Daryl. He sounded less like he meant it.

'Enthusiasm,' smiled Walker. 'Lovely. But we need to make sure you're up to our standards. Things can get pretty hairy out there.'

'I'll fit right in,' said the beagle. I fought a snigger and the snigger won.

'Charming.' Walker turned to Lauren. 'You may take over. I'll see you all later.' That frostily ambiguous smile again, then she left.

Lauren stepped forwards. 'Stanly will go first. Daryl? If you'll come and stand with me?' Daryl did so.

'Right,' said Lauren. 'Stanly. These are ten of our best soldiers. They're adept at both physical and psychic combat. They're going to attack you.' I could tell that she wasn't crazy about this little session. Possibly because I'd woken her at four o'clock the other morning, whining about hurting people.

Don't hurt these guys then.

'Got it,' I said.

'OK,' said Lauren. 'Begin!'

I felt ten synchronised psychic attacks coming towards me and the soldiers charged. Obviously the thought attacks were meant to distract me so they could get close and give me a physical pummelling.

Not happening, ladies and germs.

Calmly, without blinking or moving my hands, I built a wall to absorb their attacks and lashed out with mental tentacles, relieving them of their guns and sending all ten of them flying in different directions. I stopped each soldier inches before they could hit hard surfaces, letting them hang there, impotent and furious. I glanced at Lauren with a 'what else ya got' smirk, just in time to deflect the massive crate she'd launched at me. Then I thought the soldiers back towards me and pressed them face-down against the floor. Not too hard.

No pain.

'That's my boy,' said Daryl.

'Well,' said Lauren. 'I'd say you're ready. Stand down and re-group, everyone. Daryl?'

'I'm not sure about this,' said Daryl. 'I mean, I use my teeth to fight. I . . . well, I savage my opponents, for want of a less savage verb. If this is training . . .'

'Do whatever you would in a real-life battle situation,' said Lauren. 'We can repair injuries.'

'Are you sure?'

'Yes.'

'Are you absolutely positive?'

'I am.'

'Absolutely one hundred per cent positively sure?'

'*Yes*, Daryl. They're not going to go easy, so neither should you. Come on, let's get cracking.'

Twenty minutes later, when Lauren had re-attached a couple of limbs and the blood had been hosed away, I was still shaking my head. 'I'm glad you're on my side.'

Daryl, who had cleaned his blood-soaked muzzle and rinsed his mouth out about fifty times, shrugged. 'She said to do what I would in a real-life battle situation.'

'You bit that guy's arm off.'

'Yep.'

'And that woman's leg.'

'Yep. They're lucky I didn't *actually* do what I would have done in a real-life battle situation.'

'You didn't?'

Daryl snorted. 'Of course not. In real life I'd have bitten their heads off.'

I looked down at him. 'Really?'

'No. Obviously I'm joking.'

'Unless it's absolutely necessary, while we're working together, you bite to *maim*, OK? Not to kill.'

'I *said* I was joking.'

'Still. No *disintegrations*.'

'This deal's getting worse all the time.'

Lauren came over, looking pale. 'Well,' she said. 'That was

. . . interesting. Nothing like a spot of bracing graphic violence after lunch.'

'You did tell me to—' began Daryl.

'Yes, yes,' said Lauren. 'I know. I think we're all sufficiently combat-ready now, don't you?'

We spent the rest of the afternoon being shown the facilities. The immaculate training grounds, the dull corporate conference rooms, the call centres full of identically-suited earpiece-wearing drones co-ordinating various operations, the biology and tech labs. Lauren told us that we would have limited access to their computers and databases and that our usage would be monitored. It was all a bit like school – *why is everything always like school* – but I figured I could deal with a bit of bureaucracy if it meant I had some resources behind me.

We were also introduced to a bunch of management types whose names I immediately forgot. None of them seemed hugely pleased to see me. It seemed to be going around – at one point we also passed Danielle Dewornu, who rewarded my cheery smile with a cold glance.

Definitely like school.

After a coffee break in the building's rather epic canteen, Lauren took us to her office and gave us a list of potential assignments that had been earmarked for us. 'Obviously these are more geared towards you, Stanly,' said Lauren. 'Daryl, you caught us a bit by surprise.'

'I sympathise,' said Daryl. 'I often catch myself by surprise. Don't worry, I'm happy to sit and drink coffee while Stanly does the legwork.'

'Yeah, I bet you are,' I said.

Truth be told, I wasn't crazy about any of the assignments. There were still major construction efforts underway and I had my pick of those. There was the option to shadow a Citizen Liaison, who went out into the community and found newly registered – or un-registered – empowered and saw about bringing them into the fold. I could work towards becoming an assistant for one of various different types of psychic training instructor. I could donate my brain to science – not literally – and let some of their lab people poke and test me to see if they could find anything useful. Or there were various fast-track learning programmes.

'How do they work?' I asked.

'They're specifically for empowered students,' said Lauren. 'They basically harness your own power and enable you to learn things at a vastly accelerated rate – properly supervised, of course, and regulated so that it doesn't overload your brain.'

'You're kidding,' said Daryl. 'You mean like the frickin' *Matrix*?'

'I haven't seen it.'

'I think she does mean like the frickin' *Matrix*,' I said. *Woah.*

'It was necessary,' said Lauren. 'We needed to give very important jobs to people who didn't always have the relevant experience, and there was no time to waste.'

'Have you had it done?' I asked.

She nodded. 'Do you think I had any experience of police work, or field work of any kind, before I joined Angelcorp? I had a whole pile of crash courses. Plus traditional longer-term training, of course.'

'I can't believe this,' I said. 'The world went *crazy*. Where was I?'

'You were off on your alien spa holiday,' said Daryl. 'More to the point, Lauren, how do you know that they weren't doing extra stuff to you? When they plugged you in to the learning generator or however they do it?'

'Extra stuff?'

'Yeah,' said Daryl. 'You know, subliminal suggestion, triggers and the like.'

Lauren frowned. 'Because that's not the way we do things.'

I hoped she was right. But I made a mental note to watch out for repeated phrases or speech patterns or other weird tics anyway.

'We're hoping to take this technology out into the world eventually,' said Lauren. 'Maybe even adapt it for non-empowered use – that's the ultimate plan with everything, enabling everyone to reap the benefits.'

'What a time to be alive,' said Daryl. 'Now, re: these assignments, there definitely doesn't seem to be much for me to do.'

'The Citizen Liaison stuff, maybe,' I said. 'You could sniff out un-registered empowered.'

'Oh yeah,' said Daryl. 'Just like I used to do when I worked with Freeman, and pretended that what I was doing was a good thing when deep down I knew it wasn't, investing me with a healthy streak of guilt and self-loathing. Sounds electric.'

'Consider yourselves lucky I'm letting you choose,' said Lauren.

'We do,' I said. 'But . . . look, obviously all those assignments are important. And I'm happy to do non-crazy stuff. But . . . I kind of got the impression from what Walker said that you wanted me to be *doing* crazy stuff. All that talk about potential and power . . .'

'Everyone needs to start somewhere,' said Lauren. 'You need to prove you can do small-scale stuff before you can do . . . "crazy stuff".'

I nodded. It seemed fair. It *was* fair. It was how things worked for real people in the real world.

But, said a wheedly twelve-year-old sitting at the back of my brain with his arms folded. *But I wanna . . .*

'What about my thing I suggested before?' I asked.

'What?'

'Investigating what happened with Mr and Mrs Rogers.'

Lauren sighed. 'Stanly, you don't have *any* of the right . . .'

'But what if—'

'No,' said Lauren. 'Even if I did think there was mileage in it, you are absolutely, under *no circumstances*, taking on anything like that at this early stage. If I had my way, you wouldn't even be starting yet, you'd be under observation in hospital.' She stood up. 'Take the rest of the day. Think about which of those assignments you might be willing to lower yourself to. Then you can get started properly tomorrow.'

'This is rubbish,' said Daryl, when she had gone.

'I know,' I said. 'Sorry.'

'You said there'd be door-kicking! Badassness!'

'You got to bite some limbs off.'

'Yeah, and the day went pretty steeply downhill after that.'

I nodded. I wanted to discuss what had happened this morning, but it seemed prudent not to talk about it here. I imagined someone was always listening. So I suggested we go for a wander, and when we were sufficiently far from the lion's den I told him about following Mary and my confrontation with the policeman, manfully forcing my way past his disapproval to the juicy crux.

Unfortunately, his disapproval was pretty agile. 'You really need to be careful.'

'I *know*. But—'

'No,' said Daryl, 'I don't think you do. Stanly. You're still young, you've still got a lot of life to live. You saved the world. I feel like you're not . . . you need to work out how to have a place in it, now you've saved it. You can't be constantly butting heads with everyone. If we're playing it safe with Freeman, you should be playing it safe in general.'

'I know,' I said. 'I do. But . . . look, you know me. Fitting in was never exactly my thing. I just . . . need to try and do good.'

'There are plenty of ways of doing that.'

'So I've heard.'

Daryl sighed. 'All right, fine. I have registered my feelings, and I'm sure you will carry on regardless. So. Superpowered child.'

'Indeed. Ever seen any that young?'

'Nope. Think twelve's the youngest I've ever heard of.'

'So. Something new? Or . . .' I thought of that other Stanly, the older one, mortally wounded, bestowing powers upon a scared younger version. 'Maybe someone gave them to him?'

'*Gave* them?'

'Another empowered,' I said. 'An empowered like Tim Hart.'

'I've never heard of one empowered giving their abilities to another. Transferring them, you mean?'

'No,' I said. 'Just . . . using their own powers to make someone else's appear. Stimulating the process or something.'

Daryl breathed out, shaking his head. 'Wow.'

'Just a theory. But it fits.'

'What's it got to do with Tara, though? You said there was a connection in Tim's brain? The memories?'

'Yeah.' I frowned. 'Well . . . maybe he gives powers to people? Maybe that's his thing? His dodgy business? People would pay a lot for that.'

'You think maybe he gave them to Tara?'

'Possibly . . . maybe he thought I was using her to get to him, hence trying to wipe my mind.'

'But why would he give them to his nephew?'

'Dunno. Maybe I'll ask him later.'

'Later? Oh arse. The meeting.'

I nodded.

'You're definitely going.'

'I'm definitely going.'

Daryl sighed. 'Fine. Then I guess I'm coming with you.'

'You don't have to . . .'

'Kid, you know I'd follow you into hell. In fact, I pretty much did. But I reserve the right to whinge about it.'

'Agreed. Right, now I need to go and find some terrible clothes to wear.'

Chapter Eighteen

U GH. WORST OUTFIT *ever.*
I was sitting in a shadowy booth on Jinx Bar's upper level, sipping a beer, dressed like an absolute thundering bell-end. Shockingly white trainers, white shirt, luminous red bead surfer necklace and black jeans that were a bit too tight because I had such a visceral hatred of clothes shopping that I'd just grabbed a pair that looked vaguely the right size rather than spend a second longer in the shop. I'd also put some gel in my hair. I looked atrocious and Daryl's mocking laughter still echoed in my ears.

Oh well. At least I wasn't getting weird stares this time. I couldn't afford that kind of attention. Which was ironic, because I felt like the proverbial sore thumb. Except this thumb belonged to a giant and had a massive neon sign attached to it saying ROLL UP, ROLL UP, SEE THE AMAZING SORE-EST THUMB IN THE WORLD.

Hey, look.

Tim Hart had just appeared at the top of the stairs. Black suit, no tie, blue studs in his ears, glass of whisky in hand. *'Bout time.* I'd only been here for half an hour but it felt like days. I watched him cross the room and take a seat at the far end, making sure I didn't stare too much, sipping my beer, casual as you like. Just some empowered bozo, hanging out . . .

Well, well. Speaking of empowered bozos . . .

It was Leon, spiky of hair, sharp of suit and blank of

expression, slouching up the stairs as though he could barely muster the energy to put one foot in front of the other. He took a seat near the DJ and sipped what looked like a tall glass of water. Amusingly, I seemed to have found the only setting in the universe where Leon didn't look ludicrously out of place.

So. Business or pleasure?

I shifted in my booth, trying to manoeuvre so he wouldn't be able to see my face. I wasn't particularly in the mood for a confrontation with him. Last time we'd seen each other I'd sort of choked him, quite a lot.

Last time I saw him . . .

Eddie had just died.

No. NO. Fierce warrior. On a mission.

Aaaand . . .

Somebody had just strolled up to Hart's table. He was a little older, with dark eyes and severely receding hair, and wore a black poloneck and white cargo trousers which he'd co-ordinated with a bright green belt buckle, shoe laces and rings. He put me in mind of a Guy Ritchie version of Lex Luthor.

Right.

Concentrate.

'Evening,' said the new arrival, placing a glass of something on the table.

'Evening?' said Hart, uncertainly.

'It's Vernon.'

At that, Hart's whole face changed. 'Oh yeah,' he said. 'All right?'

Vernon took a seat. 'Yeah.'

'Still not used to this. I see you, I know you look familiar, but I've got no idea who you are until . . .'

'I know,' said Vernon. 'What's the news?'

'First perfect round,' said Hart. 'Not a single anomaly.'

'Good news.'

'It's gone from a forty per cent rate to zero. And this group has gone twice as long as others.'

'Yeah. It's a good result. Better than we hoped.' Vernon sipped his drink. 'Speaking of anomalies, though . . . some of it is unaccounted for.' He spoke like someone who fancied himself a gentleman gangster.

'Dunno what you mean,' said Hart. 'I took the leftover samples to the drop-off points.'

'Yes,' said Vernon. 'Except, you didn't take it *all*, did you? You kept some. Planning on selling it?'

'I swear,' said Hart. 'I don't know what—'

'Shh.' The word was charged, somehow. I guessed that Vernon was doing something psychic, although Tim's face betrayed nothing. He was just looking at the other guy as if vaguely interested in what he had to say.

After a few quiet seconds, both of them visibly relaxed. 'Well,' said Vernon. 'You definitely believe what you're saying.'

'I'm telling you,' said Hart. 'I dunno what you're talking about.'

'If I hadn't spent so much time inside your head,' said Vernon, 'I'd suspect that maybe you'd wiped it yourself.' He sipped his drink. 'We won't be needing your services anymore. The money will be in your account tonight.'

'Good,' said Hart. 'I don't want anything more to do with it anyway.'

'Well, that works out nicely, then.'

They talked about nothing for a while longer, presumably to avoid looking suspicious by leaving too early. Finally

Vernon said, 'Well, I'd better go. No worries about the misunderstanding earlier. *Forget* about it, OK?'

Wow. I wonder what that emphasis on the word 'forget' might have meant.

Hart nodded.

'You take it easy.' Vernon finished his drink, stood up and walked off. I was just getting up to follow him when I saw Leon doing the same.

Balls.

Looks like we might be on the same mission.

Um . . .

The beginnings of what was probably a very bad idea had just occurred to me, so I decided to see it through to its logical conclusion. There was clearly more to this than I'd thought. Angelcorp seemed to be on to it.

Is that why Danielle was here on Monday?

I was very possibly interfering with an important operation. Not the sort of thing that would endear me to my new employer.

Ah . . . fuck it.

I slid out of my booth and headed for the stairs, keeping some space between me and Leon. Vernon was already on the lower floor, striding towards the STAFF ONLY door through which Tim had led me the other night, Leon following fairly leisurely. I made a very quick calculation, split off from them and jogged towards the main entrance. As I hurried out, I glanced towards the bar and saw someone very familiar heading for the stairs. Danielle. I quickly looked away, hoping my generally non-me-looking appearance would fool her. She had to be here as part of the mission.

Was she going to get Tim?

No time.

I dashed out the front of the club and ducked under the rope. The temperature had dropped considerably, even in the short time I'd been in there. I ducked around the side of the club, trying to rub some of the gel out of my hair, found a spot where no-one seemed to be watching and flew straight up as fast as I could, alighting on top of the building. I ran across the roof and hopped over a parapet onto a lower roof, then made for the edge of that and waited, hoping I'd worked the angles out properly. Moments later a back door opened below and Vernon emerged, hurrying down an alleyway lined with bins.

Here we go.

I silently dropped down into the alleyway, facing the door.

Right. Now for the bad idea bit.

The door opened again and Leon came out. When he saw me, a look of shock actually passed across his face – OK, *that's already made this whole thing worth it* – and he followed it up with a full-scale frown.

'So,' I said, nice and loud. 'What's Angelcorp doing in Jinx Bar, eh?' I felt for the end of the alley with my thoughts and was pretty sure Vernon stopped to look. *Good, good . . .*

'Get out of my way.' Leon tried to think me aside, but I stood my ground. Once and for all, I was going to prove myself stronger than him.

'What were you doing in there, eh?'

Rather than speaking, Leon responded with a ferocious thought that hit me square in the chest. I used my own thoughts to dampen the impact but let myself fly anyway, doing a pretty convincing impression of someone being psychically punched twenty feet up an alley. I landed hard, rolled and sprawled on the pavement next to Vernon, clutching my chest.

'Ouch,' I said. 'He's not happy. Friend of yours?'

'I don't know him,' said Vernon.

Leon was stalking towards us now, real anger in his eyes and in the curl of his mouth. I jumped to my feet, moving my hands as if conducting an orchestra, and sent every bin in the alley hurtling towards him, spilling their foul, mouldering contents everywhere, a rain of filth. Leon deflected most of the bins but one struck him in the shoulder and he staggered. I glanced at Vernon. 'Get involved any time.'

'I'm good.' Vernon turned and ran and I looked back towards Leon, just in time for him to propel several bins back towards me. While I was busy deflecting them he held out his hand, and as if responding to the movement – *that's literally what's happening doofus* – one of Jinx Bar's windows shattered.

Wait, what—

Leon gestured savagely and whipped the broken shards straight at me like a horde of enraged, gleaming bats. Instinctively I raised my arms, crossing them across my face.

Son of a—

SHATTER!

Barely a foot from my head, the swarm of glass exploded, multiple showers of much tinier shards passing harmlessly on either side of me. As I lowered my arms, Leon, his mouth distorted with hatred, took the opportunity to hit me really hard in the face with his brain and I fell on my arse, stars popping at the edges of my vision. The furious anime character strode past and kicked me viciously without breaking stride, knocking me further to the floor.

OW. Goddamn shithead motherbastard.

Trying to ignore the pain, I rolled over to see what was happening. Vernon had been running but now he stopped abruptly, spun around and floated back towards us, caught in Leon's mental grip. I could hear sirens nearby.

OK. So either they were always planning to take Vernon, or I've severely bollocksed things up and now they're steaming in to try and salvage it.

Either way, it seemed as though I might as well crack on with my terrible plan. I dragged myself up, channelling all the pain and rage into an invisible cannonball, and blasted it towards Leon. Direct hit, right in the back. It struck hard enough to send him sprawling ten feet up the road, arms flailing, his hold on Vernon instantly broken.

Eat that, you goon.

I wasted no time establishing my own grip on Vernon and *flew*, accelerating up and over the high metal fence on the other side of the street, just as three police cars screeched around the corner ahead. I pulled Vernon close then dived down, hugging the street.

'What the hell are you doing?' he yelled.

'Feels an awful lot like saving you from Angelcorp. You can thank me later. Right now, we need to find somewhere safe to hide. I'm sort of between places at the moment . . .'

'Well you're not coming with me. Let me down, you little prick.'

Charming.

I slipped a thought into my pocket, quietly took out my Angelcorp ID card and hid it in my sock. Satisfied that we'd outrun our pursuers – at least for now – I hung a sharp right, taking us around a corner into a dimly lit passage. I let Vernon go and he immediately squared up to me, hissing. 'You think they can't track a flyer? You might as well wear a flashing light and a siren of your own!'

'Jesus,' I said. 'Someone's touchy. Why were they after you, anyway?'

'None of your *business*, you little—'

OK. *Not putting up with that.* I thought him into a lock and held him against the nearest wall. I could feel his furious thoughts struggling to break free, to take me down, but I was sufficiently pissed off to overpower him. 'Listen,' I said. 'I stuck my neck out for you back there.'

'Why?'

Um. Good question.

''Cos I hate them,' I said.

'Hate who?'

'Angelcorp.' I relaxed my grip on him and took a step back. He didn't run or try to attack me. *Progress.* 'Obviously.'

'Yeah?' He didn't look convinced. 'And why's that, then?'

'I have my reasons. And they're none of *your* business.' *Good one.* 'What I want to know is, why were they after you? That dude is one of their top empowered agents. And I saw another one in there. Ex-Chavenger. They wouldn't be after you unless it was for something big.'

'Why don't you read my mind and find out?'

'Fine.' I stared at him, into his eyes, into his AH! AH, NO! NO THANKS! 'Jesus!' I said. 'What's going on there?'

'What's going on there is me *not wanting people to read my mind.*'

'But . . . God, how do you just wander around all day with *that* imagery floating about in your head? That's some serious Takashi Miike sewage bondage disembowelment porn you've got going on . . .'

'You get used to it,' said Vernon. 'How about I have a look inside *your* head?'

'Go ahead,' I said. 'Knock yourself out.'

Right. Gamble. Can I show him what I want him to see and hold back what I don't?

I shifted my thoughts, making a crack in the cliffs, a gap in the fog, a slight sharpening of certain blurs. I let him see some of my history with Angelcorp, the edited highlights. Of course, there was no guarantee I could prove that what he was seeing was truthful. Although that bouncer had seemed pretty convinced by my age the other night . . . *could* people sense the truth, if you wanted them to? Or was it just a judgment call? Surely you could make it seem like you were telling the truth, even if you were lying?

Or maybe nobody has a clue what's going on, any more than they did before the entire world completely lost its shit, so everyone's just proceeding as best they can under comically insane circumstances.

That thought was actually semi-comforting.

Vernon's eyes narrowed as he scanned my thoughts. 'Well?' I said. 'Proof enough for you?'

'You're that kid.'

Um . . . what?

'What do you mean?' I said.

'The kid,' said Vernon. 'The one people talk about. People say you stopped the Collision.'

Errm . . . didn't mean to show him that . . .

'I helped,' I said, uncertainly.

'You helped.' His tone was tricky to interpret. Impressed? Hostile? Disbelieving?

Let's hope for impressed.

244

I held out my hand. 'Stanly.'

He shook it. 'Vernon.' The sirens were getting closer. Vernon looked up and down the passage, making mental calculations. 'We need to go. Follow me.'

Well.

Maybe this wasn't my worst ever plan.

Chapter Nineteen

'THIS IS STANLY,' said Vernon. 'He's OK.'

The pasty dreadlocked guy who'd just answered the door nodded and stood aside, and I gave him a rueful sort of 'oh what a silly business, eh' smile as Vernon ushered me in. We'd come to a top-floor flat in a block a couple of miles from Jinx Bar. Low, menacing dub was playing from somewhere and I was getting a fairly pungent scent of herbs.

We went through to a living room, where a shaven-headed girl a few years older than me was packing a bong. She froze as we entered. 'Chill, Wanda,' said Vernon. 'This is Stanly.'

Wanda and I exchanged nods and Vernon took a seat on the sofa while I hovered awkwardly. The dreadlocked guy came in, popping the cap off a beer using the handle of a flick knife, and threw himself into an armchair. 'Wha' gwan, Vernon?'

'Trouble,' said Vernon. 'Angelcorp.' He was texting on a battered flip phone.

'Assholes, man. What went down?'

'Better if I don't go into details,' said Vernon. 'Just needed somewhere to hide out for a bit.'

Dreadlocks frowned. 'Trouble coming my way?'

'No.'

'You sure?'

Vernon stared at him. 'Would I have said so if I wasn't sure, Troy?'

Troy held his gaze for a moment, then grinned. 'Shit, man, course not. Just, you know. Gotta ask.'

Vernon returned to his phone and Troy nodded at me. 'Have a seat, mate, you're making me nervous.'

I smiled and perched on the edge of a smaller, empty sofa, trying to look uber-confident. Apart from the sofas and armchair, there was a table covered in DJ equipment, multiple boxes of records, several ashtrays and a half-completed Lego model of a Star Destroyer.

'What's your story, then?' said Troy.

'He helped me out,' said Vernon. 'You'll get on like a house on fire, Wanda.'

Wanda jumped. 'Why's that?'

'Cos you've probably heard of him. He helped stop the Collision.'

Wanda looked even more nervous at this revelation, while Troy looked impressed. 'No shit! *That* kid? Dude!' He offered a fist bump, which I awkwardly accepted. 'Seriously, bro, you're, like, *legendary*. Everyone knows the official story's bullshit. You were right in it! Safe as fuck, man. You really got a talking cat?'

'Dog,' said Wanda, holding in a pretty heroic bong hit as she spoke.

She must read the comic.

Life is too damn strange.

'Dog, then.'

'Maybe,' I said.

'*Maybe.*' Troy shook his head. 'Bro, if I had a goddamn *talking dog*, it's all I'd talk about! I'd bring him with me *everywhere!*'

I laughed, seriously wishing I had brought him with me.

'Boy's a flyer too,' said Vernon. 'Proper one.'

Troy looked even more impressed at that. 'No *shit*! I've never even *seen* a flyer. 'Cept on the Internet. Didn't think there were any in the UK. What's it like? Must be crazy.'

'It's all right,' I said. 'Pretty fun. Not much use in the city, though. You just get stopped.'

'Fo' real.' Troy slurped some beer. 'I ain't got powers. I was *vexed*. I didn't leave London the whole time the Collision was happening, not once. Representing, start to finish. And what did I get? Had to move house on account of my old gaffe getting the tits kicked out of it by monsters.' He shook his head. 'Ain't life one cruel and unusual bitch.'

'Yep,' I said. 'What about you, Vernon? You get your powers during the Collision?'

Vernon shook his head. 'Few years before.' His phone bleeped and his eyes narrowed as he scrutinised the message.

'Really? Where were you living?'

'London.'

I frowned. 'Just . . . you were just living normally?'

'What else would I have been doing?'

'I dunno,' I said. 'I just . . . I thought that Angelcorp . . . thought they'd rounded up most of the empowered.'

Vernon snorted. 'I hate that word.'

'It *is* pretty gay,' said Troy. He'd started rolling a blunt.

'But you didn't have any trouble from them?' I was going to persist with this line of enquiry if it ended with Vernon flinging me out of the nearest window. 'You just . . . went about your life?'

'Yeah,' said Vernon. 'Like I'm trying to do now.'

I'm not sure why I was so surprised. Lauren had managed to stay under their radar. So had Sally, until she'd volunteered for the machine of course. So had we, for God's sake. 'Did you know any others? With powers?'

'Why are you so interested?'

'Because it's interesting.'

Troy let loose a weirdly high-pitched giggle that didn't fit with his look. 'He's right, V. It *is* pretty interesting.'

'Well, I'm not in the mood for sharing,' said Vernon.

'Tough,' I said. 'I let you see inside my brain.'

'Stick it up your arse,' said Vernon, casually. 'You chose to let me in. I'm choosing *not* to.'

'I *chose* to save you.'

'If you two want to just go to my room and pound this out,' said Troy, 'be my guest. Just make sure to change the sheets afterwards.'

'Watch it,' said Vernon.

'Hey, Wanda,' said Troy, punching Wanda in the knee. 'How about you shut up for once? Can't get a goddamn word in sideways.' He giggled again. Wanda let out a long-suffering sigh.

What am I doing here?

What is my plan?

Maybe I'll just ask.

'So what's the plan?' I said. 'Hide out here all night? Move on? Not that I'm not enjoying myself.' I gave Troy what I hoped was a respectful smile.

'Makes no odds to me, bro. Not often I have a bona fide superhero on my sofa. Well, 'cept for that one time.'

'We're waiting,' said Vernon. 'Meeting someone here.'

'Who's that, then?'

'You'll meet her in a little while,' said Vernon. 'She's on her way.'

She.

No way.

It couldn't be . . .

'What?' said Vernon. 'What's that look?'

'Nothing,' I said. 'Just . . . I don't like surprises.'

'You two are making some *wicked* intense eye contact,' said Troy. 'You *sure* you don't want to take me up on my offer of a room?'

'Give it a rest,' said Wanda. She was looking more uncomfortable by the minute. Whether it was because of Troy's gay jokes, the potency of the weed or my presence, I wasn't sure. Possibly a combination of all three.

'Sorry, sorry.' Troy nodded at Vernon. 'V. Word in the kitchen, dawg?'

'Fine.' Vernon got up and they left the room, followed rapidly by Wanda. They made a point of closing the door behind them.

This is pretty much definitely not a good thing.

I tried to listen out for their conversation, but I couldn't hear anything. Maybe Vernon had ordered them to think rather than speak?

He was definitely suspicious.

Had he been reading my mind?

Balls. He has. I let him read me before, established a connection, and he's probably been probing me the whole time without me even realising.

And what had I learned? Pretty much bugger all. This whole thing had been a colossal waste of time. The only thing that could be even vaguely considered an achievement was the fact that I'd pissed off Leon. And that was a somewhat abstract interpretation of the term 'achievement'.

I wonder if I'll get sacked.

I was starting to feel a creeping, oily dread seeping in, although I was pretty sure it wasn't related to the possibility of my being sacked. I felt cold. I didn't know those people in the kitchen. I didn't know this world, let alone its underworld. They could be psychos. Killers. I was powerful, but there were three of them. And I only had their word that Troy and Wanda weren't empowered. Maybe they were working out the best way to take me out. If they all came at me at once, from different sides, maybe they could get the better of me. *Kill* me. I didn't want to die. I . . . I didn't . . .

My palms were suddenly wet and I felt light-headed. I looked around the room. The walls were moving, contracting, closing in. This . . . I . . .

Hold on . . .

This wasn't my fear.

It *smelled* different. No, not smelled . . . it . . .

It was Vernon.

He was—

Someone knocked on the front door and immediately the fear was gone, like it had never been there. 'Damn.' Vernon's voice. 'That's her.' He came back through and went to open the door without even looking at me. My stomach was turning some insane somersaults. 'Evening,' said Vernon. I couldn't hear an answer. Vernon stepped aside, and . . . and . . .

Oh.

Tara and I made eye contact and several doors slammed of their own accord. I stared at her, unable to vocalise. She looked sixteen. Hell, she looked *older* than sixteen. She had a few braids in her hair and a bit of make-up on and wore a black skirt, a purple hoody and chunky Nikes. She . . . she was *Tara*.

I stood up. 'Tara . . .'

'Hold on,' said Vernon. 'You *know* each other?'

'No,' said Tara. 'No!' A blast of thought – *it came from her it came from her oh God* – sent Vernon tumbling into the corridor and me flying at the wall. I hit it hard and fell to the floor. 'You're not him!' she screamed, sending another thought my way. This one cut my cheek and drew blood and I cried out. I could hear Troy and Wanda banging on the kitchen door, trying to come through, but Tara must have been holding it shut.

'Tara,' I said, trying to get to my feet. 'It's me—'

Another thought, even more violent, right in my chest. It was like being drop-kicked.

Jesus . . .

'Which one of you is doing this?' Tara yelled. 'Vernon, why the *hell* are you—'

'I don't know what you're on about!' said Vernon, breathing heavily as he got to his feet. He looked at me. 'You *knew*. This is why you helped me.' His face was twisted with rage and now I felt his thoughts coming at me, tentacles, like mine but *black*, thick, edged with razors. Tara was thinking at me as well, lashes of confusion and terror and rage, and then there was a crash as Troy and Wanda busted the kitchen door open and ran back into the living room, yelling hysterically and brandishing baseball bats. I jumped to my feet—

—and stood up in a clearing, in another world. I blinked hard. 'What the . . . oh no. No! No no no not now!' I whirled around. No sign of Senia anywhere . . .

But there was a man. Sixties, possibly. Flat cap. Sandwich frozen mid-way to his mouth. Staring at me.

Balls.

No time no time NO TIME.

'Don't worry!' I said. 'Just a hallucination!' I turned away, thoughts spiralling. I'd found Tara. I'd found her. I'd bloody *found her.*

Back.

Got to go back.

Got to go back.

Now, please.

Back please.

Back. Please. Now.

Still here.

'Oh for God's *sake!*' I rose up off the ground, my anger surrounding me, a burning psychic tornado, *I HAVE TO GO BACK NOW—*

—and I was back in Troy's living room, my head barely a centimetre from the ceiling. Troy and Wanda jumped and cried out. Vernon was on the floor in the hall, clutching his head, muttering obscenities . . .

The front door slammed shut.

'No!' I said. 'Tara!' I dropped to the floor and ran after her, ignoring Troy and Wanda, thinking the door open before I got there. She was already halfway down the corridor.

'Tara!' I yelled.

She stopped dead, but she didn't turn around.

'Tara,' I said, feeling as though I was going to start sobbing. 'It's me.'

Her voice was barely a whisper. '*No it's not.*'

'It is. It *is* me. I've been looking for you.'

She turned towards me and the force of her expression

alone, even from here, made me take a step back. So much rage, so much hurt, tears streaming down her face. 'You're *not Stanly!*' she screamed, and I could have sworn her eyes glowed red as she lashed me with another brutal, furious, untrained thought. I stumbled backwards, grimacing at the pain, but I was *not* going to fight back.

'I'm so sorry,' I said. 'Tara, I'm so, *so* sorry that I left you. I couldn't . . .'

'STOP IT!' A couple of doors had started to open but she slammed them shut with her thoughts. 'You look like he looked! *Why would he look the same?* Do you think I'm fucking *stupid?*'

I kind of don't look the same . . .

Jinx Bar getup and all . . .

Also, Tara doesn't say the F-word . . .

'I gave you a Twix,' I said.

She went pale. 'What?'

'Years ago. When we first met. When we were in that . . . that bunker. Smiley Joe's bunker. I had a Twix on me and I gave it to you. It was all melted and—'

'NO!' Another blast of thought, this one forceful enough to plant me flat on my back, the wind rushing painfully out of me. I gasped, warm blood trickling from my nose, but forced myself to sit up . . .

She was gone.

Not only that, but there were three drones hovering on the other side of the open-air corridor, shouting at me in robot voices. And a helicopter searchlight flooding the place with blindingness. And Danielle Dewornu striding past, telling me that I'd better not goddamn move.

Message received.

Danielle stopped and turned to look into the flat, just as Troy came hurtling out. With a crazed bellow he swung his bat right at her head, hard enough to shatter her skull. I was too stunned to do anything, but I didn't need to. Without blinking, Danielle calmly raised her right arm and took the full force of the blow.

The bat snapped in half against her forearm.

She didn't even flinch.

Woah. There's that super-strength.

Troy stared at the handle of his ruined bat, his face a stunned mask. Danielle glanced at me with a 'you are *so* busted' expression and spin-kicked him without looking. Troy practically flew into his flat, past a glassy-eyed Vernon, who just sat and gawped at me like an ape who had received some news that he somehow knew was bad, even if he couldn't understand why. I had a feeling I knew the reason.

Hmm.

That went well.

Chapter Twenty

THEY DIDN'T TAKE me in the helicopter. I guessed they thought it was too dangerous, that if I was going to try anything it was better it happened at ground level. I sat in the back of the massive armoured police van, handcuffed to a bench, armour-clad officers to my left and right, Danielle and Leon sitting directly opposite me, more officers on either side of them. Leon was clearly sore that he hadn't been allowed to beat the snot out of me.

'You don't think about consequences, do you?' said Danielle. 'You just do what you want.'

Tara's OK.

'Even when I went out in that stupid superhero costume,' said Danielle, 'I was *careful*. I knew how much damage I could do. I knew that if I was going to help people, I needed to hold myself to better standards. No collateral damage.'

Tara . . . has powers?

'But you,' said Danielle. 'You just stampede around. Using your powers whenever you want, on *who*ever you want, then flying on. I know all about you. I've read everything. *Heard* everything. People remember you. You *frighten* them. You smashed them against walls, broke their limbs. As far as anyone at Angelcorp is concerned, you represent *everything* that can go wrong if we don't control ourselves.'

They were talking about a drug, weren't they? It's not that

Hart's been using his abilities to make new empowered, they've developed a drug for powers . . .

Has Tara taken it?

'Maybe it's the flight,' said Danielle. 'I've never heard of anyone who can do it as well as you. Nobody. The next best . . . it's basically really impressive jumping. You're legit, though. Maybe that's why you act the way you do. Everyone just looks so tiny from up there. Or maybe the fact that you can fly away makes it easier to forget, to leave things behind.'

I need to get my story straight. Can't incriminate Tara. And then . . .

Then what?

I'm kind of . . . arrested.

She was so angry . . .

'What does it *feel* like?' said Danielle. 'A world without consequences?'

'Trust me,' I said, not looking up. 'I'm well acquainted with *consequences*. You're not the only person who's ever lost someone.'

Neither of us spoke again.

When we reached the Shard I was escorted to the Undercells, which turned out to represent a perfect stylistic juxtaposition of old Angel Group – hiding dodgy things underground – and new Angelcorp – giving things rubbish and / or thuddingly literal names. The special holding cells that they saved for empowered prisoners were several floors below the Shard's basement level and Danielle and Leon led me down, flanked by six guards, through a maze of corridors and checkpoints and retinal scanners and suspicious-faced people in uniforms and white coats. I was on fire with curiosity and cold with

257

uncertainty, but there was also a little giggly part of me squealing *this is ludicrous. I'm a boy from Wales. And this shit is* LUDICROUS.

Finger print analysis. Another retinal scan. A guard who read your brain . . .

And then a familiar cold, disagreeable voice: 'Well, why exactly the *hell* hasn't the order been processed?'

Well, well.

Hello grouchy, my old friend.

I was ushered into the cell block itself, all blank doors and smooth panels and brown walls, and there he was, Morter Smith, looking like someone who had better things to do than interact with human beings. He wore a sharp dark suit and his hair was military short and he was berating a young guard who was frantically scrolling on a tablet, clearly looking for some misplaced information.

'Well?' said Smith.

'I-I-I'm sorry sir, I didn't—'

'Don't stutter at me, you spineless little cretin. Tell me why the transfer order hasn't been processed.'

'I'm not sure . . .'

'You're *not sure?* Shall I tell the CEO that? That you're *not sure?* Do you think that will satisfy him? Do you think that will facilitate a stress-free end to my day? *Find out,* you pathetic f—'

'Aww,' I said. 'Chill your bean, Grumpy Cat.'

Smith paused to look at me and my next witticism died in my throat. He definitely seemed to recognise me, but there was no indication whatsoever that we had extensive shared history. The way he looked at me, it was as you might look at someone you'd once shared some fairly boring classes with, years ago.

Freeman did get to him.

I'd known it, of course. It was the only thing that made sense. But seeing quite how thoroughly Smith's mind had been manipulated . . . it gave me a shiver.

'Hey,' said Danielle, giving me a shake. 'Quiet.'

Smith held my gaze for a few more seconds, a perplexed wrinkle at the edges of his eyes – *maybe?* – then turned away and resumed bombarding the poor underling with ever more colourful insults and threats. We had to wait for him to finish so that I could be signed in properly. Eventually he stalked off and Danielle exchanged words with the palpably relieved guard, and I was shown to a cell. She unlocked my cuffs, told me to wait and closed the door behind me.

I took a look around, stretching my limbs, glad to be out of the restraints. The room was fairly comfortable, as possibly-probably-definitely-not-quite-legal prisons went. It had a desk (bolted to the ground), a bed that looked sleepable in and a curtained-off area with a toilet. The first thing I did was go to the sink and wash the rest of the gel out of my hair. Then I sat down on the bed and waited.

I was feeling surprisingly chilled about the whole thing at this point, enough to let some curiosity in. These cells were for empowered, but what did that mean? Had they taken my powers away? I didn't feel any different and a quick test levitation showed that I still had my abilities . . .

How does this work, then?

Enquiring minds want to know.

About ten minutes later Walker came in, wearing an expression of mild disappointment. 'Well,' she said. 'This *is* unfortunate, isn't it?'

I did a trying-too-hard smile. 'Sooorry.'

'One day on the job and you end up in a cell.'

'I was off duty as well.'

'Would you mind telling me why you were at Jinx Bar? And why you opted to interfere in an operation, assault a high-ranking employee and flee the scene?'

'When you put it like that, it sounds really bad.'

Walker smiled tolerantly. 'What were you doing there, Stanly?'

'Can I ask a question first, please? How do these cells work? They're specifically for empowered, right?'

'Yes,' said Walker, a little less tolerantly. 'Depending on the prisoner's assigned threat level, we can dampen or negate their abilities entirely. On the default setting, power use is simply confined to the cell itself. You can use yours in here, but only in here.'

'Interesting. Thanks.' OK. *Let's have a crack at this lying thing, shall we?* 'So . . . I was there because I'd heard rumours about a drug that gives people powers. I thought it sounded interesting but I didn't want to mention it to Lauren until I could find something out. Got wind of a meeting at Jinx Bar, decided I'd follow that Vernon guy . . . fighting Leon seemed a good way of gaining his trust. Undercover thing, sort of.'

Walker nodded. It was impossible to tell whether she believed me or not. 'Not a bad strategy. Although the fact that you managed to stumble into something that we've been investigating for almost a year suggests to me that you're either much, *much* better than I gave you credit for . . . or frightfully lucky.' She smiled. 'Or perhaps neither.'

Yeah, neither to be honest. I shrugged. 'Lucky, probably.'

'I see. Well. Would you mind telling me what happened after you lost Leon and our patrols? Because what we found at that flat was something of a dead end. Vernon Pearce, as far as we can tell, has no memory of the last six months. The two non-empowered have no memory of the last twenty-four hours. Tim Hart isn't proving terribly helpful either.' Something in the way she said that last sentence suggested to me that maybe she was lying, but all I could think about right at that moment was Vernon and the others. Had Tara done that to them? Wiped their minds?

'Well?' said Walker.

'I managed to talk my way into the flat,' I said. 'Then there was a lot of sitting around, talking.' *Careful.* 'Then I think . . . I don't know, it was like they all suddenly got suspicious. The three of them went in the other room, then they came back, attacked me. Vernon with his powers, the others had bats. I fought them off but . . . I don't know, I think Vernon got a good hit in. It's all kind of blurry.'

'Blurry.'

'Yeah,' I said. 'I don't even know how their minds got wiped. Maybe Vernon tried to do it to me and I . . . deflected it? I kind of panicked when it occurred to me how bad my plan was.'

Walker nodded. 'Well, it mightn't have been a bad plan in the abstract, but the execution certainly left something to be desired. Leon is absolutely furious. As is Miss Dewornu.'

LEON'S furious? Kinda think I owe him for that dick move with the glass.

'Mm,' I said. 'Got a taste of that on the way here.'

'However,' said Walker, 'you may be able to make up for it.'

Oh? 'Really? Great, I'd like to try.'

'We think that Hart may have some information,' said Walker. 'But he'll only speak to you.'

Um . . . wut? 'To *me*?'

'Yes,' said Walker. 'I'm not sure why. He's asked for you by name. By your first name, anyway.'

How the hell does he know my name?

And why . . .

And what . . .

Huh.

Well, at least this confusion looks genuine, I guess.

'So . . . do you want me to talk to him?' I asked.

Walker nodded. 'I want you to see if there is anything that can be salvaged from this debacle. Perhaps you'll inspire me to be lenient. Save your career. Keep your freedom.'

'Sounds good.'

'Excellent,' said Walker. 'Come along, then.'

Walker took me to another cell a few blocks away, showed me in and closed the door behind me, showing a somewhat cavalier attitude towards my safety. Hart was lying on his bed, looking pretty comfortable and content, considering. He glanced at me and pulled himself into a sitting position.

'You're Stanly,' he said.

'I am.'

'You're not one of them, are you?'

'Independent contractor. How come you can remember me?'

'Saw you at Jinx Bar,' he said. 'Jogged my memory. I can only remember little bits. We'd met there before, hadn't we?'

'Yeah,' I said. 'We had . . . a confrontation.'

'You took something from my head.'

I nodded. I was half expecting him to attack me, that this was going to be a ploy to get revenge, but suddenly he was speaking in my head. (*I need your help.*)

Interesting. Clearly they didn't consider him enough of a threat to block his powers. I frowned and thought an answer. *With what?*

(*Steven.*) Hart swung his legs around and sat on the edge of his bed, indicating for me to sit next to him. (*I know I won't be able to contact anyone from in here. I've heard about this place. They're never letting me out.*)

I sat down gingerly. *You don't know that.*

(*You don't know much about them, obviously.*)

I know enough not to trust them.

He laughed out loud. (*But you're working with them.*)

It's complicated.

(*Don't care. I'm buggered now, but you can help me. Our minds connected the first time we met, a lot of stuff has come back to me. You're trustworthy. I know that. So you're about the only person I can ask.*)

So?

(*I've been helping test this drug. Gives people abilities. The people I've been working for, they've cracked it now. It works.*)

You gave some to Steven, didn't you?

He looked shocked. (*How did you know?*)

Why did you give it to him?

(*Cos of his father.*)

Who's his father?

(*A nasty piece of work. Violent. Unstable.*)

Does he have powers?

(*Yes. And he's strong as well as violent, and he's in and out of their lives whenever he likes. He's hurt Mary before. And I know that one day Steven's going to look at him the wrong way and the bastard is going to lose it. And I won't be able to*

263

protect him, and neither will Mary. I gave Steven the drug so he could defend himself.)

OK . . . and you didn't consider informing the police?

(The police?) Hart snorted. *(They didn't care before the Collision and they don't care now that they're in Angelcorp's pocket. They care about their brave new world. The people left behind?)* He shook his head. *(No-one gives a shit. No-one ever did. And plus, I'm a drug dealer who also happens to be an unregistered empowered. I'd have been buggered six ways from Sunday if I went to them. I did the only thing I thought I could do to protect Steven. Understand?)*

I nodded.

(Thing is, now they have me, they'll talk to Mary. If she hasn't reported it already, she will. And they'll take Steven's powers, and he'll be un-protected. They both will.)

OK. So . . .

Hart smiled grimly. *(Vernon always thought he was stronger than me. Like he could just walk all over my mind. But I kept things from him. Information. A name here, a face there. Just in case. If I want something hidden, it stays hidden. I'm sure there are some pretty powerful psychic torturers lined up to have a crack at me. They won't get anything. They'll turn me into a vegetable first.)*

I got what I wanted from you the other day.

(I'd had no time to prepare. Didn't know you'd be that strong. And you went after . . . unexpected information.)

OK . . . so what's the deal?

(I'll give you everything I know. You, and you alone. In return, you find Steven's father and get him out of the picture. I don't care how. Don't care if you have him arrested, or if you put him in a coma. Don't care if you kill him. Get him out of

the way, so he'll never go near them again. Do that, and bring me proof, and I'll give you what you need to find them. To find that girl. She family?)

I ignored that. *You obviously hate Angelcorp. Why would you sell your friends out?*

(They were never my 'friends'. It was a job, nothing more. And anyway, any loyalty to people like that goes out the window where family is concerned. Yeah, I could sit here and stay quiet, and Steven's father could turn up and kill Mary, maybe Steven too, and then you lot could find who you want to find anyway, and where has staying quiet got me then? Nowhere. But it's got my family killed. You understand?)

I did. *What's his name?*

(Matthew Crane.)

Crane. The surname rang a bell . . . yes, when that policeman had been bugging Mary. She'd insisted her surname was Hart, that her husband was dead . . .

Guess that gave me an insight into how she felt about him. *Where does he live?*

(Dunno. London somewhere.) Hart thought an image into my head. A tall, heavily muscled guy, blonde hair, blue eyes, forearms awash with tribal tattoos.

I nodded. *Anything else? Where does he work?*

(No idea. Like I said, he appears, he disappears. He shouts, he throws a punch, he buys a bunch of flowers. Same old story.)

OK. You do know that if I deliver and you don't, someone will probably come in here and do horrible things to you?

Another grim smile. (I'm surprised someone hasn't already. You know, you need to toughen yourself up. That was your first proper go at interfering with someone's mind the other night, wasn't it?)

I wasn't interested in getting into that. *Do you have any more useful information for me?*

He shook his head.

Fine. Then I'll see what I can do. I stood up and took a last look around the cell. 'Have fun,' I said out loud. 'I'll get them to bring you a newspaper or something.'

'A newspaper? No thanks.' Hart smiled. 'To be honest, I'm happy to get away from all that crap.' He lay back down on his bed. 'There's worse places to be than here.'

'That's incredibly depressing.' I knocked on the door and Walker opened it.

'Anything?' she said, as we walked back up the corridor. 'I assume you were speaking telepathically in there.'

'We were.'

'Well?'

'He has some information. Could be useful. But he wants me to do something for him first.'

'Oh really. And what's that?'

'A favour,' I said. 'Look . . . I know today's been a bit of a shambles.' Walker actually laughed at that. 'OK, quite a lot of a shambles. But I can get this done.'

'This is not your investigation,' said Walker. 'You're not even cleared, let alone trained, for this sort of work. I would be foolish to let . . .' *Oh, please call me a loose cannon, that would just be the best.* 'To let you do this,' she finished. *D'oh.*

'Let me at least try,' I said.

Walker stared at me as though her bullshit detector was running overtime. 'Be at Everest Tower first thing tomorrow morning. We will discuss it then.'

'OK. Um . . . do I have to stay in the cells overnight?'

'No. You can go home.' She signalled a guard. 'Escort Mr Bird to the main lobby. His little dog is waiting.'

'Thanks, Ms Walker.' I held out my hand.

She sighed, but she shook it.

Sure enough, Daryl was in the lobby, looking like he was about ready to bite some heads off. When he saw me he practically leapt out of his fur. 'What the *hell* happened?'

'I'm fine. Come on.' Once we were outside and safely beyond any listening devices, I whispered, 'I *found* her.'

'Tara?'

'Yep. Of course, then she disappeared and I got locked up. But I have a lead.'

'Well? What is it?'

'I'll tell you in the morning,' I said. 'Bedtime now. Knackered.'

'You have *got* to be shitting me. I've been waiting in there for *hours*! I never agreed to work nights! I could have been at home eating bacon sandwiches and carrying on with my *Next Gen* marathon! Tell me the lead *immediately*, you infuriating, reckless, coronary-inducing, troublesome child.'

'There's a guy,' I said. 'With info. Needs me to do something. You want to know what else?'

'Oh God, there's else?'

'I saw Morter Smith in there. He didn't recognise me. Freeman's definitely been messing with him.'

'Makes sense,' said Daryl. 'But . . . Jesus. He's been working closely with the guy for five years. That must be some killer mojo. Making Connor and everyone forget a few details once, then letting them go, that's one thing . . .'

'Maybe Smith has regular meetings with dear George,' I said. 'So he can top up said mojo.'

Daryl shuddered. 'Yeurgh. That is creepy as *balls*, yo.'

'I know, right?' I allowed myself a little shudder of my own. Much as I loathed Smith, much as we had major baggage filled with prime cuts of major beef, much as I owed him the mother-in-law of all beatdowns . . . five years of continuous brainwashing courtesy of George Freeman?

Screw. That.

'But why wouldn't he just *kill* Smith?' asked Daryl. 'Surely it's a massive risk having him wandering around? What if he broke free?'

'I reckon that Freeman might have got a wee bit carried away with his own bastardness.' I cracked my knuckles. 'Sloppy.'

'Well this is all very reassuring to hear,' said Daryl. 'Not at all terrifying. What a bloody day. Can I go home now?'

'Yes, but we need to be back here first thing tomorrow.'

'Ugh. Being whatever we are *sucks*.'

Chapter Twenty-One

'I COULD ACTUALLY kill you,' said Lauren.

'Join the queue,' Daryl muttered into his coffee.

'Look,' I said. 'I know I'm a maverick who plays by his own rules, and my methods are sometimes questionable—'

'Oh, shut up,' said Daryl.

'But . . . um . . . yeah,' I said. 'Anyway. Walker's letting me do it, so it must be fine.'

'Yes,' said Lauren. 'Apparently she's taken leave of her senses.'

'Woah, woah! That's my boss you're talking about there. Bit of respect, please.'

'Stanly . . .'

'Sorry, sorry,' I said. 'But . . . it's fine. Isn't it? Walker's signed off on me doing it my way, all is well.'

Lauren laughed darkly. 'Well, I'd run in the opposite direction if you see Leon or Danielle, you certainly haven't endeared yourself to them. And I wouldn't be so sure that this is all it seems. Walker always has an angle. That's why she is where she is.'

'I'll bear that in mind,' I said. 'But in the meantime, I need to get cracking with some detective stuff. Keen?'

'I'd love to,' said Lauren, 'but some of us have incredibly important and boring admin to do.' She showed us to a computer and logged us on. 'Be. *Careful*,' she said, as she left the room.

'I will,' I said.

'I don't believe you,' said Daryl.

'Hush.'

It didn't take long for us to find Matthew Crane on Angelcorp's database, which conveniently contained the entirety of the police's database as well. He had a record for petty theft and possession and the like, some prison time. No record of him registering as empowered, which wasn't altogether surprising.

'How about this?' I said. 'Known haunts – boxing club. South west. Owned by someone called Simmonds. Worth a try?'

'Guess so,' said Daryl. 'You're the detective.'

'Man, then we're totally screwed.'

'True dat.'

We took a train across town, debarking at an impressively grimy backwater station. Even the barriers were old, and as we emerged onto the street it seemed like the sun itself was avoiding this part of town. We hopped on a bus that smelled of the word 'tired' and I tried to work out what to do when we found the boxing club. I wished I was taller. I knew I didn't make much of an impression when I entered rooms. And I wanted to avoid using my powers if at all possible. I felt like I needed to be careful – for the sake of my own conscience, as much as anything.

We hopped off by a row of down-on-their-luck shops and wandered around back streets for almost half an hour before we finally found SIMMONDS CORNER, which seemed to be missing an apostrophe. *Sharon's eye would be twitching right now.* The faintly sad, grubby sign and uneven brickwork didn't seem to promise much.

'Like a once proud Vegas tart who's fallen on hard times,' said Daryl, almost wistfully. I squinted at him. 'Sorry,' he said. 'It just came into my head and I had to say it.'

The front door, side and back doors were locked. 'D'oh,' I said. 'Gonna have to break in.'

'That's a good first impression,' said Daryl. 'I hear the youths are obsessed with this loopy contemporary craze called "knocking", you could try that?'

'Oh yeah.' I knocked on the back door and waited. After nearly a minute – and several increasingly loud knocks – a face blurred into view on the other side of the frosted glass. 'What?' someone asked in a gruff, forty-a-day croak.

'Hello! My name's Stanly. I need . . . some information.'

'Get lost.'

'Please,' I said. 'I need to find someone. It's urgent. I know he used to come here, I was hoping—'

'Piss. *Off*.' The face disappeared.

I looked down at Daryl. 'D'oh,' he said. 'Gonna have to break in.'

The door didn't look like the toughest barrier ever, but kicking it down seemed unnecessarily thuggish – even though it would probably have inspired them to take me seriously. So I unlocked it with my brain, revealing a dimly-lit hall carpeted in sickly green, the walls lined with framed photographs of square-jawed boxers going back decades. We were halfway down the corridor when a door opened at the other end and a man, pushing seventy, head like a hairy potato, appeared, scowling. He wore a vest, trousers and braces, and looked like exactly the kind of person I'd expected to find here, which was amusing.

'Hi,' I said. 'Door was open.'

'Bloody wasn't.' The man coughed and disappeared again.

I continued up the corridor with Daryl at my side and pushed open another door. The old man was cowering at the back of a poky, musty office, next to a table that held a somewhat suspicious looking briefcase. Standing between us was a young man wearing a red shirt open over an excessively ripped torso, his thin blue eyes regarding me with a mixture of hostility and anticipation.

'You'd better get out now,' said the old man. 'Or you'll see what Pierre can do.'

Pierre? Not the most badass name ever invented.

'Show me what you can do, then, Pierre,' I said, amiably.

Pierre struck a fighting stance and did a couple of vicious-looking dummy high kicks and martial arts blows.

Hmm. He could definitely kick the shit out of me.

'If you're not careful,' said the old man, 'the next lot'll be hitting you, not the air.'

I smiled. 'You know, when I was about fifteen, I would have been mega impressed by that.' I snapped my fingers and in the space of a second I'd built a cage around Pierre using chairs, a filing cabinet and the table. The suspicious briefcase, meanwhile, was on the ceiling. The old man jumped and Pierre started vainly trying to free himself.

I grinned. 'But then I got superpowers.'

'You . . .' said the old man. 'You're one of those . . . one of those—'

'Yep.'

'You lot think you bloody own the place! Bloody *freaks*! Think you're better than us!'

'Nope,' I said. 'No we don't. Look, mate. I really don't want to fight. I don't want trouble, I don't want to damage your property, I don't want to threaten people, I don't want to steal anything. I'm guessing you're up to something dodgy but I really don't care. I just want some information.'

The old man regarded me balefully for a moment, then took a half-smoked cigarette from behind his ear and lit it. 'What do you want to know?' Pierre continued to struggle in his cage, but he wasn't getting out until I thought so.

'Matthew Crane,' I said. 'Used to box here. Remember him?'

The old man shook his head.

Honestly.

I whipped the briefcase into my waiting hands, so fast that it made the old man jump. 'Do you know what I could do to this?' I said. 'I could melt it with a look. Is Crane really worth that?'

The old man had dropped his cigarette and was fumbling around for it. 'No,' he said. 'No, I . . .' He picked it up, re-lit it. 'Yeah, I remember Crane. He came in a couple of times a week with a woman, while back. Good fighter, he was. Strong. Used to drink with some of the younger guys . . . haven't seen him in a long time.'

'I need to find him. Fast. Any help you can give me would be much appreciated.'

'He was friendly with a lad called Jamie. I can give you his phone number.'

'You'll give me his *address.*' I turned the case on its end and rotated it slowly on the palm of my hand. 'Or you'll be scrubbing melted briefcase out of your carpet for weeks.'

'All right! All right!' The man scribbled an address on a piece of paper and gave it to me. It seemed to be in the general vicinity of the boxing club, but I was damned if I was going to be able to find my way there.

'Directions, please.' I glanced down at Daryl. 'Remember these.'

Daryl nodded. The old man's eyes widened in horror at this exchange, but he gave me the directions.

'Thanks a lot,' I smiled. 'You've been very helpful. And whatever you're doing that's so dodgy . . .' I moved the chairs, filing cabinet and table that surrounded Pierre back into place. 'Maybe you should be a bit less dodgy about it. Then you wouldn't have to worry so much.'

Pierre moved to attack me but the old man barked his name and shook his head.

'See ya,' I said, turning and leaving the way we'd come, making sure to lock the door behind me.

'I'm having a problem,' said Daryl, as we headed down the street. 'I really think that I should be telling you off for intimidating ordinary people, and for the clichéd crooked-detective-with-dodgy-tactics shtick. But that was kind of awesome. Severe cognitive dissonance.'

'I know what you mean. I didn't lay a thought on either of them, though.'

'Does that make it OK? Genuinely asking.'

'Wish I knew.'

Jamie Something's house didn't yield much. His wife was immediately suspicious – and had a severely pissed-off-sounding baby to deal with – and even though I got the impression she wasn't a fan of Matthew Crane, she wasn't in a hurry to tell me anything. I rang Lauren to see if she could find out where Jamie worked, but she didn't answer.

'You could have read her mind,' said Daryl. 'The wife.'

'I know.'

'It's good that you didn't, though.'

'Yep. Lunch?'

'Plannage, Stannage.'

We decamped to a nearby fish and chip shop and bought enough greasy food to induce the quantum singularity of heart attacks. I hadn't anticipated what hungry work wandering around questioning random people was going to be, and was just dabbing up some curry sauce with a bit of sausage when Lauren called me back. I told her the latest development and asked if she could find this Jamie guy's details.

'Would have been handy if you'd got a last name,' she said, reproachfully.

What am I, the world's greatest detective?

No.

'You have an address,' I said, as though I'd not got a surname on purpose because it wasn't necessary.

'Fine. I'll get back to you.'

We sat and picked at the remainder of our food. I was starting to feel unwell.

'So,' said Daryl. 'Tara.'

'Tara.'

'She's knee-deep in some dodginess.'

I nodded.

'What are you going to do?'

'Get her out of it.'

'What if she doesn't want to get out of it?'

I shrugged. 'Then . . . I don't know. Maybe if I just talk to her, she'll . . . realise she doesn't want to be doing it?'

'Have you ever met any sixteen-year-olds?'

'Hush.' I sat back with a sigh. 'I honestly haven't got a clue. Everything is just non-stop confusing. All I know is that . . .

she's Tara. And she's lost. I could feel it, she was so . . . her powers felt so *angry*. If I can help her . . . I have to try.'

'I understand.'

My phone buzzed. A text from Lauren – James Ridley was currently working on a construction project in south London. She had thoughtfully provided the address. I texted a quick thank you. 'Sweet. Come on, Dogberry. Let's get rambling.'

'Dogberry? From *The X-Files*?'

'That's Doggett. Dogberry's the main cop from *Much Ado About Nothing*.'

Daryl snorted. 'And how the hell do *you* know about anything Shakespeare-related beyond *Romeo and Juliet*, you un-cultured heathen?'

'Mate, I am *Mr* Culture. Now come along, Droopy, spit spot.'

'I hate you.'

It turned out that I'd passed this place just the other week, on the way to Connor and Sharon's new house, but I hadn't really noticed because none of those working on it had been using their minds. It was a new community centre, about a quarter of the way to completion. We walked towards it . . . and the first person I saw was Connor, hefting a pile of wood that must have been twice his weight.

Oh joy of joys.

We clocked one another at the same time and he paused briefly to frown before taking the wood to its destination and handing it over for two more guys to struggle with. Then he strolled over to us. 'Stanly. Daryl.'

'Hi Connor,' I said. 'How's it going?'

He nodded. 'What can I do for you?'

'We're looking for a Jamie Ridley. Do you know him?'

'I do.'

'We need to talk to him.'

'Why?'

'It's . . .' I really didn't want to say Angelcorp business, but that was OK because Connor said it for me.

'Angelcorp business, is it?'

'Just need to talk to the guy.'

'What's the case?' He spoke mildly and his face and body language were relaxed, but I could feel how much he wanted a confrontation. It came off him in waves.

'We're trying to find some bad guys,' said Daryl.

'Really.'

'Connor, please,' I said. 'These are bad people we're after. It'll be much better for everyone if we can take them down. And . . . it'll help me find Tara.'

If the stakes hadn't been so serious, I might have enjoyed the way the look in his eyes changed when I mentioned her. 'We need some info,' I said. 'That's it.'

'Wait here.' He turned and walked away.

Daryl shook his head. 'Who *is* that guy? And what did he do with the Connor I used to really enjoy hanging out with?'

'People change.'

The dog snorted.

Moments later someone came striding out of the skeletal building, a solidly built guy with curly ginger hair, pointing in our direction. Connor was walking un-hurriedly after him.

'Oi!' the guy yelled. He wasn't much taller than me but he weighed significantly more. He also looked significantly angrier. 'Are you the kid who turned up at my house earlier? Threatening my wife?'

Oh thanks a bunch, Jamie's wife.

'I didn't threaten anybody,' I said, calmly.

Jamie was within punching distance now. He didn't throw one immediately, just stood very close to me. 'You don't *ever* go near my wife, my daughter or my home again.'

'I wasn't planning on it, I promise.' Connor was hanging back.

And thanks a bunch to you too. Don't worry about helping or anything.

'I just need some information,' I said. 'I wanted to talk to you but you weren't in—'

'You'd better make sure you never come near us again,' said Jamie, 'cos if you do, you're going to be shitting broken teeth for a couple of weeks.'

Well that's a lovely image.

'I just want to know where Matthew Crane is.'

'Never heard of him. Get lost.' He turned and started to walk away.

'Yeah you have,' I said. 'I know you have. And you need to tell me where he is.'

Jamie stopped and turned his head a little, clenching his fists. '*Get lost*. Right now.'

'Hey, Connor?' I called. 'The guy I'm looking for? He beats his wife. Possibly his kid. That's why I'm looking for him. To stop him from doing that.'

Connor looked visibly affected by that. *Good.* Unfortunately – *ah, not so good* – so did Jamie, who came at me, throwing a punch. I could have taken him out easily, but most of the other workmen and women on site had now gathered at the edge of the building to watch and I really didn't want to look like an empowered bully. Impressively, I managed that entire calculation in the time it took for the punch to *nearly* get me in the face, leaving time to wobble out of the way. Daryl snarled but I held up a hand. 'Chill, Daryl!'

Jamie spun and came at me a second time. I dodged again. 'Jamie! Why are you protecting this guy? He's scum. Tell me where he is. I don't want to fight *woah*—' I jumped aside, narrowly avoiding another punch that would have crushed my nose. I could hear Daryl yelling at Connor, asking him what he was playing at, telling him to get involved. That actually distracted Jamie, who turned and looked disbelievingly at the talking dog, giving Connor time to jump in and gently subdue him.

'Come on Jamie, mate,' he said. 'Calm down.'

'That dog . . .'

'Yeah,' said Connor. 'The dog talks. Now, are you going to calm down?'

'I don't know this prick from Adam,' said Jamie. 'He goes round my house, harassing my wife—'

'I didn't *harass* anyone—'

'Stanly,' said Connor, sharply. 'Give me a second, OK?' He turned Jamie around and looked into his eyes. 'Come on, mate. We all get on on this site, don't we? You start hitting people, I can't keep it to myself. You know that.'

'I don't sell out my friends,' said Jamie. 'I don't care *who* he is.'

For God's sake.

I don't have time for this.

I made a show of being impatient, looking around, while Connor tried to reason with Jamie. Nobody would have known that I was reaching out with my mind, into the thrashing sea of the other guy's thoughts. Turned out that he was really hacked off with me – *go figure* – but also with Matthew. Jamie knew he was a bad egg. He *knew* he was. But there was loyalty there. They went back a long way. Matthew had helped Jamie out of some pretty serious trouble.

'Jamie,' I said. 'I know he's your mate. But his wife and son are in danger. Whatever you owe him, whatever's making you protect him . . . is it more important than their safety?'

'Listen to him, Jamie,' said Connor.

Deep red guilt was spreading through the confused waters of Jamie's mind, like spilled blood. He could see his own family in it and he was imagining what he'd do to anyone who ever tried to lay a finger on them. This would be a dangerous gambit, but I wasn't prepared to mess around anymore.

'Imagine your wife,' I said. 'Your daughter. They've got you to protect them. Mary and Steven? They have no-one.'

Jamie closed his eyes. 'Lenny Morgan.'

'What?'

'That's who he's staying with,' said Jamie. 'Lenny Morgan. Friend of his. Cop. I don't know his address.'

Cop . . . Morgan . . .

Holy crap. That policeman who's been hassling Mary?

Crane must have put him up to it.

Son. Of. A. Bitch.

'OK,' I said. 'Thanks. You're doing the right thing.'

Jamie grunted and slouched off. I smiled warily at Connor. 'Cheers for that.'

He nodded. 'Yeah. Well . . . good luck. Hope Tara's OK. If you . . . let me know if you need any help. See ya.'

Jesus. Did he actually just say that? 'Thanks,' I said. 'Bye.'

I clicked my tongue at Daryl. He gave me a murderous glare in return and we headed off.

'So,' said Daryl. 'You totally went into Jamie's brain, didn't you?'

'Yeah.'

'So this was one of those times when it was OK? What's the policy? No women, no kids?'

I shrugged. 'Trying to find a way to appeal to someone who was protecting a domestic abuser who could be the key to a vital clue to find my vulnerable young friend and also track down the distributors of an illegal drug that gives people superpowers? Seemed legit.'

'You could have just said "yes".'

I phoned Lauren again and asked her to get an address for Lenny Morgan, hoping that she wouldn't realise that he was a policeman, but obviously she did because obviously she was always going to.

'Stanly,' she said. 'Leonard Morgan. That's the policeman you . . . aggravated.'

'Yep.'

'Matthew Crane is bunking down with a *policeman*?'

'Kinda.'

'Stanly . . .'

'Lauren, this is our *only* lead.'

'If I don't give it to you, you'll just ask someone else, won't you?'

'I actually hadn't thought of that . . . but probably.'

She sighed, but she gave me the address. 'Please, *please* be careful. Do this properly. I can't protect you from everything.'

'I will. Thanks Lauren. I owe you approximately a shitzillion favours.'

'Oh, don't worry. I'm keeping a tally.'

'I have a bad feeling about this,' said Daryl, as we neared the block of flats in which Lenny Morgan lived. It was a posh construction, within spitting distance of the river. Seemed more expensive than someone on a policeman's salary should have been able to afford.

Presumably being a hired thug and bully helps with the extra.

'Make up your mind,' I said. 'One minute you're down with extreme methods, the next you're up in my grills all cautious like . . .'

'This is a *policeman's flat* we're about to bust into, Sergeant Steam-Ahead.'

'He's harbouring a criminal. A criminal I need access to, in order to further a vital investigation.'

'Wow. That sentence really just came out of your mouth. You're properly into this maverick detective bollocks, aren't you?'

'Aren't you?'

'Maybe a bit. But like Lauren said, this isn't a game. We need to be careful.'

I stopped. 'OK then, Captain Cautious.'

'Good one. It's like what I said except different and also higher ranking.'

'What do you suggest?'

'See who's there first,' said Daryl. '*Without* them realising. If it's just Crane, then by all means, bust in and rendition the crap out of him. If it's Morgan, either forget it and wait, or try to explain.'

'I can already see explaining not working. And being cautious takes time we literally don't have.'

'Literally?'

'Well . . . probably.' I kept walking and Daryl ran alongside me.

'So,' he said. 'When you asked my opinion, you never really intended on taking it on board, did you?'

'I did, actually. But then reality came a-knockin'.'

'Fine. What's your plan, General . . . some sort of synonym for reckless that starts with a G.'

'Good one,' I said. 'Higher ranking again. If they're both there, I want you to corner Morgan. You don't need to hurt him, just keep him occupied. If I don't actually assault him, hopefully everything will be OK.'

'Or I'll be sent to the pound.'

'In which case, I will bust you out of there in highly awesome fashion.'

'Promise?'

'Probably.'

We got to the building and I bypassed the lock with barely a thought. Morgan's flat was on the twelfth floor.

'I actually assaulted a policeman once,' said Daryl, conversationally, as we rode the lift up.

'Really?'

'Yeah. In New York. Bit his hand off. Well . . . actually it was an assassin posing as a male stripper *disguised* as a policeman . . .'

'Bit his hand off, eh?'

Daryl looked sheepish. 'Lost my temper. They stitched it back on . . .'

We arrived on the twelfth floor, which was incongruously carpeted in baby pink, and headed to Morgan's door. I pressed the side of my face against it and listened, trying to enhance my hearing with my powers, feel my way into the flat, along the walls . . . definitely voices . . . no, that was the TV . . . no, now a human voice.

Morgan. 'Coffee?'

Second voice. Deep, harsh. Another man's. 'Nah.'

Has to be Crane.

I looked down at Daryl. 'What do you think? Kick the door down?'

'Knock,' said Daryl. 'Christ alive, child, you should at least *try* to do this without breaking, entering and assaulting an officer of the law.'

'You're no fun.' I knocked. Footsteps came up to the door and Morgan's voice asked who it was.

Bums.

Uh . . .

'Let me in,' I said.

'What?'

'Let me in. Uh . . . please.'

'You *what?*'

'Let me in, now. Please.' I really wanted to add *asshole* but managed to restrain myself.

'Wait a minute, that's . . .' The door opened and Lenny Morgan stood there looking just as disagreeable as he had the first time we'd met. 'It *is* you. What the hell are you doing here?'

'I need to have a word with your flatmate.'

'I don't have—'

'All right, if we're going to dance the semantic ballet, I need a word with the other man who is inside your flat and is called Matthew Crane.'

Morgan looked suspicious, furious, worried and threatening

all at the same time, which was quite an achievement for one face. 'You listen here, you little shit. I'm a *police officer*. I don't have to let you in here. I don't know who Matthew Crane is. And you'd better hop it if you don't want me to arrest you.'

'You're off duty,' I said. 'You can't arrest people.'

'Actually, I can,' said Morgan, smiling nastily. 'But it's tedious and complicated, so I'll probably just batter you. I don't give a shit if you're Angelcorp.'

'I know he's in there,' I said. 'I also know he's been using you to spy on his wife and son. Well. I say spy. Harass might be more appropriate. Highly unprofessional behaviour, not befitting an officer of the law. I'm sure your bosses would agree. Now I don't have any quarrel with you . . . well. Yeah, I do, actually. But it's secondary to my quarrel with Crane.'

I'm glad Morgan isn't empowered too. He's looking really angry.

'If you're not gone in five seconds flat,' said Morgan, 'I am going to break your arms.'

'Daryl,' I said. 'Sic him.'

Daryl growled and leapt at Morgan, pinning him to the ground before he could blink. The beagle snarled pretty terrifyingly in his face and I walked in, closing the door behind me and skirting around the struggling policeman. 'Get out of here, Matt!' he yelled.

Someone in the living room stepped into view. Matthew Crane. Tall, spiky blonde hair, white shirt with the sleeves rolled up to reveal his tattoos . . . and his muscles. *Woah. I know who to question if there's ever a spinach shortage.*

Crane glared at me. 'Who the hell are you?'

'I've got a message for you.'

'Len!' he called. 'You all right?'

'Yeah! Get *out* of . . . oof . . .' *Nice one, Daryl.*

'A message, is it?' said Crane. 'From who? Murray? Gobstopper?'

Gobstopper? Who the hell is called Gobstopper? 'Well,' I said. 'Actually . . . it's from me.'

'And who are you?'

'No-one,' I said, uncertainly. *Crap. Currently sucking at this.* 'Look. Basically, the message is . . . you need to stay away from Mary and Steven.'

Crane suddenly looked about five hundred per cent angrier. Crimson splattered across his face like someone had chucked paint over him, his jaw tightened into a granite wedge and his body tensed, ready for fighting.

What's he going to do? God, I hope his powers aren't as nasty as he looks.

'You'd better get out of here,' he said. 'Or I'm going to ruin you.'

What a weird turn of phrase.

'Ruin me?' I said. 'What does that even mean? Isn't that what blokes say about girls they want to . . . you know . . .'

'*I'll break your bloody spine is what I mean!*' Crane bellowed, the words exploding out of his face like a valve had just burst.

'No you won't,' I said. 'In fact, you won't even try. You're going to stay away from Mary and Steven. Leave town. And tell your friend to stay away too. You do that, and I won't hurt you. Or have you arrested. Or worse.'

Crane lunged at me, letting loose a strangled loop of random vowel sounds. *OK, this is happening.* I caught him with my mind and threw him across the room quite a bit harder than I'd intended and he smashed into a painting on the wall, shattering the glass and breaking the frame. He sprawled to the ground in a heap.

Why isn't he using his powers?

'Stay down,' I said. He didn't. He jumped up and went for me again and I flipped him over onto a wooden coffee table, which broke under his weight. I could hear Daryl and Morgan struggling in the hall, Morgan shouting, Daryl barking. Crane grunted in pain but quickly got back up again. *Man. He's lively.* I grabbed him, held him, turned him upside-down and levitated him until he was at eye level with me.

'Where are your powers?' I said, unable to stop a slight taunting edge from creeping into my voice.

'I don't have any *powers*,' he said, fighting to free himself.

'Whatever,' I said. 'Come on. Might as well make this a fair fight, if you're not going to listen to reason.'

'I don't *have* powers, prick. Why are you here? What are Mary and Steven to you?'

'I'm acting on behalf of a concerned third party,' I said. 'You've hurt Mary before, haven't you?'

'You f—'

'HAVEN'T YOU?' The force of my outburst sent Crane flying into the kitchen and he landed hard on the counter, breaking some china and sending condiments flying everywhere.

Woah. Calm down, kid.

Crane rolled off the counter and immediately came at me again but I threw him back across the room, stopping him just before he hit the wall. 'Answer me,' I said. 'You've hurt her before.'

'I was . . . it was just . . . I was drunk, she wouldn't—'

287

'Shut up,' I said. 'Shut up *now*. You hurt her. So how do I know that one day you're not going to hurt Steven? He won't do as he's told, won't go to bed, and you lose your temper? Or maybe you're just drunk and you're pissed off and he's just *there*—'

'I would *never* hurt my son—'

'Don't believe you.'

'Did Mary put you up to this?'

'Nope.'

'I haven't seen either of them for months—'

'But you've been having your pal watch them,' I said. 'Your pet policeman.'

'He's just keeping them safe—'

'Stop *lying*.' I spun him around several times. 'Now, I can keep doing this all day,' I said. 'I can break bits off you one at a time, or two or three at a time. I don't want to. I want your solemn promise that you're going to stay away from Mary and Steven.'

'Why are you doing this?'

'*Swear.*'

'No!'

I breathed deeply. *Seriously, Stanly. Chill.* 'Fine. How about this, then? I go inside your brain and I remove every memory you have of them.'

Now there was fear in his eyes. Very real fear. 'You wouldn't . . . you *can't* . . .'

'I can and I will. I'll reach into your mind, find every memory, your son's birth, if you bothered to turn up for it, his birthday parties, every happy moment you had with your wife, and I'll take it all. Wipe it away. As if they never existed.' *Shiiiiiit. What am I saying?*

288

'You can't.' He started to cry, which I definitely hadn't been expecting.

He doesn't have powers.

He's just a bully.

Hart lied.

'I can,' I said, trying to keep the rising uncertainty out of my voice. 'Promise. I can.' As I spoke, I went into his mind, trying to find proof, to make sure I was doing the right thing, make sure that Hart had only told me one lie, about Crane's powers. I needed to know that this was a bad guy. Through and through. I dived in . . . and I saw everything. I saw blind drunk rages, I saw him raising his hand to Mary, I saw him bellowing while his son sobbed in a high chair, I saw all the times he'd messed up, all the people he'd hurt, all the horrible things he'd done and all the things that had been done *to* him, all the things he'd seen, from when he'd been Steven's age, younger, the path that had led him here, led him to be this, and I felt a tiny stab of pity for him . . .

No. No pity. Not for this guy. So he'd had a horrible life. So did lots of people. They didn't all turn into thugs. 'I promise you,' I said again. *Come on. Resolve. Let's hear it in your voice.* 'So . . . there's your choice. Stay away and keep your memories of your family . . . or you stay and I take them all.' My phone started ringing but I reached into my pocket and clicked it on to silent. Crane lay on the ground, panting and crying.

I . . . I broke him.

'Your choice,' I said again.

'I'll go,' he whispered.

Thank crepes for that.

'Good,' I said. 'Come with me.'

He nodded. I let him up and he grabbed a rucksack and slung it over his shoulder. We walked down the corridor, where Daryl still had Morgan pinned.

'Let him go,' I said. Daryl jumped off and Morgan leapt to his feet. 'Your friend's going now,' I said. 'Say bye.'

'You'll pay for this,' said Morgan.

'Unless you want the boys down the station to know that you spy on vulnerable women and their children as a favour to your scumbag mates,' I said, 'you'll forget that I was ever here. I can help with that, if necessary.' I tapped my temple.

'You'd better watch yourself, you cocky little—'

'*Say bye, Lenny.*'

I took Matthew Crane to the nearest station and put him on a train that terminated a good few hundred miles away.

'They're important to you,' I said. 'Mary and Steven. Otherwise you wouldn't be doing this. That means something. Think about it.'

Crane said nothing.

'Well, that sort of went well,' said Daryl, as we headed back to the Shard. 'Except now we've made a mortal enemy of a really nasty policeman. And you threatened to wipe a man's mind.'

'I wasn't actually going to do it.'

'No?'

'No! Of course not.'

'Why?'

'Threatening is one thing. Invading someone's head like that . . .'

'You did it with Hart.'

'That was . . . different. There are degrees of it. I made Hart forget *me*. Five minutes of his life. Five minutes in which he'd already tried to do it to me, to stop me from trying to find Tara. That's one thing. Removing someone's wife and child? Completely? No.' I shook my head. 'It was . . . an effective threat. But I would never have done it.'

I almost sound sure.

I rang Lauren to tell her I'd done what needed to be done, but before I could even speak she was already yelling. 'Where have you been? I've been trying to phone you!'

'Sorry, my phone was on silent—'

'Walker let Rosie in with Hart.'

'She *what*? When?'

'About half an hour ago. I only just found out.'

'Rosie tortured him?'

'Yes.'

'God . . . *DAMN IT!*' I almost hurled my phone to the floor but managed to restrain myself. 'Did it . . . did she even get the information?'

'You'd better get back here.'

'Lauren, what—'

But she'd already hung up.

Chapter Twenty-Two

'**D**ID SHE GET *anything* from him?' I asked, as the lift plunged down towards the Undercells.

'No,' said Lauren. 'At least, I don't think so. I'm not even supposed to know it happened.'

'How *do* you know?'

'Danielle told me.'

'Danielle? How does *she* know?'

'I don't know.'

'Did she say what kind of state Hart is in now?'

Lauren just gave me a severely Meaningful Look. I slammed my fist against the wall. 'For Christ's *sake*! I had it! I had it under control!' *Well. Ish.* 'Crane's on his way out of town, it was all fine!'

'I'm sorry,' said Lauren. 'I couldn't . . . I didn't know.'

My knuckles were white, my body fizzing with furious adrenaline. We hurried through the security checkpoints and the guard unlocked Hart's cell. I stepped inside and froze.

Oh.

Hart was curled up on his bed, shaking. He was soaked in sweat, his face frighteningly pale, paler than anything. I knelt down next to him. 'Tim? Tim? Can you hear me?'

He looked at me, but I couldn't see any recognition in his eyes. 'Tim,' I said. 'It's me. Stanly. Remember?'

He just looked at me.

'Mary and Steven,' I said. 'You remember Mary and Steven?'

Something flickered in his eyes, but he still didn't speak. 'They're safe,' I said. 'I did what you asked. Crane's gone, he won't hurt them again. I promise.'

Still, Hart just stared.

'Tim,' I said, 'I'm remembering now. I'm remembering Crane getting on the train. Look into my mind. Come on. It's OK, I don't mind, you can come in. Look. See? I'm telling the truth.' I stared into his eyes and he stared back and I thought maybe I felt a slight tickle in my brain, but I wasn't sure. I might have just been imagining it. For a long, long minute we just stared at each other, and then, amazingly, beautifully, I saw the faint ghost of a smile on his mouth. It was definitely there. Definitely.

'You saw,' I said. 'See? I did what you asked. I'm so sorry about what Rosie did to you. I didn't . . . I'm sorry, Tim. Can you speak?'

Finally he opened his mouth. 'She . . . showed me . . .' His voice wasn't his voice. There was nothing in it.

'I know.' I didn't know. I didn't want to know. 'I'm sorry. I . . . if I'd been here . . .'

'She . . .'

'Tim,' I said, 'I will help you get better. I promise. I swear. I will help you. But I need to know what you know. Please.' *Please. For Tara. I have to find her. This can't have been pointless.*

He might have nodded. 'Thank you,' I said. 'Can you tell me?'

He opened his mouth but no words came out. He shook his head. The movement looked agonising. 'Can you think it?' I asked. 'Put it into your mind, front and centre. And let me in.'

A nod? Maybe?

'Thank you,' I said. 'It's all right. You'll be OK. And Mary and Steven will be fine.' I reached out with my mind and found his, stepping gently and politely in, as though entering a vast blackness with things zipping back and forth like tiny fireflies, leaving trails so complex and bursting with variables that it was dizzying. And there, right at the very front, hovering in the air, were two thoughts. The essence of thought. Brightness, potent with meaning and memory and so many other things . . .

They painted themselves into my mind and I drew back. 'That's it?' I said, a shake in my voice.

Another microscopic nod.

'I . . . thank you,' I said. 'I'll make sure you get help. Don't worry.' I stood up and knocked on the door and Lauren let me out. 'He needs a doctor,' I said, striding back towards the lift. 'And someone needs to check on his nephew. Steven Hart. Even if the drug is safe . . . he needs to be looked at.'

It couldn't be . . .

'Did he tell you?' Lauren asked, hurrying after me.

'Yes.'

Could it?

'What was it? Stanly?'

'A face.' My brain was still turning hyper-cartwheels, trying to process and rationalise and reconcile. 'And an address.'

'A face? Whose?'

'Alex.'

'You know you nearly ballsed this whole thing up,' I said, resisting the urge to slam my hands down on Walker's desk, lean forwards and shout in her face.

Walker stared me down frostily. 'And *you* should know that I don't appreciate young, inexperienced freelancers – or anyone, for that matter – bursting into my office and dressing me down.'

'Well, tough. I said I had it under control. I asked for a reasonable amount of time to do what I needed to do, time *you granted*, but then you jumped the gun and sent Rosie in to vandalise his brain and now he's a wreck. We're lucky I managed to get any information out of him.'

'Rosie?' said Walker. 'You think I sent Rosie in?' She was barely bothering to feign ignorance.

'I *know* you did.'

'Well, good luck proving it.'

'The doctor will prove it.'

'I will decide if Mr Hart requires a doctor.' Walker took a deep, irritated breath. 'And as for the *information* you think you obtained, you don't even know that it's genuine.'

'It's a good deal more genuine than the big fat wedge of nothing *you* got.' I could tell that Lauren was itching to jump in and drag me out, but she just stood there, radiating awkwardness. 'And I think I've got a solid lead now. If you'd just listened to me—'

'Let's get something straight,' said Walker, remaining seated but somehow growing in stature using just her tone. 'I do not take orders from you. I do not recognise any authority you think you might have. You have your uses, I'll give you that. You are powerful and you have half a brain and you may yet be a real asset. But you have also been reckless and overly opinionated, charging into situations with no regard for procedure or the safety of co-workers. You yourself have "ballsed up" *several* delicate situations. You are *not* in charge.

You do not tell me how to run things. And you do not come marching in here, talking to me like this. Are we clear?'

'My methods may be unorthodox,' I said, 'but *damn it*, I get results.' I didn't actually say that, but I was sorely tempted. What I actually said was, 'OK. Fine. So you always intended to send Rosie in. That's it, isn't it? So why let me go off pointlessly? Was it a test? Or were you just keeping me occupied?'

'I don't have to answer any more questions,' said Walker. 'I'd suggest you go away, calm down and have a long, hard think about your future.'

'Trust me,' I said. 'I've done a lot of thinking. And a lot of *seeing.* I've seen that you're perfectly happy to torture someone who was ready to give me information, torture him until he's a broken shell shivering in the foetal position. Congrats. In less than twenty-four hours you've pretty much convinced me that *nothing* has changed round here. Same old *Angel Group.*'

'You know nothing,' said Walker, 'of what is necessary.'

'Necessary my—'

'Enough of this,' said Lauren. 'Are we going to discuss this new information?'

'Oh, I see,' said Walker. 'Stanly, special Stanly, is allowed to talk to me in such a way and then simply carry on as he wishes?'

'He aired a legitimate grievance,' said Lauren. 'I'm tempted to do the same.'

A film of ice covered Walker's desk and eyes. 'Don't play games with me, Lauren.' She turned back to me. 'So. The *information* you extracted.'

'The information he *gave* me.'

'An address and a name,' said Walker, ignoring that. 'Alexander DePierro. I've read his file. Fascinating ability, controlling animals, if somewhat twee. Do we have any record of him after the Collision?'

'No,' said Lauren. 'I'd assumed he was dead.'

'And we're certain it's the same person?'

'Yes,' I said. 'The picture in Hart's mind – it was from a distance, like he was spying, but it was definitely Alex. A few years older, obviously, but I'd recognise that face anywhere.' *I spent enough time punching it, after all.*

'And the house . . .'

'We thought we'd check it out first,' said Lauren.

'*You* did, did you?'

'I feel as though Stanly would benefit from some supervision.'

Walker uttered a cold, utterly humourless laugh. 'We're certainly in agreement there.'

'You're going to let me carry on, then?' I said.

'I haven't yet decided how to proceed,' said Walker. 'I'm sorely tempted to lock you up and throw away the key.'

'Jane—' Lauren began.

'It's *Ms Walker*, Lauren. Don't push me. I know you like to think that you're in charge around here—'

'And I know you like to think your psychotic pet is going to take over from me one day—'

'*Enough.*' Walker banged her fist on the table. 'Stanly, go away and make a concerted effort not to cause any further disasters. Good luck. Lauren? Watch your step, my girl. I'm sure you'd rather we remained uneasy allies than enemies.'

'She's lovely, isn't she?' I said, as we walked down the corridor. I could feel the fury coming off Lauren in sizzling waves.

'One of these days . . .' Lauren took a deep breath. 'If she didn't have Rosie and half the Board in her pocket . . . I've had to fight hard to get where I am. Tread on toes, make friends with the sorts of people I'd *never* . . . I've sacrificed things. And I'm *not* going to let Walker and that nightmarish . . .' She took a deep breath. 'Sorry.'

'It's OK,' I said, offering a hopefully not too patronising pat on the arm. 'Anyway, first things . . .'

Lauren's phone rang. 'Hold that thought,' she said. 'Hello? Yes, this . . .' She frowned and handed it to me. 'It's for you.'

'Me?' I took the phone. 'Hello?'

A click. A buzz. Then . . . 'Stanly!'

Um . . . 'Freeman?'

'How are things?'

'Yeah,' I said, trying not to sound as uncertain as I felt. 'I'm . . . fine. How are you?'

'Splendid. I'm very well, thank you. I just had a somewhat heated phone conversation with Jane Walker. She seems to think that we should be letting you go.'

'Oh really?'

'Well. In the sense of terminating your employment. But not in the sense of, you know, you ever leaving the building again.'

'You haven't got a cell strong enough for me.'

'Trust me, we have. But that's not why I'm calling. I'm calling to say that I calmed her down and informed her that you have my backing, one hundred per cent. You are to proceed with your little investigation.'

Um what. 'That's nice,' I said, maintaining nonchalance in the face of severe confusion. 'Thanks, mate. May I ask why?'

'Because you're doing well,' said Freeman. 'And your somewhat haphazard strategy is . . . entertaining.'

'Cool. So it has nothing to do with you having some kind of nefarious master plan that involves me?'

'No,' said Freeman. 'Believe it or not, I regret all that has happened between us, Stanly. I don't want us to be enemies.'

'OK . . .'

'This is a brave and intimidating new world. For I, as well as you. There is still much to do. I would much rather work alongside you than against you.'

'Aces,' I said. 'Well . . . yeah, great. Cheers *mate*. Speak to you soon, yeah?'

Freeman chuckled. 'Yes. Bye for now.'

'Laters.' I hung up. Lauren's face was one huge question mark. 'Seems I have a green light from the powers that be,' I said. 'Or the power that is.'

'You're joking.'

'I am not.'

'*Freeman* is letting you proceed?'

'He is.'

Lauren shook her head. 'I don't get it.'

'Right there with you.'

'Well . . . I suppose we'd better get on with it—'

'Hey.'

I turned. It was Danielle. 'Um,' I said. 'Hi. What do you—'

She ignored me and checked that there was nobody in earshot before speaking to Lauren. 'Did you confirm? Walker let Rosie loose on that suspect?'

Lauren nodded. 'How did you hear about it?'

'I just . . . I heard.' Danielle glanced at me, then hurried off before Lauren or I could say anything else.

'The hell was that about?' I asked.

'No idea.' Lauren looked troubled.

'Do you have much to do with her?'

'A bit. She keeps herself to herself. Anyway . . . Alexander. I'm not letting you go after him alone, you know that don't you? I'm coming with you. And you should take Daryl too.'

'Use your loaf.' It came out more unkindly than I'd intended. 'What's the one thing we definitely know about Alex? Apart from the fact that he's a fairly troubled individual?'

'Power over animals.'

'Exactly. It'd be like . . . I don't know . . . if I went to fight a Jedi, and I brought a lightsaber . . . except I wasn't very good with one . . . or . . . no, that's a crap analogy. Forget it.'

Lauren laughed. 'Don't worry. I know what you mean.'

'I know Daryl's not a normal animal,' I said, 'but it's just too risky. I'm not putting myself in a position where I might have to hurt him. He can be nearby, in case of emergency. That's it.'

'All right,' said Lauren. 'Well. Shall we go to the house?'

'Yeah. But let's grab the aforementioned beagle first.'

The three of us had been sitting in a car on a pleasantly nondescript North London street for the best part of two hours before somebody finally emerged from the house. It was a young guy, maybe my age, maybe a couple of years older, with light brown skin, wearing a blue hoody, dark jeans and white skate shoes with bright red laces. Daryl and I remained still in the back, not as convinced by the safeness of blacked-out windows as Lauren was, while she pretended to read a map, listening out with her brain.

The guy walked past us, showing no sign of

noticing anything. When he'd rounded the corner I whispered, 'Anything?'

'Bits and pieces,' said Lauren. 'He had barriers up. Walls, smoke, mirrors. But I did get the name Tara.'

Tara . . .

'So she is involved,' said Lauren.

'Yeah.'

'I knew you were hiding something.'

'Lauren . . .'

'It's fine. We'll talk about it later. I also got a time, which kept changing. He was obviously scrambling it in case someone tried to read him.'

'No idea what it was?'

'It switched about ten times,' said Lauren. 'But they were all between now and eleven o'clock.'

'Great,' said Daryl. 'So that's a window of what, about seven hours?'

'We should just follow him,' I said.

'He's going to notice a car with blacked-out windows keeping track of him,' said Lauren.

'Yeah,' I said. 'But . . . hmm. Daryl . . . how loud can you think?'

Daryl barked and the young man started. He looked down and Daryl looked up at him, wagging his tail enthusiastically. He barked again.

'All right there, boy?' said the guy. He got down on one knee to pat Daryl and the beagle did a very good job of looking like your standard brainless mutt. I smiled. *At least this dude's a dog person.* Lauren and I kept watch from our vantage point, extending our hearing,

Lauren keeping her mind open to receive whatever Daryl projected.

'He's thinking that he couldn't be more humiliated right now,' she murmured.

'I bet.'

After a while our suspect stopped petting Daryl and walked off. Daryl wandered after him, keeping up the charade, and Lauren and I followed, keeping our distance. It took a minute for the guy to notice that the dog was following him.

'What's up, mate?' he said. 'You want to come with me? Nah, off you go. Go on. Now.' He shooed manfully, but Daryl just sat and stared at him, wagging his tail and barking.

'He really isn't enjoying pretending to be a normal dog,' said Lauren.

Tough, I thought, chuckling to myself.

'Go on,' said the guy. 'Off you go!' He shooed Daryl away and carried on walking, but the dog continued to follow. The guy chanced a look behind, rolled his eyes and changed tack, ignoring Daryl in the hope that he would go away. We followed him for nearly fifteen minutes, until he stopped to wait for a bus.

'We're going to lose him if he gets on a bus,' said Lauren.

'Can you tell Daryl he has to stay with him?'

'I am. He's saying he'll get on the bus.'

'Good.' I flagged down a taxi and we got in.

'Wait a minute,' Lauren told the driver, showing him her Angelcorp credentials.

Three buses came and went before the guy finally boarded one, and Daryl got on as well. 'OK,' said Lauren. 'Can you please follow that bus?'

'Can you hear him now?' I asked.

'No,' said Lauren. 'I told him to stay silent as long as he's on the bus. Too risky. He'd have to broadcast really loudly, and that could risk our guy hearing him.'

'Really? Is that how it works?'

Lauren shrugged. 'Maybe.'

I knew it. Not even Lauren has a clue what's going on these days.

I wondered how Daryl was getting on. Whether he was being petted, whether the guy had sussed him. At least we knew our suspect wouldn't think to read a dog's mind.

Hopefully.

The bus pulled in and the young man jumped off, still pursued cheerily by Daryl. Lauren ordered our driver to stop and we got out and followed after them.

This had better get us somewhere.

After another ten minutes, Lauren said, 'Stop.'

We stopped. 'What's happening?'

'They've reached a house. It looks like our guy's going to go in . . . he's shooing Daryl again. Daryl is . . .' She laughed.

'What?'

'He's whining.'

I could only imagine how the dog must have been feeling then, having to whine pathetically at a complete stranger as if all he wanted was a bit of love and a biscuit.

'The guy's annoyed now,' said Lauren. 'He's telling him to piss off.'

'Tell Daryl to piss off, then,' I said. 'Make it look natural.'

She nodded and a few moments later Daryl appeared at the other end of the road, rounding the corner with his tail between his legs, generally looking pretty droopy and unwanted.

'Was that fun?' I asked, as he trotted up to us.

'I know it was for the good of the mission,' said Daryl, 'but please, next time, can someone else play the part of dumb, needy dog? I nearly died of shame.'

'He didn't suspect?' asked Lauren.

'Hopefully not. I mean, I don't think a stray would usually follow someone this far. But I managed to look as pathetic as possible.'

'And he went into a house?'

'Yeah. Number twelve on that street.'

'Did you see anyone else?' I asked. 'Tara?'

Daryl shook his head.

'What now?' asked Lauren.

'How about I walk in?' I said.

They both looked at me. 'I'm sorry,' said Daryl. 'What?'

'Listening in covertly without being noticed is going to be tricky. How about I just play it straight? March up to the door and say I know what they're up to and I want in?'

'That's ridiculous,' said Lauren. 'We need more information before we do that. And if you take them by surprise, they might wipe your mind.'

'Tara wouldn't do that.'

'Stanly, we don't know how deeply she's involved. You can't assume anything.'

'Fine. We need to do something, though. The longer we stand here, the longer Tara and that dude get to have an interesting conversation without us hearing it. What if I fly? Land on the roof? Listen in?'

'I don't know,' said Lauren. 'You'll be so exposed . . .'

'Worst-case scenario,' I said, 'they notice me and I fly away. I can be in the clouds before they even think to attack me.'

'I'd say that's worth a go,' said Daryl. 'More than just walking up to the door and knocking on it, which, by the way, I can't believe was a plan you actually came up with.'

'That sort of planning's got us this far, hasn't it?'

'Barely.'

'And I thought you loved knocking, anyway?'

'Don't you—'

'*Guys,*' said Lauren. 'Banter later, OK? Stanly, fine. Go and land on the roof and we'll wait at the end of the street. As soon as anything bad happens, you think in my direction and we'll come.'

'I like your assumption that it's definitely going to go bad.' I lifted off of the ground, trying not to think about how sketchy it was flying in the middle of the day in a residential area, zipped over a row of hedges and houses and alighted on the house's damp roof as softly as I could. At least there were no drones to be heard.

I lay across the tiles, pressed my ear against them and thought *in.*

Through.

Attic, like the idea of a wireframe in my head . . . fibreglass . . . spiders . . .

Down.

Bathroom. And echoes from—

—*down*—

—stairs . . . hallway . . . echoes from—

—kitchen—

—two people sitting at a table. One voice speaking, my projected thought processes picking up the vibrations and transferring them back up, up, up, through the floors . . .

My stomach wobbled. It was Tara's voice. 'There was someone else there.'

Young man: 'Who?'

Tara: 'I . . . I'm not sure. Someone . . . they were messing with my brain. I got away, though.'

Young man: 'You get Vernon's info?'

'Yeah. One hundred per cent success. We should tell Alex.' *How the hell does she know him?*

'What do you think his plan is?'

'Dunno. That's the point.'

'Are you sure about all this?'

'What do you mean?'

'I mean that I'*m* not really sure about all this. Drugs . . . that's exactly the sort of thing I used to fight.'

'It's different. These drugs will *help* people.'

'I guess . . . so are we meeting today?'

'Saturday.'

Yes. Yes! YES!I tried to hear a location but there were no rogue thoughts. Or maybe I just couldn't hear as much as I could normally. It was taking a hell of a lot of concentration to do this, and the fact that it was Tara wasn't helping.

Young man: 'He wants us both there?'

Tara: 'Yes. Scales' place.'

Young man: 'I don't know where that is.'

Tara: 'Neither do I. Well . . . I don't remember, anyway. But it's fine. Alex will call me two hours before we need to meet, tell me where to go. I'll meet you here on Saturday afternoon. One o'clock.'

'One o'clock Saturday. Cool. So this place is definitely safe?'

'Yes. Alex made the owner go on holiday.'

'Mind messing. I hate it.'

'I know. Me too.' I could hear in her voice that she knew about her parents. That she was guilty. Had she done it herself?

Oh Tara . . .

Young man: 'Gotta be done though innit.'

Tara: 'Yes. Alex did pay for the guy's holiday, at least.'

Young man: 'Which makes it all OK.'

Tara: 'I don't know.'

An awkward-sounding pause. Then the young man spoke again: 'Right. Well. See you Saturday.'

Tara: 'OK. Be careful.'

'Yeah, you too.' The young man's shape moved, mass transferring through the kitchen to the hall. Out to the front door, down the path. Tara stayed where she was for a moment then headed somewhere else . . . where . . . the back door? I heard it unlock, open, shut, lock again . . .

Aaaand I pulled my thoughts back into my head. They rushed in like blood and I felt momentarily dizzy and had to cling on to the tiles, because it felt like the roof had turned upside down. I held on until my head had cleared, keeping my eyes scrunched tight shut. Once I felt sufficiently stable I lifted off, trying to see Tara . . . but I couldn't. She was nowhere to be seen.

Damn it. DAMN IT. Stupid useless BASTARD brain.

Girl's really good at disappearing, to be fair.

I flew back to Daryl and Lauren, but we didn't discuss anything until we were back in the car. 'So we have two days to come up with a plan,' said Lauren.

'I already have a plan,' I said.

'Let me guess,' said Daryl. 'Turn up and knock on the door.'

'Quiet, you. And no, that's not the plan. Plan is, we stake out that house, wait for them to leave and then I follow them, *alone*, to wherever they're meeting Alex. In the meantime—'

'You're *not* going alone,' said Lauren. 'I'm—'

'*In the meantime*,' I said, 'we're going to do some intensive training. I did pretty well with the listening up there, but it's still new territory and it takes a lot out of me. In fact, I lost Tara because of it. So I need you to teach me everything you can about mental resistance and attack, all that stuff. I need to be psychically bulletproof by Saturday afternoon.'

'Fine. Obviously it's nowhere near that simple, but fine.' She shook her head. 'I do not like you going alone.'

'Lauren,' I said, 'these guys don't like Angelcorp. So they've probably done their homework. You're high profile, they'll know you. Me? Tara knows I'm no friend of the company. So does Alex. So even if I do get caught, I might be able to at least talk to them. But *only* if I'm alone. And like I told you, I am not taking Daryl. It's too risky with Alex's powers.'

She wasn't happy. Neither was Daryl.

But it was true.

'Fine,' said Lauren. 'I need to go and have several awful meetings now, so I suggest you go home and rest because we are training *all day* tomorrow. Eight o'clock sharp at Everest Tower. And you'd better be prepared to work really, *really* hard.'

'Promise. Just . . . call it the Shard, please?'

'Oh, do shut up.'

Chapter Twenty-Three

FRIDAY PASSED IN a blur. I got to the Shard at half eight for training – and a telling-off – and we were on it for most of the day, with only a few breaks for food, coffee and leg-stretching. I eagerly swallowed every piece of advice Lauren gave me, attacking every new strategy and discipline as hard as I could, and by the end of the day I certainly felt like I had a whole new set of tricks up my sleeve: I was repelling all of Lauren's attacks, even her sneakiest mental ones. I was *not* going to balls this up.

Throughout the day, Lauren kept reminding me what she'd said when we'd trained together years ago. We were basically capable of anything. It was just a matter of convincing ourselves that it was true and exploiting that certainty. Making the power work for us at its most basic level. 'There's no limit,' said Lauren, and it was a testament to how seriously I was taking things that I didn't immediately picture us engaging in a training montage set to 2Unlimited's 'No Limit'. Although obviously it did occur to me later on.

No limit . . .

I just needed to stop thinking there was, and then there truly wouldn't be.

(*I heard from the clinic.*)

My eyes snapped open. Lauren and I were meditating to unwind. Her eyes were still closed, so I closed mine again too. *Yeah?*

(*The Rogers are all right. Confused and upset but all right.*)

Good.

(*The doctors found more than one anomaly, though.*)

My stomach wriggled. *Oh?*

(*The Tara-related commands are very recent. But there was another irregularity, in both Oliver and Jacqueline. Memory related. Older, more integrated, more subtle. The doctors are still examining them, the therapy is ongoing. It's very delicate, especially as they're older, and non-empowered.*)

OK . . .

(*But the memories apparently have to do with you. And Freeman.*)

My eyes opened again. This time hers were open too. *Really*, I thought.

(*We need to talk, don't we?*)

I wanted to say yes. I wanted it so much. But I just shook my head and closed my eyes again. *There's nothing to talk about.*

(*I don't believe you.*)

I didn't answer. I couldn't. Lauren didn't say anything else, and later, as I left the Shard, I called Skank. 'Are you still a man who can get stuff?'

'Very possibly.'

'Are you also still a man who can hide things that need to be hidden?'

'See above.'

'Great. I have some stuff on tomorrow, and when it's done I might be needing to hide some . . . things.'

The following afternoon I was lying face-down on a roof, wishing it wasn't so cold. A persistent, niggling breeze slipped under my hoody and jeans, fiddling with my hair, trying to annoy me, and I could smell the possibility of rain. *Bugger off, wind. And rain.*

Tara and Faisal (Tara had said his name earlier and he'd told her off) were sitting in the kitchen, waiting quietly. I wondered who owned the house. Why Alex had chosen him. Lauren said she'd make sure he got some help when he got back; I was just wondering how many other people were out there in the world, brains invaded, memories changed, thoughts altered.

Surely this world isn't going to be recognisable for much longer.

My hands kept going purple and numb and I had to concentrate on making them warm again. It was distracting. I needed to listen. I had been there for over an hour and Lauren had assured me that she and Daryl would be close at all times, but that they wouldn't let me know where, just in case. All I had to do was think loudly and they would be there. I knew they didn't like my backup plan of trying to convince Alex that I was friendly. To be honest, I wasn't mad keen on it myself.

But I was significantly less keen on the idea of handing him and the others over to Angelcorp.

A phone rang, the sound rising up through the floorboards and slates. I focused, the whole house becoming a bright blur of not-quite-thought. Focused on the phone. On Tara's voice.

'Hi,' she said. 'Yes, we're here. OK.'

Focus.

Focus.

Behind her voice, lurking, were her thoughts.

Mostly they were closed off.

But when he told her where to meet, it would have to appear.

Just for a second, it would have to—

'OK,' she said again.

But beneath that . . .

Beneath that 'OK' . . .

A thought.

The Gyptian. *Blue house boat. Embankment Gardens* . . .

Then nothing once again. Blank.

Didn't matter, though.

Got 'em.

I kept listening, heard Tara say goodbye. 'Boat,' she said to Faisal. 'Half seven. We'll leave in an hour.'

An hour?

I am so not lying on my front on this cold-ass roof for another hour . . .

But what if they say something else? Something relevant?

I doubted they would. They hadn't done much talking thus far and even if something useful did come up in the meantime, missing it felt like a risk worth taking. I needed to be at that boat as early as possible. Be ready.

I launched myself into the air and powered upward, and when I was sufficiently high I turned and darted towards the river, enjoying the fact that the omnipresent drones weren't following me. As I flew, I gave Lauren a call and let her know the location.

'A boat?' she said.

'Yeah. I'm heading there now. Do what you guys have to do to be ready, but under no circumstances do you show yourselves. Not without my say so.'

Ooh, get you, Mission Commander.

'OK. Good luck.'

'Thanks.'

I landed on a tall building and peered over the parapet. I could see plenty of boats from up here . . . red boat . . . restaurant boat . . . official boat . . . blue boat . . . no, that was called *Judith* . . .

Yes!

Gyptian. A large house boat with a fading, dirty blue paint job. I scanned the vicinity. There was nowhere nearer where I could hide easily, so I ducked down where I was and waited.

Over an hour later I saw Faisal and Tara walking down the road, both of them with their hoods up. They made their way down to the decking where the boat was moored, knocked and waited. A hatch popped open, words were exchanged – *Alex, is that you* – and they disappeared inside.

Right.

I leapt over the parapet, dropping as close to freefall speed as I could manage without damaging myself, and headed across the building's lawn to the road. Keeping my hood up, I jumped over the wall, landed silently on the wooden decking and stepped off, stopping myself so I was floating barely six inches above the cold dark water. I hovered swiftly around the edge of the boat, attached myself to the side, limpet-like, and thought my way inside, feeling the cramped geography, searching for people, following my mind.

They were in a room at the rear of the boat and I crawled along the outside as quietly as possible, all the while keeping my thought processes blank, keeping my walls up. A black, in-visible shape on the outside thinking black, invisible thoughts on the inside.

I stopped, held on, listened.

Tara: 'What's happening?'

Another voice: 'Next stage. I wanted to talk to all of you.'

It had to be Alex. Had to be. He sounded older, more sure of himself, his voice a little more bassy, but it was definitely him.

Faisal: 'Where's Scales?'

Alex: 'He's just finishing his dinner. He'll be through in a second.'

Silence. Waiting. I concentrated on being invisible.

Come on.

Footsteps. A shape moving in. Tara's voice: 'Hi, Doctor Scales.'

A new voice, low and oily: 'Hello Tara. Faisal.'

'What's happening, Alex?' said Faisal.

'The latest tests were all effective,' said Alex. 'Totally. Which means we can get ahead of Angelcorp. We know they've been investigating us, but they've got nothing. And now we're ready, weeks ahead of them.'

Get ahead of Angelcorp . . .

'So what are we going to do?' said Tara. 'I don't remember . . .'

'The water supply,' said Alex. The way he emphasised the words suggested that they were accompanied by a psychic reminder.

Hold on . . . the water supply?

He doesn't mean . . .

'Seriously?' said Faisal.

'Yes,' said Alex.

'But,' said Tara. 'Do we even . . . is there enough? Doesn't it take a long time to manufacture?'

'I have reached out to . . . appropriate parties,' said Scales.

'But we can't be *sure* it's safe, can we?' said Faisal. 'I mean . . . obviously it *looks* good, but don't you need to test it on hundreds of people before . . .'

314

'Proper field tests would take years,' said Scales. 'If we were developing this for the open market, it would be half a decade or more before anyone would dream of making it available. That's why we need to bypass normal channels. And as Alex has stated, we are working to a vastly reduced timescale. Necessity must be our master.'

'I just don't want to hurt anyone,' said Faisal.

'Nor do I,' said Tara. 'You said—'

'I know,' said Alex. 'No-one wants to hurt anyone. But they're forcing us. You know Angelcorp. You know they won't stop. We need to do this.'

'I know,' said Faisal. 'And I . . . I'm with you. Just . . . can't quite believe it's got this far so fast, you know what I mean?'

'Are you telling the others?' asked Tara. 'Everyone else? Kurt, Vernon . . .'

'Vernon's gone,' said Alex. 'He wiped his own memory rather than let Angelcorp torture him. His two friends' too. He'll get paid. Kurt's on his way to Switzerland. Tim's in prison, sadly. I would have helped him if I could, but . . . everyone else, taken care of. They've either forgotten, or Faisal has dealt with them. Outside this boat, no-one knows anything. We're all that's left. It's safer that way.'

If only he knew . . .

'I heard that,' said Alex.

A porthole flew open and I found myself dragged unceremoniously through and deposited on the floor. It happened too fast for me to be surprised, let alone resist. The porthole snapped shut behind me and I looked up at Alex, Faisal, Tara and Scales.

'All right, guys?' I smiled.

Balls.

Chapter Twenty-Four

S CALES LOOKED LIKE an old, scatty Frank Zappa in stolen librarian clothes, peering at me through glasses that made his eyes look tiny. Alex had grown. He was now taller than me, although he was as skinny as he had been before, and his hair was short and he wore jeans and a plain white T-shirt with a grey suit jacket over the top.

Smart. What happened to that green coat, I wonder.

He stared down at me and although his face didn't betray much, I could tell that he was spectacularly flummoxed by my appearance.

'Who on earth is this?' said Scales.

'I'm Stanly,' I said.

'No,' said Tara. Her hands were shaking and she'd gone completely pale. 'You're *not*.'

'I am,' I said. 'Tara. You know it's me.'

'You're *lying!*'

'It is him, Tara,' said Alex.

Tara's eyes were wet. 'But *how?*'

'Yeah . . . good question.' Alex managed a smile, although it didn't look particularly comfortable on his face. He still seemed like someone struggling to come to terms with having to communicate with other people. 'How *did* you do it? With your powers? Did you use them to stay young?'

'Not exactly,' I said. 'It's quite a long story.'

'To be honest,' said Alex, 'I thought you were dead.'

'I thought you probably would be as well,' I said. 'Sorry about all the face punching.'

He smiled ruefully. 'I probably had it coming. Sorry about . . . everything else.'

'What the hell are you *doing* here, Stanly?' Tara cried.

'Alexander,' said Scales, 'what is going on? Why are you speaking to him? He overheard everything! Wipe his mind and get rid of him!'

'Seriously,' said Faisal.

'Everyone calm down,' said Alex, mustering a lot more authority than I'd ever have imagined he was capable of. 'Scales, Faisal . . . can you give me and Tara a minute with Stanly please.'

'But—' said Scales.

'Doctor,' said Alex. 'I've done you lots of favours. Made you lots of money, with more to come. Please.'

Scales nodded reluctantly and left the room. Faisal lingered. 'You guys sure you're OK?'

'It's fine,' said Alex. 'Thanks, Faisal.'

Faisal nodded and followed Scales.

'You can stand up if you want,' said Alex.

'Might just sit somewhere more comfortable, if that's OK?' The cabin was small and I took a seat on one of the few chairs. 'This your boat?'

'Belongs to Scales.'

'Is that really his name? Doctor Scales?'

'Stanly,' said Tara, tearfully. 'What the *hell*.'

'I'm sorry,' I said. 'I . . . I did try to tell you the other night . . .'

'I thought you were an illusion. Someone messing with my mind.'

'I'm not. I swear.'

'I'd heard about someone flying around the city, causing trouble,' said Alex. 'I actually wondered if it might be you . . . but I figured it couldn't be.'

'Accept no substitutes.' I couldn't take my eyes off Tara and she couldn't seem to take hers off me, although her expression wasn't exactly warm. I wanted to hug her, but I guessed maybe it wasn't appropriate.

'So how are you here?' said Alex. 'Alive, no older, eavesdropping.'

'Mm,' I said. 'Yeah, sorry about the eavesdropping. You guys are about the most interesting thing going on since I got back.'

'Thanks,' said Alex. 'So . . . how?'

I explained. Tara, who I presumed had only been given the Cliff Notes to an already heavily censored version of my story, didn't seem to know how to respond to anything that I said. Alex seemed vaguely impressed.

'So,' I said. 'I came back. And then I went to see Tara and found her foster parents brainwashed.'

'They're not *brainwashed*,' said Tara. 'They're fine.'

'Really?' Anger flared in my stomach. 'You messed with their minds, Tara. What would *you* call it?'

'It's no different than if I'd lied to them and they'd believed me.'

'It's *very* different . . .'

'It wasn't her, anyway,' said Alex. 'She didn't know how, for a start, but she didn't want to. I gave them just enough . . . probably should have done more, to be honest. But I made sure it wouldn't hurt.'

'Tara,' I said. 'They're your *parents* . . .'

'My *foster* parents,' snapped Tara. 'My foster parents who *freaked out* when they found out I'd developed powers. I didn't want to tell them. I kept them secret for *ages*. And then somehow our neighbour saw me. She told them and they went mad.'

Eesh. 'I'm sorry,' I said. 'That must have been horrible. But messing with their minds—'

'*You don't get it.* When you revealed your powers, you just ran away, and everyone who saw got on with their lives, and pretended they hadn't seen anything. Nowadays? Your neighbours report you. To your parents, if you're lucky. More likely to your school, or the *police*. You get put on a database.' Tara took a deep breath. 'Screw that. And screw staying at home for one second, after the things they said. Alex had to do it. If anyone found out about me, there'd be police . . . our whole plan . . . it had to be done.'

OK. Let's maybe move on. 'How did you two meet, anyway?' I said.

She chewed her lip. 'Through Faisal. As soon as my powers started showing, I started going to places where empowered hang out. Wanted to talk to people.' She stared mutinously at her feet. 'People who didn't remind me of you.'

Ouch.

'I met Faisal at Jinx,' said Tara. 'He introduced me to Alex.'

Jinx . . .

'That reminds me,' I said. 'Someone told Tim Hart to wipe me. Cos I was looking for Tara. Who gave that order? Out of interest?'

'I don't know anything about that,' said Alex. 'We did have one of the bar staff keeping an eye out for suspicious types. Could have been him. His memory's been wiped now, though.'

'Fairish. Sorry, so. Faisal introduced you guys . . .'

'I was already working on this plan,' said Alex. 'I'd got to know Doctor Scales, he'd told me he was close to cracking the formula, and I'd been looking for others to help. Me and Faisal already knew each other pretty well. Tara said she wanted to help.'

'Superpower drugs?' I said. 'Yeah, good plan there.' *Calm down. You'll lose her.*

'Fuck off, Stanly,' she said, with real venom. 'You have no idea. You've got *no idea* what it's been like.'

'You're right,' I said. 'Sorry. So . . .'

'Tara's good at hiding,' said Alex. 'Passing unnoticed. She can basically make herself invisible. Handy for a messenger.'

I looked at Tara. 'You do know he pretty much *caused* the Collision, don't you?'

'So did you,' said Tara. 'And Sharon and everyone.'

Again, ouch. 'Yeah, but . . . we didn't *know.*'

The barest hint of shrug. 'Everyone messes up.'

Wow. OK. So he gets forgiven and I get shouted at.

Seems fair.

'Right,' I said. 'Well . . . I'd really love to talk to you about all this some time. You and me.'

Another microscopic shrug.

'But for now . . .' I sat back in my chair and raised my hands. 'What the hell, guys?'

'I could ask *you* that,' said Alex. 'Why are you here? Are you working with Angelcorp?'

'You could say I'm using them to my own ends. Mostly I've been looking for *her.*' I nodded towards Tara, who shrank away as though trying to hide in her hoody. 'But I can't say I'm not intrigued, perturbed and

320

'. . . mystified by your plan. So lay it on me. The grand scheme.'

'What,' said Tara, 'so you can judge me? Tell me what's right and wrong like I'm still ten years old?'

'No,' I said. 'I'm sorry, I shouldn't have come in here lecturing you, I know I don't have the right—'

'*Fucking* right you don't! You left me in the woods! You promised you'd come back to us!'

'And I *couldn't*,' I said. 'I know I shouldn't have promised, but . . . I couldn't come back. I had to . . .'

'Save the world, yeah,' said Tara. 'Except then you got to skip what happened *after* the world got *saved*. The rest of us had to live through it.'

'Then tell me,' I said. 'Tell me what happened. Tell me why you would want to give everyone powers, without their consent.'

'You think things work better now?' said Tara. 'Is that what they've told you? Lauren and Sharon and everyone? *They're* all fine, *they're* comfortable. What about everyone who came out of their hiding places when the monsters disappeared and found that the people who'd been ruining their lives before now had *superpowers*? What about the . . . the prostitutes whose pimps can now smack them around with their minds, or just give them endless nightmares, not even leaving any evidence? You thought predatory guys were bad before? Imagine what they can do when they get rejected by a girl now.'

'Did something happen to you?' I said. 'Did . . .'

'No,' she said, and thank God I believed her. 'But it's all happened to other people. I heard stuff. I saw all the new cruelty at my school, weak ones getting victimised worse than ever. You know that it's easier for an empowered to mess with the mind of a non-empowered?'

'Yes.'

'Whole new food chain,' said Tara. 'So there you go. There's your *why*. Come on. Tell me I'm wrong.'

Just like Tim.

Just trying to protect people . . .

'I understand,' I said. 'I do. But—'

'No,' said Tara. 'No! You don't. Because you're immediately saying *but*.'

'Tara—' began Alex.

'No,' she said. 'I don't . . . I can't.' She turned and left the room, slamming the door.

'Sorry,' said Alex. 'She . . . she took it really hard. You disappearing.'

'I understand.' I slumped in my chair. 'Are we going to fight? Unfinished business?'

Alex laughed. 'No. I don't really do much telekinesis anyway. Can't fly. No monsters or rabid dogs for me to take over.'

'You haven't tried to take your power in other directions?'

'I have. But I like to keep it in here.' He tapped his head. 'Never much for fighting. Well . . . not for a very long time.'

'What happened to you? After I last saw you?'

He sat down and shrugged. 'Did a lot of hiding. Mixed with some pretty dodgy people. Useful contacts for when the plan started coming together . . . I know Tara and Faisal weren't happy about some of the people I brought on, some of the . . . stuff I did. I wasn't happy either, really. But to persuade certain types of people to work with you . . . you kind of have to behave a certain way. Do things. Scales is ex-Angelcorp, pretty serious player. I needed to show him I was serious too.' He smiled the faraway smile of someone who had *done stuff*. 'To be honest, working mostly with criminals . . . it makes some things easier. Looking them in the eye, wiping their memories. Taking their money, so we can put it to better use.'

Wow.

'And some of the really bad ones,' he said, 'I'd hand over to Faisal to sort out, once we were done with them.'

'Sort out?'

'He used to be a Chavenger. Have you heard of them?'

'Really? One of the survivors? No shit! Which one?'

Alex frowned. 'Um . . . Captain England?'

Again, wow. 'So when you say sort out . . .'

'Take down their operations,' said Alex. 'And leave them for the police. Sometimes with injuries. He's got some pretty serious skills.'

I nodded. 'OK . . . not a bad system, I guess. So this plan of yours. What Tara said. Does she speak for you? Are her reasons your reasons?'

'Partly,' said Alex. 'I like the idea of levelling the playing field.'

'Lots of people got powers after Monster Day, and they're choosing *not* to use them.'

'But everyone deserves that choice.'

'You're not talking about choice, though, are you? And . . . *everyone* deserves them? I seem to remember you being pretty pessimistic about people, in general.'

'OK. Maybe *deserve* is the wrong word . . .'

'I wonder if *people* was the wrong word.'

Alex stared at me for a moment, then smiled. 'OK. It's

not just about people. More about changing things. Things *seemed* to change after the Collision, but they didn't really. The system just shifted around what happened and kept going. Angelcorp use empowered when they want them, but they haven't tried to use the powers for anything *big*, apart from a bit of construction work. Imagine what people—'

'There's that word again,' I said. 'People. Sorry Alex, I'm not buying it. You becoming *less* cynical, wanting to give everyone the gift of superpowers? Dude, you tried to *end the world*. This isn't going to fly with me. No pun intended.'

He didn't seem angry. He just shrugged. 'OK. There are rumours that Angelcorp is planning to release a new version of their power suppressant into the water supply. It's been tinkered with and tailored so there'll be no noticeable side effects. It's untraceable . . . but powers will just disappear. Gone.'

My stomach did a flip and a flop. *Seriously?*

'These powers are the key to things changing,' said Alex. 'This world is still as corrupt as it ever was. I thought that when powers came into the open, when people started to realise there was something else, something bigger and better, things would change. We'd shed the old system, bring in something new. But it didn't happen. And Angelcorp want to ensure it doesn't happen by removing the problem entirely.'

'Are you sure about this?' I said. 'It sounds . . . far-fetched. And you say rumours . . .'

'There's plenty of evidence,' said Alex. 'If you know where to look. And I know people who've talked to Angelcorp personnel. It's true – but either way, the risk is too big to ignore.'

Dear sweet fluffy Odin, he believes what he's saying.

'Look,' said Alex, leaning forwards, warming to his theme. 'You're right. I still hate this world, a lot of the time. Not all the time . . . which I guess is progress. But I don't want to destroy it, not anymore. I want to *change* it. Because it's all still the same. George Freeman tries to act like the whole world is becoming this big interconnected open democracy where important things come before profit, but it's a lie. The people in charge don't want normal people being *empowered*. Give everyone powers, and we could be looking at a complete change in attitudes, values, structures.'

Jeez. Sounds like he rolled up one of Weird, Sister's weirder press releases and smoked it all to himself.

'Or the world collapses into superpowered barbarism,' I said.

'I prefer my version,' said Alex. 'Obviously Angelcorp knows that a different world might be a better world . . . but they also know that if the world changed that much, that'd be it for them. They wouldn't be left standing. They know that removing the empowered entirely will be better in the long run than keeping them around and potentially losing all their money and influence. The last few years have basically been an experiment, and they're not keen on the results.'

'So you're going to flip it on them,' I said. 'Give *everybody* powers.'

'London to start off with,' said Alex. 'Then we'll expand. It'll create chaos for a while. But it means things will *have* to change.'

I nodded.

'So what do you think?'

'Everyone with powers,' I said. 'It'd be interesting. Chaotic, like you said.'

And it's not everyone's choice.

'Heard that,' said Alex.

'Sorry,' I said. *Ach, be more careful, idiot.* 'I'm just . . . it's a big thing. A big idea.' As I spoke, I reached out with my mind, keeping it small and quiet, subtle, searching for Alex's thoughts. There had to be something. A tell-tale sign. Something to let me know that it was all true, that Angelcorp really were planning what he said they were planning, that his scheme really did have merit, that he *knew* for a fact and wasn't just trying to convince me of some horseshit conspiracy theory . . .

But he wasn't giving anything away. It made sense. Here he was, on his turf, lecturing me about his plans for the world. He had the best hand. He had the high ground. Of course he was going to be comfortable and stable in his head. Of course he wasn't going to give me an inch.

Unless . . .

'What would Leila think?' I asked.

And that was all it took. Just for a second, he slipped. The blank veil, the absence of even a sign that something was being hidden, slipped. And I saw through him.

He had doubts.

'You're not sure, are you?' I said. 'You're not *certain.*'

He stared at me.

'Alex,' I said. 'I know you've got no reason to listen to me. As history goes, ours is pretty complicated. But seriously, mate, if you're not one hundred per cent *certain*, if you don't have evidence, you *can't* do this. I mean, even if you do know for a fact, I'm still not sure you can do this, but . . .'

Something crawled up my back. I jumped and felt for it, ready to brush it away. It felt like a spider . . . no . . . there was nothing there . . .

Something crawled up my leg. 'Ah!' I patted my leg, wanting to squash it before it got any further . . .

Nothing . . .

What?

I suddenly felt cold. Very, very cold. I could feel little itches all up my arms, all across my back, on my neck, on my scalp. I tried to flick them away but every time I reached for one it danced out of sight, scuttling across me, nibbling.

I looked at Alex for help . . .

Looked into his eyes . . .

No . . .

He's doing this . . .

'Nice try,' I said. *Ignore them.* 'Nice . . . nice . . .'

The boat flickered around us. One second we were here, sat in the cabin, the next we were in the woods, deep and dark, with a baleful half-blood moon sighing down on us and spiders coming from every direction, and Alex wasn't there, he was *in* the spiders, his mind was their mind, their joint mind, hive mind, their living breathing thinking psychic flesh web, and they were coming at me, coming at me—

No.

Remember what Lauren taught you.

I fought to get him out, but he'd got pretty far in already and it was tough. He must have been doing it the whole time we were talking, without me even noticing. I couldn't even feel his thoughts when they entered my brain, just realised they were there when it was too late, when the spiders were on me —

No.

No.

Get out.

'I'm sorry,' said Alex. 'I really don't want to do this.'

No . . .

NO.

'What would Leila think?' I asked, and for a second the impossible, crushing weight of Alex's thoughts lifted and I could climb out of the pit he'd put me in, claw my way up, out of the oily dark, out of the spidery, wasted nightmare of grime and horror, the blizzard of images, of spiders laying their eggs in my brain, of the eggs hatching, of more invasive many-legged thoughts pouring out of them and out of *me*, like black blood from my ears and nose and eyes—

NO.

I thought Leila's name, again and again. I wished I knew what she looked like, wished I could fling her at him in that way, but her name was enough. Even now, even years later, everything he did came from her, the girl he had lost.

I opened my eyes and I was sitting on the chair in the cabin, facing Alex. We were both shaking, sweating. He stared at me and there was fury in his eyes, because I'd made him remember. And fury made him sloppy. And sloppy meant I could go in—

Reach into his mind with mine—

And there she was—

Leila—

Tall and beautiful and dark-haired and sad and so far away, smiling at him, and I could feel what came with that smile, the absolute love it inspired in him, but also the sadness, because he couldn't get close, because she was damaged, because—

NO, he thought. He thought it like a punch, lined with razors, and I recoiled and my brain bled and I felt him reach in and try to snatch her out, but I held onto her, held onto her—

Something flashed between us, a thought Alex was sending back at me, one I'd inspired in him without even realising—

I saw Leila dead, bled out.

I saw him find her.

I felt what he'd felt.

My whole body filled up with it.

I gasped because it hurt so much.

No . . .

He's using it against you . . .

I conjured up living Leila, alive and beautiful and untouchable but still alive, and I used her to beat back the image he'd sent towards me, the memory he was terrified of, the memory that defined him, and more flurried between us, things he'd been too frightened to say, times when they'd just sat in silence, times when they'd communicated so deeply that they didn't even need words, the times he'd tried, the times she'd tried, it was all there, spilling out of him into the room, and I grabbed it all and I threw it back, threw it back into him, into his head—

Spiders filling up the room, eating the memories—

No.

A spider so big and ancient it had slept at the bottom of the Thames for millions of years, opening its jaws, ready to swallow the boat—

NO.

I'm not scared of spiders anymore.

I could see his thoughts now, their colours, the way they burrowed down through the cracks in my mind, the cracks that had still been there, even though I'd convinced myself they hadn't been, I could see them, smell them, feel what he poured into them.

I imagined Leila's face when she realised what Alex was planning to do.

He recoiled in his chair, his thoughts recoiling with him – out of my mind *out of my mind* – and I gripped him hard with my brain, staring him down, telling him I was the strong one, I was the strong one, but he was strong too, strong and so driven by pain. I could see how he had masterminded all this, wiping people's memories so they couldn't pose a threat. I could see why Tara and the others had been drawn to him, the trust they'd built, the connections he'd made . . .

I could see exactly why Alex wanted to do what he wanted to do. In his own deeply weird, counter-intuitive way, this was his attempt to make up for what he'd done five and a half years ago.

I could see it all. See him, feel him, understand him. I knew exactly who he was.

And he didn't.

And that made me stronger.

I held him in his chair. 'Alex,' I said. 'Please. You can't do it.'

He struggled, his face spasming, lip trembling. He didn't want to cry, but he was so full up with what he'd tried to bury . . .

'I know why you want to,' I said. 'I know. Things do need to change. But not everyone wants to have these abilities. And it should be *their* choice. I can't let you do it.'

He was sending every kind of *no* in my direction, a silent, deafening stream, but I flipped them on him, buried them in sand, cement on top. 'You can't do it,' I said.

'You . . . have no right,' he said, his voice strangled. It sounded as though it was a colossal effort to force out each word. 'No *right* . . .'

'Neither do you.' I sighed. 'Same old whinge, isn't it? Boo

hoo, the world isn't what it's cracked up to be. Boo hoo, things aren't the way I want them to be. So I'm going to do something massive and stupid and see what happens, see what emerges from the chaos.'

'Need chaos,' said Alex. 'For stuff to change . . .'

'You need to start thinking outside your own box,' I said. 'Yeah, sure, create chaos and stuff will change. But how many people will be hurt in the process? *That's* your problem. You don't think about them. You never have. You lost someone. It's shit. Deal with it.'

It was only now, as he opened his mouth, that I realised we'd both been talking in our heads. 'Haven't lost everyone,' he smiled.

Hold on . . .

Are those sirens I can hear?

'*Help me!*' Alex shouted.

Once again, balls.

Chapter Twenty-Five

IN THE TIME it took for the door to burst open and the others to pile in, I made several impressively quick calculations. Of course, there was the nagging feeling – if a feeling that appears and is then dismissed in less than two seconds can be described as 'nagging' – that this was the latest in a long line of terrible plans, but they'd got me this far.

And if it ain't broke . . .

'Don't fix it,' I said, because few things are more off-putting than someone finishing off their own private thought process out loud.

And *up* we went.

The force of the boat lurching out of the water, ripping free of its moorings and screaming skyward sent Tara, Faisal and Scales tumbling, although I whipped a rope of thought towards Tara so that she wouldn't get bumped around too much. I managed to keep myself stable, locking my axis to that of the boat and keeping Alex where he was, secure in my psychic grip, and sent my thoughts out into the air, just to make sure we weren't going to hit a plane or anything – and to check how high we were going. I didn't want to take us *too* high, after all. I very much doubted that this boat would protect us from the heat of the atmosphere.

Plus, won't we, like, run out of oxygen way before we get there? Or something?

I wish I knew science.

'What the hell are you doing?' screamed Tara.

'Exactly what it looks like!' I yelled. 'So I don't want to feel *one* stray thought on me, OK? Not from any of you! Otherwise we've got a long fall ahead of us! Or below us! Or . . . whatever!'

Scales was cowering in a corner, terrified. Tara and Faisal were looking to Alex.

All he said was, 'Wait'.

'Yeah,' I said. 'Wait.' My phone had just started ringing and I brought us to an abrupt halt and answered it, Homer Simpson-style. 'Y'ello?'

I'm not going to lie, I felt *buzzed*.

'Stanly,' said Lauren, 'I don't know what exactly you think you're doing, but I thought you should be aware that there will be drones up there with you in less than a minute. Drones with guns. And police down here.'

'Cheers,' I said. 'I'm . . . kind of improvising. I'll get back to you.' I hung up. 'Right. To re-iterate. *Nobody* lays one psychic *finger* on me, OK? If you try, then with my last thought I will send us back down as fast as humanly possible. And somehow I doubt that you guys will be able to stop it.'

'You'll die if you do that,' said Scales. He sounded more pleading than anything. '*And* you'll kill her.' He pointed at Tara.

'Maybe,' I said. 'Or she and I might conveniently vanish and re-appear safely in another universe, cos I do that sometimes. So . . . probably best not to test me, yeah?'

'What do you want?' said Faisal.

'Honestly,' I said, 'I want all this over and done with. Your plan is kaput. It was kaput before I even arrived today. I'm not the only one who knows about you. It's finished.'

'You have no right to do this!' Tara yelled.

'Tara,' I said. 'Please, *think*. This is not, by any stretch of the imagination, a good plan. You say you want to help people. I understand that. But this isn't the way.'

There were tears in her eyes. 'Things have to change . . .'

'I know!' I said. 'I know. But not like this. The world's had enough new problems to deal with since the Collision and it is a bloody *miracle* that it's still even vaguely in one piece. You do this, things will unravel. I guarantee it.'

'Who the hell do you think you are?' said Faisal. 'Coming here and telling us what to do?'

'Dude,' I said. 'You were a *superhero*. A real one. Surely you don't *really* think this is a kosher scheme?'

'You don't know me, dude. Yeah I've been a superhero. Didn't go so well. It's kids' stuff.'

'Maybe,' I said. 'But let's be honest – so is this. All you're doing is sticking a firework in a wasp's nest and closing your eyes.'

'So what? I should just sign up to this new world that I don't agree with? Get a job with *Angelcorp*?'

'Danielle did.'

Faisal's face darkened. 'Yeah. Danielle sold out.' *Ooh. Beef there.*

'She's just trying to do some good,' I said. 'Look, guys, whatever happens, your plan is not going ahead. It never was. They nearly had you on Wednesday, the only reason you're not currently in off-the-books forever prison having your sanity sucked out by a walking nightmare is cos I blundered in and ballsed it all up. I bought you time, but they're on to you. There is no way that you get out of here with plan A intact.'

'So?' said Alex, quietly.

334

'I can keep you safe,' I said. 'My friend Skank has places you can hide. Away from Angelcorp. You get to keep your freedom . . . but you abandon the plan.'

'How do we know they won't keep coming after us?' said Faisal.

'Because I will stop them,' I said. 'They want me for something. I don't know what. It's probably bad. But if anyone can bargain them out of chasing you, I can. I *will*. I just need to prove to them that you and your drug are no longer a problem.'

'What if they just put *you* in prison?' asked Tara.

'Honestly,' I said, 'I probably deserve to be there.'

'Stanly—'

BOOM. The boat rocked hard and we all sprawled to opposite corners of the cabin. I thought my way outside and saw that there were now six drones surrounding us . . . and one had just fired a missile, blowing away the front of the boat.

OK.

Time to go, methinks.

'What's happening?' said Scales. 'What on earth . . .'

'Everybody hold on!' I yelled.

Aaaaaand DOWN.

We dropped just as a second missile passed harmlessly over us. My phone was ringing again and I thought it to my ear, using my hands to try and steady myself against the wall, concentrating on diving as fast as possible. 'Hello?'

'Stanly!' said Lauren. 'What are you—'

'We're on the way down! We're kind of having a bit of trouble—' The boat rocked again as another missile exploded nearby.

'Bloody right you are! There are more drones on the way,

335

and helicopters, and Embankment Gardens is swarming with police!'

Oh great. 'OK,' I said. 'What do you suggest I do?'

'*What?* Are you actually asking me—'

'I'm bringing us down, but I am *not* handing these guys over to Angelcorp!' Outside I saw the drones diving after us, lethally sleek blank-eyed torpedoes. They were quieter and meaner looking than the standard ones.

'But—'

'Non-negotiable!' I said. 'I'm not handing them over, not after what Rosie did!' We weren't far from the city now and the drones had given up firing missiles. Presumably their operators – or artificial intelligences or whatever the hell dictated their missile-firing choices – had at least some concern for people on the ground. 'So I guess I'm going to have to outrun them!'

'Oh for God's sake . . . let me get back to you!'

'Rightio! In a bit!' I hung up.

'What are you *doing?*' Tara screamed.

'Literally no idea!'

This is so awesome right now.

NO IT'S NOT. NOT AT ALL. *The most likely outcomes are death, arrest or torture. Possibly all of them in a certain order.*

OK . . . *well if it's not even a* bit *awesome, how come I can barely hear myself think over the sound of how awesome it is?*

Because your brain is broken, that's why.

Two helicopters were waiting for us, hovering low above the water where the boat had been, and I could see police cars and Angelcorp personnel all the way along the dock. *Wow. They were fast.* We were definitely falling too rapidly to go around the helicopters so I flipped the boat on its side, passing between them so narrowly that I could hear the chug of their rotor blades.

'What the hell are you doing?' yelled Faisal.

'Can everyone *please* stop asking me that! I am trying to get us to safety!' I glanced at Alex . . . and I couldn't believe it.

He was *grinning*.

He's having fun too!

I couldn't help it. I grinned back.

Hey, maybe we'll be buddies now—

SLAM. The boat hit the water. For a second or less I considered starting the engine, but then I remembered that whole thing with the front of the boat having been blown to bits.

So I did what any sane person would do. I kept the boat about a centimetre above the surface of the water and used my brain to send it powering off upriver – *or downriver* – accompanied by the howl of sirens, the buzz of helicopters and the roar of angry voices through megaphones.

'This is intolerable!' Scales cried.

'Shut up!' I said. 'Now, everyone conscious with powers, I need you to think a shield around this boat. People are going to start shooting at us.' I was interrupted – *cracking timing guys* – by a bullet shattering one of the portholes. 'OK, they've started shooting at us! Think a shield around the boat! Do it now! Think *away*, deflect everything! Please! Thanks!'

Tara, Faisal and Alex nodded, braced themselves and visibly started concentrating.

Hopefully that'll work—

AARGHBOAT!

I swerved, narrowly avoiding clipping the end of a house

337

boat that was executing a painfully slow turn in the water, and kept us going. Ahead, police boats were roaring towards us, practically bouncing across the waves.

Nope.

Wishing I could see the occupants' faces, I lifted us up and glided straight over them, quickly and not entirely delicately plonking us back down on the water. Then I yanked us as far over to the other side of the river as possible, *just* getting us under a bridge and bursting out the other side as missiles tore up clouds of hot spray behind us.

Now THIS is podracing!

Something clattered on the roof of the boat with a thump and I flipped my out-of-body gaze to see a pair of black-clad soldiers, proper ninja-looking dudes, inching along. *Nice one Tara et al, great shield there.* I tried to dislodge them with my thoughts but they must have been empowered because I could feel them resisting.

'Hey!' I said. 'We've got company! On the roof! Anyone?'

'No problem,' said Faisal, with a smile that immediately made me want him as my new best friend. He ran to the porthole through which I'd been dragged before and climbed nimbly out, as though we weren't hammering up the river at insanity miles per hour, and I watched him with my thoughts as he flipped up onto the roof and scissor-kicked the two soldiers in their chests, knocking them off opposite sides of the boat. The dark water swalllowed them and I couldn't resist a grin of my own.

That was BAD. ASS.

Faisal swung back in through the porthole, but before I could express my appreciation, my phone rang again. 'Hallo? Anything?'

'You know that thing you do where you cause a massive and totally unnecessary problem?'

'That attitude isn't *helping*, Lauren—'

'You need to keep going for a bit. Try and lose as many of the pursuers as possible. I can't help you there, you're on your own. Then you need to find a way to abandon the boat – all of you – but keep it going, so it looks like you're still on board. That'll buy you some time.'

'OK . . . right. Cheers. I'll get back to you.' I hung up.

'Any news?' asked Alex, dryly.

I made a noncommittal noise, opened the door and headed into the next cabin. This ought to have led to another door and a smaller front cabin, but instead there were just ripped, blackened boards and a gaping hole opening onto a chaotic blur of water and flashing lights. Overhead, another helicopter swooped.

Right. Er . . .

I ran back to the rear cabin, keeping as much of my brain outside as possible so I could steer us without crashing. 'Can anyone swim?'

'No,' said Alex.

'No' said Tara.

'No,' said Faisal.

'Yes,' said Scales.

'OK,' I said. 'Well . . . I'm afraid we're all going to need to go in some water very shortly. But . . . actually, don't worry about swimming, I'll deal with that. Y'all are just going to have to hold your breath.'

'Please,' said Scales. 'What is *happening*?'

'Don't worry, it's just a really awesome chase scene. Right. Now.' I grabbed my phone and found the location of the safe house Skank had arranged. 'Alex?'

'Yeah?'

'Do you know where this is?'

Alex rolled his eyes at my incompetence. 'Yeah.'

'Anywhere near here?'

'No. We'll need to head back the other way.'

Oh, great plan Stanly.

'For God's sake . . . OK.' I went back outside with my brain. There were a number of police boats in pursuit, gaining ground – *or water or whatever* – and two helicopters overhead. If I kept the turning circle tight, maybe . . .

'Hang on!' I yelled. Everybody hung on and I braced myself physically and psychically, thought around the boat and killed our speed, simultaneously pulling the mind-driven waterborne equivalent of a handbrake turn. The G-force sent us all flailing against the wall, the police boats swerved out of the way to avoid hitting us and the helicopters whomped by, ripping the air apart with the chunky *thok* of their rotors. I wasted no time and sent our increasingly decrepit vessel hurtling back along the river in the opposite direction.

My phone rang again. 'Hiya!'

'Oh, you'd better hope you don't survive this or so help me I will *beat* you to within an inch of your life for using that jaunty tone—'

'Lauren,' I said in a sing-song voice, 'helping now, bollocking later *please* . . .'

'I *can't help you*! I just want to know if you have anything resembling a plan, apart from driving that bloody boat up and down the river all night!'

'I have somewhere safe for us to go. I'm going to dump the boat ASAP, get us off the river, go dark for a bit. I'll find you.'

Haha, I said 'go dark'.

'Where?'

'I'll come to Angelcorp.'

'*What?*'

'Gotta face the music sooner or later. Best do it early. I'll explain to Walker that all this business, this chase, was me trying to overpower them or something. Then I'll say the whole thing is sorted, no more threat of bad super drugs. Then I'll tender my resignation or whatever I need to do. Badge, gun, the full thing. Then . . . then we'll see what happens, I guess.'

'This is your plan?'

'Yep.'

I must have been on speaker because Lauren said, 'Daryl wants me to tell you that you are the worst ever at plans. I'm inclined to agree.'

'Tell him I wish he was here because this shit is another level of awesome.'

Lauren exhaled for an improbably long time. 'So . . . what do you want us to do?'

'Go back to Walker. Say that I went off-book.' I was trying to hide my glee at using phrases like 'go dark' and 'off-book' in a genuine reality-based context. Maybe not very well. 'I'll see you when I see you.'

'Stanly . . .'

'Sorry Lauren. I know this has all gone a bit silly.'

'I really am going to kill you.'

'Later, OK? Bye.'

'Bye.'

I kept us speeding down the river, pushing as fast as my brain – and my reflexes – would allow. The helicopters were back on us, raking the boat with bullets, and I barked at the others to keep the shield up. The jumble of megaphoned voices telling us to stop and do this and do that was so cacophonous that I couldn't really make out individual instructions at this point. For several minutes we continued, me pushing the boat as fast as I could while still maintaining some semblance of control, giving Alex periodic updates as to where we were in relation to the location I'd shown him. After a little while he said that we should probably get off shortly, as though we were on a relaxed sightseeing tour.

'Right,' I said. 'Everyone, stand there.' I pointed at the edge of the cabin. Everyone obeyed, but Tara came over to me first.

'You've totally screwed this all up,' she said.

'I'm sorry,' I said. 'Genuinely.'

'You're not forgiven.' She hugged me. 'But I really missed you.'

'Missed you too, kiddo.'

'*Ugh*. Don't call me that.' She went and stood with the others, Alex putting comforting hands on her and Faisal's shoulders. I positioned myself on the other side of the room and psychically smashed my way through the floor of the boat with a splintering grind of wood, tearing as much of it away as possible to reveal rushing, bucking waves below. Scales winced. We kept going and I told Alex where we were.

'About a minute,' he said.

'OK,' I said. 'All of you. In about a minute, I am going to use my power to drop all of us through that gap and into the water. I'm going to have to do it really fast to avoid taking our heads off. I'm talking *really* fast. So it'll be disorientating. Then we're going to be underwater. Possibly for an uncomfortable length of time. So start calming your breathing down now, OK?'

'You're insane, mate,' said Faisal. 'Legit bonkers.'

'Very possibly,' I said. 'But if you knew my whole story, you'd probably be impressed that I'm this functional.'

'Don't worry, I'm definitely impressed. You're *that* Stanly, aren't you? The Collision Kid?'

I laughed. 'Is that what they call me?'

'Don't, Faisal,' said Tara. 'It'll go straight to his head.'

'Quiet, you,' I said. 'Now. Is everybody clear on the plan?'

Reluctant nods.

'Cool. And breathe in.' Impressively they all seemed to be doing as I asked, despite the fact that we were screaming along the river in a smashed-up boat, surrounded by a din of bellowing police voices and gunfire.

I should probably be more stressed about this.

There was a bridge up ahead. That would be the place. I split my thoughts, keeping half in control of the boat and half snaking around Alex and the others, and leapt over the hole in the boat to join them, tearing it a bit bigger. I also raised the boat a little higher off the water. Just enough to help.

'Ready?' I said.

Nobody was ready.

'Well,' I said. 'Here we go anyway.' I took a deep breath. 'Three. Two. *One!*'

Water.

Cold.

Cold.

Wow, cold.

And dark.

I sent the five of us plunging down as fast as I could, very *very* narrowly avoiding the boat as it passed over us. I could hear the muffled sound of police boats passing over in pursuit, as well as helicopters. I waited. Five seconds. Ten seconds. I saw the boat pass under the bridge.

Aaaaand up.

The boat left the water, ascending so fast that the police boats and helicopters were at a loss. At the same time, I flew us up to the edge of the river, pressing us against the wall. We broke the surface and I allowed everyone a few precious seconds of air before taking us back under, through the dark, bitter-tasting water towards the bridge. Once we were safely under I let us back up again and levitated us so that we were standing on the thin ledge at the base of the bridge's inner arc. Everyone was gasping and spluttering and shivering. I was still concentrating on the boat. My grip on it was fading, I wouldn't have control for much longer . . .

And then it was gone.

Come on, come on . . .

The sky lit up, splashed orange by a bright fireball that puffed out a cloud of burning wooden splinters and concentric Saturn rings of smoke.

Thank you, Mr Drone.

'Right,' I said. 'That was . . . a thing. Shall we hop it?'

Chapter Twenty-Six

SOMEHOW I MANAGED to shepherd everybody through the darkened streets to the safe house without us getting arrested. Skank met us outside the grimy building, which seemed to be on a slight lean, greeting Tara as though they hung out regularly. 'Hi, Skank,' she said, shyly.

We followed him down some intermittently-lit stairs to a tiny basement flat with four locks on its door. It was pretty spartan inside: a couple of mattresses on the bedroom floor, nothing on the walls, one sofa that had seen better days.

'Thanks for this,' I said.

'Not a problem.' I'd filled him in on most of the details already. He'd been fairly Skank-like about it.

'So,' said Faisal. 'Now what?'

Scales coughed loudly. 'I do not wish to have any further part of this,' he said, mustering an impressive level of snootiness. 'You *destroyed* my boat, after all. Which, I don't need to remind anyone, had over half of the latest batch of Prometheus on board.'

'Prometheus?' I said.

'Greek god,' said Faisal. 'Stole fire, gave it to humans. Scales' name for the drug.'

'Oh.' *Kinda pretentious.*

'What do you want, then, Doctor?' said Alex.

'I was rather hoping to get paid and then leave the country.' *He kind of needs to be arrested . . .*

But then again, so do the others, probably.

And if I'm letting some of them off the hook, I have to let them all off the hook.

AARGH THIS IS HARD.

'How soon can you be on your way out of the country?' asked Alex.

'Within the hour,' said Scales. 'I have contingencies for—'

'Do it,' said Alex. 'Get going. The money will be in your account by midnight.'

'I need to go to my lab first—'

'No,' said Alex. 'You don't.'

'Why?'

'Cos we're going to burn it down.'

Scales went pale. '*What?*'

Alex looked at me. 'All the remaining samples are there. If we burn down the lab, it's gone. More importantly, Angelcorp don't get their hands on it.'

'You cannot be serious!' said Scales.

'This was always about money for you,' said Alex, mildly. 'You literally said that to me. And you were going to skip the country anyway.'

'But . . .'

'Look,' I said. 'Your research isn't falling into the wrong hands. And you're most likely not going to end up tortured in prison.'

'*And* you're getting paid,' said Faisal.

'Pretty good deal,' I said.

Scales spluttered for a few moments, but quickly seemed to realise that this was as good as it was going to get. 'Fine.' He nodded forlornly.

'Good,' I said. 'Now I need to go to Angelcorp and do

some damage control. And you guys need to go and burn down the lab. Right now.'

Alex nodded.

'Tara,' I said. 'You'll . . . I guess you'll stay with these guys for now?'

She nodded.

'I'm sorry . . .'

'Don't,' she said. 'It's . . . we'll talk at some point.'

I nodded. 'All right. Um . . . so if I don't get locked up for the rest of my life, I'll come by here when I can.'

'I'll go with them,' said Skank. 'If they're happy with that.'

'I'm happy with that,' said Tara. *Jolly good.*

Faisal nodded. 'If she's happy, so am I.' *Hmm . . .*

'Cool,' I said. 'Um . . . all right. I'll see you all tomorrow then. Hopefully.'

'Thanks, by the way,' said Alex.

'*Thanks?*' I said. 'What, for steaming in and bollocksing up your plan?'

'Like you said, it was going to go wrong anyway.'

Do I believe him?

Why would he just abandon his whole scheme like this?

Maybe cos he's just as confused as he ever was.

Maybe maladjusted young men aren't necessarily the best candidates for superpowers.

'Right,' I said. 'Laters, then.' And even though my whole brain and heart were screaming at me to take Tara, I left.

Let's hope this idea isn't as bad as it definitely is.

'You arrogant little shit,' said Walker, by way of a greeting.

'Nice to see you too, Jane.'

She grimaced. I was sitting cross-legged on the bed in one

347

of the many Undercells and Walker was standing by the locked door, flanked by Leon and Rosie. Leon was obviously itching to get his brain on me, although I'd noticed that the cell's power-negating technology was on, so he couldn't have even if they'd let him. I was quite enjoying the fact that I seemed to have permanently broken his inscrutable mask. Rosie was just standing there, barely even present. Even though she couldn't hurt me without her power, she was still incredibly creepy.

'You know nothing,' said Walker. 'Of this organisation, this city, this world. Of your power, or the responsibilities that come with it. You are a child, lurching from one disaster to another, leaving a trail of destruction, chaos and heinously complicated paperwork in your wake. I'm partly to blame, of course, for pushing to take you on in the first place. For allowing you free reign. But this latest debacle—'

'Hold on,' I said. 'I think you'll find that I solved your case. The drug is off the streets. *Permanently.*' *Ha ha I just said that in real life and it was appropriate.* 'And the gang won't re-surface.'

'*Not good enough*,' said Walker. 'You were supposed to bring them in so we could—'

'Torture them?'

'*Question* them.'

'Well, sorry,' I said. 'But to quote . . . um . . . *you* . . . I don't recognise any authority you think you might have on that front. I've seen what *she* can do.' I nodded towards Rosie, who stared right through me. 'I was not going to let you subject anyone else, guilty or otherwise, to that. It's barbaric.'

'That was not your decision to make,' said Walker. 'Need I remind you of the property damage, the—'

'Oh come on,' I said. 'That chase was *amazing*. Leon? Were

you watching? You kill monsters with a psychically-propelled *sword*; surely you love shit like that!'

Leon just stared at me like a wolf whose dinner had danced out of reach and started insulting his mother.

'Suit yourself.' I shrugged. 'Look, my methods may be unorthodox, but damn it, I get results.' *Oh God. Stop it. Stop it! It's too much.*

'Oh shut up, you stupid boy,' snapped Walker. 'As far as *results* go, we have your word and nothing else. No actionable evidence. No witnesses, no suspects. Just a pile of very expensive chaos. And you aren't going anywhere until—' Her phone rang and she sighed exasperatedly. 'Yes? Oh, sir, I . . . oh, I didn't realise. I . . . really? Are you sure?' She scowled at me and I smiled sweetly back at her. 'But sir, you are aware of what has . . . yes, of course. But . . . yes, sir.'

She put her phone way. 'You're lucky you have friends in high places.'

'Don't I know it,' I said.

'You haven't heard the last of this.'

'Cool. Can I go, then?'

'You can *go* and speak to Mr Freeman,' said Walker.

Oh. That took the wind out of my sails. 'He's back?'

'He is.' She smiled nastily. 'I wouldn't keep him waiting, if I were you.'

I was escorted out of the Undercells by Leon, Rosie and several guards, up through the Shard, into the lift, up to the very top floor. A special code was required to open the lift doors, then I was marched up a grey corridor lined with blank doors. At the very end was another door, except this one wasn't blank. It had a bronze plate on it, with G. FREEMAN, CEO embossed on that.

My stomach was bubbling and I was fighting to stop my hands from shaking.

Leon knocked.

'Come in.' That *voice*.

Leon opened the door, shoved me over the threshold and closed it behind me.

The office was disappointingly functional. No captured enemies hanging from the ceiling by their toenails. No world-domination charts on the walls. Not even a frickin' laser shark tank. Just shelves, a drinks cabinet, a swish photo-copier and a big desk bearing a slim computer and two piles of papers, set-square neat.

And behind the desk, in the big chair, the man himself. The main event. He might have been wearing the same grey suit he'd worn when I'd last seen him. His hair was the same. His face was slightly more lined, but apart from that . . .

Then he stood up and smiled at me and I wanted to be sick in my own head. And also all over his office. 'Stanly,' he said. 'It's been a long time.'

I stared at him. Unperturbed, he came out from behind the desk and stood in front of me, barely a foot away, hand outstretched. Not taking my eyes from his, I accepted the proffered hand and shook slowly. 'Somewhat different from our last meeting, eh?' said Freeman. 'From the depths of an alien world to this office, high above our fair city.'

I nodded.

'Drink?' Freeman indicated what looked like an expensive bottle of Scotch, not that I would actually know an expensive bottle of Scotch if I fell over it.

I nodded again.

'Ice?'

'Yeah.'

Freeman poured us two glasses, one with ice and one without, handed mine over and sat down on the other side of his desk. 'Well,' he smiled. 'I must admit, even after having spoken to you on the phone, seeing you again is . . . quite something.'

'Likewise.'

'Quite a result, too. The case of the superpowered drug dealers.' He chuckled.

'Not really . . .'

'You took some dangerous people off the streets. Along with a dangerous illicit substance. And all without compromising your core principles. Bravo.'

'You believe me, then?'

He looked genuinely surprised at the question. 'Why wouldn't I?'

'I didn't exactly operate within . . . established guidelines.'

Why am I talking to him? Why aren't I killing him?

Why isn't he killing me?

Freeman tipped his glass in a shrug-like gesture. 'Honestly, Stanly? Between you and me? I was never hugely bothered about Alexander's little gang. And if you say that the whole episode is over, then that's good enough for me.'

'I would have thought you'd have wanted to get your hands on the drug.'

'I'm sure we'll come up with our own version sooner or later,' said Freeman. 'Although, of course, we will comb what remains of the laboratory for anything useful. But I know you better than Jane Walker does, and I'm willing to take you at your word and . . . close the case.'

351

'OK.' I took a sip of my drink. It was absolutely foul, but I tried not to show it.

'Of course,' said Freeman, 'I can't be letting *everyone* run around willy-nilly, doing whatever takes their fancy. That way lies chaos.'

'What's so special about me, then?'

'Well,' said Freeman. '*You*. You're what's so special about you. You're a special individual.'

'The most talented, most interesting, and most extraordinary person in the universe?' I snorted. 'Pull the other one. I dimly recall a psychotic megalomaniacal speech from you to the effect that you *made* me into your chosen one, as part of a messed-up Machiavellian scheme to use me to . . . well. Get here.' I indicated the room with my glass.

'Psychotic and megalomaniacal?' said Freeman. 'Is that really what you think of me?'

'Kinda.'

He sighed and sipped his drink. 'I suppose I sympathise. It's . . . all been terribly strange. Although I would be interested to discuss our respective interpretations of the word "Machiavellian".'

'Maybe later,' I said, opting not to let on that I didn't really know what the word meant anyway. 'Look . . . I'm not special. I'm not a chosen one. Chosen ones are not a thing. I just happen to have developed my powers faster than a lot of other people. I'm willing to bet there are hundreds more potential mes around the world, just waiting to be snapped up and manipulated.'

'Very probably,' said Freeman. 'But who has time for all that admin? I've wandered the world searching for empowered before, with your dog at my side.'

'Definitely mini-series potential there.'

'And it's *exhausting*,' said Freeman. '*You* are already on my radar. And I genuinely feel that you would be an asset. That you could make a difference. But first you need to stop *fighting* us all the time. That's why I have allowed you to go about your business, finding your feet. It's why I have waived the various charges and punishments that many within Angelcorp have urged me to visit upon you. It's why I have called you here now, why I am happy to accept your assurances that you've solved the problem of Alexander and his gang. Call it a gesture of goodwill.'

Is he serious? 'I would have thought I was too dangerous,' I said. 'Too much of a liability.'

'I let your friends live, didn't I?'

'They don't know what I know.'

'Granted,' said Freeman. '*But* I think you're also smart enough to realise that acting upon the knowledge you have would be foolish, futile, and ultimately counter-productive. You could do so much more good by accepting that terrible things have been done, terrible things that cannot be undone, and working, as I have, to ensure that they are never again necessary.'

'Say I do accept that,' I said. 'What's the catch?'

'We are at work on something enormous,' said Freeman. 'And not what you might think. It's not a top-secret universe-destroying scheme, an infernal machine, a devillish plot. My primary objective has always been to save this world.'

Not stroking your own crazy ego? 'Go on.'

'I get the feeling that you're disappointed with what you've come back to,' said Freeman.

'Seems like the same old thing,' I said. 'People struggling, doing horrible things to each other. Powerful people forgetting about the little ones.'

'Spend some more time here,' said Freeman. 'Do some research. Travel around a bit. Really *look* at what we've been doing. Of course, it's a work in progress. You flatter me if you think I could have sculpted a perfect Eden in less than six years. But look at what *has* been achieved. At what we're doing. And I'm not just talking about improving Britain's standing in the eyes of the world, although I consider that a minor miracle in itself. Sustainable energy is at the top of the global agenda – the reign of corporate oligarchy will soon be well and truly over. Politicians and corporations the world over are slowly but surely turning away from short-termist, profit-driven thinking, and going about the business of *humanity*. Of making the Earth a better place. We have it in our sights – a high-tech, prosperous, connected global society, people and technology working in harmony with nature rather than burning it down. There are still villains in this world, of course there are. Enemies. People that must be fought. But more than anything, what we are working to defeat is *chaos*.' He smiled. 'This is not hyperbole, Stanly. This is not hot air. A ten-minute Internet search will prove me right.'

Christ alive. 'OK . . .'

'The first eighteen months or so after the Collision was a dark time,' Freeman continued. 'People did not react favourably to the knowledge that there were hell-beasts lying in wait, that supernatural powers were a reality. There was rioting. There was fury. But mostly? There was fear. Simple, human fear. Possibly the most dangerous of our species' motivations. And Angelcorp worked hard to win hearts and minds around the world. With targeted, logical, rational, compassionate, inclusive thinking, we are turning things around. At the rate things are going, before long, global levels of peace will be at their highest since records began.'

'Well done.' I think I actually meant it, almost. 'So . . . you don't want to introduce a chemical into the water supply that takes everyone's powers away?'

He blinked owlishly. It almost made me laugh. 'I *beg* your pardon?'

'Just a rumour I heard.'

'Well, whichever crackpot came up with *that*, I wouldn't want to be within breathing distance of what they were smoking,' said Freeman. 'The empowered have always been key to my plans. That was why using you the way I did, distasteful and painful – perhaps even unforgivable – as it may have been, was essential. I needed to show Angelcorp the consequences of marginalising the empowered, of setting ourselves against them, of *disempowering* them. You were the worst-case scenario. And then you saved the world. A fairly compelling narrative. It's just a shame the world at large couldn't know the real story.'

I thought of *A Boy And His Dog* and fought a smirk. 'Got to shield people from those uncomfortable truths.'

'Sometimes,' said Freeman. 'You remember London's old mayor, for example? Derek Brooks?'

'I remember he got eaten by a wall.'

'He did,' said Freeman. 'Rather an undignified end. And he didn't exactly conduct himself with distinction before that. Embarrassing, really. But as far as the world knows, he died heroically, helping to save the city to which he dedicated his life. There was a wonderful, moving interview with his proud daughters in the *Guardian*. Would it have been better for the world to know that the blustering imbecile died as he lived – ineffectually and with no grace whatsoever?'

I shrugged. 'Who knows. So you *don't* want to take everyone's powers away . . . do you want to work out how to move between parallel universes so you can enslave them?'

Freeman let out a hearty laugh, the heartiest I'd ever heard from him. 'Oh, Stanly. You are wonderful. No, that's not my plan. I am, of course, fascinated by parallel universes. How could anyone with an enquiring mind not be? The paintings in the Kulich gallery, naturally occurring doorways that closed and locked of their own accord long ago . . . those are the only routes I have ever seen to worlds beyond this. I would love to find others one day. But it is a purely intellectual concern, anthropological, if you will. There is far too much to do in this world before seriously turning my eye to others. I only have so many hours in the day, and you'd be surprised how busy it can get, running a global, billion-pound company operating at the forefront of future-bound thinking.'

'Future-bound thinking,' I said. 'Another bit of Freeman phraseology that makes me want to swallow my own fist and puke-punch myself in the face.'

'Charming.' Freeman chuckled and finished his drink.

'I notice that you hide your powers,' I said. 'Care to tell me why?'

He didn't seem at all irritated that I'd bought it up. 'Isn't it obvious? Do you think that any world leader, or any head of security worth their salt, would allow themselves to be in the same room, the same *building*, as me, if they knew I was empowered?'

'I guess . . . but how have you done it? Aren't there tests?'

'Of course,' said Freeman. 'I undergo them regularly. But I

have always had a knack for using my powers to . . . well. To hide the fact that I have powers.'

'That's how you fooled Daryl.'

He nodded.

'So *do* you use them? On world leaders?'

'I've never ruled out the possibility,' said Freeman, 'but I prefer to rely on diplomacy, logical thinking, civilised debate and *quid pro quo*.'

Good answer. Doesn't actually really tell me anything. 'Fairish,' I said. 'So . . . what's the upshot of all this? What do you *want* from me?'

'For now,' said Freeman, 'nothing. I still consider myself, Angelcorp, the world, all of us, to be in your debt. If you wish to take a year to travel the world and see what's happening, get a better idea of the big picture, of your potential place, of what you can do, then please do so. We will fund you, happily. If you wish to stay in London and immerse yourself in community projects, do so. If you wish to seek out a slightly less violent niche at Angelcorp, be my guest. The *upshot* is that I want you to fulfil your potential. Your *true* potential. Potential that doesn't involve fighting and boat chases and monsters. Although if you decide that you wish to train to join our psychic commandos, parachuting into remote areas to eradicate empowered terrorist cells, then feel free, although admittedly I would be a little disappointed.'

I nodded. 'Wow. That's . . . quite an offer. I was kind of expecting this conversation to end in a fight. Or a death. Maybe two deaths.'

'That couldn't have been further from my mind. I don't want us to be at war. I really don't.'

And do you know what? I believed him. 'OK,' I said. 'Well

'. . . yeah. Thanks. I need to go and think. A lot. Actually, I think I need to go to *sleep* first, because today has been totally bonkers.'

'Take as much time as you need.'

'Thanks. I can't say I don't still have a massive problem with you . . . I doubt that will ever go away. But it seems like the sort of thing I'm going to have to see past. Look at the bigger picture.'

'That's good.' Freeman toasted me with his empty glass. 'You've taken your first step into a larger world.'

Special, I thought, as I walked down the corridor to the lift. *I'm powerful and special. I can do what I want. No consequences.*

Down the elevator went.

Anything I want.

I met Lauren and Daryl in the lobby and once we were out in the cold, dark city I told them in the briefest possible terms what had occurred. They wanted to talk more, but I was too tired and said I'd be in touch. 'Thank you, both,' I said. 'For everything you've done. I'm sorry for all the trouble I've caused you. I need . . . I have to go and do lots of thinking.'

What I actually did was go back to the flat and ring my mother.

Chapter Twenty-Seven

T HE GRAVEYARD WAS quiet. Was that unusual, for a
Sunday? I didn't know. A lethargic drizzle fell, light wind
rustling a thousand different breeds of flower, and I stood and
stared at the stone, hands tucked into the pockets of my new
black coat. Maybe going out in a black coat to fight evil wasn't
my style anymore, but coming here? It seemed appropriate.

The grave was nice, as graves went. Light grey, not
shiny and fake-looking like some of them. EDDIE BIRD.
BELOVED FRIEND, COUSIN, NEPHEW. Dates. They
were the worst thing. *How can they be so close together?*

I hadn't been planning to speak, but suddenly I found
myself speaking. 'Hey. I . . . you know I like films. Quite a
lot. And this is something people always do in films. They
come to important graves and they talk. They apologise and
explain and . . . and I wasn't going to do that. Cos it's a
cliché and it's trite as fuck and what the hell would I say?'
First tear. 'What can I say to you? You're dead and it's my
fault. It's my fault because I wanted to be . . . to be fighting.
To be flying around and walking away from explosions and,
and, instead . . .' Second tear. 'Instead of being happy. Being
content with what I had. I had a girl who I loved and I had
friends who I loved. I had you. But I *had* to be out fighting.
And now I've done too much fighting and I don't want to do
any more, but it's too late to be realising that, it's too late . . .'
Third. Fourth. More.

Sod it, might as well stop counting.

'It's too late, because you're gone. You're gone. And yes, it's Freeman's fault too. Mostly his. It's Alex's too, but I can . . . I can forgive him. Because he lost someone. He lost someone who he loved, in a different way than I loved you, obviously . . .' A laugh.

I think he would have laughed at that too.

'And that, losing that, I can see why it would make you feel like there was no point. Forget that there were others who hadn't lost people yet. It's not OK, of course . . . but . . . anyway. So it's not just my fault. But it's a lot my fault. And I just . . . I know you'd forgive me. I know if you could Force ghost yourself here, go all Obi-Wan on me, you'd say you forgave me, and that I saved the world and that makes up for it, and you'd mean it. And *damn you*, you shouldn't forgive me.'

I took a deep breath and looked up at the sky. The rain had stopped and there was a brightness behind the clouds somewhere.

'But you would. And . . . thank you. Thank you for everything. Thank you for doing so much. I'm sorry I didn't . . . sorry I didn't take more time to . . . to ask you stuff. What you were up to. What you wanted to do with your life. How you felt about things. Sorry I was so ungrateful, so . . . wrapped up in myself. Too stupid to realise what I had, that I was going to lose it. That I was *trying* to lose it.'

I crouched down and stared at his name. 'I talked to Freeman yesterday. I *talked* to him. I shared a *drink* with him. He told me he didn't want to fight, that he wants to work together. He's . . . he's insane. But . . . he's also done good that I can't deny. Even if I can't forgive him, even if I can't justify what he's done . . . I think I understand it. Is that OK? Is that enough for me to . . . to let it slide? Would it even be my place to go after him? Do I have the right? This world . . . I barely understood it before. Now I'm totally lost. Even if I did decide to take him down . . . how would it work? Would I just make things worse again? After everything I said to Tara and Alex . . .'

I stood up again. The tears had stopped. 'I feel like I'm in danger of accepting his offer. I really feel like it. And I need to know if that's OK. Because I don't know if I trust myself to decide.' I kept staring at his name, letting the whirlpool swirl inside. 'But Angelcorp . . . the things they do . . . surely one evil act is too many? Or is it just the price you pay? I don't *understand*. I don't know what to do.'

I stood there, staring. Waiting. I don't know what for. A sign?

Yeah, cos those happen.

I took another very deep breath. The air was damp, earthy. Real. For a second, I couldn't believe I was breathing it.

I shouldn't even be in this world.

'I love you, Eddie,' I said. 'And I'm sorry. I'll try to be better.'

I turned and walked away, through the lines of graves, through the monuments to loss and broken dreams and darkened lives . . . and probably, in some cases, perhaps, relief. I passed a few people, some dressed in black like me, laying flowers, crying, smiling, talking as I had. A few times, I made eye contact. Swapped smiles. It was nice.

I was barely out of the gate when my phone rang. I answered without looking. 'Hello?'

'Hi.' It was Sharon.

'Oh! Hey. I was going to call you, actually.'

'You were?'

'Yeah, I . . .' I suddenly registered her tone. She sounded . . . wrong. 'Are you OK?'

'I need you to come round.'

'What's wrong? Are you all right? Has something—'

'Just come. Please.'

'OK. I'll be right round.'

'Thank you. Bye.' She hung up and I ran for the nearest Tube.

Connor answered the door before I'd even had a chance to knock. He looked . . . perturbed.

'Are you guys OK?' I said.

'Yeah, we're all right. It . . . it's upstairs.'

It?

He led me in and I saw Sharon sitting on the top step. Her complexion was usually pretty fair, but she appeared particularly ghostly white right now. I looked uncertainly from her to Connor, who hugged himself and looked uncertainly from me to her.

OK. *Guess I'm taking the initiative.*

I slid off my shoes, went up the stairs and knelt down a few steps below Sharon. 'Hey. What's happening?'

'I found it on the way home.' Her voice was as drained as her face. 'I heard it. I think it's . . .' She stood up and I followed her up and around, across the landing, to the bathroom. The door was closed but I could feel something. Energy.

Familiar energy.

Sharon opened the door, not all the way, but enough for me to poke my head around. 'Brace yourself,' she said.

I leaned in and for a second I had an impression of something lying in the bath, partially submerged. A spindly-limbed creature, watery blue, reclining painfully . . . but as I focused I suddenly became aware, no, not aware, *certain*, that if I stepped any closer someone was going to stab me, drive a knife right into my back and *keep* driving it in, pull it out and stab me again, tear me, tear me . . .

I yelped and jumped back, spinning around to see who was behind me, yanking the door shut with a panicked thought. Sharon grabbed me and forced me to look at her, at her eyes, the most comforting eyes ever invented, scared as they were right now . . .

And the fear was gone, just like that, like it had never been there.

'Holy crap,' I said.

'It's a shimmer, isn't it?' she said.

'Yeah . . . you *found* it?'

She nodded and beckoned for me to follow her back downstairs. We went to the kitchen and Connor made three cups of very strong, sweet tea. My hands trembled as I gripped my mug.

'I was on my way home,' said Sharon. 'I teach a group in Brixton some Sundays. I was walking, and I heard . . .' She frowned. 'It's so hard to describe. Like crying . . . but in my head. And not human. But there was . . . language there. Like the crying had meaning. Something wanted help. I looked around, there were plenty of people about, but nobody else seemed to have noticed anything . . . so I followed it. I don't know how I heard it from so far away, it's like it was calling for me, specifically. A frequency only I could hear. It was at the bottom of a hill, near a drainage pipe, lying in some rubbish. I thought I recognised it. But when I got closer, it . . . it showed me things. Terrifying things. Sickening things. Like a defence mechanism. I nearly ran, but I could still hear the crying. And I tried to soothe it, you know, with my mind. So it would know I was there to help. And after a while it stopped trying to defend itself and it let me pick it up. I wrapped it in my jacket . . .' She closed her eyes tightly and squeezed out several tears. I took her hand.

'It *clung* to me,' she whispered. 'Like a child.'

I looked at Connor. 'Have you been able to get near it?'

He shook his head. 'No. I can barely get to the bathroom door before it . . . you know. Does its thing.'

'Sharon? What about you?'

'I've managed to get in there a couple of times,' said Sharon. 'I've been trying to read it, to find out where it came from, what happened to it . . . the thoughts are like nothing I've ever . . . seen? Heard? I don't . . .' She took a deep breath and sipped her tea. 'It's traumatised, I know that much. Abused. I had a flash of something. A room . . . like a lab. There were more of them. More shimmers.'

'Angelcorp,' I said. 'It has to be. They've been experimenting on them.' *Of course they have.*

The only survivors . . .

'That's what we're thinking,' said Connor. I'd been expecting some kind of dig, but maybe we were past that now.

God, I hope so.

'I don't know what to do,' said Sharon. 'I thought you might, as you . . . you know. You've spent time with them.'

'Yeah . . . quite a bit. But I'm not . . . I guess I'll give it a try.' I finished my tea, steeled myself and headed back upstairs. Sharon and Connor followed me, Connor staying behind Sharon, gripping her hand. I thought the bathroom door open from the other side of the landing and gingerly took a few steps towards it. Nothing yet. I turned back, taking some comfort from their faces, scared but strong. My friends.

Friends.

Both of them.

I stepped into the bathroom and closed the door behind me. The shimmer lay in the bath, maybe looking at me, maybe not, it was impossible to tell. I tried to radiate calm thoughts, kind thoughts. I wasn't here to hurt it. And there was nothing it could show me. It didn't seem to be trying . . .

Something moved out of the corner of my eye. I glanced towards it and saw a fat glob of something wet and black dribbling down the white wall of the bathroom. It stank of death. I looked away but there was more dripping down the opposite wall . . . no, *all* the walls, loads of the stuff, pouring, surrounding me, and God why had I shut the door, why had I shut myself in here, and . . .

Oh no.

I knew what it was. The black stuff.

It was *them.*

The other shimmers.

The ones who had died when I'd left their world.

All of them.

'No!' I cried. 'Please! I didn't . . . I didn't mean for that to happen! It wasn't me, I swear! Please!' And now I saw, crawling amongst the torrents of black filth, spiders, hundreds of them, thousands, their legs spasming as they tried to climb over one another, they were coming *for me*, to punish me for what I'd done, for everything I'd done, and I ran to the bathroom door, pounding on it, screaming to be let out . . .

'Stanly!'
'Stanly!'
'Stanly!'

The bathroom door slammed and I was on my knees on the landing, hyperventilating, and Sharon was hugging me, pouring calm thoughts into my head like cool water into a scalding hot bath, subduing the fear and leaving me drained and light-headed.

'Jesus,' said Connor. He'd gone as white as Sharon. 'What did it . . .'

'It . . . it read my mind,' I said. 'Or maybe I showed it without wanting to . . . the rest of them. Back in their world. Dead. It thinks I killed them.'

'Did you?'

'Connor!' said Sharon.

'Sorry,' said Connor, 'I didn't mean . . . it was just a question.'

'I don't know,' I said. 'Genuinely. Whatever pulled me out of their world, *it* killed them. And I thought that it was something else, some kind of external force, someone controlling me. Messing with me. But maybe . . . maybe it *was* me, after all. Maybe I did kill them.'

Connor leaned over and gave my shoulder an awkward pat. I smiled weakly. 'Um . . . either way, I don't think it's going to be accepting any help from me. Sharon, you're going to have to do it. Try and soothe it as much as you can, see if you can get any more information. About where it was, what was done to it . . . who was involved.' *Of course it was Freeman. Of course it was.* 'Sorry. It probably won't be fun.'

'It's fine.' She nodded and I saw that steel, steel like no-one else, and God I was in awe of her. 'I'll do what I can.'

'Wait a minute,' I said. 'I'll see if I can . . . Lauren might be able to help.' I took my phone out, then immediately put it away again.

Connor frowned. 'Changed your mind?'

'I think I'll just go round there,' I said. 'Talk face-to-face. There . . . might be other stuff.'

Sharon and Connor exchanged Meaningful Looks. 'Stuff . . .' said Connor. 'About Freeman?'

I frowned. 'What . . . what do you mean?'

He didn't seem to know how to proceed, so Sharon stepped in. 'Stanly, we both . . . the shimmer got inside both our heads. And afterwards, it was like . . . it was like we both remembered things. About Freeman. About what happened. Things it seems . . . ridiculous that we would have forgotten. Impossible.'

Oh God. I didn't know what to say.

Do I confirm?

Think you just did, sport.

'It's true,' said Sharon. 'Isn't it?'

I nodded.

'Freeman . . . changed our memories?'

I nodded again.

Connor turned away and very nearly punched a hole through the wall, his fist stopping millimetres away from it. 'Son of a . . . goddamn *bastard*.'

'I'm sorry,' I said. 'I'm so sorry I didn't tell you. I got back and nobody knew . . . I felt like it was safer to keep it that way. If you didn't know, he'd have no reason to come after you.'

'He did it to all of us?' said Sharon.

'Yeah,' I said. 'Except . . . it didn't quite work on Daryl. Or it wore off quickly, or something. Beagle power, I guess.'

'Daryl's known?' said Connor. 'All this time?'

I nodded. 'And he did the right thing. He kept you all safe.'

Sharon took a deep breath. 'So . . . I assume there's more we don't know.'

'There is.'

'Well,' she said. 'Shall we have something to eat while we discuss it?'

'I love you,' said Connor.

She smiled.

There was a lot to talk about. I started with the horrible stuff. Freeman's scheme. The way he'd manipulated me, us. Our endless, awful conversation in the shimmer world. We cried and raged and hugged and then I told them that I periodically disappeared and materialised in another universe, which led to more questions and a conversation about whether we could take the shimmer home, along with its brothers and sisters. If we could rescue them, that is.

'If I can, I will,' I said. 'For now, though, I have no idea what we can do with it, beyond looking after it as best we can. It's not like there's a habitat we can send it to.'

'So . . . what?' said Connor. 'We're just going to have to keep it here?'

'For now.'

'You want us to keep a disturbed, violent telepathic creature from another universe in our bath until further notice?'

'I'm sorry,' I said. 'I can't think of any other—'

'It's fine,' said Sharon. 'It's fine. We can keep it. I'll . . . we'll work it out. OK, Connor?'

'Yeah.' He nodded. 'OK.'

By now Sharon's chilli was ready and as we ate, I filled

them in on everything that had happened with Tara and Alex. They'd heard about the boat chase on the news and Connor actually laughed. 'I should have known you'd have been in the thick of that. You crazy little bastard.'

Sharon, for her part, kept trying to apologise for not taking my worries about Tara seriously, and for not keeping a closer eye on her, and all sorts of other things, but I wouldn't let her. No apologies today. The food went down fantastically well, and it got dark outside, and presently the conversation turned back to Freeman.

Well. It wasn't a conversation, exactly. It was Sharon, holding my right hand and Connor's left, blue supernovas blazing behind her tears, saying, 'He has to pay.'

And Connor nodding and saying, 'Damn right.'

'Hello,' said Sally, frowning uncertainly.

'Hi,' I said. 'It's Sally, isn't it?'

'Yes . . .'

'I'm Stanly. Has Lauren . . .'

Recognition and a nervous smile. 'Ah,' she said, running a hand through her long black hair. 'Yes. She did. Do you . . . did you want to see her?'

'Is she in? Really sorry for just turning up like this.'

Sally nodded. 'Yes, she's in.' She turned and called into the house. I could smell Chinese food and hear soft piano music. 'Babe! Stanly's here!'

Lauren appeared at the end of the hall, frowning. She was wearing a big, creased T-shirt and denim cut-offs. It was odd, seeing her so casual. 'Stanly?' she said. 'Are you all right? What's wrong?'

'I'm fine. Well . . . kind of. Sorry, I would have called but I didn't want . . . I mean, I thought you might be at Angelcorp, and . . . sorry, is this a bad time?'

'It's fine.' Sally smiled. 'We'd just finished eating, actually.' She stood aside and ushered me in. I felt awkward and guilty for intruding. There were paintings all the way along the hallway, impressionistic scenes of harbours and oceans and seasides, all clearly by the same artist. I wondered if it was Sally. Or maybe Lauren. I still knew so little about her.

'Would you like some tea?' asked Sally.

'Um, yeah,' I said, 'if that's OK. Thank you.'

'Babe?'

Lauren nodded. 'Please.' She pushed open a door to a lovely, cosy little living room and ushered me in. There was her piano, polished and gleaming, some ludicrously complex-looking sheet music spread out across the stand. I took a seat on a red sofa – *phwoar, now THAT is a sofa* – and Lauren pulled out the piano stool and perched there.

'What's wrong?' she asked.

I told her everything, from the beginning. The truth about Freeman, the reason I'd stayed quiet when I got back, Mr and Mrs Rogers, Morter Smith, and now this latest development, the shimmer, all wrapped up in my own concerns about Angelcorp's methods, the Undercells, Walker, Rosie.

Lauren didn't give much away as I talked, not even when I told her that Freeman had messed with her memory, but when Sally came in with our tea she squeezed Lauren's shoulder gently before leaving the room again, and the only thing that betrayed how Lauren must have been feeling was the way she held on to her girlfriend's hand. It was brief but . . . *desperate*. As though without those few seconds of contact she might not have been able to handle it. Then she was quiet again, listening, impossible to read.

'So it all adds up to serious badness,' I said. 'And I feel like
. . . I feel like we can't ignore it. Not now.'

Lauren stared at me for a very long moment. Then she
started to cry.

Oh no. Oh dear. Oh bollocks. 'Lauren,' I said, getting up and
moving towards her, but she shooed me away, hiding her eyes,
so I sat back down and waited. She got herself under control
quickly and looked up again, wiping tears away, shaking her
head.

'I'm so sorry,' she said.

'What? What do you mean?'

'I should have known. I should have *known*. But I didn't
. . . I never even realised . . .'

'How could you have known?' I said. 'The guy's superpower is manipulation. He changed your *brain*—'

'It's not just that, though . . .' Lauren took a deep breath.
'Obviously that's disgusting and horrible, and I'm going to
need to shower for a week . . . but it isn't just that. I've ignored
things, I've put up with . . . I looked you in the eye and I
said we were doing good work, that . . . that we have to make
compromises. *Sacrifices.*' She shook her head. 'It's obscene.
Talking to *you* about sacrifice. I had no idea that he . . . he
made you . . . God, the least we could have done for you was
keep fighting.'

'You didn't know,' I said. 'You didn't . . .' And then I did
something weird. I laughed. I couldn't help it.

Lauren frowned and asked me what could possibly be
funny.

Good question.

'You *have* kept fighting,' I said. 'You've done . . . you got on with it. With life. For better or worse, triumphs and screw-ups all mashed together. You've done what was necessary.'

'But—'

'Look.' I reached out and took her hands in mine. 'We can do all the soul-searching and hand-wringing in the world, we can sob and talk about how much we've messed up, everything we're ashamed of. God, I could write a trilogy about my screw-ups. And a spin-off about the questionable things I've done in the last week. We can do all that . . . *once we've done what needs to be done.* Yes?'

Lauren nodded. 'Oh yes.'

There was a knock at the door and Sally poked her head around. I realised that I was still holding Lauren's hands. *Does this look bad?*

Or is it fine?

It's probably fine.

'Everything all right?' asked Sally, coming over and putting her arms around Lauren's shoulders. Lauren pressed her face into her side and cried a bit more and I looked apologetically at Sally. She just smiled. A strong smile. The kind of smile you'd want to come home to after a day at that infernal place.

'It's . . . complicated,' I said.

'Basically,' said Lauren, her voice a little muffled by Sally's dress, 'we're going to take down George Freeman.'

Sally's eyes widened. 'Oh dear. Sounds like you might need some more tea.'

There was more tea and more discussion, late into the night. Lauren said that we needed lots more information before we even thought about moving against Freeman and Walker, and that she would put out some tentative feelers and see if anyone knew of a lab anywhere near where Sharon had found the shimmer. At some point, it would also be essential to isolate Morter Smith, although that was tricky because he very rarely travelled alone.

We also agreed that under no circumstances could we discuss – or even *think* about – what was happening while at the Shard. It was far too risky.

It was crazy late when I finally left. Lauren gave me a hug and apologised for the hundredth time and I told her she was not allowed to apologise ever again. Then Sally walked me to the end of their garden path.

'You helped Lauren rescue me, didn't you?' she said. 'From that machine?'

'Yeah,' I said. 'Well, sort of . . . I thought you volunteered?'

'I did,' she said. 'But thank you anyway.'

Chapter Twenty-Eight

I OPENED MY eyes in the clearing, but rather than being scared, I felt happy, like I'd just remembered something excellent was supposed to happen today. It was damp, although it wasn't raining, with a vague threat of sun behind the rolls of grey.

I stood and looked in the direction from which Senia always came, but I couldn't see her. Panic rose in my stomach.

What if she doesn't come?

What if that old guy told everyone?

What if he was her dad or something?

What if—

For several minutes I stood and *what if*'d and I'd almost given up when she appeared, hurrying through the trees, smiling, dressed in green.

'Hi,' I smiled.

'Hi.' She giggled. 'Nice pyjamas.'

'Thanks. They're new.'

'How are you?'

'Not too bad, actually,' I said. 'But, um, I have something to tell you.'

'I thought you might.'

I frowned. 'Why's that?'

'Well, my dad was at the pub last night with a few of his friends. And one of them said he was sure he'd seen someone appear up here yesterday, at around this time. A boy, looking confused and angry. Apparently the boy told him not to worry, it was just a hallucination. Then he vanished.' She raised a significant eyebrow.

'Ah,' I said. 'Yeah. I might have . . . kind of . . . that might have been me.'

Senia rolled her eyes. 'Really?' She chuckled. 'Poor old Hem said he was worried he was losing it. My dad thinks he probably is. But people talk in my town, it's a very small place.'

'Sounds familiar.'

'There were plenty of theories about that mysterious broken tree too. Obviously it doesn't look like someone chopped it down. There've been no storms. And now Hem's tale . . . odd goings-on at the top of the wood . . .' She smiled. 'It's quite fun, being the only one who knows.'

'Anybody anywhere near guessing what's actually happening?'

'Not at all.' She reached into her woollen jacket, which might have been a jerkin – it looked like something an elf might wear anyway – and withdrew a silver hip flask. 'Want some?'

'What is it?'

'Ember,' she said. 'I brew it at home. I'm technically not supposed to, but my dad doesn't say anything, and in return every now and then I find about a bottle's worth has mysteriously gone missing.' She took a nip from the flask and smacked her lips. 'It'll burn your whole self.'

'Sounds great. Although it *is* first thing in the morning for me.' I took a nip. It tasted sort of like what Freeman had given me, but less mature, more burn-y, more like it had been stirred up in an old copper bathtub. 'Phwoar.' I coughed. 'Punchy. Isn't it lunchtime for you?'

'I have the afternoon off.' Senia took another swig and put the flask back in her jacket.

'Got plans?'

'I'm pretty sure I'm close to getting my car started,' she said, taking a seat on some dry grass beneath a tree. I joined her. 'So that's the plan for the rest of the day, after you vanish. I'm hoping that if I can get it road-worthy by the weekend, I can drive to see a band. They're playing about twenty miles away and the trains aren't too great round here.'

'Cool,' I said. 'What's the band?'

'Don't laugh. They're called 56423098652.'

'Wow. What sort of music?'

'It's really intense, technical crash rock built around mathematical scales.'

'Sounds awesome.' I meant it.

Senia laughed. 'It's good for losing yourself to. To be honest, I'm just looking forward to getting away from Dramawn, even for an evening. I love it here, don't get me wrong, everyone knows each other, families go back generations. But you start to . . . itch.'

'I sympathise.'

'Also, generally people get out when they're about sixteen, maybe seventeen,' said Senia. 'I'm nearly nineteen and I'm still here. It's an unwritten rule that if you don't escape by your early twenties at the latest, you're stuck here forever. But I can't really leave my dad . . . I mean, I don't *want* to . . . I just don't want to be here anymore, either.'

I nodded. 'Sounds spookily similar to where I grow up. Little rural time-warp, I used to call it. You have to get out eventually, though. It makes the place nicer to go back to . . . at least, I imagine it would. I've only been back home once and the circumstances were kind of bonkers. But I remember it much more fondly than I thought of it when I lived there. It means you can go somewhere else and you start to forget the bad aspects, you just remember the good stuff.'

'That makes sense.'

'Of course, I wouldn't advise my method of escape,' I said. 'Using your secret superpowers to attack someone in front of a hall full of people, then stealing a car and high-tailing it to the city.'

'I probably wouldn't do that.'

'Sensible.'

'So what have *you* been up to?' she asked. 'I'm sorry I wasn't here yesterday, I couldn't get away. Although that might have been a good thing, what with Hem seeing you.'

'No need to apologise. You've already come to meet me more times than I would have expected. And . . . what have I been up to. It's been fairly . . . a lot. I found my friend. Beat the gang, foiled the plot . . . but that was basically the warm-up act. Now we're going to be taking on the *big* bad guys. We've found out some stuff . . . it's probably going to be messy.'

'Wow,' said Senia. 'Aren't you scared?'

'I am,' I said. 'Which is good. It means I'm taking it seriously. In the past, I've got carried away. Hell, in the last few days I've got carried away. When you feel like you're living a superhero action film, it's easy to get swept along, to feel like you're invincible. But things are getting serious now. And . . . I don't know. I went a bit far trying to find my friend. Did some things . . . yeah. It all got hectic. Could I have some more of that stuff?'

She handed it over. I nipped it. It burned. She laughed. 'Your life really is insane.'

'It is a bit.' Now it was my turn to laugh. 'You know . . . I'm sorry.'

'For what?'

'The image you must have of me, at this point, is of a possibly unhinged, *definitely* mega self-absorbed basket case. I accidentally transport myself between universes, you take time out of your day to come and meet me, and what do you get in return? Me constantly bitching about how hard my life is. It's . . . disrespectful.'

'The novelty hasn't worn off yet,' said Senia. 'When it does, I'll let you know.'

'You don't mind that I travel all the way across universes just to have a moan?'

She laughed. 'If you don't mind, I don't mind. Although it might be nice if we . . . did something sometime. Other than sitting down. Going for a walk maybe. Or you could take me to see your world.'

'I'm not sure how that would work,' I said. *Plus . . . am I ready for that?* 'I did sort of crack it the other day . . . yesterday for you . . . I *think* I made myself go back. Although it was more like sheer force of will than actually *knowing* how to do it . . . but yeah. I'm going to work it out. And I'd be happy to show you round some time. I'd like you to show me round here. I know it might be complicated . . .'

'It would be. But it would be fine too.'

'I'd also love to take you for a fly,' I said.

'A fly?' Her eyes widened. 'You can *fly?*'

'Yeah,' I said. 'I was going to show you, one of the times before I disappeared.'

'I don't believe you.'

'I'm serious,' I grinned. 'It's pretty awesome.'

'I'm so jealous.'

'I'd love to take you . . . but I can't risk it. If I suddenly vanished, you'd just drop out of the sky. Which . . . bad.'

'I get it,' said Senia. 'So yes, maybe let's not try that. You could show me, though?'

'I could,' I said. 'But . . . thinking about it? I'm not sure how that would work if I disappeared. I might reappear stuck halfway through my ceiling or something.'

'Oh,' said Senia. 'Yes, I see what you mean.'

'Sorry. I can definitely fly though, promise.' I smiled. 'Hey, you didn't bring your bow today, did you?'

'No, sorry.'

'Shame. I'd like to have a go.'

'I can teach you sometime. She shoots beautifully.'

'Cool. I'd like that.'

We sat quietly and looked at the trees. I liked that trees were the same in other worlds. Trees were solid. They stayed the same. You could rely on them to be sturdy and gnarled and to have leaves that came and went. It was bizarre how immeasurably better I felt, knowing that trees were the same everywhere. It hadn't really occurred to me before. I was half-expecting my brain to take the piss out of me, call me a hippie weirdo. But it didn't.

And when I re-appeared back in the flat, I felt better.

I almost felt ready.

'I don't understand it at all,' said Sharon. 'It doesn't seem to want food, water, anything like that. It just lies there.' She sighed and drank some tea.

'Have you managed to get anything else from it?' I asked.

'I saw Freeman.'

Knew it.

'I think it was trying to tell me that he was in charge,' said Sharon. 'It's still so hard to interpret what it means with its thoughts. It doesn't use words.'

'Really? That's odd. I've definitely heard them use words before.'

'Maybe it just doesn't want to,' said Connor. 'Can't imagine it's a huge fan of humans at this point.'

'All the patterns are so strange,' said Sharon. 'The thought processes aren't . . . they're not linear. It shows me something that must have happened recently, and at the same time all these other images, tangled together. A place that I think must be its home. A red cave?'

'Yeah,' I said.

'And things,' she said. 'Monsters. Huge. Just . . . wandering.'

'They make them. Create them from pure thought.'

Sharon nodded, as though this were a conversation that normal people might be having. 'One of the many reasons I imagine Freeman wants to control them,' I said. 'Interdimensional travel *and* creating horrific monsters out of thin air? That's some doomsday shit right there.'

Connor shook his head and muttered something fairly obscene.

'Is it still attacking?' I asked. 'Lashing out?'

'Not at me,' said Sharon. 'I think . . . I can't be sure, but it *feels* as though it's happy to see me when I come in.'

'It's let me get close a couple of times,' said Connor. 'I get this kind of . . . paranoia, like I shouldn't be there. Or like there's someone behind me. But it's pretty mild. Think it's getting used to me, at least.'

'I try to give it reassuring thoughts,' said Sharon. 'This

morning, before I went out, I spent about half an hour just sitting, thinking nice things. Beautiful scenery, happy memories, songs.' She laughed. 'It sounds like hippie nonsense. So silly . . .'

Hey, I was seriously vibing with the concept of trees this morning, I can't judge.

'No,' I said. 'Really not silly, actually. Did you get any idea of what Freeman was doing? What happened to the others?'

'No. I think maybe it doesn't want to remember.'

'Fairish. I probably wouldn't either.'

'I'll spend a bit more time with it tomorrow,' said Sharon. 'Don't think I can face any more today. It *is* amazing, connecting with it. Beautiful, in a way. But it's intense. Draining.'

'Don't worry,' I said. 'It's incredible what you're doing. Thank you.'

'Any news at your end?' said Connor.

'Lauren's on board,' I said. 'With doing . . . something. She's doing some recon today, digging around. I'm going to head over to Skank's safe house in a bit. Daryl's given Skank the low-down. You know. On everything.'

'Bet that was awkward,' said Connor. 'What with them living together. Daryl knowing.'

'I thought that,' I said, 'but believe it or not, Daryl said Skank was totally Skank about it. Took it in, nodded, got right on with shit. He's sourcing us some old-fashioned untraceable phones. That'll make it easier to discuss things when we're not face-to-face.'

Connor nodded, stood up and wandered through to the kitchen. I looked at Sharon. 'Mind if I go and talk to him?'

She smiled. 'I'd love it if you did.'

Connor was leaning against the counter, staring out into

the back garden. It was a bright day, sunny, serene. I hovered awkwardly, not entirely sure of what to say.

Feels like I should make the first move . . .

'I know this isn't what you wanted,' I said.

Slight inclination of the head. *Interpretation – questioning.*

'Going up against Angelcorp,' I said. 'Against Freeman. I know you've always wanted to just . . . to stay out of trouble. You thought I posed the biggest risk of bringing all that danger back. You . . . were probably right.'

He seemed to be building up to something, so I stopped talking. *Come on. Throw me a bone.* 'Yeah,' he said.

OK. Good start. Maybe.

'But . . .' he said. 'No.'

OK . . .

'When you first came to us,' he said. 'Me and Eddie . . . we wanted to keep you safe. So we searched for Smiley Joe. To kill him, get him out of the way. Somehow, Eddie knew what would happen. So we tried . . . we didn't want you to have to fight. Obviously that all turned out how it turned out . . . I guess I was angry you didn't show us the same courtesy later on.'

'You had every right to be angry. I shouldn't have pushed to be involved.'

'I get why you did, though. I understand. And I know you never wanted anything bad to happen. I *know* that.' He sighed. 'Look, there's issues . . . we'll either work 'em out or we won't. I've definitely been unfair to you since you've been back. A lot of it . . . I'm not sure I could articulate why, exactly. And I didn't know the full story, although it seems a cop-out to blame it on that. The thing is, I did miss you while you were gone.'

'I think the reality of me isn't quite what it's cracked up

to be.'

Connor laughed. A real laugh, like we used to share. 'Same goes for everyone, I think.'

'I'm sorry,' I said. 'For everything.' Considering what a wide-ranging sentiment that was, it still seemed hopelessly inadequate, but Connor nodded.

'I know,' he said. 'Me too. But . . . yeah, I was building up to a *but*. All of our stuff aside? Freeman has to go.'

'He really does.'

'Eddie wouldn't want him in charge.' Connor's voice shook a little. 'I owe my friend that.'

I nodded.

'And getting rid of the bastard is step *one*. We might well get hurt. Prison . . . who knows. But you can be my witness, right here. Whatever happens . . . it's *my* choice. To do this. To help.'

I nodded again. Partly because I felt like I might cry if I spoke.

'So even if I am a prick again in the future,' said Connor, 'I've admitted in advance that it's not necessarily all your fault.'

I had to laugh at that. 'Cool.' I held out my hand.

We shook.

Skank answered the door, haloed by weed smoke. I raised an eyebrow. 'Afternoon.'

'Afternoon.'

'How's it going?'

'Same as always.'

'That bad, huh?'

We both laughed and he let me through. The weed smell didn't get less pungent. Alex, Faisal and Tara were all sitting on the sofa, surrounded by ashtrays, takeaway cartons and magazines. They all looked, to put it mildly, fucking blazed. And even though it was all flavours of wrong for little Tara to be smoking marijuana, I couldn't help but smile. *Aww. Mates.*

'All right, guys?' I said.

Variously stoned nods.

'How goes it?'

'Better than prison,' said Faisal. 'Seriously, Skank's green is some next shit.'

'Cool.' I nodded at Alex. 'Never pegged you for a smoker.'

He shrugged. 'Used to be, when I was a teenager. Getting back into it.'

'Are you going to lecture me about how I shouldn't do it?' said Tara.

'Nope.'

'Oh. OK. Thanks.'

'No worries.' I took a seat on the floor and Skank pulled up a chair. 'Right. So.' I told them what had transpired between me and Freeman, that I had successfully negotiated them out of prison sentences.

'Awesome,' said Faisal. 'Much appreciated. So . . . we're good?'

'Not exactly,' I said. 'I think you might need to leave town.'

'You what?'

'A group of us . . . we're going to take Freeman down. For good. Which means that whatever deal I struck with him may not apply much longer. So it's probably in your best interests to be elsewhere.'

'Take him down?' said Tara. 'How?'

I gave them a bit of detail, not that there was much at this point, and they listened attentively, passing a joint between them. 'So,' I said. 'I can't guarantee that the deal will hold. I'm sorry.'

Tara didn't seem to know what to say. Alex was as hard to read as ever. Faisal was frowning.

'Skank, I figured you might be able to facilitate this?' I said. 'Getting them somewhere far away?'

'I can,' said Skank.

'Cool,' I said. 'I know it's not ideal, but—'

'Thanks,' said Faisal. 'But I'm staying. And I don't know about these two, but I'd be keen to help.'

I hadn't been expecting that. I'm not sure why. As soon as he said it, it seemed blindingly obvious. 'Help?'

'Strength in numbers, innit,' he said. 'And if I'm honest . . . taking down a legit villain? Kinda more my speed than what we were doing before. No offence, Alex.'

Alex chuckled. 'None taken, mate. It was only my master plan that I spent years working on.'

'Shit plan, bruv.' Faisal let out a stoned giggle. 'Totally awful.' His laughter spread through the other two like wildfire. It even reached me and Skank.

'You could have told me that a year ago,' said Alex, his eyes wet.

'But you were so into it!' said Faisal, who was clutching his sides. 'I felt bad!'

'You're such a prick.'

I caught Tara's eye and she shrugged through her laughter. 'See what I have to put up with?'

It felt good to let the laughter do its thing. By the time it had subsided, I felt like certain important things had been said, like we'd found a cheat code and skipped through a bunch of emotional nonsense.

'But I thought you said all that superhero shit was kids' stuff?' I said.

Faisal shrugged and grinned. 'Why does that have to be a bad thing?'

Legend.

'You realise,' I said, 'that we could all end up in prison. Or worse. I don't even know how it's all going to work. I can't guarantee anyone's safety. Tara . . .'

'You don't need to guarantee anything,' said Tara. 'I'm in.'

Faisal looked at Alex. 'What do you reckon?'

Alex took a deep, thoughtful drag on the remains of the joint. Then he stubbed it out in the ashtray and shrugged. 'Why not? I did sort of help put him in charge. Guess I owe it to . . . everyone.'

Blimey. Three more recruits.

'If you guys are sure,' I said, 'then . . . cool. Awesome.' I grinned at Faisal. 'Be an honour to have Captain England on board.'

He looked away, embarrassed. 'I can't believe I went by that.'

'It's not the worst of the names you guys picked,' said Tara. 'Thor Blimey is *bad*, man. Shocking pun.'

'I quite like Iron Brew,' I said. 'Which, speaking of . . . what happened to her?'

'Skipped town,' said Faisal. 'After we got arrested, she busted us out of the cells. Then said she was leaving the country. Off to fight bad guys. Little Scottish mentalist.'

'How did she bust you out?'

'Crazy shit,' said Faisal. 'Seriously, she was always . . .

y'know. *Crazy.* Pretty sure she teleported us.'

'*Teleported?*' said Skank, sounding as though he'd only just woken up.

'Can't explain it any other way,' said Faisal. 'One minute I was in my cell, next minute me and her appear outside. First time she'd ever done it. She was pretty freaked out. Didn't stick around long.'

'You weren't tempted to go with her?' I asked.

He shrugged. 'London's my home, man.'

I wanted to stay. I had more questions, for all of them. I wanted to share a joint with an ex-Chavenger, and a guy who I had nearly beaten to death for unleashing a plague of monsters on the world, and Tara, who was now nearly the same age as me.

But this seemed to have turned into a recruiting mission.

Which meant I needed to speak to a certain journalist.

He walked along an uneven stone path suspended between two cliffs, beneath a dark purple sky laced with spiders' legs of lightning. The air was heavy, sulphuric, and somewhere he was sure he could hear singing.

'Nice place for it,' he said, knowing he would be heard. 'Pretty dramatic.' He reached the end of the path and ran his hand over the wooden door set awkwardly into the rock. It was marked with some arcane inscription. It would have taken barely a thought for him to tear the door to splinters, but he knew his quarry wasn't behind it.

He looked up, kicked off and flew, taking his time. There was no need to rush; he would derive no pleasure from what was to come. When he reached the peak of the cliff he stopped, hanging in the garish sky, its colours reminding him of the cover of some cheap, lurid pulp fantasy novel.

His quarry sat on a throne of bones atop a carpet of skulls, his red velvet cloak crumpled around his hunched shoulders. An apple flew from his left palm to his right palm, as if of its own accord, and before him lay a dead girl in a lace coffin, her lips frozen in an eternal smile. He was crooning a lullaby, too softly for the new arrival to discern the words.

'You have to stop,' said the new arrival, floating forwards, hands behind his back.

The boy in the cloak took a bite of the apple and glanced up at the being who shared his face. Another boy, who was not really a boy. 'Why now?' he asked. 'After everything? Why was this the last straw? Why not the world before this? Or the one before that?'

'I don't have to justify myself to you,' said the other, calmly.

388

He dropped out of the air and landed nimbly on the macabre, makeshift floor, skulls cracking beneath his boots. 'I gave you more than enough chances. You chose to keep destroying.'

'Destruction's all there is,' said the boy. 'Ultimately. Nothing lasts. Everything dies, one day. Except us. So obviously our role is to destroy. What other conclusion could I come to?'

'Something a bit less fucking bleak, possibly?' said the other.

'Let's just fight, shall we?' The boy stood up. 'I've had enough conversations with you for infinite lifetimes.'

'All right,' said the other. 'If we must.'

The battle that followed lasted for days. They fought with their brains, with the elements, with the very mountains through which they flew, tearing apart jagged peaks and hurling them like great javelins. They drew blood without touching, striking with false memories and anger concentrated into great glowing abstract shapes that split the sky like lightning. By the time the battle was over, the sky was burning and the world itself – or what was left of it – bled.

The survivor looked at the debris, the silent smoking chaos, for a few seconds, then closed his eyes. He knew what he was looking for and found it with ease.

He disappeared . . .

. . . and reappeared, floating outside a window. It was the only lit window in this house, a nondescript house on a quiet country street, with dark woods on one side. Through the window he saw a boy lying on his back, in the throes of an incandescent headache.

The boy who was not a boy smiled and murmured something that nobody heard.

'Happy birthday, Stanly. We hope you like your present.'

Chapter Twenty-Nine

'Hello?'

'Hi, Stanly. Sorry, did I wake you?'

'Lauren? No, I've been awake for a while. Weird dreams. You OK?'

'Don't let anything on from your side of this conversation. Non-committal responses, no detail, no information. Your flat *is* bugged.'

'OK . . .'

'I'm sorry. I was sure it wasn't. It . . . well technically it's the flat below that's bugged, but Freeman can still hear everything you say, loud and clear.'

'Cool.'

'I think that must be why he wants to keep you around, why he let you off after the whole thing with Alex. He heard our conversation the other day, you talking about travelling between universes. That's his goal. That's what he wants to use you for, and the shimmers.'

'Probably.'

'I have more information. Lots more. But we all need to meet, everyone who's going to be involved. Tonight.'

'OK.'

'You said Sharon and Connor were happy for us to congregate at their place?'

'Uh-huh.'

'Seven tonight. Can you arrange that?'

'Sure.'

'If I don't hear from you, I'll assume we're on.'

'Cool.'

'OK. Thanks. I . . . I can't believe we're doing this.'

'Same here.'

'See you later.'

'Yep. Bye.'

I evacuated post-haste so I could talk freely, confirming to-night's meeting with Sharon then informing the rest of the Justice League when and where we would be assembling (yes, I know the Justice League don't assemble, so don't bother writing in). Plans made, I suddenly had a whole day to fill. I didn't really want to return to the flat, so after nearly an hour of mindless non-planning over a greasy fry-up in a nearby café, I decided to have a wander around the city. See what was afoot. Plus, it always used to work when I felt pensive and loose end-y like this.

It was a nice day, not terribly warm but bright, and as I strolled, hands in pockets, I just let my brain do its thing, whirling back and forth between the conflicting, confusing thoughts that jostled for position. I still hadn't worked up the courage to call Kloe, which was fairly unforgivable, although at least I'd spoken to Mum finally. That had been an intense conversation, one I hadn't really allowed myself to dwell upon. She'd cried so much, made me promise to come home. She couldn't understand why I wasn't there already.

You and me both, Ma.

I made myself promise to do the right thing and phone Kloe soon, and my thoughts turned naturally to Tara. Little em-powered badass. Well, not so little. Was I being irresponsible, bringing her on board? Undoubtedly. But then again, it wasn't really up to me. She'd have fought to be included anyway.

Just like me.

What were the consequences going to be, though? An unregistered empowered involved with something like this? And then there was the matter of Oliver and Jacqueline. What would become of Tara when the smoke cleared?

Which led my tumble of thoughts to Angelcorp. As powerful as any organisation on the planet and in dire need of taking down . . . or was it? Did it just need new management? *Could* it even be taken down? Were things actually that easy in reality? Defeating the bad guys? Surely if there was one thing I'd learned, it's that things just weren't that simple?

Leading us back to . . . me.

Stanly Bird. Confused, eighteen. *Going on twenty-three.* Out of time, superpowered and unable to decide on anything. Occasionally disappearing and reappearing in some clearing and chatting up a rather fetching local parallel-universe dweller. Stanly Bird, who liked to think of himself as a crusader for good, a moral person, a force for smiles. Stanly Bird, who fought dirty and threatened to wipe precious memories in order to get . . . where?

I walked across a pedestrian bridge, trying to remember why it looked familiar . . .

Of course. An assassin tried to hurl me off here once.

That made me laugh. An assassin paid for by Freeman to make me think the Angel Group were after me so I'd help to take them down so he could take over.

He couldn't have thought of a simpler plan?

I walked through a market full of clothes and food stalls, empowered performers juggling and playing instruments with no hands, tall men and women in bright outfits showing off gadgets whose functions I couldn't begin to fathom. Superpowered London. My London. Not my London. *She's sort of yours but never quite yours.*

Kinda like before.

I passed 110th Street, or what should have been 110th Street, now just a spot where two half-constructed buildings met.

Moments and times of your life just fall from the tree and get swept away . . .

And suddenly you don't have a clue what's going on.

Except you do.

One thing. One definite. Maybe the only one.

Freeman goes.

After that . . . we'll see.

I stayed out all day, wandering, entirely losing track of time. When I checked my phone on the way back to the flat, I saw that Sharon had texted me a while ago. Apparently Tara had gone round early with Skank. They were having tea. It was 'a bit awkward but lovely too'.

I smiled. *Sweet . . .*

And BALLS it's nearly seven.

I rode the elevator up, fumbling in my pocket for my keys and thinking *shit, gonna be late for my own do, need to grab stuff.* I felt like I should have been tired from the walk, or that I should have come to some conclusions, or both, or neither. But all I really felt was vaguely more cheerful and slightly confused as to why.

I stepped into the flat and an invisible force dragged me to the living room. It flipped me over, smashing me through my coffee table, and for a second I thought I *should be defending myself,* but now I could see that there was oil dripping from the ceiling, filling the room with the stink of dead fish and dead cities and dead *people*, and the things that lived in them, and the walls were old ripped wood with rusty nails poking out, nails on which people had hung and suffered and died . . .

Something made me stand up and walked me to the centre of a cold, bloody brick room. I could see faces, huge faces, big as worlds, laughing screaming insane eye-popping gouged-cheek clown faces, gargantuan tongues unrolling in spattering streams of acid saliva. I stared, transfixed, knowing this had to be it, this had to be it, I was gone, I had lost myself, I was . . .

Two people stepped out of the darkness, taller than anyone I'd ever seen before. Two . . . no, *three* . . . one was tall, spiky black hair . . . *Leon* . . . *should have recognised the smell of his power* . . . and then there was a girl, hair as black as Leon's, blacker, if that was possible, but long and impossibly silky, skin so pale . . . *Rosie.* She wore a red skirt and a white hooded top and there was nothing in her eyes and behind her danced an army of shadows, each one the shape of an atrocity: this one the mad glare that burned down an orphanage, that one the black static in a killer's mind . . .

I recognised the third person too. He stood, towering above me, the law in human form, all blue and shining, eyes full of deathly light.

Morgan.

'Surprise.' He smiled and his smile filled the room, swallowed the room, regurgitating us on top of a mountain that rose from a hissing boiling stinking fetid blood sea, a mountain that had stabbed its way up through the heart of the Earth and let the world decay and dissolve around it, leaving nothing but blood, endless blood, *oh God, so much blood* . . .

Morgan stood over me and aimed a kick that reverberated

through my past, present and the darkness that was my lack of a future. The girl, Rosie, just stared down, implacable, not smiling, not scowling, not enjoying what was happening, not *not* enjoying it, she was just *nothing, nothing nothing nothing* . . . at least I could feel Leon's anger and his satisfaction, at least that was *something* . . .

'You thought you'd got away with it, didn't you?' said Morgan. 'Thought you were above the law.' The law was above me now, a rising beast, all claws, tearing at my clothes, shredding them around me, leaving me a quivering naked child, unable to speak, unable to even think, too full up with horror, with terror, with with with with—

'You never know,' he said. 'Maybe they'll give me your job now.'

Rosie just stared at me, blank-faced jailer at the head of a nightmarish crowd, all the writhing pitiful victims of every crime I'd never stopped, all the whimpering sobs that faded into the blackness when no-one came to help them, all the unanswered tragedies and agonies, they all danced for Rosie and they cowered because they were scared of her and oh God I was so scared of her, *so* scared—

Flash.

There I was, looking.

Flash.

There I was, looking at *me.*

Flash.

There I was, my own ghost, smiling.

Flash.

Winking . . .

FLASH!

I opened my eyes. I was in my living room, lying on the

shattered remains of the coffee table, three unconscious figures on the floor around me. I got unsteadily to my feet, my heart racing as though I'd just woken up from a night terror.

I looked down at them. Morgan, although he wasn't any-where near as tall as he had been a minute ago. Leon, quiet and crumpled, breathing regularly. And next to them, in white hoody and red skirt, Rosie. I didn't want to imagine the sort of things she might dream about.

What did I do?

Must have . . .

'Ha,' I said, weakly. 'That'll teach you to mess with me.'

'Yes,' I said. 'It will.'

Eh?

It was me who said it. My voice. But it wasn't *me*, or any of the voices that lived in my brain, jostling for attention.

It came from behind me.

I turned around, already kind of knowing what I was going to see.

'All right, Stanly,' smiled Stanly. 'How's it going?'

PART THREE

Chapter Thirty

'HI,' I SAID, perfectly normally, as anyone would in such a perfectly normal situation.

He was me. Utterly me. Well. Slightly different. He might have been a couple of years older, though I couldn't be sure, and he either took even less care with his hair than me or took an awful lot of care making it look like he didn't take any care with it. Was he taller? Possibly. Or I might have been imagining it. He was wearing all black – black trainers, black jeans, black suit jacket and hoody over a black T-shirt – and he was grinning. It was quite a grin, too. Not a shit-eating grin, exactly. It was a grin that knew a lot. An awful lot more than me.

'Sorry,' he said, nodding at the three unconscious figures on the floor. 'Have they been here long?'

I looked down at them. I'd kind of forgotten they were there. 'Um . . .'

'I'd have taken them out before, but I was tied up. Something overran.'

Something overran . . . huh? 'Um,' I said again. 'It's . . . um . . . do you know why they're here?'

'They came to take you out.'

Evidently.

'Don't suppose you noticed that the security guard was AWOL?' said Stanly. I hadn't. 'All the bugs have been de-activated too. Local drones re-directed. Nice quiet murder scene. Looks like Angelcorp have decided you're one loose end too many.'

'Looks like.' For some reason, I didn't feel terribly bothered about that. The unutterable terror I'd felt barely a minute before, the realisation that Freeman really did want me out of the way . . . it was all a bit *meh* now. 'So,' I said. 'You're me. From another universe.'

'I am.' He held out his hand. 'Pleased to meet you.'

Defo should have said 'pleased to meet me'.

I shook hands with myself. It was as shaking hands with oneself was probably supposed to be. Possibly.

'Pleased to *officially* meet you, I should say,' said Stanly. 'I've actually been watching you for a long time.'

That's not weird at all. 'Really? Why?' *And how long, exactly?*

'I like to keep track of my counterparts in other realities,' said Stanly. 'Make sure they're keeping well.'

My mind flashed back to the others I'd seen. The Stanly who was shot in the public toilet, before calmly removing the bullet. The Stanly fighting tanks in the desert. The older Stanly, overwhelmed by monsters.

'You showed me them,' I said. 'It was you, wasn't it? You sent me on that trip through the other universes.'

He nodded. 'I had a feeling you were about to have the rug swept out from under you.'

'So you thought you'd pre-empt it with some rug-sweeping of your own?'

'Yeah,' he said. 'I plucked your consciousness out of your body. Took it for a ride.'

As you do. 'OK . . . but . . . Senia. In her world, I could speak. I had a body.'

Stanly nodded. There was a hint of something in his eyes. Was it embarrassment? 'Yeah. That wasn't supposed to happen.'

'Oh?'

'Accident,' he said. 'You put up more resistance than I was expecting. I had a much longer, wider-ranging trip planned, but you kept managing to break free, bring your body and your consciousness back together. Obviously you didn't really know what you were doing, so you ended up materialising randomly in another world.'

'But I keep on materialising there.'

He nodded.

'Why?'

'You've tied yourself to it, somehow,' said Stanly. 'I'm honestly not totally sure how it works. Dimensional travel is some pretty out-there shit. All I know is that part of you is linked to her world.'

'So it *is* me. I've been doing it.'

'Subconsciously. I think maybe you feel safe there. They're fascinating, those sorts of connections. You've probably dreamed about other Stanlys without even really realising it. Maybe you thought you were dreaming about yourself. Maybe you saw something before it happened. Ever get the feeling that you've encountered *slightly* too many coincidences?'

Holy what. 'OK,' I said. 'Well . . . yeah. Um. Maybe before we get into that . . . you pulled me out of the shimmer world, right?'

'I did.'

'Which, presumably, you could have done whenever you wanted?'

He nodded.

'Why did you let it go on for so long, then? Why didn't you just—'

'I didn't want to interfere, at first.'

'But you had a nice long think about it then decided you would?'

'Let's go on another trip,' he said. 'I'll show you some more stuff. Stuff that'll make your head go . . .' He made his eyes spin around and around in their sockets. It was deeply creepy.

'Um,' I said. 'Kinda got some stuff going on here . . .'

'It's fine,' he said. 'I'll bring you back to this point. You won't miss anything.'

Jeeeeeesus. Is he serious?

'If you really don't want to go . . .' he said.

'You'll take me anyway?'

That grin again.

'Fine,' I said. 'Let's go.'

We didn't move, but we were suddenly somewhere else, floating in the air, hundreds, thousands of feet above the ground. It was glorious daylight and there were bright red birds in the sky and a city below. Stanly was flying next to me and I was glad to see that I had a body, he hadn't just taken my mind for a quick jaunt. He winked at me and started to descend, fast.

Rightio, you feckin' smartarse.

Let's see who's faster.

I dived, shooting past him easily. Wind and space, thermals, gravity and lack of same. These essentials, things I understood so well, made my confusion and anger fade.

A little.

'This way!' he called, overtaking and descending rapidly. I followed and we levelled off, flying about fifty feet above the spires of the city. It looked sort of like Dubai, or possibly a Dubai that had been spliced with Las Vegas, because the astonishingly tall, svelte skyscrapers were covered in gaudy holograms and neon adverts for things that I couldn't imagine going down too well in Dubai. After a minute we stopped in the air in front of an apartment building, and through a massive picture window I saw another Stanly sitting cross-legged a few feet off the floor, juggling shiny black balls with his mind. He was older than both of us, with very long hair and an expression of such deep contentment that I felt chilled out just looking at him.

'I gave him his powers,' said Stanly. 'Ten years ago. He was travelling across Eurasia at the time, backpacking, getting into scrapes. He'd lost someone back home. He was drinking. Fighting. Well . . . mostly getting his arse handed to him, to be honest. I found him, showed him a few things. Unlocked the power in his mind. Now he teaches younger people how to control theirs. He's been instrumental in bringing powereds and non-powereds together here.'

'Ten years ago?' *You've aged pretty well.*

'From his perspective. At this point.'

'What do you mean?'

He shot back up and I followed, matching his pace, flying alongside him, two halves of my brain battling between *what in the name of everything is going on* and *this is* COOL.

'I've travelled through more parallel universes than I can count,' he said. 'Well . . . technically not, I can remember all of them. But it's a fearsome number and as far as I can tell, they keep coming. And they don't move in relation to one another. At this precise moment in *this* universe, everything that has ever happened and will ever happen in other universes is happening at the same time. When I travel, I can pick which point I want to go to. Requires a bit of finesse, but . . .' He turned and sailed gracefully back down and I darted after him.

'So you can basically travel in time,' I said.

'In a manner of speaking.'

Holy shitbiscuits. 'How old are you?'

'Old. But I keep myself looking young. And I don't get ill. Any time anything in my body starts to decay or malfunction or generally become unhealthy, I just look inside and repair it. Anything, from a stab wound to the effects of alcohol to a cancer, it can all be reversed. I just *think* . . . and it's gone.'

So he's pretty much immortal, too.

No wonder he's a bit up himself.

'Let's go somewhere else,' he said. As with travelling to Senia's world, I wasn't aware of anything changing, but all of a sudden we weren't flying anymore, we were standing on some huge structure, overlooking a desert. I could see pyramids.

'You brought me here before,' I said.

He nodded. 'The Stanly here is a legendary hero. A warrior. We're standing on—'

'His statue?'

'They're all over the planet. Everyone in this world knows his name.'

Sounds great.

Must be a nightmare going to the shop.

Now we were in the air a few hundred feet above another city. This one looked like somebody had thrown the *Star Wars* prequels and *Blade Runner* into a blender.

'There's a Stanly here who fights for the rights of mutated humans,' said Stanly.

'You're screwing with me now, surely?'

'I'm not.' He laughed. 'I was pretty gobsmacked when I first got here, to be honest. Thought the likelihood of finding another Stanly in such a different world was slim to non-existent . . . but I immediately knew there was one. I can always tell. So I sought him out. Turned out, funnily enough, that *he* was from a different universe in the first place. He'd just set up shop here, staying anonymous, fighting the good fight. I didn't reveal myself to him. He was getting on just fine without me.'

'So you travel across worlds and give power to Stanlys who don't have it? Why? Are you putting together a League of Stanlys? In case one day there's an impossible multiverse-threatening crisis that needs the combined might of all the Stanlys to defeat it? Do we get masks and capes and rings? Is there an oath?'

He laughed again, louder and longer. 'I wish. That'd be pretty sweet. We could all meet on a beagle-shaped space station or something. No, to be honest, world-ending threats like that are few and far between. Your monster apocalypse is one of only a couple of honest-to-God Armageddons I've ever witnessed. Mostly, it's just day to day dangers.'

'Then why do you do it?'

'To make sure that we're special,' said Stanly. 'To know that we're making a difference. There obviously isn't a Stanly in every world, but there are still plenty to go round. And I want them all to have the opportunity to be amazing. You see, when I first worked out how to travel between worlds, I just had fun. Bags of it. Went from world to world, having adventures, meeting people, getting into trouble. It was wicked. Sort of like *Doctor Who* but with way more sex and violence. But eventually I started to wonder: were there other versions of me? What were they doing? So I sought them out, and I kept finding them frustrated. Wishing for more. Like I had been, once. And it gave me an idea.'

'Give them powers.'

'Potential superheroes in each of their worlds,' said Stanly. 'I was starting to feel the *great power, great responsibility* burden at this point, after a *lot* of superpowered hedonism. Thinking seriously about re-styling myself a world-saver. And I figured, what the hell, if I couldn't save every other world, I could at least give other Stanlys the opportunity to save them.'

Fair point. Entirely monumentally catastrophically mental, but fair.

We were somewhere else now, standing on a beach watching a cerulean ocean sweep away into the distance, the reflections of a moon and sun shimmering in the blue.

Shimmering . . .

'Did you kill them?' I asked.

'Who?'

'The shimmers. They saw something, just before you took me out of the dream. A shadow. Then when I got back, they were all dead.'

'Ah,' said Stanly. 'Yeah.' He was staring at the water, making waves rear up in horse shapes with his mind. 'That was an accident.'

'You like your little accidents, don't you?'

'No. I don't. But if you never have them, it makes them that much more unexpected when they *do* happen. As far as I can work out, the shimmers killed themselves. The shock of your mind suddenly disappearing sent them into overload. Like feedback, discharging through them. A sudden wave of nightmares, frying them all. I didn't realise until it was too late.'

'So it *was* you.'

'I said it was an accident.' Stanly shook his head. The sea rose, parted and fell. 'I couldn't possibly have known it would happen.'

I felt sick. 'A whole species. Dead. So you could take me on a little trip through your favourite parallel worlds.'

'Don't,' said Stanly.

I glared at him. 'What if I don't believe you?'

'What if you don't believe me.'

'My presence was the main thing stopping the shimmers from unleashing the monsters again. You probably wanted to avoid that side effect. Maybe you killed them on purpose.'

'You really think that?' I couldn't interpret his tone at all. Defensive? Guilty? Nonchalant? All or none of the above?

'I really don't know, mate,' I said. 'We've just met. I mean, I'd like to think you wouldn't have done it on purpose . . .'

'Thanks for that.' He snapped his fingers and we were in another sky, a night sky filled with billions of stars, above miles of foreign countryside.

'How long have you been watching me?' I asked.

'Since you first got your powers,' said Stanly. 'I've been keeping an eye. Watching your progress.'

'The whole time?' *Creepy.*

Also . . . is that a bell ringing . . .

'Well,' said Stanly. 'Obviously not the *whole* time. I'm not a weirdo.'

'Could have fooled me.'

'I kept coming back to check,' he said. 'See how you were doing. And bloody hell, you've done well.'

'Have I?'

'You're the only Stanly I've ever encountered who came by his powers by accident,' said Stanly. 'Apart from me.'

Now I remembered. A dream I'd had the other night, like a remixed version of an older dream, a battle between two Stanlys, huge and terrible . . .

And then one of them, the victor, *this* one, I was sure of it, floating outside a window.

My window.

Did he give me my powers?

'The only one?' I said.

Why is he lying to me?

'Every other Stanly has either had his powers as a gift from me or from another Stanly.' My doppelgänger looked at me, and his smile was gone and his face was suddenly hundreds of years old and I didn't understand him at all.

'What about that one you were talking about before?' I said. 'The one who fights for mutants, or whatever? You said he already had his powers.'

'Yes,' said Stanly. 'And I traced him back to a world practically identical to yours. He even had the same bedroom as you. And there I saw *another* Stanly – one I recognised, because I'd given him *his* powers – secretly gifting him with his.' He smiled. 'Told you this stuff would make your head spin.'

Is he reading my mind?

Probably.

So he could well be lying.

But why?

Why is he trying to make me feel special?

'So you see,' said Stanly. 'I've had a particular interest in you from the beginning.'

'Why are you showing me all of this?' I said. 'Why have you suddenly decided to reveal yourself?'

'Because it's time you started thinking big.' We were

408

elsewhere again, flying across the ocean at dawn. The cold salt breeze was heady.

'I know you've been feeling it,' he said. 'What we all feel eventually. Like you've hit a wall, like the world's suddenly got too small, too tight, too constrictive. When you've started to just play the part you think you should be playing.'

'What part should I be playing, then?'

'You could *rule* your world,' said Stanly.

'Whatever, mate.'

'Why not?' he said. 'I ruled mine.'

Never mind heady, now I felt dizzy. *He's mad.*

'Not in an evil way,' he said, so mild, so matter-of-fact. 'But I saw what was wrong. I saw problems, errors of judgment, appalling failures and misconceptions at every level. And systematically, I made it all better. Nobody wants for anything in my world anymore. Because I realised that this power, this thing we have, this impossible presence in our minds, it is *ultimate*. Ultimate mastery over matter, over mind, over *everything.*'

We were still flying, but now we were above a mountain range, majestic peaks crowned with snow. Stanly pointed at the top of one mountain and with a deep rumble its jagged top started to rise, ripped from its foundations, its ancient link to the Earth severed. We slowed down to watch as the broken peak began to rotate.

'Matter,' said Stanly. 'I can do whatever I want with it. Thoughts. Not matter, exactly, but I can do whatever I want with them. Part of it is affecting neurons and synapses and poking the right bits of brain, but it's also understanding, having the subtlety to manipulate things so beyond the physical that words aren't adequate to describe them. Marching into a building where the world's richest men are planning another round of exploitation, looking them in the eye and filling their minds with something different. Sucking out the greed, the hunger for profit regardless of cost. Replacing it with something better.' He replaced the peak gently on top of the mountain.

'You have the right to judge that?' I said. 'Whose brains you can alter? Which impulses shouldn't be allowed?'

'You're still thinking small.' I squinted, my eyes adjusting to new brightness: we were walking across a field in broad daylight, a tank battle blazing around us. Explosions everywhere, tearing hot clods of flaming earth from the ground and scattering them. Somehow, I wasn't worried. The sounds were slightly muffled and Stanly spoke clearly over them.

'You've done a bit of mind messing lately,' he said, 'but it's small-scale stuff. Necessary evils. Using an "unfair" advantage to get the correct result. Because in *your* perception, you don't have the right to just make up their minds for them. Change their thoughts. Because you're still operating at their level. You could have gone into Matthew Crane's brain and made him the best, most loving father and husband ever. But you didn't. The fact is, you have the power to reshape the *planet*. And the minds of everyone on it. Normal rules absolutely, one hundred per cent *do not* apply to you anymore.'

'Everyone has the potential to have this power, though . . .'

'You got there first.' Stanly raised his hands and fifty tanks were blasted backwards, but before they had time to hit the ground we were standing next to a waterfall, overlooking an endless expanse of jungle. Somewhere amongst the trees, I was sure I could see a dragon moving. 'Your friend Alex made some good points,' said Stanly. 'Your world isn't just going to change because an opportunity gets dropped in its lap. Unfortunately, the majority of the worlds I have seen work along the same lines. Our power is the next step. Alex's plan was just a bit too . . . dunno. Un-planned. Did he really think that once everyone had powers, they were all going to sit down and carve out a new future? No. Never going to happen. Humans need to be led. They need to be shown. Occasionally they need to overthrow whoever is leading or showing them, but that only happens if the person in question is weak enough to be overthrown. You don't have to be weak. You can be grand, powerful, on a cosmic scale. You can be the emperor of your world. Not just a kid from Tref-y-Celwyn who used to draw zombies.'

'I can't be that big,' I said. 'Even if I wanted to be, I don't have it in me. I don't *know* enough. I don't know how the world works, how the hell am I supposed to change it on that kind of scale?'

'You know right from wrong.'

'Barely.'

'All it takes is will,' said Stanly. 'The will to *think big*.'

'Well sorry, but I don't have it.'

'Give it time. You were itching already. I could feel it, you could feel it. You wanted something different. Something that wasn't meetings and secrets and corporations and vested interests and little puny plottings. You wanted something else.'

'That could just have been to move to the country and settle down.'

'It could be,' said Stanly. 'But that would be a shocking waste of potential.'

'So this was your plan? Wait for me to start getting itchy

411

feet and then pluck me out into the multi-dimensional wilderness for a lecture on thinking big?'

'I just wanted you to realise that you're special.'

'People keep telling me that.'

'People like Freeman?'

'Yeah.'

'Because it's true,' said Stanly. 'He recognises it. That's probably why he's decided to turn on you now. And your plan? To take him down, because he's a bad guy? You could be going *so* much bigger with it. Angelcorp may be trying to push things in the right direction but it's still as riddled with corruption and conflict as ever. You could take control of it, if you wanted. Drive it forward into a *genuinely* great future.'

'Take control?' I said. 'Rename it Stanly Inc, or something? You must be joking. And anyway, I'm taking down Freeman because his crimes are too great to go unpunished. Because he's *dangerous*. If he manages to harness the power of the shimmers . . . can't let it happen. He has to go.'

The other me shook his head. 'You're built to be bigger.'

'I'm just another person with powers. It could just as easily be Lauren. Could have been Alex, eventually.'

'It's not them, though,' he said. 'It's you. You. Can. Do. *Anything.*'

'I *know* that.' I flew off and he came after me but I sped up, ducking and diving, rolling, flying as fast as I could between the jagged peaks and majestic curves, watching the remains of the sun bleed on the snow.

'You *don't* know it,' said Stanly, out loud and in my head. 'You've touched the surface. Flying. Moving things. Affecting people. But it doesn't stop there. It doesn't *stop*, period. You can level entire mountain ranges and re-form them into

Möbius strips. Reverse global warming with your *mind*, rather than scaring politicians and energy companies into doing the right thing. Go inside a murderer's head and turn the urge to kill into the urge to paint. Delete cancer from someone's body.'

'I'll have to try that.' I dived, down, down, down, pulling up at the last minute, then as I flew across the snow I gathered it up with my mind, building great balls and rolling them along, leaving flurries dissipating in the chilled air. Soon I reached another titanic drop and stopped, alighting softly on the snow, making sure I barely made a footprint.

'I'm not saying you'll be ready immediately,' said Stanly. 'You need to travel. Learn. Practise. Of course. But your brain holds the power to re-make universes. Nothing is impossible for you anymore.'

'Maybe,' I said, building a snow Stanly with my brain. 'But . . . I can't comprehend it. I just can't. Maybe I don't have the software. The hardware, yeah. That can re-make universes, or whatever. But I'm just running a regular eighteen-year-old geek operating system. I'm not ready.' I looked at the snow-Stanly's confused face for a moment, then let the wind blow it away.

'Key word there? *Ready.*' Stanly smiled. 'Maybe you're not now. But you could be.'

'I don't know if I *want* to be.'

'And that's OK,' said Stanly. 'I'm not going to make you. You'll do extraordinary things, whatever happens, whether you decide to pay attention to me or tell me to get knotted. But I just want you to understand.'

'I do.' I *thought* I did. Who the hell knew, though?

We stood on the snow and watched the sun set between the mountains. After a minute, Stanly spoke again. 'There's so much awesomeness out there. So much to see. It's frustrating, seeing you still rolling around in the dirt with animals.'

'Animals? Do you mean people?'

'Poor choice of words.'

'Revealing, more like.'

Another new world, a great red rock plain beneath a swirling pre-storm sky. It was heavy with psychic stink, a crushing atmosphere of melancholy, the residue of ancient atrocities.

'Where's this to, then?' I asked, trying to sound bright.

'I didn't say all the awesomeness was good,' said Stanly. 'I mean, you know what the word "awesome" actually means, don't you?'

'Inspiring of awe.'

'Yeah. And bad stuff does that too.'

'You mean there are bad guys out there. Bad people. Bad *animals*.'

'And more,' said Stanly. 'Worse. You remember the shimmer world? That's nowhere *near* as weird as it gets. There are places out there in the wilderness that would turn your heart cold and drive the light from your eyes. And the things that live in them . . . that rule over them . . . you can't even imagine.'

I shivered, remembering that place. It felt like a dream, rather than somewhere I'd walked through, run through, flown through. The shapes I'd seen, indistinct grumbling giants. *Alien gods . . .*

And now there were footsteps coming from behind us, footsteps that shook this world, wherever it was. I moved to turn around but Stanly put a hand on my shoulder.

'Don't look behind you,' he said.

With pleasure. 'I think I get the point of this exercise,' I said. 'Can we go now?'

He nodded and we were gone again, flying above the sea.

OK, breezy subject change to distract me from the mind-melting cosmic horror.

'So,' I said. 'Got a girl?'

'Had a few.'

'I'm sure. Any special ones?'

'Of course,' said Stanly. 'In one world, I lived a whole life with a girl called Olivia. Loved her. Grew old. She said she wanted us to live normally, free of power. So I agreed, and we did. And when she died . . . I grew young again. And I left.' The feelings behind the smile he wore made me feel nauseous, they ran so unfathomably deep.

So much for a breezy subject change.

We flew without speaking for a few minutes while I tried to think of more questions. Not that there weren't billions to be asked . . . I just didn't know where to start.

And I'd been struck by an image, like a memory but not quite, of an old man watching an old lady quietly pass away, then shrugging off his age, becoming young again.

Disappearing.

Another dream . . .

But not for him.

Chapter Thirty-One

I SKIMMED A stone, using my power to continue the skim long after it should have sank, making it flip and skitter all the way upstream, bouncing off mossy, half-submerged rocks like a little hard fish at play. Stanly was lounging on the grass building a pile of rocks, lazily conducting them with one finger. It was a good forty feet high by now.

We were in his world, in his favourite city. Hope City. Yeah. I know, right? I'd sniggered and he'd shrugged. 'I asked the people what they wanted it to be called. They voted overwhelmingly for Hope City.'

'Sometimes maybe the people shouldn't be allowed to decide things. In fact, you may have just convinced me that superpowered dominion over the affairs of all is actually the most humane approach.'

Stanly had laughed and we'd skimmed stones. This park was at the very centre of the city, an enormous area of greenery bigger than any in London, with some of the most astounding plant life I'd ever seen. Great purple flowers that looked like they should have been growing at the bottom of the sea, yellow bushes that flexed in time with the movement of the sun, spindly silver trees around which wound bright red creepers, secreting a velvety lavender smell. People ran back and forth, frolicking with chattering pets and playing complex games with hovering balls, while a crew of colourfully-dressed vagabonds on a cathedral-shaped bandstand played some indecently funky music, all bass and brass.

'I love this park.' Stanly let go of his tower of rocks, watching it tumble into the river as if in slow motion.

'It is pretty sweet,' I said. 'Why aren't people running up to you? Getting on their knees and thanking you for turning their world into a paradise?'

'I've changed our faces. Don't want any distractions.' He took a deep, contented breath. 'Do you want to see some more?'

I kind of did, but I was also starting to think about my world again. 'There'll be repercussions,' I said. 'Freeman, Angelcorp . . . I should get back. Try and sort them out.'

'You want to go back now?' He sounded disappointed, like he didn't want his playmate to go home.

'Miles to go, yo.'

'I can help, if you want.'

'How?' I didn't necessarily hate the idea of having an all-powerful superbeing on my side, but I was far from sold on his trustworthiness.

'I could take you back to an earlier point,' said Stanly.

Huh? 'Like when?'

'Whenever you want,' he said. 'I could take you back five and a half years, moments after you closed the doorway to the shimmer dimension. You could rejoin your friends. Find Kloe. Live the years you lost. Or I could take you back further. I could put you back in your own head when you were sixteen. The night of *Romeo and Juliet*. You'd know not to use your powers on Ben King. You could carry on with the play, with your normal life.'

With Kloe . . .

'Or I could drop you back a few days,' said Stanly. 'You could get a head start on Freeman.'

I was still mired in thoughts of myself at sixteen, triumphantly leaving the stage after the first act, flushed and excited. The way people had come up to me bearing bright-eyed congratulations. The way it felt like my life was just beginning. The way Kloe had looked at me, even if I hadn't been sure it was the look I thought it was . . . although now I knew it *had* been . . .

I could go back there.

No Freeman. No Smiley Joe. No apocalypse. No fear and heartbreak and uncertainty. No violence. No stains on my soul. I could live the meandering indie version of my life rather than the insane superhero blockbuster.

But . . .

'I'd remember everything,' I said. 'If you took me back. I'd remember everything that's happened since.'

'You wouldn't have to,' said Stanly. 'I could take those memories, if you wanted. Pluck them out like grey hairs.'

Jesus . . .

'It would mean giving up, though,' I said. 'Everything that's happened since. Good *and* bad. No monsters, no Smiley Joe . . . but no Tara, either. No Connor or Sharon or Skank. No Lauren or Nailah. No saving the world.'

But Eddie would be alive.

I didn't want to admit to Stanly how sorely tempted I was. Hell, I didn't want to admit it to myself.

Go back.

Be normal and young and in love, with who knew what in front of me.

'Personally,' said Stanly, 'I'd rather not send you back to

your youth. I think it would be a waste. I like to think you'd still find your way along the path to greatness . . . but it would mean I'd wasted a good few years. Not that a few years means anything when you're me . . .' On the face of it those words sounded haughty and arrogant. Like a god talking to a mortal, trying to make his incredible gifts sound like a burden.

Underneath, I wondered if they really were.

'I could take you back a little bit, though,' he said. 'You'd have the benefit of hindsight, or foresight, to tackle whatever's coming next.'

I still couldn't stop thinking about the night of the play.

Stop it, Stanly.

That ship has sailed.

It didn't have to have sailed, though. I still dreamed of that night, sometimes. Dreamed it as though the event were re-running in my head, every word, sound and image note-perfect. And each time, I woke up and it burned because I'd never have it again.

Except I *could* have it again.

I could just be selfish and have it again.

But Tara . . .

And not just Tara. Kloe. I'd lost her, that was true, and it hurt . . . but it would hurt less. And she'd had five years to get over me, find herself, be happy, fall in love again. To live.

I couldn't just take that from her. Just like I couldn't risk rewinding the happiness of everybody else who had survived the Collision, everybody else across the world who had built amazing things for themselves. The thought of being with Kloe when we were younger, when we'd really been meant for each other, was astronomically painful and beautiful. So beautiful it gave me a headrush. But we weren't meant for each

419

other anymore. I had no right to re-write her life. And for me to go back even ten minutes . . .

'It would be cheating,' I said. 'Going back in time. Things have happened the way they've happened . . . got to face the consequences.'

Plus, now that I thought about it, it would mean I wouldn't be there to save Tara from Smiley Joe . . . as well as a whole other heap of messiness that I couldn't even begin to untangle.

My stomach twisted around itself, like a sponge being wrung out, because more than any of it, more than giving up Kloe . . . I was giving up Eddie. I was saying *Eddie stays dead*.

But I felt sure that it was the decision he would have made.

Of course it is.

He probably wouldn't even have been tempted.

'No,' I said. 'Thanks . . . but no.'

Stanly nodded. 'Honestly? I kind of hoped you would say that . . . although I do want you to remember that the possibility is there. And that's the point. You don't *have* to use your powers to bend reality to your will, to re-write things and make them better. You don't *have* to think on the kind of scale I'd like you to think on. But I want you to know that it's possible. And I think you do now, don't you?'

'I do,' I said. 'And I'm not ruling it out . . . but I'm just not ready yet.' I kicked off from the ground and Stanly and I flew up and across the city, all gleam and shine and domes and solar collectors beneath warm, benevolent sun, and beyond it hundreds of miles of open country criss-crossed by monorails running on some strange energy I didn't understand, and beyond the countryside more towns and villages and silver domes and glass towers, all of them as bright and perfect-looking as anything could be, and although somehow I doubted that Stanly had really gone from one end of his world to the other making everything right, at this moment, in this light, it certainly looked like it.

Even my world, in the right light, looks perfect sometimes.

'How many people did you have to brainwash?' I asked. 'To make your perfect world?'

'Some,' said Stanly. 'But I didn't want to just bend everyone to my will. I *could* have climbed inside every brain on the planet and told them to make peace and do things right, but it felt like cheating. I wanted to *convince* people. Some were convinced. Some were too scared to resist me. Many were already on my side, in their own heads, they'd just been too weak or frightened to take a stand. Some . . . I had to chip a few things away. It was sad that I had to scare a lot of the most powerful people into . . . not even giving up their power, but sharing it. Took time. But within a few years, everything was on the up. People still keep themselves to themselves and they still argue, but they've had to find their way around major conflict. Find new ways to deal with stuff.'

'Because they know you'll come crashing down and enact vengeance.'

Stanly didn't answer.

'Do you ever wonder if they're *just* doing it because they fear you? Rather than because it's the right thing to do?'

'I'm sure it's that way for some people,' he said. 'But civilisation, time, they're funny things. Within a few generations, humans can often forget why something's being done. It's just . . . how things are done.'

'So the ends justify the means.'

'I think so.'

'I imagine Freeman does too.'

421

The other me shrugged, jumped and dived down through the clouds and I followed. We flew around one another in a double helix and I had to laugh with the sheer joy of ruling the sky. Stanly laughed as well and although he was a certified mental case with the mother-in-law of all god complexes, I couldn't help but think we could have been quite good friends, given time.

How much of a messed-up narcissist that made me was a debate for another day.

'How old are you?' I asked. We were sitting cross-legged a few metres above the sea, watching dolphins frolic.

'Old,' said Stanly, 'and still quite young in some ways. Can we just leave it at that?'

'Fine.' I watched a dolphin rise, clicking happily, then disappear below the waves again. 'Show me space before we go back?'

'We can take as much time as we want,' said Stanly.

'But . . . oh.'

We were sitting, as we had been, but now we were hanging in space, hundreds, millions, billions, unimaginillions of miles above the Earth, which curved away towards the stars, a perfect ball of blue and green and white with a halo of sunlight sparkling behind it. I could hardly breathe – although in the vacuum of space, I guess hardly was pretty good. For who knew how long I just stared at the world, so big it made me look like a speck, but so small I felt like I could reach out and pluck it from the sky and munch it down.

'Wow.'

Stanly grinned. 'Innit.'

'This is your world? Your Earth?'

'Yep.'

'It's nice.' I looked beyond the Earth to the endless dark robe of space, sewn with flaming jewels that had cooled and dimmed before humans had even emerged from the soup, and felt a kind of vertigo, which was also a comforting hug, an assurance. Who knew what was going on down there on the planet's surface? At least out here it was quiet. Out here, things went on. 'How are you doing this?'

'Brought oxygen with us. Holding it in place. Pretty easy, really. You bring air with you inside a spaceship. I'm just doing the spaceship's work with my brain. Just got to make sure you bring enough. You could learn to do it. You could learn to travel between worlds as well. No more accidents. Just appear and disappear at will, like me. I can teach you.'

'That . . . would be good.' I looked at him. 'As badass as a super-duper Stanly and normal Stanly team-up adventure would be, when we get back to my world I'm going to sort things out myself.'

'I assumed you would. As I said, before I took you out of the shimmer dimension I'd not interfered.'

'Because you knew I wouldn't appreciate it?' *Or because you're lying and you have actually been interfering.*

'Of course,' said Stanly. 'I wouldn't have appreciated it were the positions reversed. Even when you were having the crap beaten out of you, even when you were terrified for your life, even when you almost died . . . I left you to it. Because I knew you'd want to find your own way.'

'Did you think about leaving me in the shimmer world?'

'I did,' said Stanly. 'You made your sacrifice. Noble as shit. But it seemed like there was unfinished business. And like I said . . . potential. Couldn't bear to see it go to waste.'

I thought back to the Kulich Gallery. Pandora's bullets in

my chest. 'And when Pandora shot me, years ago. Would you have let me die?'

'I nearly saved you,' he said. 'I might have done it . . . I'm not sure.'

'I don't think you're being entirely honest.'

'You'll have to be more specific.'

'I think I *have* seen you before.'

'If you're about to say something incredibly naff like *every time I look in the mirror . . .*'

I couldn't not laugh at that. 'No. But that time. When I died and came back . . . you were *there*, weren't you? You appeared. I could see you. And you gave me a little smile. Obviously I was out of it, I just figured it was my dying brain showing me myself, doing something weird. But it was you, wasn't it?'

He didn't answer, which pretty much told me everything I needed to know.

'And you did it again,' I said. 'When I met the shimmer in the forest, I saw myself, smiling. Just a little thing, to let me know that something was . . . not what I thought it was. And then when Smith was torturing me, or pretending to torture me, with Alex and that shimmer. You appeared.'

Again, he didn't answer.

'Why?' I said. 'Why those little helping hands?'

'Not really helping,' said Stanly. 'Just . . . reassuring. All of those times, you saved yourself. It was entirely you. Your power, your skills, your determination. I just . . . kept you company. It's important to be able to go it alone. Sometimes when you're alone you can reach your highest point, because there's no-one else to fall back on. But . . .'
He trailed off, as though he couldn't find his words. It was

strange. At no point since we'd met had he seemed lost for words.

'Imagine,' he said, 'that you had a younger brother. And you wanted him to learn to be tough, to sort out his own problems, to rely on himself and not on you or anyone else. But in order to do that, you had to watch him go through horrors. And the absolute *least* you could do was to allow him a little flicker of your presence. Barely more than a photo of yourself in his pocket, or just the mental image of you, in his mind's eye, to look at, to hold on to. To let him know that he wasn't alone, even when he was. To help him find that tiny, extra bit of strength.' He shrugged. 'Couldn't help myself.'

'I appreciate it,' I said. 'But . . . it's still hard to trust that you haven't been doing other things. Behind the scenes. Pulling strings, helping me along. You're a walking *deus ex machina* as it is.'

'I haven't,' he said. 'I swear. Apart from appearing to you those three times. And that was barely anything. I mean, you thought I was you. Kind of handy really, if I *wasn't* you it would have been a major distraction.'

'It sort of messes up your brother analogy though, doesn't it? You didn't really show me that I wasn't alone, cos I thought you were just me, projecting.'

He laughed. 'Sorry. I'll go back in time and think of a better analogy and we can have this conversation again.'

I laughed too. Cos you had to, really.

'Honestly,' said Stanly, 'do you really think that you'd have bollocksed things up quite so spectacularly quite so many times if you'd had a god helping you out the whole time?'

So he's self-identifying as a god now.

Reassuring.

425

I nodded. 'Fair point. I'm choosing to believe you. And you'd better be telling the truth. If you respect me half as much as you seem to think you do . . .'

'I'm telling the truth. I swear on that big stupid beautiful blue and green ball down there, and everyone on it.'

'OK.'

I sat with myself and watched the world turn, drinking my fill of this planet which wasn't even mine, but sort of was. But even with the majesty of the situation, I kept coming back to something. It didn't matter how friendly the two of us got, what wonders he showed me, how much he taught me.

I kept coming back to the shimmers.

'Did you kill them?'

He didn't answer.

'You knew they'd die, at least.'

Nothing.

'Just tell me,' I said. 'Please.'

'I knew that if you were to leave, they would do it all again,' he said, finally. 'Break through to your world, flood it with monsters. Not for revenge, not out of anger, but because with you gone, they'd forget that they shouldn't.'

'So . . .'

'So yes,' he said. 'I let them die.'

Shadow, I remembered.

My shadow.

Him.

'Thanks for that,' I said. 'Now I have the death of a whole species on my conscience.'

'I—'

'Turn it back,' I said. 'Turn the time back. Put me back in the shimmer world. What exactly has it achieved, me being back? I didn't *need* to come back. Not at this cost. Not at the cost of a species.'

'No,' said Stanly.

'What?'

'No, I'm not taking you back. It'll be cheating, you said so yourself.'

'Don't you dare—'

'All right,' said Stanly. 'Full disclosure – I don't give a piss about cheating. Time and space, mind and matter, I snap my fingers and they dance to my tune. That's how things work for me. So I don't care about re-writing things to suit my own purposes. The universe is my Etch-a-Sketch and if something doesn't look right I'll happily give it a shake and start again. If I wanted to, yes, I'd send you back and undo what I did. But I *don't* want to. As far as I'm concerned, the death of an interesting but ultimately pointless species of brain parasites is a price worth paying for bringing you back to the world. You're needed there.'

'*Pointless?*' I said. 'A pointless species? Jesus Christ, *listen* to yourself. And how exactly am I *needed?* Needed, my arse.'

'*Tara* needs you,' said Stanly. 'As does the rest of the world. I know you agreed with Alex. You *do* want to change the world, no matter what you say about not being ready. You are far more important than those shimmers.'

'You don't get to make that decision.'

'Why not?'

'Take me back to my world,' I said, dangerously close to punching him in the face. 'Bored of space. Bored of you.'

'You seem to be forgetting that the shimmers quite happily unleashed Armageddon on your city,' said Stanly. 'They would have kept doing it as well. You don't owe them anything.'

427

'They did it benignly. That's just . . . how they work. They're not evil.'

'Neither is cancer,' said Stanly. 'It still destroys.'

I'm so going to smack this douchebag at some point.

'Take me back to my world, *now*,' I said. 'Got stuff to do.'

'Fine,' said Stanly. 'Let's go.' He snapped his fingers.

You don't need to do that.

Tit.

We reappeared in my living room with my broken coffee table and Leon, Morgan and Rosie lying unconscious on the floor. Looking down at Rosie, I couldn't help but shiver. The way she'd entered my mind . . . it was like she'd taken everything bad in the world and suddenly made me aware of it. That was some fearsome skill. It made Alex's attempts seem childish.

I'm sure she's really nice when she's not at work.

Stanly was standing next to me. 'You really pissed Morgan off the other day.'

'I figured as much. Let me guess. He went to Angelcorp and kicked up a fuss. Said he'd take me out in exchange for a job. Walker, who was already pretty pissed off with me, put it to Freeman, who had already decided I was a liability. He said yeah, sod it, let's cut our losses, and they deployed the Three Stooges here to batter me.'

'Something like that.'

'I'm almost offended,' I said. 'Would have hoped that Freeman would have wanted one more face to face with me before the end. A last rant or patronising speech to book-end our epic relationship.'

'Some people,' said Stanly. 'Amiriiite?'

I started to laugh, but stopped myself. 'Look. Thanks for

the lesson. If that's what it was. I think maybe you can be elsewhere for a bit now.'

'Roger that,' said Stanly. 'Here endeth the lesson.'

'Awesome. Bye then.' I gave him a little wave. He just looked at me, reached into his pocket and held something out. It was a tiny USB drive.

'What's that?' I asked.

'Next lesson.' All the humour had gone from his face. He looked so serious that I felt a dip in my stomach.

'What do you mean?' I took the drive.

'This is the reason I got here late,' said Stanly. 'When Rosie was attacking you. This is what I was preparing.'

'What—'

'Like I said. Next lesson.' He took a step backwards. 'If you continue to think and act on their terms, this is what's going to happen.' He smiled sadly and the last shred of warmth vanished from inside me. 'Good luck.'

And he disappeared.

I stood uncertainly for a moment, slightly unsteady with the headrush of what had happened, and not at all happy about Stanly's parting shot. Then I summoned some clothes to tie up my unconscious would-be killers and ran to the computer. The USB drive felt cold in my hand.

When the machine was ready, I inserted the drive. There was one thing on there, a movie file. I opened it and the screen filled up.

A windowless room. Three people. Walker, with Rosie standing behind her . . .

And someone tied to a chair, shaking.

Lauren?

'Oh no,' I whispered.

Rosie's blank gaze was fixed on Lauren, who was trembling, biting her lip, sweating. There were no visible wounds, but I knew what was happening to her. Walker's face was set grimly.

'I didn't want this, Lauren,' she said. 'I really didn't. But you couldn't just carry on being a good worker, could you? If you'd just stuck to your duties, I wouldn't have to do this.'

'Please . . .' It came out of Lauren's mouth, but it wasn't her voice.

'Nobody can know about the shimmers,' said Walker. 'Nobody can know about any of it. You shouldn't have gone digging. Not only did you burn your last bridge with me, you managed to irritate Mr Freeman enough for him to sign your death warrant. Yours, Bird's and the others'.'

The others . . .

Walker shook her head. 'Investigating me *and* the CEO? You've got some brass neck, girl.'

'You . . . *knew*,' said Lauren. Forcing the words out looked and sounded so painful that my chest hurt. 'All along. What he . . . did . . .'

'Lauren.' Walker's tone was almost pitying. 'If you really thought we could build a new world without getting our hands dirty, you're even more naive than I thought you were.'

'Freeman . . . *made* it . . . caused . . . Collision. Killed . . . all those . . .'

'And how many will live, now?' said Walker. 'How many will live *better lives*? The scales balance, Lauren. They always balance.'

'*Stop* . . .' Was it Lauren's voice, or mine? I wasn't sure.

'Stop resisting,' said Walker, 'and it will stop. I may never have really liked you, but I felt that you were owed an explanation. What a terrible thing, to die without knowing the truth that got you killed.'

No . . .

'Those creatures are the key to unlimited power,' said Walker. 'Power that makes people like you look like *ants*. The shimmers can break the laws of physics. Create something from nothing. They are the definition of a game-changer. So you see. Somewhat valuable to Mr Freeman, to me, to Angelcorp. And whatever you and Bird were planning, it ends here.'

'You . . . you . . . won't . . .'

'I'm sorry, Lauren.' Walker turned her back and spoke to Rosie. 'Do it. And then take Leon and that bloody policeman and sort the rest of them out. The boy and his friends are too dangerous. Kill Morgan once you're done, too. If he really thinks he's going to bluster his way into a job he's got another thing coming.'

Rosie's face didn't change, but Lauren slumped in her chair, instantly inert. Walker and Rosie left the room and the video stopped, frozen on the image of Lauren, tied to her chair, dead.

I turned away from the computer and threw up on the floor. My body felt numb but my mind was racing. Thoughts were firing off, exploding and bouncing and colliding, orbiting one central image, Lauren, dead, Lauren, dead . . .

Oh God.

Lauren.

I'm so sorry.

'Where are you?' I yelled. 'Stanly! Come out! Change it! Take me back!'

He filmed it.

To show me.

'If you continue to think on their terms, this is what's going to happen.'

He wasn't going to appear. *Cheating . . .*

I walked unsteadily to the next room, in time to see Rosie stand up, shrugging off her makeshift restraints. I didn't even have to think. It was deeper than thought. I just looked at her and she flew backwards as if yanked off-stage, crashing through my recently repaired window and disappearing into a killer plummet.

She didn't even scream.

I walked over to Morgan, thought him to his feet, ordered him to wake up. His eyes snapped open, his mouth trembling, and I proceeded to stuff his brain full of all the things I would do to him. All the essential components I would remove or re-position while keeping him conscious.

'Where were you going after this?' I would have been surprised at how calm I sounded, if I had been capable of emotions like surprise at that moment.

'We . . . we . . . we . . . please—'

'Walker said to sort the rest of them out,' I said, thinking that I was going to feed him to himself if he didn't tell me what I wanted to know, gifting him with that image in full glorious psychic 3D. I knew I could climb into his head and retrieve the information I needed, but I wanted him to tell me. I wanted him to beg. 'She means my friends, doesn't she? Where were you going first? Who . . .'

A creeping coldness.

We told them all to meet at Sharon's . . .

No . . .

I felt thoughts coming at me from behind. Leon's. I tossed

Morgan aside, turned and caught Leon's psychic assault easily, turning it back against him a hundredfold, a thousandfold. He left holes in two walls, shaped like himself, like a cartoon. I didn't bother to think about where he might end up, I just turned and advanced on Morgan. He was cowering, shrinking into the corner, terrified. I noticed with disgust that he was pissing himself, right in front of me.

'Where were you going first?'

'We've already been!' sobbed Morgan. 'You . . . you were the last stop . . .'

Oh God.

One thought and Morgan was slammed against the ceiling so hard that part of it shattered. He fell back to the floor in a shower of dust and plaster, unconscious again. I didn't think he was dead. It didn't exactly matter.

I jumped out of the window and flew, unable to even think the thought that . . .

It couldn't be.

Couldn't possibly.

I flew faster than I'd ever flown, faster than any drone, faster than anyone could see, landing clumsily on the pavement outside Connor and Sharon's house. It felt like only seconds had passed. I ran up to the door, blood and desperation and denial pounding in my head and heart and stomach. It was closed. No sign of a forced entry.

Rosie's style.

I thought it open, ran along the hall, calling their names. The hall seemed longer than usual, extending endlessly in front of me as I ran on the spot . . .

I got to the kitchen.

Stopped in my tracks.

433

No thought.
Nothing.
I think even my blood stopped flowing.
Then I screamed and every window in the house exploded.

Chapter Thirty-Two

SHARON HAD BEEN sitting at the table. Her head lolled against the fridge, her arms hung slack at her sides. Her face looked peaceful. Connor was slumped over the back of a chair, as though he'd been about to stand up. It looked awkward and uncomfortable. Further up the kitchen, Skank was spread-eagled on the floor and Daryl was half in the sink and half on the counter, his neck at the wrong angle.

This is a nightmare.

It's a lie.

I'm still in the flat.

Rosie's doing this to me.

But she wasn't. I knew she wasn't.

I fell against the wall and slid down, down, down, a hundred miles down. Hugged my knees to my chest. Stared. Connor. Sharon. Skank. Daryl. Skank. Sharon. Connor. Daryl. SharonSkankDarylConn—

The front door creaked and I snapped back to reality so fast that I felt momentarily dizzy. I was in the hall within seconds, striding or maybe flying, reaching out with my thoughts. I didn't see a face, not immediately, I just saw the shape of a person and a gun. Instinct took over and I whipped the weapon away, yanked back the hammer, emptied the clip, tossed it and the gun to the floor. *Whoosh.* The gun's owner came flying past me and I pinned them against the wall. Looked into their eyes . . .

Her eyes . . .

'Bird!' said Danielle Dewornu, struggling to free herself. 'What the hell are you doing?'

'What the hell are *you*—'

Somehow, through sheer physical force, she managed to break out of my psychic grip and throw a punch that would undoubtedly have dented my face inward, had it landed. I flew clear and grabbed her in another mental lock but I could feel how strong she was, feel her trying to break free. 'What are you doing here?' I yelled, hovering about a foot above the floor, not really on purpose, just because that's what I was doing.

'I had a message—'

'Oh yeah? How's this for a *message*?' I hurled her savagely into the kitchen. For a second she seemed about to come at me again, but then she registered the horror movie scene in front of her and froze.

'What . . .' she said. 'What happened . . .'

'You don't know? You didn't come to finish the job?'

'No!' She ran her hands through her hair, shaking her head, like she couldn't believe what she was seeing.

YOU can't believe it?

'Rosie did this?' she asked.

'What do you think?'

She shook her head. 'I can't . . . on whose orders?'

'Freeman.'

'*Freeman?*'

'And Walker. Lauren's dead too.' Lauren. Connor. Sharon. Skank. Daryl . . .

Oh no . . .

Where's . . .

'Tara!' I ran into the next room, dragging the sofa away from the wall with my mind, checking under the table. Nothing. '*Tara!*' I dashed upstairs, ran in and out of the bedrooms, throwing beds aside, opening cupboard doors. Nothing . . . no Tara . . .

No body, though . . .

And she wouldn't have left already . . .

'Tara! TARA!' My voice was too loud and I sucked it back inside myself. Stopped breathing.

I could hear something.

So, so quiet . . .

Crying.

The bathroom door was open. The crying was coming from the bath. Soft, desperate . . . but I couldn't see anyone . . . or anything . . . but the crying . . .

Oh thank everything.

'Tara,' I said. 'It's me.'

'No,' I heard her whisper. 'You're her . . . it's her . . .'

'It's me, Tara. You know it's me. You know it is.'

For a second she flickered into view, then she was gone again. 'It's all right,' I said. *It's not all right.* 'She's not here. I got her.'

'No . . . you . . . you were her . . . all along . . .'

'*Tara.*' The thoughts behind the name were so fierce that they must have overridden her power, because suddenly she was there, sitting in the bath, scrunched up as small as possible, shaking. Then there was another flicker and I blinked: she wasn't alone. The shimmer was there too. Both of them, sitting in the water, water that hadn't been there a second ago. I tentatively reached out to the shimmer with my thoughts and got a savage *flash* of its dead brothers and sisters in the cave, a flash that made me recoil.

No, I thought at it. *Please. I want to help you. It wasn't me. It was the other one.*

With my real voice, I said, 'Tara. Look at me.'

She shook her head.

It was the other one, I thought at the shimmer. *The other me. Do you . . . can you understand?*

Something like yes? Something like understanding?

How am I functioning right now?

'It helped me,' Tara whispered. 'Helped us stay hidden . . .'

I thanked the shimmer with my thoughts, hoping it understood, then gently levitated Tara out of the bath and into my arms, hugging her to me, carrying her like a child rather than a sixteen-year-old, my mind taking most of the weight. I felt like I needed to fall apart. Scream and scream and scream. Break the walls, when my last scream had merely broken the windows, or maybe just disappear into myself, fold away, leave this nightmare behind . . .

Can't.

I hugged her harder, probably too hard. 'It's all right.' It wasn't all right. 'It's OK.' It wasn't OK. It would never be OK again.

'She . . .' Tara sobbed into my neck. 'They . . . I couldn't . . . I should have tried—'

'You did what you should have done,' I said. 'Hid. If they . . . if Connor and Sharon couldn't . . .' *Oh God. Don't think. Don't think, because then it's true.* 'If they couldn't fight her, then you couldn't have. And you're alive. You're . . .'

Alive.

But they're not.

Connor. Sharon. Skank. Lauren.

Daryl.

Oh God, Daryl.

'I need to go downstairs,' I said. 'You . . . you stay here. I'll be back—'

'No,' she said, wriggling out of my arms. Standing. *How is she standing?* 'I'm coming.'

'You don't want to. I promise you don't.'

'I don't care.'

She doesn't care.

I wouldn't have.

As we crossed the landing, I heard a knock at the front door, then a creak, then a voice. 'Uh . . . hello?'

Alex.

'Wait,' I whispered. I went to the top of the stairs and saw him standing in the doorway, looking uncertain. He wore jeans, a red T-shirt, a jacket. Normal clothes. Like a normal person. Faisal was there too. He was dressed normally too. Jeans. T-shirt. Normal. Like the world was still normal.

'Sorry we're late,' said Alex. 'We were a bit stoned, we got lost . . . what happened to the windows?'

Before I could answer, I heard Danielle speak. '*Faisal?*'

Faisal saw her and his eyes widened. 'Danielle? What are you . . . Stanly? Why is she here?'

No idea.

'Why are *you* here?' said Danielle. 'I haven't seen you for . . . I thought you . . .'

'Yeah,' said Faisal. 'How's things at *Angelcorp?*' There was so much venom in his voice . . .

They're talking like the world is still normal.

I don't understand.

'Stanly?' said Alex. 'Is everything all right?'

'No,' I said. 'Come inside. Close the door.' My brain started working a bit, amazingly. Had to assume they were going after everyone. I took out my phone, called Nailah. No answer. No. NO.

What if . . .

No. Focus on what you know.

But . . .

Lauren . . .

And that made me think of Sally. *Oh no.* Lauren had given me their house number and I found it, rang it. It rang and rang before going to an answer phone message. *Their* answer phone message that they had recorded together. I felt like I was going to be sick, but I forced it down.

Thinkthinkthink.

I took Tara's hand. 'Come on.' Slowly down the stairs. One step at a time.

'I should call this in,' said Danielle.

'Don't you *dare*,' I said.

'What's *happened?*' asked Faisal. 'Tara . . .'

'Angelcorp,' I said. 'They . . . were here.' I moved towards the kitchen but Tara stopped, pulling at my hand.

'I can't,' she said. 'I . . .' Her free hand flew to her mouth, stifling a sob.

'It's fine,' I said, possibly the most hilarious sentence anyone had ever said. 'Wait here.' I let go of her hand, although I could feel that she didn't want me to, and tried to give her a reassuring smile, which felt perverse and horrible on my face. She fell against the wall and slid down, barely seeming aware of the others. Faisal knelt down next to her, took her hand, whispered something. Danielle and Alex hovered awkwardly. I walked to the kitchen . . .

And once again, it was true.

I walked to Connor. Looked at him. Remembered. Walked to Sharon. Remembered. Felt the tears begin. Walked to Skank. Remembered. More tears.

Walked to Daryl.

Touched his head.

Remembered.

At the other end of the room, miles away, I heard Tara gasp and start to howl. I was crying too, but silently. Then I heard Faisal's voice. 'Oh shit,' he said. 'Oh man . . .'

'Jesus,' said Alex. I wondered if he was having flashbacks.

Guess we've got something else in common now.

'What are you doing here, Danielle?' I said, figuring she was probably there too. I couldn't turn around, though. Couldn't turn my back on Daryl. Not yet.

'I . . .' she said. 'I've been investigating Walker. And Rosie. On behalf of Lucius Hamilton. He's concerned about what she's being used for. Torture . . . I got word she'd been sent out to do something . . . I wasn't expecting this.'

Lucius?

'This is what your company *does*,' said Faisal. 'Murders people in their homes. *Tortures* people. This is what you decided to be.'

'No it isn't,' said Danielle. 'This *isn't* what we—'

'Shut up,' I said. 'Everyone *shut up*.'

Everyone shut up.

'Have some *respect*,' I said. 'If you want to shout at each other, punch each other, be my guest, but *get the hell out of here first.*'

Nobody moved.

He must be watching.

I know he's watching.

'Show yourself,' I said. 'Show yourself, or I swear on my life I will track you down and *destroy* you. And I'll make it last.'

'Uh,' said Faisal. 'Who are you talking—'

A chorus of shocked breaths.

'What the *hell?*' said Danielle.

'Stanly?' asked Tara's tiny voice.

'Don't worry,' I said. 'It's all right.' *It's not. Stop saying that. I have to say it cos it's what you say.*

I turned and faced him. Stanly. The self-appointed god. 'You knew,' I said. 'About this. About all of it. The whole time we were talking, the whole time you were telling me to think big, taking me from world to world. You *knew.*'

He nodded.

'Why? Why didn't . . . you made that video . . . why . . .'

'Because I knew you weren't going to change your mind,' said Stanly. 'Not immediately, anyway. I knew you were going to cling to your status quo. Your day-to-day, within-the-box reality, where people do unspeakable things to each other, and you have powers but they're not of any use, not *really,* because people are still people. I knew you were going to stay on their level. I knew it was about to get really horrible. And I knew you needed to see it. See the consequences. See *this.*' He gestured at my dead friends.

'But the video . . .'

'You want to take Freeman down. And Walker.'

'Of course.'

'But you won't think big enough to do it the way I would have. You're not going to truly destroy them.'

I bloody am. 'How dare you,' I said. 'They *killed*—'

'You're just not ready,' said Stanly. 'And that's OK. It's OK. But you *are* determined. You're focused now. You are going to do something. And you need to do it on your terms . . . which are their terms. So I made the video.'

The penny dropped with an atonal, head-splitting clang. 'Evidence.'

'Evidence,' he said. 'Or at least, the beginnings of it. Evidence that Walker killed one of her own. That she was going to have Rosie kill you and all your friends. That there is a laboratory that needs hiding, and a bigger conspiracy beyond that. All on Freeman's orders.'

'You watched her kill Lauren,' I said. 'You *filmed* it. To . . . to *motivate* me? You could have *saved* her!'

'It was necessary,' said Stanly. 'A horrible but necessary first step for you. This time, you'll fight them in the normal way. By taking that evidence and bringing it into the open. But you'll remember what they did. You'll remember Lauren. Your friends. These memories will be burned into your soul. And in time, you'll understand that *this*, this *obscenity*, is what happens when you play humans at their human games. This is what happens when you think *small*.'

'Help me,' I said. 'Turn back time.'

'You don't mean that,' said Stanly. 'Even now. Even here, surrounded by the bodies of your dearest friends, you don't mean that.'

'Fine,' I said. 'Then get lost. I've got work to do.'

Stanly smiled. 'Yeah, you do.' And he was gone.

'Seriously,' said Danielle. 'What the *actual* hell.'

'Ultra-powerful dickhead version of me from another

dimension,' I said. 'Tara? I—' We all jumped, because somebody was banging on the front door.

Christ, more?

'Everybody *wait here*.' I ran out to the hall. I could hear a familiar voice calling my name.

Oh thank God.

I yanked the door open with my mind, pulled Nailah inside, slammed it again, grabbed her in a hug. 'You're OK,' I whispered.

'Yeah,' she said, returning the hug. 'Just. Christ, flyboy, what the hell are you into?'

'Bad stuff.' I pulled back. 'What happened?'

'Some dudes turned up at my office,' said Nailah. 'Pretty sure they came to kill me.'

'How did you get away?'

'Security system stalled them. And I made sure when we moved into that office that there was at least one extra exit.'

'I tried to call you . . .'

'Yeah,' said Nailah. 'Tossed my phone. For safety. Half thought I should skip town entirely, figured they'd have sent people here too. But I guessed you guys could take whatever was thrown at you, thought I'd be safer here . . .' She looked into my eyes and immediately knew that something was terribly wrong. 'What happened?'

'They killed them,' I said. 'They killed Lauren, they killed Daryl . . . Sharon . . . all of them.'

'Oh my God. I . . . I'm so sorry . . .'

I noticed that she was clutching a laptop. 'What's on that?'

'I . . . had an email,' said Nailah. 'From Lauren, earlier this evening. Encrypted. Haven't had a chance to get inside it yet,

444

I had to reach out to some people, get them to send me the right software.'

'Get cracking on it,' I said. 'Living room's through there. I'd . . . avoid the kitchen, if I were you. Danielle?'

Danielle came out into the hall. 'Danielle, Nailah,' I said. 'Nailah, Danielle.'

'Yeah,' said Danielle, 'we've met.'

Of course. Idiot. I handed Nailah the USB drive. 'There is footage on here of . . .' *Keep speaking. Hold it in.* 'Of Lauren's murder. It's horrendous, but Danielle needs to see it.'

'What are you planning, Stanly?' asked Danielle. 'You know I can't . . .'

'You *listen to me*,' I said. 'You've been investigating Walker. You think that's as bad as this thing gets? Freeman has ordered, what, *seven* murders tonight? He has been performing illegal, invasive experiments on aliens. He has been brainwashing Morter Smith for the last five years. And trust me when I say that that is the *tip* of the atrocity iceberg. I do not give a shit about procedures. I do not give a *shit* about "by the book" or whatever you think you're about to lecture me on. I am taking Freeman down, *tonight*, and he cannot see it coming or he will destroy every piece of evidence, wipe every mind, make it *impossible*.'

'You can't kill him . . .'

'I never said anything about killing him. But I ain't making an official complaint.'

'Stanly, I want to help,' said Danielle. 'Genuinely. I know we've not . . . I've not exactly been super friendly. But this is exactly why Mr Hamilton assigned me to this. To uncover this sort of thing. I need to know everything.'

'Fine,' I said. 'Brace yourself.'

Lauren had said that empowered brains could handle lots of information at once. So I put it to the test. I summoned all my memories of Freeman, our confrontation, the truth about the Collision, and I fired them into her brain with mine. It hit her so hard that she staggered backwards into the wall.

'Oh *God!*' she moaned, clutching her head. 'What did you . . . you *bastard*, how *dare* you . . .'

'I'm really sorry,' I said. 'But you need to know what he is. What he's done. And I don't have time to sit down and go through it all.'

'Danielle.' It was Faisal. He put a hand on her shoulder. 'This guy is *bad*. He needs to go. Remember why we decided to be superheroes? Remember Marlon? Dude, *this* is why we did it. To stop scumbags who reckon they can hurt whoever they want. You do remember, don't you?'

Danielle couldn't seem to form words. Faisal helped me transfer her to the living room, where I sat her next to Nailah.

'Crack what's on that laptop,' I said. 'And show her everything.'

'OK.' Nailah glanced nervously at Danielle, who was still holding her head. 'What are you . . .'

'Something I need to do. Faisal?' We went back to the kitchen, where Alex and Tara were sitting side by side. Alex looked up at me as though he didn't have the faintest idea what thought he should be having, let alone what words to say. I tried a sympathetic smile, which was blackly amusing in its way, and crouched down next to Tara.

See the consequences, Stanly said.

'Tara?' I said. 'I need you to help me.'

'What?' Her voice was tiny and broken, her face red and swollen from crying.

446

'Dude,' said Faisal. 'She's freaking out . . .'

'I know,' I said. 'And I'm sorry, but Tara? I *need* you. Right now.'

'What . . . what are you doing . . .'

And what did Danielle say? 'You don't think about consequences . . .'

Actually, I do think about consequences.

Know what I think about consequences?

I think bollocks to 'em.

I took Tara's hand in mine. 'I'm going to bring them back. All of them. Back to life.'

'Can you do that?'

'Yes I bloody can.' *Because I can't not. It's impossible for me not to.* 'But I have no idea how. And I have a feeling that it's going to take a lot out of me . . . so I need you to hold on to me. I need you to keep me anchored. And if I start to go . . . I need you to bring me back.'

'I don't . . . I don't know if I can . . . I've only been . . .'

'You can,' I said. 'It doesn't matter if you've had powers for five years, five minutes or five centuries. It's always there. You can do it. Just hold on.' I gripped her hand.

This has to work.

It has to.

'Can we help?' asked Alex.

'Yeah,' said Faisal, 'if you need us . . .'

'Yes,' I said. 'Please. In fact . . . idea . . .' I half-ran, half-flew out of the kitchen, up the stairs, to the bathroom. There it lay. The shimmer.

I knelt down next to the bath and thought at it, as gently as I could. *You can understand me. I know you can. You can look into my head. You can see that I never wanted to harm any*

447

of you. I lived with you, for years. See? Look? I felt something in my head, the strangest feeling. Like a trickle in my brain. I could feel it in there, looking. *See? I'm not your enemy. I want to help you. So please, help me. My friends have been killed too. By bad people. The same people who kept you trapped. We can rescue your friends. We can send them home. Send you home. But first, I need you to help me. Please. I'm begging you.*

It lay there, glowing inscrutably, for so long.

Then a thought, a single thought, a single word, although it wasn't a word, it was a feeling, spelled out in summer breezes and unrolling fields and weird, alien shapes . . .

Help.

I scooped the creature up in my arms, tingling at how strange it felt, and ran back downstairs. Alex, Tara and Faisal were standing next to one another, Alex looking grave and kind of awkward, Tara shell-shocked, Faisal troubled but resolute.

'Woah,' said Alex, his eyes widening. 'Is that . . .'

'Yeah.' I sat down and motioned for them to do the same, forming a circle. The shimmer climbed out of my arms and onto my back and I felt it press its soft, warm hands, or whatever it had instead of hands, against my temples. I reached out and took one of Tara's hands and one of Alex's, with Faisal bridging them opposite me.

'I seriously have no clue what I'm supposed to be doing,' said Faisal.

'Neither do I,' said Alex.

'Honestly, neither do I,' I said. 'I'm totally making this up as I go along. I just need all the power I can get. So . . . do what you feel like you should do, I guess?'

Alex and Faisal nodded uncertainly. I looked at Tara. 'I need you to keep me here, OK? You're my anchor. I know this is all a bit mystical hippie drum circle, but . . . I don't know how else to do it. You with me?'

'Yes.' She made her voice strong, made her face strong. I was reminded, strangely, painfully, of Sharon.

'Right.' I could feel something coming from the shimmer. A crackling in my brain, subtle but already rising. I imagined this was what it felt like when the drugs started to kick in. Alex had closed his eyes and I could feel his thoughts as well. They had their own colour, a dark tarnished gold, their own particular shade and texture, a roughness stitched with vulnerability. I could feel Faisal's too, except his were blue against black. They reminded me, inexplicably, of the opening credits of the 1978 *Superman* film.

That John Williams march wouldn't go amiss right about now.

Oh well. Here goes nothing.

The first thought had to be that they weren't dead. Surely. If I thought that they were dead and that I was bringing them back, I was admitting that they were dead, and therefore they couldn't be alive.

Was that it?

Oh God, how the hell am I supposed to know?

My brain buzzed and I forced myself to picture them as they were now, lying here, broken, silent, gone. And then I thought of them as they had been. Connor backflipping, guns blazing, mowing down Smiley Joe in a hail of bullets, calm and collected and completely *alive*. I imagined him in his living room, picking away at his guitar, singing softly, heard the music in my head, and it surged through me like pure light. I imagined him as he had been, as my friend, and how he had been when that friendship had started to suffer. I imagined him shouting at me when Eddie died. I imagined the way he'd looked at me when I'd come back. I imagined our conversation in this kitchen just yesterday. Our handshake.

Alive.

My body jerked. I could feel Alex's power, Faisal's, my own, the shimmer augmenting it all, Tara wrapped around us like a protective web, and *woah* . . .

ALIVE.

I imagined Sharon's smile. Her eyes. The way she was a perfect illustration of the word *alive.* The way she had immediately accepted Daryl, the way she'd welcomed us into her home. I remembered her telling me the story of how she had destroyed the Worm, the way she had seemed to glow, the images, vile, amazing, ludicrous, that had been conjured up in my head. I imagined her fighting on the night the monsters came. Twirling lampposts around with her mind, battering monstrous invaders. I imagined the way she radiated goodness, whether she was battling, cooking, smiling or crying. I thought of every time she had stood by me, put up with my rubbish, the way she'd stayed loyal when I'd had no right to expect it.

I imagined her expression, and the hug she'd given me, when she'd seen me again for the first time in years.

Alive.

She was alive. She couldn't not be.

Skank. The oddity. The loyal, eccentric millionaire. I remembered his test when I'd come to work at 110th Street. The way he'd asked me who my favourite Doctor was, assuming I had one. Now I could actually talk to him about *Doctor Who.* Maybe we would argue. I imagined him arguing with people over their interpretations of superheroes. Over the Silver Surfer's various illustrators. As heated as I'd ever seen him, pretty much . . . *except for arguing Han vs. Indy with Nailah.* I remembered us sitting together smoking weed and watching Buffy. Skank with his mad, semi-sentient beard, his sandals and 2000 AD T-shirts.

Alive.

And Daryl. I shook as I remembered. No, I was already shaking, my whole body trembling with the raw concentrated *power* flowing through it. It was overwhelming . . .

No.

NOT overwhelming.

Daryl.

Focus.

Finding him by the side of the road as I ambled intoxicatedly home.

Chattering away as if a talking dog was the most normal thing in the world and very quickly deciding that it *was* the most normal thing in the world. More normal than the world, in fact.

Sharing my space and my thoughts.

Watching endless films.

The look on his face when he'd found out about my powers.

Our first training session in the woods behind my house . . . so long ago . . .

So much life in him.

Alive.

More alive than all the trees in the woods put together.

Jumping up and down.

Cracking wise and swearing and bawling his eyes out over *Casablanca.*

And what I'd thought was a betrayal, the way it had cut me so, *so* deeply, because he was my friend, my first and best.

I imagined him running all over that giant blue dog, tearing it a new one. My superpowered beagle.

I imagined all his different looks.

The way he smiled.

The way his eyes could be so soulful.

The way his acid tongue could burn.

Alive.

My dog . . . no . . . *my friend* . . . who also happened to be a dog . . . alive.

All of them.

Alive.

I jerked, my eyes flying open for a second, and the others jerked as well, like a current had passed around the circle, and then I burst into bright blue flames and started to *run*, rushing *into* my friends, through silent arteries, abandoned castles criss-crossed by darkened corridors, in and out of veins and hearts and organs, into brains and minds, a tiny giant made of fire, gold for Alex's power and blue for Faisal's and *red* for mine, kicking and screaming, breathing and laughing. I imagined black blood shining, becoming scarlet again, red and white blood vessels churning, breath coming back to hushed mouths. I ran through my friends' minds, hurling my memories at them, using them like hammers to batter the great bells in their heads that had fallen so horribly silent, crashing them into wakefulness, electrifying them with everything that they meant to me, because they meant too much, *too much* to not be alive, liquid thought pouring into abused, empty shells, shells that now had to be re-filled . . .

No.

Not filled.

And not shells.

Flames.

To be re-lit.

Just enough to start them simmering . . .

Shimmering . . .

Glimmering . . .

They're still in there, or nearby at least, somewhere.

They have to be.

They haven't had time to leave yet.

All the information, everything they are, everything they've been and said and done and loved and hated and hoped and regretted and lost and found, it's all still in there, or nearby at least, it's just gone quiet, gone dark, just need to shine a light on it, into the corners, if my consciousness can go walkabout then that means theirs can come back, they can, they can . . .

Because I can't not have them in the world.

Can't.

They cannot be dead.

It is a physical impossibility, a psychic impossibility, an existential impossibility, and it is not happening BECAUSE WHAT I SAY GOES AND I SAY IT'S NOT HAPPENING.

If I have to break science into a billion pieces then I will FUCKING DO SO.

Seeds watered, blossoming. Trees sprouting new, bright leaves. Kindling catching, becoming fire.

My mind ran through them, through everything they were, at the speed of light. *Faster* than the speed of light.

Running.

Running.

Never stopping running.

Not until they were here, until they shone again.

Miles to go . . .

And then, out of the light, up they came. What they were. *What they are.*

I saw Daryl smile.

I saw Skank smile.

I saw Connor smile.

I saw Sharon smile.

And I knew. I knew those smiles. I knew they were smiling, truly smiling, and I knew they knew I loved them, that I wasn't going to let them go. I saw them in a great dark hall, standing tall again, dwarfing me, laughing down at silly Stanly, silly little Stanly with all his silly little thoughts, laughing, because they loved me, because I'd brought them back . . .

And now I was done. Now I could rest.

So tired.

Haven't slept a wink . . .

Sooooo tired . . .

My mind is on the blink . . .

I wonder should I get up . . .

Nah . . .

So little left of myself.

Never stopping running?

Stopping running.

Stopping.

Stop—

'No,' said Tara.

I looked up. The others had faded into the vague, blurry black, but Tara was there, bright as day, brighter in fact, standing above me, extending her hand.

'Come on,' she said. 'Come on. Don't give up. Don't you dare.'

But I'm TIRED, I said, in my sulky little kid voice.

'You're *not*,' she said, in her stern grown-up voice. So grown-up. *Crazy* grown-up.

I am . . . I'm so tired. Just let me have a little sleep. Please?

'No.' I could see her *no* in front of me. It was quite small, barely the size of a cat, but it was there and it fizzed with energy, except, no, it was bigger, about the size of a horse, no, bigger, the size of a house . . . no . . . bigger than that, much bigger . . . city-sized . . . *everything*-sized . . .

NO.

'No!' she said. 'You come back. You bloody come back *now*! *You always come back to me!*'

AAAAAAAAAAAA—

I shot straight up with a yelp, hit the ceiling and dropped back down to the kitchen floor with a *thump*, a small sprinkling of dislodged plaster raining down on my head. The shimmer jumped off me and skittered over to the wall, the air full of its thoughts . . .

It was *giggling*. As far as it was concerned, this was just another game.

'Stanly,' said Tara. Tears were running down her face . . . but she was smiling. So was Alex. So was Faisal.

'What?' I said, because it couldn't possibly be true.

'Look.'

I looked.

They were there. Daryl, manoeuvring himself out of the sink, his ears twitching. Skank sitting up, rubbing his neck. Sharon sitting forwards in her chair, blinking slowly.

Connor standing.

I started to laugh. Tara started to laugh. Faisal started to laugh. The shimmer was laughing even louder than it had been before, lovely chiming silken telepathic laughter. Even Alex joined in. We all laughed, filling the room with a feeling I couldn't even describe.

Sharon looked at me. 'You,' she said. 'You . . .'

'Bloody hell, kid,' said Daryl, jumping down to the kitchen floor and running over to me. 'That was fucking *mental*.'

'A bit,' I said, hugging him to me.

'Some power you got there.'

I looked at Tara, at Faisal, at Alex. 'I had some help.'

'I didn't do anything,' said Tara.

'Yeah you did,' I said.

'I ain't got a clue what I did,' said Faisal.

'You did it, though,' I said. 'Thank you.'

'No problem!' He scratched his head. 'I guess . . .'

'Stanly—' said Sharon.

'Sorry,' I said. 'We can talk later. We can talk forever, hopefully. But there's no time now. Nailah! Have you got into those files?'

'Yeah!' she called. 'You're going to want to see this. I think Thor Blimey is having a Road to Damascus moment. Or a Darth Vader throwing the Emperor down a big hole moment. Whatever you want to call it.'

Skank chuckled at that, which was rather amazing.

'What are you going to do?' asked Connor, reaching out and helping me to my feet.

'I'm going to go big,' I said.

Chapter Thirty-Three

THE SHARD PUNCHED its way up like some unsightly growth with delusions of grandeur, still buzzing with activity, even at this time of night. No rest for the wicked. Above the city of London, still standing after so much punishment, grey clouds shifted restlessly; they could have been seconds from raining, or they might stay dormant for days. The air was mild, but there was an edge to it, a sliver of cold. A threat.

Suddenly, silently, something broke through the clouds and descended towards the city. The screaming was a Mexican wave. Once one person saw, so did everybody else, and they all screamed because of course you would. Inside the Shard, Freeman's citadel, people ran to the windows, pointing, crying out, grabbing one another, hysterically demanding confirmation that others could see what they were seeing.

What they were seeing was me, three hundred metres tall, Godzilla-like, eyes burning fiery scarlet like furious suns, hair blowing in a new, unholy wind.

The giant Stanly landed next to the Shard, the ground trembling beneath his enormous feet. He smiled and spoke in ten thousand voices, a monstrous roaring boom. 'FREEMAN. I WOULD HAVE WORDS WITH THEE.'

Inside the building, all those who stood near a window were knocked back a few feet, pushed by an invisible force. Then all the windows, every single glass panel that stretched across the building like a reflective skin, exploded outwards in a jagged blizzard. The glass shards didn't fall, though, they hung in the air for a few seconds before flying towards Stanly like obedient, glittering birds. He put his two great hands together, holding the glass between them, and it turned to liquid, re-forming into a huge, perfect reflective sphere. Stanly stared at it and let loose an earthquake chuckle, tossing the ball from hand to hand, rolling it around his palm, twirling it on one finger like a basketball. Then he placed it carefully, almost daintily, on the ground.

Alarms were howling and people were exiting the building in a chaotic scramble, screaming. A voice called to another voice and now came the soldiers, rushing, raising their weapons, but they didn't even have time to fire before they were pressed swiftly to the floor, overpowered by Stanly's thoughts, clips ripped from guns, bullets popped from clips and sprinkled on the ground with a pretty ringing sound.

It didn't take long for the sirens to come. That noise that I'd always associated with this muddle of a city. Police cars roared up and loudhailers tried to tell Stanly off.

Stanly just stood where he was, waiting.

Then one of the voices I wanted to hear most rose up over the din. Walker, amplified by a megaphone. 'That's not him! It's an illusion! He's projecting it from somewhere, into your minds! *Find him!*'

Yeah, good luck with that.

Some people fired at the giant Stanly anyway, but he stopped their bullets, blinking and smiling as he disintegrated these strange, pathetic projectiles with his thoughts. The giant chuckled again, then bellowed, 'FREEMAN! COME OUT!'

Another wave of soldiers, readying their powers, all

thinking at me – or wherever they thought I was – in puny little bursts. I didn't really need to defend myself but I did anyway, pushing them effortlessly to the floor as I scanned the crowd for Walker. Couldn't see her, but I could hear her.

'Somebody bloody *kill him!*'

'FREEMAN!' bellowed giant Stanly again. 'YOU'RE OUT OF TIME!'

I smiled in my hiding place and thought of the *other* Stanly. Remembered the mountain he'd broken.

I thought my way inside the building, up through its lift shafts, along its corridors and in and out of its offices. There were a good few people still in there, frozen with terror, and I pulled each one through their nearest broken window and deposited them on the ground, not roughly, but not gently. A stray bullet whizzed uncomfortably close to me but I melted it into driblets before it could hit anything. Then I thought another wave outward, snatching more guns from hands, flooring their owners.

When will they take the hint?

'You can't win, Stanly!' bellowed Walker. 'For the good of this city, we will kill you!'

LOL.

For one second giant Stanly's face became a great yellow smiley emoticon.

More screams.

Right. Let's do this.

I thought, because that's all it took. Just a thought, a quick little think, and stuff happened. Whatever I wanted happened.

Finally, said a voice that wasn't quite mine. *You're getting it.*

Stanly reached out, planted one hand on either side of the Shard and gripped it hard . . . or at least that's what it looked like. The building buckled and a few stray tonnes of rubble fell, but I caught them before they could hit the floor or hurt anyone.

I stared at the building.

Thought of a rocket blasting up.

The sound was incredible. Like a beast taking a bite out of the Earth. Like a nuclear explosion in reverse. Stanly ripped the Shard free of the ground and started to rise upwards, lifting off with the building clasped in his hands. More screams, more shouting, more bullets, harmless as flies. The giant kept rising with the building in his grip, the structure shaking, cracking, shedding its steel and concrete flesh, but each piece was in my mental grasp before it could hit the ground. Up it went, towards the sky, until it was so high that the whole city would be able to see it, that ludicrous landmark, that testament to ego and corruption, that symbol of Freeman's rule . . .

'Stanly!'

Ah. Heeeeeere's George.

He had appeared in the crowd, running, looking up at the impossible apparition in the sky. Stanly looked down, regarded him momentarily with the burning eyes of a murderous genie, then *flew* back down so fast that people screamed and ran, stampeding in all directions. The giant landed, great feet kicking police cars aside with ease, thoughts taking care to protect their occupants from injury, twirling the Shard around and around above his head on one finger.

'THERE YOU ARE,' he boomed.

'Stanly—'

'DIDN'T I TELL YOU WHAT WOULD HAPPEN IF YOU HURT MY FRIENDS?'

Freeman was sweating. His hair was unkempt, his suit rumpled. He was scared of me. Terrified.

'Bout.

Time.

'I'm sorry!' he cried. 'I didn't—'

'NO!' Stanly cracked the Shard in half and started tossing the two halves from hand to hand. 'NO APOLOGIES! NO EXCUSES! YOU ARE A MURDERER!'

'I—'

'YOU KILLED THEM ALL! YOU TRIED TO KILL ME! AND YOU SHOULD HAVE TRIED HARDER!' Stanly roared, before throwing the two bits of building into the air so that both of them split again. Before they could fall, he started to move his huge hands like a magician performing a trick, causing the four ruined husks to circle around and around one another in a crazy orbit.

'Stanly, don't do this!' Freeman yelled. 'This is not who you are! You are not—'

'WHAT AM I, THEN? AM I A SUPERHERO? ARE YOU MY SUPERVILLAIN?' Stanly stopped juggling the remains of the Shard and I sent a thought towards Freeman, snatching him up into the air. He was too scared, too taken aback to resist, to do anything. He hadn't planned for this.

He hadn't planned for *me*.

Stanly held out one of his hands and I placed Freeman down on the palm. I made him *feel* it, made him feel flesh beneath his shoes, even though it wasn't there, and then I showed myself, perched on giant Stanly's shoulder, grinning Puckishly, a crazy, frightening light in my eyes.

'Or maybe *I'm* the supervillain,' I said. I jumped, dropped and landed on the great palm, facing Freeman.

461

'I know this is an illusion,' said Freeman. His voice almost sounded like it might one day believe what it was saying.

I walked towards him, shrugging. 'Doesn't matter, mate. You messed up. You killed the people I love. And I seem to recall promising you destruction like you could never imagine. Well.' I indicated the giant that I had created, the ruins of Freeman's palace, the chaos below. 'How d'you like *them* apples?'

'I don't,' said Freeman. 'And . . . I'm sorry about Lauren and the others. I *am* sorry.' He started burbling on, pathetically trying to justify what he'd done, he'd just been defending himself, looking out for the company, the world, blah blah blah, and all the while I stood and listened with my best unimpressed curled-lip teenage sneer.

At the same time, I was also listening to what was going on down below.

'Hey,' said a soldier. 'Look at this . . .'

'Please, Stanly,' said Freeman. 'Your friends . . . they wouldn't want this, would they? They wouldn't want you to . . . to dishonour them, and yourself, with behaviour like this? You are a *good* person. Far better than I. Do not disgrace yourself by—'

'Hold that thought.' I walked to the edge of the great hand and called down to the crowd below, using my power to amplify my voice. 'You seen it yet, Walker?'

'No,' she said, from wherever she was. It sounded suspiciously like 'yes'. 'No!'

'Has she seen what?' said Freeman.

'Just a little recording,' I said. 'Which is currently playing . . . let's see . . . everywhere.'

'I—'

'*Shut up,*' I said, channelling thunder into my voice and rooting Freeman to the spot with a thought. 'I'll deal with you in a minute. Walker! *Where is she? Where's Lauren's body?*'

Walker was spluttering pathetically somewhere. 'She . . . she . . . I don't, this is . . . it's fake! It's a forgery!'

Heads were beginning to turn.

'Take her down!' I yelled. 'Arrest her!'

'*No!*' Walker was hysterical. 'This is an outrage! I never said these things! I have never—'

I rolled my eyes and giant Stanly mimicked the motion, bringing the four pieces of the Shard hurtling back down from the sky. I let two pieces fall onto one of the adjacent fields and dropped the others back where they used to lie, amongst the rubble. Pathetic, ruined piles of nothing.

'It's over, Walker!' I yelled. 'Where is Lauren's body?'

'She—'

'WHERE?' Stanly and I screamed, filling the air with our voices, our booming tornado bellows.

Freeman clutched his ears at the terrible sound. 'Stanly . . .'

'I *said* shut up.'

'Miss Walker,' said a voice in the crowd. 'I think you need to come with—'

'No!' Walker yelled. 'No!' A gunshot. She was firing into the air, trying to escape.

'What are you doing, Stanly?' said Freeman.

'There's a little video playing down there,' I said. 'A video of Walker killing Lauren. On your orders. Pretty neatly implicating herself.' I turned to look at him, daring him to protest, to laugh it off.

But his eyes just narrowed, because he hated not knowing. 'How?'

'With a little help from a friend.'

'I was not present,' he said. 'There is nothing to connect me with Jane Walker or any actions she or anyone else may have taken . . .'

'Apart from the fact that you're the boss of the company. Also, she calls you by name.'

'Circumstantial at best.'

I let my face fall, as if I hadn't thought of that. I looked up at giant Stanly. His face also fell. Big glum giant. It was enough to make me giggle, but I fought hard to maintain my poker face. 'Well, shit,' I said. 'D'you hear that, big guy? Guess we might as well go home.'

'AWWW,' said Stanly, in a huge, ridiculous sad voice.

'Don't play games,' snapped Freeman.

I turned back, walked towards him, stood so that we were nose to nose.

'To re-iterate,' I hissed, 'you killed *all my friends*. Even Tara. Little Tara. Dearest daughter. Rosie snapped her *neck*. So when I say this is *not* a game, when I say I've got *nothing* to lose, when I say that there is *no reason whatsoever* for me not to absolutely *fuck. Up. Your. World* . . . you know I'm being serious.'

'Stanly.' His voice was soft now. Placatory. 'This will accomplish nothing. Do the right thing. Just leave.'

'Leave?'

'Go,' said Freeman. 'To another world. Somewhere else. Anywhere. Just go. There is no place for you here. Not any more. I'm sorry about that . . . but there isn't.'

'Yeah,' I said. 'I know. But I still got things to do, yo.'

'Just go, please. You know I can't follow you.'

'I wouldn't be so sure about that. You'll find a way.' My

phone rang and I gave Freeman an apologetic smile. The confused look on his face was priceless. "Scuse me, I have to take this. Hello? Uh-huh. Great. Get him to the safe house. I'll call you later.' I hung up.

'Who was that?' asked Freeman.

'Wrong number.' At that moment a sniper tried to shoot me in the head, but the bullet stopped several feet away and turned inside-out.

'Stanly,' said Freeman. 'What is—'

My phone rang again and I smiled again. 'Ooh! Someone's popular! Sorry, I'm really sorry. Hold on. Two secs, yeah? Y'ello? Ah, excellent. Cracking job. Laters.' I hung up, turned back to Freeman, rolled my eyes like anyone would if wrong numbers kept interrupting them while they were trying to perpetrate ginormous revenge. He looked pissed-off now, I could feel his power crackling . . . but it didn't work on me any more. He wasn't the supervillain now. I wasn't the underdog. I was large and in charge.

'What the *hell* is going on, Stanly?' said Freeman. 'I *demand* that you tell me *now!*'

'If you insist,' I said. 'Do you remember that time we hung out in the shimmer world? By the lake?'

'Of course I do.'

'Of course you do. Good times. Remember how you bored me to tears going on and bloody on about your awesome-sauce master plan and how diabolical it was and how much you'd manipulated me? Remember how it literally went on forever?'

'What's your *point*, Stanly?'

'My *point* is that I'm going to do the same thing in about one paragraph,' I said. 'This whole thing, with big me and the Shard, has been a diversion. My friends aren't dead. Connor and Daryl just kidnapped Morter Smith and we're going to remove the mental blockages you put in his brain and use him to implicate you in a whole mess of quite heinous shit. Oh, and also, speaking of heinous shit my arch nemesis does, the *rest* of my very not-dead friends just busted into your secret shimmer lab to rescue its occupants. And they'll be following up their little Walker broadcast with a special report, coming live from the scene of *how epically screwed you are.*'

I held up a fist and giant Stanly fist-bumped me with his enormous one. 'Party on, Wayne!' I yelled.

'PARTY ON, GARTH,' boomed my skyscraping doppelgänger.

Freeman's lip curled. His eye twitched. His hands shook.

'How's that for a master plan, arsewipe?' I said. 'And I literally threw it together in one evening, after being back in this world for, like, a fortnight. I think maybe *you* might want to exit this plane of reality stage left and piss off to another dimension sharpish, rather than me.'

'You . . .' said Freeman. 'You . . . you little . . .'

'Little?' I indicated giant me with my head. 'Don't forget about the Stanly Megazord here. You'll upset him.'

'You won't get away with this!' Freeman's eyes flashed with pure rage and burning red thought smashed into me, knocking me backwards. My head clouded with static and giant Stanly's hand flickered . . . then he vanished entirely and I started to fall.

No. Flying.

I stopped myself and turned, hoping to see Freeman falling too . . . but no. He was flying. Hovering in the air, arms spread wide.

'Well,' he said, with one of the scarier smiles I'd ever seen on a human face. 'Look at that. It seems that all I had to do was *believe in myself.*' The way his voice distorted on those last three words made me shudder. It was a sneer that could have curdled milk.

'You've lost, Freeman!' I said. 'You are *over.*'

'*Don't count on it!*' I must have been weaker than I'd thought because suddenly he was in my brain, raw thought streaming in, cascading through my defences, looking for . . .

No . . .

Not . . .

'*Where is your safe house?*' he hissed, an enormous serpentine beast towering over me, transforming me with less than a finger snap from huge to *tiny*, powerful to powerless . . .

NO.

I forced him out, hit him with a blast of brainpower and sent him spinning through the sky, up, up, up. He wasn't used to flying and had trouble righting himself, but then he was swooping back towards me, hands pulsating with energy, firing invisible lightning in my direction. I tried to catch it, loop it around and send it back at him, but he was *so* furious, so so furious and *aaargh* he was back in my brain, ransacking it, turning it over and over, his face huge and everywhere, Joker-like, hysterical screaming cackling clown face and . . . *nnnNOO* . . .

'Ah,' said Freeman. 'There we are. Or there *they* are. Not so safe now, eh?'

And he was gone, flying off faster than I could have imagined a first timer flying. Towards the safe house. Our haven.

He left me with a thought:

I'll kill them all again. I'll make you watch. And then I'll kill you. And nobody will ever know.

I didn't have time to catch my breath. I flew after him, banking left and right between buildings, running along walls, ducking under concrete outcrops and arms of steel and brick, trying to think the essence of every super-fast living flying running sprinting thing into my own movements, to keep pace with him, but God he was fast, and within seconds, or at least that was how it felt, I could see it, less than a mile away. Blue Harvest. Or the husk of the wonderful beast that was once Blue Harvest, hunched and dark, a blunt manifestation of everything I'd lost. As I tore through the sky after Freeman, hurling vicious thoughts that he shrugged off like a light rain, I couldn't help wondering if I was going to lose more. If history was going to repeat itself, all my friends murdered . . . except this time I'd have to watch, he'd *make* me watch . . .

But no . . . I'll just save them again . . .

But then he'd kill them again. Over and over again. And then me.

No.

NO. *You shut up. You shut-* WOAH.

A car came spinning through the air towards me, lobbed in Freeman's wake. I barely dodged it in time, feeling the wind of the thing as it passed by. It crashed down into the road somewhere behind me in a catastrophe of abused metal and tinkling glass and I heard somebody scream. *God I hope that didn't land on . . .*

Doesn't MATTER . . .

All that matters is getting him . . .

AAAGHHNOTHERCAR. I stopped this one with my brain and sent it right back at Freeman like a torpedo, but it changed course before it reached him and demolished a second floor window, half of it sticking out, almost comically, as I flew past. Freeman was so much faster than me . . .

He's the villain.

I'm the hero.

I'm the underdog.

He dropped out of the sky and landed on the road ahead and I followed suit, landing about thirty feet down the road from him. I started to stride in his direction and he stopped.

Turned.

Looked at me.

Smiled.

All around us cars were swerving, jacknifing, sent out of control either by their own panicked reactions or by our thoughts, a deafening chaos of breaking glass and wailing horns and squealing rubber. It had started to rain heavily and a low purr of thunder trembled in the distance. *Nice touch.*

'You shouldn't have gone against me, Stanly!' said Freeman. 'This world is *mine* now!'

'You're insane!' I spat, coiling and springing a whip of crackling white thought towards him.

'I'm perfectly sane. You're just too small and stupid to understand.' He caught the thought, twisted it around and around his arm, trapped it and let it dissipate in the rain, then hurled another car my way. I grabbed it, spun it, threw it back; Freeman split it in half with a thought and the two halves passed harmlessly on either side of him.

'Yes,' he said, 'I've done terrible things. History is *littered* with terrible deeds. Everything, from this city, to the industry that produces those films you love, to the very language we speak, *everything* is built on foundations of spilled blood and shattered bone and hideous action and compromise. I am under no illusions about what I've done. But securing the future of our species? Of this planet? I'd do it all again, without hesitation. And what's more, I would kill every single person who died during the Collision *myself*, with my own hands, rather than letting the monsters do it. If that's what it took.'

He thought chains towards me, trying to wrap them around my neck, to break it, but I snapped every psychic link and pushed on, teeth gritted, through the blizzard of barriers he was thinking between us. It was like walking into a howling, hundred-mile-per-hour wind, but I'd almost reached him. Almost . . .

Then, just as an almighty eruption of thunder heralded the rain's transformation from heavy to torrential, he screamed one more vicious attack my way that blasted me clean off my feet. I lost control of my limbs, twitching, flying – *no, not flying* – falling . . .

AAH.

I landed on the ground hard and something cracked. I coughed up blood, spewing it down my front, moaning low in my throat. Freeman looked down at me. Shook his head.

Turned and glided towards Blue Harvest.

I heard the door open and shut and forced myself to my feet. Gurgling blood and dizzy with pain, I half-ran, half-flew through the chaos of the street. *No. You're not getting them. You're not getting away with this, not this time. Not again.* I reached Blue Harvest, tore the doors clean off their hinges with my brain, staggered in.

Freeman spun to face me, turning his back on an empty room. 'Where are they?'

Oh. That little thing.

I smiled. A chuckle rippled up my throat, emerged, became laughter. Freeman started to advance on me, eyes bulging crazily, but then a voice spoke, disembodied, filling the room, making him jump and look around in total bewilderment.

Danielle's voice. 'Stanly? It's done.'

'Promise?' I gasped.

'Promise.'

I staggered over to Freeman, popping bones back into place and sealing wounds as I did so, and stopped a few centimetres from his face, which was just the most amazing mask of confusion and fury.

'Check. Mate. *Mate.*' I grinned and tapped my temple, then looked up at the ceiling. 'Computer? End program.'

Chapter Thirty-Four

I OPENED MY eyes and the first thing I felt was nausea, deep in the pit of my stomach. Coming back to reality felt so *weird*.

Jesus, got a bit too into that . . .

No time, NO TIME.

I jumped to my feet and looked around. The shimmer had hopped off Freeman's head and retreated towards the office door. Alex was getting up, his consciousness fully back in his body, Tara was standing between us, hugging herself nervously, and Danielle was standing by the desk with one hand on the gun that hung at her hip, staring at Freeman, face set. The big boss, for his part, blinked and groaned.

'Everybody out,' I said. 'Tara? Alex? Danielle? Go. He'll have had a jump start from contact with the shimmer.'

'Nope,' said Danielle. 'I'm staying.' She had one of the most effective 'don't argue' tones I'd ever encountered.

'Fine,' I said. 'Tara? Alex? Outside. *Now.*' I thought the office door open and ushered them out with my mind, cutting Tara off as she tried to protest. The shimmer followed and I slammed the door behind them.

Freeman looked at me.

Realised what I'd done.

'You . . .' he began to roar.

I caught him before he could get up, before his furious thoughts could reach me, and built a cage of intention around him, pinning him to his chair. It was hard, though, he was struggling powerfully, his thoughts a tangle of violently spitting cobras, colours shifting so fast they hurt my eyes, or whatever instruments I was using to pick up the frequencies. Danielle was giving me a helping hand with what felt like fairly basic telekinesis, but it was still a pretty major struggle.

'You've lost,' I said, through gritted teeth. 'You have *lost*. We have the video of Walker, a video of the shimmer lab. Smith is in custody.' *Haha I said 'in custody'.* 'Our star witness,' I said, managing a grin even though my face was begging me not to place it under undue strain. 'Loose ends, mate. Sloppy.'

'You won't—'

'Get away with this?' I filled a smile with all the triumph it deserved and sent it his way. The shimmer had certainly made him more powerful . . . but it didn't matter now. 'I already *have* got away with it. We'll be in some trouble, yeah. Maybe serious trouble. But you are *finished*.' He almost managed to break out when I said that, but I slapped him down hard with memories of Eddie. 'For my cousin,' I said. 'And for everyone else you killed.'

'Nicely done, boyo.'

'Oh, bloody hell, not you.'

Stanly stepped forwards and stood next to me, arms folded. He'd changed into a black suit, complete with shirt and tie. 'Yep. Me.'

'What's he doing here?' asked Danielle.

'Yeah, what do you want?' I said. 'Because I owe you some severe—'

'You got him, then,' Stanly interrupted, not taking his eyes off the big boss.

Freeman's face creased momentarily with confusion. Then he smiled. 'Oh, I see. More illusions? Dreams within dreams?'

'No,' I said. '*Inception* is *well* 2010. This is real. He's a version of me from another universe.'

'Really.' He didn't believe me. I didn't care.

'What do you *want*?' I said.

'I want to know what you're going to do now,' said Stanly. 'With him.'

I looked at Freeman, who seemed to have forgotten to struggle. In fact, he was watching us with an expression of such genuine, human fascination that I almost warmed to him, momentarily, before remembering that under no circumstances was I ever going to warm to him, ever.

'Hand him over to Angelcorp,' I said. 'There's plenty of evidence . . .'

'Angelcorp,' said Stanly. 'The same Angelcorp to whom you refused to hand over Alex and his gang, for ethical reasons?'

'This is different.'

'How?'

'He's . . .' I trailed off. Freeman was looking expectantly at me. 'What do *you* reckon I should do, then?' I asked. 'If we really have to do this?'

Stanly snapped his fingers and the two of us, along with Freeman, were suddenly standing on the edge of a copper cliff beneath a glowering obsidian sky. In the desiccated grey valley below, hundreds of monsters were tearing into one another with berserker fury, tentacles and bladed tails swinging, horns and spikes and razor wings tearing, soaking in every colour of blood.

'Charming,' said Freeman, audibly trying to sound nonchalant and not quite managing it.

'So what?' I said. 'I should throw him to them?'

'For instance,' said Stanly. 'Or is killing against your code?'

'Kind of is, yeah.'

'Why?' he sneered. 'Because Superman doesn't kill? Well. Unless Zach Snyder's involved . . .'

Jesus, is this clown actually serious right now? 'No,' I said, 'not because *Superman* doesn't kill, you twat. Because murder is bad and should be avoided as much as possible. *Obviously.*'

'So you'd never kill a bad guy? Never ever? Even one like this, a mass murderer? One who could still cause so much damage?'

'Never?' I shrugged. 'Honestly, I don't know. I would like to think that it would never be necessary. I'd like to think I'd never choose to do it. But I don't *know*. What I do know, right now, is that killing is not the way to deal with Freeman. He needs to pay *properly* and people need to *see* it.'

'Boring,' said Stanly. 'Plebeian. Small scale. You could choose *any* punishment for him. I know of worlds free of any life whatsoever, where we could leave him to wander alone, forever. Worlds ruled over by entities that would make Cthulhu piss his tentacles and scurry home - entities that would *love* a puny human to play with.' He advanced on Freeman, who took a few nervous steps back. 'Or I could reach into his brain right now,' said Stanly, 'and just *pluck* his powers out. Gone. What's more, I could permanently damage the specific part of the brain that allows them to manifest. George Freeman reduced to a normal, boring human for the rest of his natural life.'

'No!' I said. 'He needs to have his powers if he's going to stand trial. Everything he's done, to Morter Smith—'

'Stand trial?' Stanly whirled around with flames where his

eyes should have been. '*Stand trial?* I'm offering you multiple universes of punishment! Justice as ironic, as painful, as humiliating, as existentially horrifying, as *infinite* as you want!'

'It's not *about* what I want!'

'Isn't it? Why the hell not? I think you're as good a representative of the wronged party, aka *humankind*, as we're likely to find! This piece of trash happily fed your world to the monsters but you won't do the same to him?'

'No,' I said. 'I won't.'

'Well done, Stanly,' said Freeman. 'I knew your inherent—'

'Shut. *Up.*' I gave him some major eyeball. 'Seriously.'

Stanly tutted impatiently and waved his hand.

Oh Jesus.

We were back in the shimmer cave. The lake was black, the whole place full of an utterly rancid smell, stinking worse than anything should rightfully stink, worse than the biggest pile of rotting rubbish, worse than all the sewage refineries in the world emptied out and left in the hot sun, worse than . . . well, anything.

'So?' I said. 'What now?'

'You want him imprisoned like a normal person in your world?' said Stanly. 'How can you guarantee he won't make a deal? Worm his way out? You can't be sure he'll stay imprisoned, but you won't kill him. Why not this?'

'This?'

'I can bring the shimmers back to life,' said Stanly. 'Easily. Like *that*.' He snapped his fingers. 'Then we just chuck him in and leave him here. Like he left you. I'm sure they'll even make sure he has nightmares forever, if we ask them nicely.'

'They wouldn't take him before,' I said. 'They said he wasn't powerful enough.'

'Shimmers understand more than they let on,' said Stanly. 'I'll convince them to keep him. Either that, or I'll super-charge his powers so they'll be *desperate* to keep him here. Best battery ever.'

'Great idea,' I said. 'Make the maniac even *more* powerful.'

'He'll never get out of here.'

'I did.'

'Because of *me*.'

'Boys,' said Freeman. 'Now come on, let's play nice shall w—'

Stanly and I both turned and snapped 'Shut *up*' in unison, before turning back to one another. 'You don't *get* it,' I said. 'I'm not looking for poetic justice. I don't *want* to decide his fate. I *shouldn't* decide his fate.'

'Why?'

'Oh for God's sake. Why d'you think? Surely you've come across the term "conflict of interest" before?'

'Oh *stop* it,' said Stanly.

'Stop what?'

'The maturity act! Like you're above feeling vengeful! Like you wouldn't *love* to see him torn to shreds by monsters, or sleeping away here for eternity, or—'

'Of course I would! I *hate* him! That's the *point!*' I shook my head. This was really starting to piss me off. 'I'm not . . . I don't have the authority or the knowledge . . . he needs to be *tried*, by . . . by objective . . .'

'You don't have the *authority?*' Stanly clapped his hands and the three of us were hovering in the air above his favour-ite mountain range again. 'You can do *this!*' he yelled, his enraged, suddenly awe-inspiring voice echoing between the peaks. To punctuate the last word he raised his fist in the air and clenched it. In tandem with the movement, one mountain peak was crushed, as though gripped in his closed fist. It crumbled, rocky debris tumbling into the abyss, making a truly spectacular sound.

'I thought you wanted to be a superhero?' Stanly said, whirling in the air to face me. 'What exactly does being a superhero entail if not taking the law into your own hands, delivering the smackdown, delivering the *judgment?*'

'OK,' I said. 'With the two of you as my witnesses, I would like to officially state now and for all time that I am *not* a superhero. I don't have the faintest idea *what* I am. I'm just trying to do my best, to do what's right. And what's *right* is handing this piece of human garbage over to the authorities—'

'The authorities who you didn't *trust* with—'

'It's *different!*' I said. 'They will *change.*'

'Don't count on it,' said Stanly.

'Hear hear,' muttered Freeman, glancing interestedly at the epic drop beneath us.

'Take us back,' I said. '*Now.* I mean it. I have had enough of this. I have had enough of *you*, very much in a William Shatner kicking Christopher Lloyd into an exploding planet way. Just take us back, then piss the hell off.'

'Fine,' said Stanly, and we were back in the office. Freeman was slammed back into his chair and regarded the room. For someone whose plans had been fairly comprehensively screwed over, he'd recovered his calm, contemptuous demeanour pretty well.

Danielle, who had been standing by the door talking on her phone, jumped and cried out. 'Aah! Where the hell did you go?'

'Don't ask.' I looked expectantly at Stanly. 'Well? Get lost, then.'

'No,' he said.

'Stanly,' said Danielle. 'We need to—'

'Be *quiet*,' said Stanly, irritably. Danielle obeyed and the other me turned towards the door and called, 'Tara! Can you come in here?'

'I beg your pardon?' I said. 'You *don't* speak—'

The door opened and Tara popped her head around. 'What's wrong?' She frowned. 'You've . . . changed your clothes.'

'Tara,' I said. 'Go back outside right now and—'

'Yeah,' said Stanly. 'Long story. Brain stuff. Can you come in a sec? I want to ask you something.'

Tara came in, her gaze passing right through me. He was hiding me from her. I tried to yell her name, but no sound came out at all. I tried to move, to touch her shoulder, but I had no control over my limbs. I looked at Danielle, who was just watching proceedings with vague interest. *He's in her mind. Bollocks.* I looked at Freeman, who was *smiling* as he realised what was happening.

No . . .

'What's up?' asked Tara.

'There are a few things I haven't told you,' said Stanly, 'that you deserve to know.'

You son of a bitch. Don't you DARE—

'Now?' said Tara. 'Shouldn't we . . .'

'Yes,' said Stanly. 'Now. It's important. Mr Freeman here has an employee named Morter Smith.'

No . . .

'Morter Smith,' he continued, 'is your father.'

Tara blinked. Her hand flew instinctively to her hair, tugging at it. She shifted uncertainly on the spot. 'What?'

'Freeman and a woman named Pandora took you from him when you were a baby,' said Stanly, 'because he's . . . a bad guy. They thought you'd be safer with Mr and Mrs Rogers. Then, when you were kidnapped by Smiley Joe, Freeman decided that he'd use you to pit me against the Angel Group. He and Pandora convinced me that I was your father and Kloe was your mother, and that we'd brought you back in time to protect you from the Angel Group.'

'What the hell are you on about?' Tara scowled, her eyes glassy.

'I'm sorry,' said Stanly, 'but you need to know.'

DAMN YOU! STOP THIS NOW!

'Freeman forced Oliver and Jacqueline to go along with the story,' said Stanly. 'Threatened them. You remember when we went to the cabin in the woods? They helped convince me that I was being guided by my future self, when actually it was all part of Freeman's plan to manipulate me.'

'Why are you telling me all this now?' Tara's voice caught in her throat.

'Because you need to know the extent of his crimes,' said Stanly. 'This, all this, manipulating me, bullying your foster parents, *all* of it, was so that he could unleash the monsters on London and take control of the Angel Group. He then wiped Mr and Mrs Rogers' minds, so they have no memory of ever going along with his scheme. He also wiped Morter Smith's memories, wiped you from his mind, and he's been keeping Smith around as his own brainwashed lackey, just for his own amusement, to remind himself how much power he has. How *brilliant* he is. How untouchable. Freeman here has played with your life, with my life, with your foster parents' lives. With our *minds*. And the lives and minds of everyone in London and God knows who else around the world. He's manipulated, lied, murdered. He's unleashed literal hell on this city. He's kept shimmers in his own private lab, torturing them so he can find out how to travel to other worlds, to gain *yet more* power. And his reward for all that? He gets to live in luxury, have global influence.'

Tara was staring at Freeman, her hands shaking. *No. Please. Don't.* I tried to think at her, think through what Stanly was doing, but I was stupid if I thought that he was going to let me overpower him. If he didn't want me to, I wasn't going to. He really was beyond anything I could imagine.

'So what should we do with him?' asked Stanly.

'What?' she whispered.

'I want you to help me decide. How he should pay. The whole reason you went along with Alex's plan was to help people, wasn't it? Solve problems that *Freeman* caused? He's the source. What do we do? How do we make him pay?'

'I don't . . .' Tara scrunched her eyes tight shut. 'Why didn't you tell me all this? You knew who my real *dad* is? You . . .'

'There hasn't been time,' said Stanly. 'I only found out the whole story just before I went away. I'm sorry, we can talk about it soon, but right now we need to decide what we're going to do with *this* evil sonofabitch. Think about everything he's done. Everything he's been allowed to get away with. We have superpowers. Do you really want to just hand him over to the police? To Angelcorp? The judicial systems in this world are *decades* behind the crimes he's committed. You think he's going to get a trial that's worth shit?'

Tara continued to stare at Freeman. Her trembling fists kept clenching and un-clenching and a few tears escaped her eyes, running freely down her cheeks. At least Freeman was having the decency to look uncomfortable. I was bellowing silently with my mind, trying in vain to get through to Tara, to my bastard double, but to no avail.

This is not how I pictured my super awesome plan working out.

'What would you like to do with him?' said Stanly. 'Torture him? *Kill* him? He deserves it, doesn't he?'

Tara put her head on one side, then on the other. Then she turned. 'Where is *Stanly?*' As she said my name, a raw blast of thought crossed the room, almost bright enough to be visible. Stanly staggered backwards, caught off-guard.

'YES!' I yelled.

Tara jumped. 'Oh my *God,*' she said, 'where did you go?'

'I was here,' I said, turning to face Stanly. '*This* piece of crap hid me from you.'

Danielle too was shaken out of Stanly's influence and she spun and trained her gun on him, eyes blazing. 'Don't you even *think* about going in my head again, you little wanker.'

'You are *done* here, mate,' I said.

'I don't think you understand,' said Stanly. 'You have no control, no influence *whatsoever*, over what I do. You can't threaten me. There is nothing you can do to me that I won't shrug off with a yawn. There—'

'All right,' said Tara. 'Whatever. You're a badass. But if you're Stanly, then hopefully there's some non-dickhead in you, somewhere, deep down.' *Aww, thanks.* 'So can you just go away, please?'

Stanly looked at me. At Tara. At Freeman, whose expression had shifted to bemused and slightly tired. Then he looked back at Tara and smiled impenetrably. 'Fine,' he said. 'I'll leave you to it. But sooner or later, you're going to need to understand. You can't just go on living like normal people. Not really. Not any more. These powers? They change *everything.*'

And while I was pretty sure it happened by accident, there was a note of desperation in that last word that made me soften towards him a bit. Maybe he did it on purpose. Who knew.

Stop warming to complete nutboxes.

That's an order.

'We'll jump off that bridge when we come to it,' I said, moving to stand next to Tara.

'Yeah,' she said. 'And then *fly away.*' She stuck out her tongue.

Stanly laughed. 'You know what, kid? You're all right. But Stanly, I'm serious. If you don't sort this guy out, permanently, you have no idea what's in store.'

I frowned. 'What do you mean?'

Stanly didn't answer. His smile had gone. He glanced at Freeman and his eyes became icebergs. 'Be seeing you.'

And he was gone.

Well . . . crap.

'Tara,' I said.

'It's fine.'

'I'm sorry, I didn't . . .'

'We'll talk about it later.' Tara nodded towards Freeman. 'So what *are* we going to do with him?'

'What do you mean?'

'Asshole Stanly was right. He's *evil.* And no-one in this world is going to try him properly.'

'We don't know that.'

'Yes we do.'

Maybe we do.

Maybe we should take care of him ourselves?

But . . .

'We have grounds to arrest him,' said Danielle. 'To start an investigation. Angelcorp—'

'I don't *trust* Angelcorp,' snapped Tara. 'I trust *us*.'

'Tara,' I said. 'We can't. Exposing what he's done, making sure the information gets to the right people, that's our job. And we've done it. Now it's for other people to do the rest.'

'Which other people? Who are they?'

'I don't know. That's the point.'

'But isn't this *why* we have the powers?' asked Tara. 'To do things like this?'

'I don't think that's how it works. I don't think we have them for any particular reason. We choose what we do with them. And we have to choose what we *don't* do. Maybe that's more important.'

'It's not good enough,' said Tara. She was crying, but she spoke with strength. I tentatively tried to take her hand and was so glad that she let me.

'I know,' I said.

Freeman raised a tentative hand. 'Excuse me? Don't I get to have a say in my fate?'

'No,' snapped Tara.

'*Obviously* not,' said Danielle, with a spectacularly withering look.

'Well,' said Freeman, 'maybe I don't *want* a huge public trial. Maybe I'd rather not give you the satisfaction of handing me over to whomever you think will be able to deal with me . . . once you stop dithering like a child who can't decide which flavour of sweets to stuff in his bag, that is. Maybe I'd rather

484

not suffer the indignity of hearing my so-called "crimes" listed by self-righteous individuals who can neither comprehend my motivations nor do them justice.'

I shrugged. 'Your point being?'

'Perhaps I shall simply wipe my own mind,' said Freeman. 'Render myself a blank slate. Can they prosecute a total amnesiac? Will it matter? It certainly won't be half as satisfying for you. Which is a victory, as far as I'm concerned.'

I walked towards him and leaned across his desk. He cringed slightly, which was good. 'Go ahead,' I said.

'What?'

'Stanly . . .' said Danielle.

'Do it,' I said. 'Go on. Wipe your mind. Do it now. Be my guest. Come on. *Do it.*'

He just stared at me, opening and closing his mouth.

'I knew you wouldn't,' I said. 'You love yourself too much. Come on. Get up. We're taking you . . .'

'Where?'

'I don't know,' I said. 'Somewhere.'

Sick exit line, kid.

Gimme a break. I'm bloody knackered.

We stepped out into the corridor, where Alex was waiting. 'Everything OK?'

'Ish,' I said.

'You won't get away with this,' Freeman hissed. 'None of you.'

'Save the Scooby Doo bullshit,' said Tara.

I sniggered. 'Good one.' She looked at me and we exchanged a smile, but she very quickly stopped smiling and looked away. Seemed that I was in the dog house.

Sigh.

'Right,' I said. 'Alex? You and Tara need to go now. Danielle's exit, like we discussed. Find Nailah and Faisal, get to the safe house. Take the shimmer too.'

'Stanly . . .' said Tara.

'I'll see you soon,' I said.

'Promise?'

I shouldn't have promised. Not again. But the fact that she was asking me to, even after what she'd just learned . . .

'Yeah.' I smiled. 'Thank you both. Seriously good job. Now go.'

They nodded and hurried off. 'OK,' I said. 'Come along, George.'

Danielle and I frog-marched Freeman down the corridor, containing his psychic and physical struggling with our brains.

'I called Mr Hamilton before,' said Danielle. 'Nailah sent him everything, once the other two groups got their missions done. He's on his way here.'

'So you've got Lucius on your side, have you?' said Freeman. 'That slippery, pious traitor.'

'He's been on to Walker for months,' said Danielle. 'It was only a matter of time before we got to you.'

'Really.' Freeman didn't sound impressed.

'You can thank Lauren for all this as well,' I said. 'Right before you had her killed, she transmitted a massive bundle of extremely useful information to Nailah. The location of your lab, for example, and Morter Smith. Security details. Couldn't have done any of this without her.'

'Well, at least I killed *someone* who deserved it.'

I yanked him away from Danielle and slammed him against the wall, barely aware that I was channelling my power into my arms. *'Don't you f—'*

'Stanly!' said Danielle. 'Don't let him goad you. We need to take him alive, remember?'

'You need to take me alive,' said Freeman. 'That must sting, mustn't it? How many of your friends have you let die, Stanly? And how many times will you save my life? I see you've not brought *Lauren* back. Forgotten her already, have you?'

'As soon as I have Walker,' I said, 'I'll find Lauren's body and I *will* bring her back. In the meantime, you piece of sh—' Before I could finish the sentence, Freeman sent out a ferocious thought that blasted Danielle and I in different directions. We hit opposite walls, hard, Danielle's gun flying down the corridor. Freeman looked around desperately for a few seconds . . .

Then he vanished.

Son of a—

'Where the hell did he go?' said Danielle. 'Where *is* he?'

'Shh.' I closed my eyes, feeling with my thoughts. He had to have left some kind of residue, some colour, a mental clue, a . . .

THERE.

Like the idea of a grey curtain, with a world beyond . . . the curtain closing, falling back . . .

No.

Not yet.

FOLLOW—

Chapter Thirty-Five

—FREEMAN.

OK. Easier than I was expecting.

I was standing on crimson rock in a narrow, uneven passageway between a pair of onyx-black cliffs. The air smelled like loose electricity. Up ahead I could just see the suggestion of movement vanishing around a corner. 'Freeman!' I yelled, running off in pursuit.

The passageway was narrow so I had to awkwardly hold my arms in front of me so I didn't scrape my elbows on the sharp walls. I emerged from the corridor into a huge basin of red rock, stretching out and down in a majestically ugly sweep. Freeman was standing about ten feet away, staring up at the mauve-grey sky.

'Pretty impressive,' I said.

He turned his head slightly. 'What?'

'Didn't think you'd worked out how to travel between universes.'

'I . . .' Freeman shook his head. 'I'm not coming back with you.'

'I think you are.' I took a few steps towards him and he took a few away.

'I'm not even sure how I did it,' he said, shaking his head again. 'It must have been instinct. A defence mechanism . . .'

Idea . . .

'Maybe,' I said. 'Maybe not.'

'What does that mean?'

I took a few more steps towards him, but he raised his hand and the air rippled around me as his thoughts halted my progress.

'It means,' I said, 'that I got you *again*.'

'What are you talking about?'

Ha ha. OK this could be fun.

'Come on,' I said. 'You really think I'd bring *Tara* with me to take down my most hated, dangerous foe? You think I hang out with alternate universe versions of myself, bickering like twin brothers? You think that you can suddenly travel between parallel universes, just because it's convenient?'

Freeman frowned, sweat glistening on his brow. He looked around at the great rusty cliffs, the crimson floor, the unsettled sky.

'Another illusion,' he said.

I smiled. 'Bingo.'

'Why? To what end?'

'To buy us more time,' I said. 'From the beginning, I've had the least important job. My friends are the ones doing the really important, awesome stuff. Rescuing the shimmers from your lab, finding and isolating Morter Smith, sorting out various incriminating videos. Honestly, I'm gutted I missed everyone else's missions. Bet they were sick.' I shrugged. 'Drawback of not being omniscient, I guess. My job has always been to distract you for as long as possible. With the help of our shimmer friend. A shimmer that escaped from your lab, and is currently sucking on your noggin, pumping *this* in.' I indicated our surroundings.

'No,' said Freeman, the colour in his face rising. 'No! It can't be!'

'I'm afraid it is, buddy. And what's more, you don't get out until I say so.' I walked towards him. He backed away, holding up his hands, creating a wall between us, but I thought myself insubstantial and passed through his barriers, continuing to advance on him. He scrambled away, trying to run, but I just walked, calm as anything, like a Terminator, like Michael fricking Myers.

'You can't outrun me,' I said. 'You can't get away. I'm *creating* this entire world, as we speak, with my brain.'

Freeman stopped again, turned. 'What do you *want* from me?'

'I'll let you in on a secret,' I said. 'For all my talk of doing what's right and saving the world, I've always been a bit petty. It's a weakness of mine. So how could I possibly pass up the opportunity to mess with your head? Why wouldn't I make it my *business* to screw with you as much as humanly possible? I *despise* you. And you will face justice.' I grinned, my eyes flashing dangerously. 'But until then . . . I'ma have me some fun.'

'I'm sorry,' said Freeman. 'I'm *sorry*, Stanly. For everything. Please. Just . . .'

'No. Nooooope. None of that.' I indicated a zip being pulled across my lips. 'I want to know the truth. The *real* truth. No begging, no bargaining, no bullshit. *Truth*.'

Freeman collapsed to his knees, which I hadn't been expecting. 'Can't you just go into my mind and take what you want?'

'Yes. But I want to hear what you have to say.'

'What I have to say isn't necessarily truer than what's in my mind.'

'I know.' I felt uncomfortable standing over him, so I crouched down. 'Do you feel guilty?'

'About what?'

'You know. About what you did. Unleashing the monsters. Do you lie awake at night? Do you sit in your office at three in the morning, staring out of the window, thinking about the people who died?'

Freeman shook his head. 'No.'

OK. *Wasn't expecting that.* 'Not at all,' I said. 'No guilt.'

'No,' he said. 'I feel . . . remorse. I wish it hadn't been necessary. But I meant it when I told you that I would do it all again. I feel justified in what I did. Entirely. I'm sorry if that's not what you expected to hear, but you wanted the truth.'

'Yes, I did.'

'I do sometimes look out of my office window, late at night,' said Freeman. 'I look out across the city of London and I think of everything that has changed in the last five and a half years. Everything that I have done, everything that I have set in motion. And I feel *vindicated.*' He thought for a long moment, then got to his feet. He was smiling again. 'And that is what I will tell the world. If you can find a judge and a jury who will sit and pass judgment on me, I will tell them until the end, until they string me up or lock me away and throw away the key, that I did what was necessary. For the world.'

He turned away and took a few steps, looking around. 'I admire you, Stanly. I do. This whole ruse was masterful. To think that right now, I am merely wandering around inside an illusion, within my own mind . . .' He turned back. 'Do you remember our conversations? When we first met?'

'Yeah.' He'd slightly taken the wind out of my sails, but I was trying not to let on.

'I meant it all,' said Freeman. 'There is no winning. No

good and evil, ultimately. There is just the unstoppable onward march of time. Cause. Effect. And we simply do what we can to dictate the terms of that march, the course it takes. That's all. I am secure in the knowledge that I have done that, to the best of my abilities. So if today was my last day in office . . . I will go to my cell, or to my death, a satisfied man. Fulfilled.' He took a deep breath and nodded approvingly. 'My, my. This world even *smells* real. How much longer must we stay here, as interesting as it is?'

'Well, actually—'

BOOM.

The ground shook beneath us, hard enough for us to stumble drunkenly, like a building had just fallen somewhere nearby. And I suddenly realised that I had been here before.

Oh no.

The sound came again, from the other side of those black cliffs, but this time it was closer and I staggered back so I was side by side with Freeman. He was actually *chuckling.*

'Well,' he said. 'My my. What fresh hell have you cooked up for me now, eh, Stanly? What's this latest illusion?'

'It's not an illusion.'

'Oh.' He nodded, although I could tell by his tone that he didn't believe me in the slightest. 'I see. Well, then . . .'

'I'm serious!' I grabbed his arm, trying to pull him back, because now I could see the suggestion of a shape through the gap between the cliffs. 'This whole thing was real! I think that the other me might have brought you here, we've been here before . . .'

Freeman laughed. 'Oh, Stanly. You are funny.'

'I'm *serious!*'

He pulled a mock serious face, pouting like he was

humouring a stroppy four-year-old. 'Oh, well, if you're *serious*.'

'Damn it,' I said. 'STANLY? Where the hell are you? Exit now, please? Please? Hello?' *I am going to kill him. So much.* Everything in me was saying *turn, run, fly as fast and as far as possible . . .*

But I couldn't.

Have to see . . .

Don't want to . . .

But have to . . .

Another BOOM that made this world, wherever it was, tremble, and then something huge, *gigantic*, launched itself up from beyond the cliffs. It moved incredibly fast, despite being enormous, passed over us in a weirdly graceful arc and landed a little way away, rearing up, bathing us in cold shadow.

Oh.

My.

Elder.

God.

'Well,' said Freeman, chuckling. '*Very* impressive. You must have dug deep in your childhood nightmares to come up with this.'

The biggest thing I'd ever seen was a monster in the shimmer world. This might not have been quite as tall, but as far as dreadfulness went, it was something else entirely. In fact, as I took it in, I felt . . . different. Like . . .

Like this is the end.

It was humanoid and jet black, with four huge, impossibly muscled arms ending in cruelly clawed hands. On its back were two great wings that swept up to bladed points, and around the edges of the wings were tentacles, thick and clammy and lined with suckers, writhing and twitching as though they had minds of their own. Its head was diamond shaped, with a pair of enormous horns, but its face . . . its face kept *shifting*, as though it was made up of different, separate creatures, writhing around a pair of almond-shaped eyes that stayed mercifully still. Or not, actually . . . in fact, no, they weren't eyes, they were *holes*, gaps, tunnels leading somewhere that I didn't want to look, event horizons from which nothing could escape. All over its body, from its arms to its chest to its belly to its – OK *I didn't need to see that* – to its legs, were *bits* of other creatures, a foot here, half a screaming face there, protruding, like it had absorbed hundreds of other beings but not bothered to do it properly, so parts of them were just left there, like ghastly piercings. As I stared up at it, I felt cold and shaky, freezing sweat breaking out all over my body. I wondered if Freeman was still convinced that this was an illusion, or if this sudden awful, stomach-deep terror had hit him too. Surely no-one could feel what I was feeling now and still smile? Could I smile, ever again? Even if I got away?

Who are you kidding, kid? You ain't getting away from this.

This is it.

End of you.

Not just you.

Everything.

Nothing can survive, not after this.

'Impressive indeed,' said Freeman.

Oh God . . .

He still doesn't know . . .

I couldn't take my eyes from the thing, the beast, whatever it was, as it stood there, maybe breathing, maybe regarding us, maybe not, who knew, but I could see, just out of the corner of my eye, that Freeman was walking towards it, one arm raised . . . *waving*.

'Hello!' he called. 'Hello there! Beast of Stanly's most wonderfully absurd and disturbing imagination! It's a pleasure to meet you! If we're going to be stuck here for a while, maybe we should get to know one another!'

I wanted to tell him to come back, to stop. I wanted to fly away, fly us *both* away, but I couldn't speak. Couldn't move.

Oh God, its face . . .

Oh God, its HAND . . .

The thing held out one of its four hands, which could have comfortably held multiple cars in its palm, and Freeman started to rise up from the ground.

Jesus, this thing has powers *too?*

Freeman turned to look at me as he rose. 'More giants, Stanly?' he laughed. 'You need to come up with some new tricks! Must I now stand on this one's hand as well?'

He landed on the creature's outstretched palm, turned back towards me and shrugged as though he were acting in a pantomime. 'It seems so!'

He turned back to the immense black behemoth, which was staring at him, I think. It was hard to be sure. It also felt like it was staring at me. Like it was staring at *everything*. Like this universe, *every* universe, could be trapped and swallowed by its gaze. I felt as though I wouldn't be able to stand for much longer, but I also felt as though I couldn't possibly fall to my knees, not unless the beast wanted me to, because . . .

Cos . . .

Wait . . .

I could feel something. The tide. That insistent pulling.

Stanly. He was trying to take me out of here.

NO.

I shrugged him off and took a step towards the beast, even though my legs were both cement and mist. Stanly was *not* robbing me of the justice I wanted. He was *not* going to undercut me, to have this creature eat Freeman or tear him apart molecule by molecule or absorb him or whatever it wanted to do. This was not happening.

I forced my eyes shut and *flew* towards them, focusing on the sound of Freeman's voice, taunting this unimaginable horror. I could still see the creature, even though my eyes were closed, but it didn't matter, it *didn't matter—*

Nothing matters anymore—

NO NO THAT'S JUST THE UNIMAGINABLE TERROR TALKING—

I could feel its power, older and darker than any I'd yet encountered, it was trying to stop me, but *no no no no no no I can't let it—*

EXIT!

EXIT!

NO NO NO NOT THIS FACE NOT THIS FACE NO LET ME GO DAMN IT LET ME GO LET ME NO NO NO NO—

'No no no no . . .'

'Stanly?'

I opened one eye. Two eyes. I was lying on grass, beneath sun, gripping someone to me hard . . . someone . . . *Freeman?* I recoiled, rolling away, practically backflipping on to my feet, barely in control of what I was doing.

Freeman frowned in confusion. 'What exactly was that in aid of?' He looked around. 'More illusions?' Confusion parted like curtains, revealing white-hot rage beneath. 'Damn you, Stanly, I *tire* of this!' He jumped up and thought at me furiously, savagely. I didn't have time to defend myself. I felt like I didn't know how to anymore. Freeman's thoughts hit me and I sprawled on my back on the grass, my body burning as though an electric current had passed through it.

'What if I kill you here?' Freeman yelled, pinning me to the ground with his thoughts. 'What if your mind dies? Will your body follow suit?' Black, serpentine rage tore into me, biting, burrowing, and I screamed in agony. 'You couldn't just leave things alone, could you?' His eyes were glowing white, spewing lightning into mine. I couldn't breathe through the pain, could hardly even scream. 'You had to interfere! *I owe you an eternity of* AAAH—'

The first thing I noticed was that my face was suddenly wet. The second was the arrow sticking through Freeman's shoulder, the wickedly sharp arrowhead shiny and black with blood. Freeman looked down at it, confusion returning. 'This . . . what . . .'

He sprawled, shaking, on the grass. I looked past the space where he'd been standing, across the clearing, to Senia, pale, frozen to the spot, her longbow raised. Even from here, I could see her hands trembling.

'Hiya!' I called, weakly.

Chapter Thirty-Six

F REEMAN WAS JUST starting to come to when we flashed back to our world. Or my world. Or his world. Or whatever it was. We reappeared in the corridor and everybody – that is Danielle, Lucius and a contingent of armed police – jumped. If I hadn't been so drained, and if Freeman hadn't still been insisting on bleeding on me, I might have laughed.

My punctured companion groaned.

'Don't shoot!' Lucius yelled, as an uncomfortable number of guns were trained on me. He wore an unspeakably expensive suit and his hair was significantly greyer and his face even more severe than I remembered. His eyes widened as he noticed the arrow sticking out of Freeman's bloodied shoulder. 'What on *earth*—'

'It wasn't me,' I said. 'Promise. I've been trying to stop the bleeding, didn't think it was a good idea to remove the arrow. You might want to get him some medical attention.'

Lucius looked flustered. 'Well . . . yes. Of course. Er . . .' He nodded to two of the officers. 'Take him to the medical centre in the Undercells. Block him, highest setting. Miss Dewornu, go with them. Don't take your eyes off him.'

'Yes, sir.' Danielle helped Freeman to his feet and escorted him away, flanked by two police officers. I felt like I should have shouted something pithy and badass after my vanquished nemesis, but all I really wanted to do was go to bed.

'OK,' I said. 'Can I go now, please?'

'You can't be serious,' said Lucius. 'I should be arresting you as well! Along with your other friends.'

'Hasn't Danielle filled you in on everything?'

'Yes, she has, but still—'

'Fine,' I said. 'Arrest us, if you must. But first, I need to see Jane Walker.'

'She is in custody, she will—'

'You need to get me in a room with her,' I said. '*Now.*'

'Why on earth would—'

'She killed Lauren.'

'I'm aware of that, and I'm very—'

'I need to know where her body is.'

'Ms Walker will be questioned in due course,' said Lucius, clearly not enjoying being interrupted every time he tried to finish a sentence, 'but in the meantime—'

'If I find out where Lauren's body is, there's a chance I can bring her back!' I said, not really caring if he was enjoying being interrupted every time he tried to finish a sentence.

Lucius practically did a double-take.

'Please,' I said. 'Let me try and get her back. I don't know how much time we have left. *Please.* I swear I will co-operate with you. If you choose to lock me up then that's fine, I will go quietly, but let me try and save Lauren.'

Lucius looked even more flustered. This whole thing obviously wasn't unfolding exactly as he'd planned. 'You really think you can bring her back?' he said. I wondered whether the notion interfered with his Christian beliefs.

'Ask Danielle,' I said. 'Phone her right now. My friends were dead, and now they're not.'

'I *will* ask Miss Dewornu,' said Lucius. 'Later.' He sighed. 'Fine. Jane Walker is in a cell downstairs.'

Come on.

Please.

I heard Walker before we got to her. She was demanding to speak to her lawyer, asking how dare anybody keep her here without counsel, that she had rights.

Well. It's like raaain on your wedding day. Except it's not cos this is actually bloody ironic.

A security guard unlocked the door and Lucius showed me in. As soon as Walker saw me she shrank back against the wall, her face going pink. 'No!' she cried. 'Lucius, you keep him away from me! Keep him *away!*'

I advanced on her, ignoring her protestations. 'Where's Lauren's body, Walker?' She didn't want to tell me, but easily, effortlessly, I reached inside her mind, slipping past her fear, her hatred of me, the knowledge that she was finished, all that tasty but currently useless surface fluff.

Found Lauren . . .

Recoiled.

'You . . .' I said.

There was no body.

She had seen to that.

'*You.*' I thought a pair of hands around her neck, lifting her off the floor and slamming her against the wall. She tried to cry out, gurgling and clutching her throat, eyes bulging like a frog's. 'You evil bitch,' I said, my voice trembling, cracking, strained. 'I will *end* you. Like I ended your pet Rosie. Except with you, I'll make it *last.* I'll pop your eyeballs in their sockets, then I'll gradually pull your brain out through your ears and nose, one bit at a time, so you lose everything, but *nice and slowly,* you'll *feel* yourself trickling away, and then, when you're a dribbling vegetable—'

'*Stanly!*'

I turned my head. Lucius had his hand on my shoulder. I hadn't even noticed. I wasn't entirely sure that I'd been speaking out loud. I also hadn't noticed that the door was now open and that there were several policemen standing there with guns and thoughts trained on me.

As though I couldn't take them.

'What?' My voice seemed to have discovered a new bass frequency.

'Stop,' said Lucius. 'Don't make it worse for yourself. Let *us* take care of her.'

'You won't. She's one of yours. She'll get a deal.'

'She won't,' said Lucius. 'You have my word.'

'Let's be honest, Lucius. With our history, I have no idea what your word is worth.'

'The recording you gave us implicates her in multiple conspiracies,' said Lucius. 'Serious breaks in protocol, highly illegal activities, the murder of one of our own and the attempted murder of several others. She will pay. Everyone involved will pay. I can promise you that.'

Do I believe him?

'But you must stop,' he said, firmly. '*Now.*'

Justice, remember.

That thing.

Reluctantly – but by no means gently – I dropped Walker. She fell into a heap on the ground, crying.

I turned to Lucius. 'Now what?'

'Now what' turned out to be me waiting in an Undercell.

My initial reaction to that suggestion was 'Presumably you've gotta be fucking kidding me right now', but Lucius made a persuasive point.

'It's a formality,' he said. 'It will placate some very high-up individuals who, while they may be relieved that George Freeman is in custody, are furious about the unsanctioned operation that landed him there. I am on your side, Stanly. I will vouch for you. I will ensure that he and Walker are punished. But in order to do that, I need to go about things a certain way. Procedures. Process. *By the book*. If you fight us, you damage the whole case. You understand?'

I was too tired to argue. And to be fair, I did understand. So I let a squad of soldiers lead me to a cell, where I cleaned Freeman's blood off my face, took a seat on the bed and closed my eyes. I felt as though I could have gone straight to sleep.

'Well. There's that, then.'

Oh no. Not now. Seriously.

'Piss off,' I said, not bothering to open my eyes.

'Oh, come on,' said Stanly. 'No need for that.'

That made me open my eyes. 'I beg your pardon?'

Stanly smiled. He was leaning against the wall, still in his black suit, the dictionary definition of nonchalant. 'You got your result, didn't you? Freeman locked safely away. And you pretty much managed to save everyone.'

'Not Lauren. My friend whose death, let's not forget, *you watched*.' I wanted so much to let him have it, unleash an infinity-pack of psychic whoop-ass on the smug bastard. But I knew it was pointless. If he didn't want me to hurt him, I wasn't going to hurt him.

'It helped your case, didn't it?'

'Don't you *dare*—'

'And speaking of dying,' he said, 'I thought you might like to know that both Leon and Rosie survived after you blasted them through a wall and a window, respectively. Not exactly intact, but they'll live. Like the rest of your friends. You found your way around their deaths, I'm sure you can find your way around Lauren's too. I have faith.'

'We're not talking about this.' I drew my legs up onto the bed and crossed them beneath me. 'We *could*, however, talk about you interfering with my mission. Your little intervention? Multi-dimensional courtroom speeches? Telling Tara about Smith? Where the *hell* do you get off? You had no right.'

Stanly rolled his eyes. 'I do what I want, kid. Thought if any of my lessons had made a dent in that skull of yours, it would have been that one.'

'Yeah. Never any consequences for you.'

'Not if I don't want there to be.'

'Well,' I said. 'As far as lessons go . . . I think my main take-away from this whole episode is that I would rather spend the rest of my life rotting in here than end up like you. So thanks for that. Might not have been deliberate, but I'm pretty sure it'll stick.'

Stanly looked up at the ceiling, frowning. 'You might yet end up spending the rest of your life in here. They just switched on the power blockers.'

OK . . .

He raised his eyebrows. 'Not a good sign.'

I shrugged, even though I was inclined to agree. 'Happy to sit and wait, for now. Been a tiring day.'

'I'm serious,' said Stanly. 'I would not be so blasé about—'

'Was it you?' I said. 'Before? Freeman hopping dimensions? Did you help him?'

'No.'

I shot him some serious side-eye. 'I don't believe you.'

'I . . .' Stanly sighed. 'He did the escaping bit. Transporting himself elsewhere. Amazing what people are capable of when they're desperate. I just . . . maybe I funnelled him somewhere I didn't think he'd last very long. I genuinely didn't think you'd follow him.'

Son of a goddamn . . .

'So it basically *was* you.'

He just stared at me mutinously, looking oddly like a fifteen-year-old getting a telling-off. 'I tried to get you out. Seemed fair. Leave him with that thing.'

'And *that thing* is . . .'

'Bad.'

I nodded. 'OK. So you tried to help me. Thanks. But you also tried to unilaterally . . .' Am I *using that word right?*

'You really think handing him over to *Angelcorp*—'

'How many times do I have to say it? Who I choose to hand *my* arch-enemy over to *is none of your bloody concern!*' I leapt to my feet, rounding on him. He recoiled, taken aback by my sudden ferocity.

'How *dare* you?' I said. 'You arrogant, condescending prick. You make this big noise about showing me my potential, but if the decision I make isn't the one *you* want me to make, you sweep in and overrule me?' I was almost nose-to-nose with him. With myself. It was kind of weird.

'Step back,' said Stanly.

'Make me,' I said. 'Go on. I'm sure you still have full use of your abilities. If anyone can shrug off Angelcorp's power blockers, it's you. Mr God Complex. Jesus, if you're the logical endpoint of having superpowers, maybe I don't bloody want

504

them. Did you feel *anything*, when you watched Lauren die? Did it bother you *at all?* Or was it just a *means to an end?*'

'Step. *Back.*' Stanly shoved me in the chest.

I frowned. His tone . . . there was panic there. 'You . . . have they blocked your powers too?'

Stanly smiled a trying-far-too-hard smile. 'Whatever. Be seeing you.' He snapped his fingers.

Nothing happened.

I made a big show of looking around the room. 'Sorry. Did I miss something there?'

Stanly frowned. He snapped his fingers again. Nothing.

I started to laugh.

'Damn it!' Stanly yelled. 'How is this . . . they can't . . . no *prison cell* can hold me! This is—'

I'm not sure how long it had been since he'd been punched. A while, it seemed, because the look of shock was something special. He sprawled in the corner of the cell, hand flying to the side of his mouth. I'd drawn blood.

'Well.' I stared down at him, making sure not to let on how much my fist was hurting. 'Fancy that.'

'What the *hell?*' Stanly spat blood on the floor. 'What was that for?'

'Do you really need a bullet-pointed list?'

'You stay away from me!' He scrambled to his feet.

'I knew I didn't have any hope of fighting you with powers,' I said. 'But if we're reduced to doing things the old-fashioned way . . .'

'You want to *fight* me? With *fists?* You really are an animal.'

'Says the guy looking very much like a cornered animal.' I cracked my knuckles for effect. 'Honestly, I'm trying my best to avoid fighting these days, generally. I don't really like

505

what it brings out in me. That being said . . . you have this coming, in a big way. Maybe it'll inspire you to keep your nose out of my business in future.' I shrugged. 'And maybe punching myself a bunch of times will fulfil some messed-up psychological need. Who knows.'

Stanly looked around, as though someone was going to materialise and help him out.

No-one did.

'What do you know?' I said. 'About Freeman? Why were you so desperate to punish him *your* way? I don't believe this was all about teaching me a lesson. You know something. Tell me what it is, and maybe we can skip this next bit.'

He just stared at me, fury . . . and *fear* . . . in his eyes.

Set his jaw.

Raised his fists.

I sighed. 'Fair enough. You asked for it.'

A good couple of hours went by, during which I dozed fitfully, never quite allowing myself to sleep properly in case my bloodied doppelgänger tried to smother me with the pillow I'd – pretty thoughtfully, in my opinion – given him. My fists and face ached and while I knew the longer I was in here the less likely it was that Lucius' request had been entirely on the level, I was also totally exhausted, and could barely form a coherent theory as to what might be going on.

'You dislodged one of my teeth,' said Stanly.

'I'm sure you'll be able to re-attach it.'

'*If* we ever get out of here.'

'We will. Now shut it.'

As if on cue, the door opened and Danielle ran in. She was sweating and her hair was messy.

'What happened to you?' I asked.

'I . . .' She noticed my semi-beaten-up face. 'What happened to *you*?'

'Oh. You should see the other me.' I pointed at him.

'Okaay,' said Danielle, in a tone that suggested she simply didn't have space in her brain to process this. 'Well . . . anyway. You need to come with me. Right now.'

'Why?' I stood up. 'What's . . .'

'Lucius betrayed you,' said Danielle. 'Connor, Sharon, Daryl, Skank, they're all in the Undercells too, and he plans for you all to stay here. For good.'

'For *good*?'

'Freeman too. They've decided that a trial is too dangerous. If his crimes come out, they're worried that everything he's done, including the good things . . . and there *are* lots of good things . . . will be undone. All the reforms, the progress. So they're just going to lock him up and throw away the key. Along with everyone else who knows the truth.'

I think I'm going to have a heart attack and die from not surprise.

'What about you?' I said. '*You* know the truth.'

'Lucius thinks I'm on his side. Loyal to the company. I also might have led him to believe that. He talked about the big picture, ends and means and stuff, like we both didn't know the whole thing was a power play. I swore to him that I was with them. Then I headed down here.' A brief, humourless smile. 'Come on, we haven't got long before—'

An alarm started to blare, a horrendous BWAAM, and red lights flashed in the corridor outside.

'Before that happens,' said Danielle. 'Come on.' She ran out. I followed, stopping momentarily in the doorway to look at the other Stanly. He'd pulled himself up into a painful-looking sitting position. He looked pretty pitiful.

'I'll leave the door open for you,' I said.

'Gee, thanks. You're a real pal.'

'Yeah, I know.'

I turned and followed Danielle down the corridor, past two unconscious guards, the air a pulsing storm of sickly light and angry noise.

Really wish I'd slept properly now.

Chapter Thirty-Seven

'THEY'RE WATCHING US right now, presumably?' I said. 'Listening? Cameras and the like?'

'Yep.' We reached the door to the next block and Danielle reached into her pocket, pulled out a phone and scrolled furiously. She punched a code into the computer next to the door and it slid open, revealing a pair of guards, their guns raised. As though we'd planned it, Danielle took the guard on the right and I took the guard on the left, she executing a fairly awesome double kick that swatted her opponent's gun away *and* sent him crashing to the floor, me disarming mine and propelling him up the corridor with a thought.

The first cell we reached was Connor's. He was on his feet as soon as the door opened, seemingly ready to fight. Even when he realised it was us, he didn't relax.

'Stanly?' he said. 'What the hell's happening?'

'One of the less fun worse case scenarios,' I said. 'We're busting out.'

Connor sighed. 'Great.'

More corridors, more doors, more guards. I was getting some quite serious flashbacks to the last time I'd had to escape from a dodgy Angel Group black site . . . except this time at least I wasn't alone. I concentrated on maintaining a shield of intention around us, occasionally using it as a battering ram to force our way through clumps of guards, or extending it around Connor and Danielle while they leapt forward to lay swift, surgical beat-downs. I'd forgotten quite how fe-rocious Connor was, and while I knew he'd not bargained on doing anything like this ever again, he was still in his element, flipping up onto walls to dodge bullets and confuse opponents, shrugging off blows from stun batons with barely a flinch. We tried to limit the amount of actual fighting as much as possible, concentrating on overpowering guards long enough to lock them in empty cells, but not everybody was co-operative.

'That gravity shifting thing you do is pretty nifty,' said Danielle, as she unlocked another door.

'Thanks,' said Connor. 'You're . . . really good at punching people.'

She chuckled grimly. 'Thanks.'

We heard Daryl before we reached his cell. It sounded as though he was hurling himself against the door, hefty thumps interspersed with furious barking: 'What the hell is going on? What's with the alarms? Why have I been locked in this cell for about a month? Whose arm do I need to chew off to get a bloody bacon sandwich around here?'

'Sit down, partner!' I yelled, as Danielle unlocked the cell.

The door opened and Daryl stared up at me, his head on one side. 'Aren't you a little short for a stormtrooper?'

'Look who's talking. You OK?'

'Fantastic. Jail break, is it?'

'Yep. Keen?'

'Nah, reckon I'll just stay here.'

'Cool.'

Whichever angry industrial DJ was mixing the soundtrack to our jail break had decided to switch it up and was now lay-ering vocal samples from Lucius over the top of the screeching siren. Silly stuff like 'Stand down' and 'You're only going to make things worse' and 'Severe consequences'.

Oh yeah? More severe than being locked up without trial FOREVER?

Good one, Lucius.

You douche canoe.

Skank was sitting calmly on the edge of his bed. 'I assume things have gone sour,' he said, mildly.

'Kind of a lot,' said Daryl.

Skank nodded. 'Right. Well. Let's go, then, I suppose.'

Sharon's cell was in the final block. She and Connor embraced briefly and she touched my shoulder and smiled as though the situation was a lot more chilled than it actually was, then it was time to head back the way we came. Danielle had enlisted the help of a friendly tech to interfere with the locks at the main entrance to the Undercells, which meant that we wouldn't encounter major reinforcements as we went back through the cells.

They'd just be waiting on the other side of a single door. Along with all the other layers of security that were hard to get through at the best of times.

It wasn't exactly a great situation . . . but having Connor, Sharon, Skank, Daryl and Danielle at my side certainly made me feel a bit better.

Unsurprisingly, the other Stanly was nowhere to be seen when we passed the cell where I'd left him.

When we eventually made it to the first entrance, Lucius's voice came over the intercom again. 'I am giving you one more chance to stand down,' he said. 'I have thirty highly trained soldiers on the other side of this door. They are empowered, and they are armed. You are a formidable group, granted, but there is no way that you can break through. This ends here. Surrender now, come quietly, and we can avoid further violence.'

I glanced at Danielle, who glanced at her phone and shook her head. 'Not yet.'

Great.

I looked up at the accusing black eye of the CCTV camera above the door. 'Are you on the other side of that door too, Lucius?'

'I am.'

'If we open the door – just for a face-to-face, I promise – are you going to shoot us?'

'Don't give me a reason to, and I won't.'

'All right. Opening the door.' I nodded at Danielle, who did something technical. The door slid open.

There was a collective intake of breath from the rest of us. The next corridor was *rammed* with soldiers. They'd somehow managed to arrange themselves so they could aim the most amount of guns at us, and I could feel the flexing of their brains as well, thick waves of power in the air. Getting through them would definitely be challenging, if not impossible.

Guess we don't get through.

Lucius was at the very back, standing on a raised platform. 'Well?' he said, his voice surreally amplified by the intercom.

I looked at my friends, who all looked at me.

Right. I'll do the talking, then.

I cleared my throat. 'Um,' I said. 'We . . . didn't want this. We didn't want to pit ourselves against Angelcorp. We didn't want to be fighting people like *you* again.' I pointed at the soldiers. 'We know you're just doing your jobs. Trying to do the right thing.' I coughed. 'Um . . . I might well have encountered some of you before. I might have fought you. I might have hurt you. It seems kind of ludicrous for me to apologise, as though an apology will make it better . . . but I am sorry. I thought that we were enemies. I thought I was saving the world, and you were helping to destroy it.'

'Stanly,' said Lucius, warningly. 'I don't like where this—'

'*But* that wasn't what was happening,' I said. 'I was lied to. I was manipulated. And lots of people got hurt. The thing is, *you've* been lied to as well. You've been manipulated. I don't know what you think happened that night, but George Freeman is *not* who you were led to believe he is. He made it happen. He caused the Collision.'

This is going to be difficult.

'Silence!' yelled Lucius. 'Subdue them! Now!'

I had erected a shield in front of us, just in case of that eventuality, but funnily enough, nobody tried to subdue me. In fact, many of them were looking uncertainly at one another.

'He wanted to take control of Angelcorp,' I said. 'So he caused the Collision. *He* is responsible for everything that happened. Everyone who died, died because of him. My friends and I played our part, yes. But we *thought* we were doing the right thing. Helping. Doesn't make it better. Doesn't fix anything. Doesn't let us off the hook. But . . . anyway.'

Can I do this?

There's a lot of them . . .

'Freeman has done good things,' I said, raising my voice over Lucius' shouting, his orders to take me down by whatever means necessary. 'The world's in a hell of a better shape than it might have been. But that doesn't change what he did. The lies he told, the people he killed. And since then, he has brainwashed people. Morter Smith. My friends. He has sanctioned torture and murder. And he has experimented illegally on an endangered alien species.'

I think I'm almost ready.

'We tried to work with Angelcorp to bring him to justice,' I said. 'Do things properly, by the book or whatever. But Lucius and other company higher-ups decided that it was too risky for any of it to come out. They plan to bury it. Lock Freeman away for all time, along with me and my friends. So nobody ever finds out. I can understand why. It will cause problems. People will find it hard to deal with.'

'Somebody shoot him!' bellowed Lucius.

Wow, that escalated quickly.

'But they have the right to know!' I yelled, suddenly righteously pissed-off. 'They have the right to know what this new world was built on! They have the right to choose whether they want to support it! *And Lauren died for this, Lucius, you son of a bitch!* Her death will *not* be meaningless, I will not *bloody allow it!*'

'Stanly?' said Danielle. 'It's done.'

'OK!' I took a deep breath. 'Everyone? I'm really sorry about this.'

And *tseew.* From the depths of my brain, which I visualised as a huge cannon on my shoulders, I fired thirty bursts of information, feeling, insight. My confrontation with Freeman, everything he had said to me, including the new stuff from this evening, everything I had felt, so concentrated and intense that there was simply no way it could be a lie. Pure truth, just like with Danielle earlier, except multiplied by thirty and launched straight into the brains of all the soldiers in this corridor.

It was, unsurprisingly, chaos.

And at the same time, exploiting the diversion that we had created, all of Angelcorp's eyes turned inward rather than outward, Nailah quietly uploaded every single scrap of information we'd found – the video of the shimmer lab, the video of Lauren, and all the bits and pieces that she had managed to find – to the company's intranet, for all employees to see.

No going back now.

I looked up the corridor, over the mass of soldiers clutching their heads, staring at one another in disbelief, to Lucius. We locked eyes. He seemed to have just received a call that was making him very angry. The hand that held the phone was shaking.

'So, Lucius,' I said. 'Again, I ask . . . now wh—'

'—at?'

The corridor was gone. The soldiers were gone. Lucius was gone. In their place was a familiar street, a dark sky, a light drizzle.

'Uh,' said Connor. 'That's . . . our house.'

We were all standing, in the same formation, in Connor and Sharon's front garden. Everybody looked spectacularly confused.

I feel sorta not confused.

'What the hell?' said Danielle. 'Did we *teleport?*'

'I feel a bit sick,' said Sharon.

I turned to my right and looked up the road. There he was, silhouetted by grubby orange street light. His bruises were already gone. I wondered how much time had passed for him.

We exchanged a nod.

He vanished.

'Ahem,' said Daryl, sniffily. 'Who's your mate?'

'He's not my mate,' I said. 'He's . . .'

Wait, what?

I turned. Daryl was nose to nose with a cat, sleek and silvery grey. It was sitting on the doorstep, as though it had been waiting for us to get back.

'Er . . .' said Sharon.

'I'm generally fairly tolerant of cats,' said Daryl, 'but I kind of don't like the way this one is looking at me—'

(*Guys, it's me.*)

Everybody jumped. It was . . . it couldn't be . . . couldn't possibly—

(*It's me. It's Lauren.*)

'Where?' said Connor. 'Where are you? I mean . . . you're . . . it's . . .'

(*Down here!*)

No . . .

She doesn't mean . . .

We all looked down. At the cat. The cat that was staring up at us, as if it knew something we didn't.

Except I *did* know.

We all knew.

The cat did a pretty fair approximation of a nod. (*Yes. It's me.*)

'Lauren,' I said. 'You're . . . a cat.'

(*It seems so.*)

Lauren's a cat now.

Cos of course she is.

516

Chapter Thirty-Eight

'MAY I SUGGEST,' said Skank, breaking the five or so years of silence that had followed Lauren's bombshell, 'that we evacuate? Somewhere off the grid? I think we all count as fugitives at this point.'

That was definitely a plan everyone could get behind, so our motley crew of humans, animal-ish humans and human-ish animals hurried off into London's darkened labyrinth. It was after five in the morning, so quite a good time for clandestine manoeuvrings, and I imagined our sudden disappearance – plus the various freshly-uploaded revelations – had been distracting and confusing enough to give us a decent head start. Nailah and the others met us at another of Skank's many safe houses, and the first thing that Skank did – after ensuring the place was totally secure – was make a round of tea.

Tara ran over to me. It looked as though she'd been dozing. 'Are you all right?'

'Yeah,' I said. 'All got kind of hectic. They wanted to put us in jail forever. We broke out.'

'Wow.'

'What about you guys? All OK?'

'Fine. Just . . . we were worried.'

I smiled. 'Thanks.'

Tara glanced around awkwardly, then ushered me over to a quiet corner. 'Um,' she muttered. 'I . . . I'm sorry.'

Sorry? 'For what?'

'Ever since you've been back, I've been ... harsh. Angry. It wasn't fair. I just ... everything that happened ...'

'It's all right,' I said. 'It is. I'm sorry. I'm sorry I left you in the woods. I'm sorry I never came back. I'm sorry for everything I didn't have time to tell you ... I'm sorry I wasn't here to look out for you. That's all I ever wanted to do.'

'I know.' She smiled. 'I do. Oh, also, why do you guys have a cat?'

(*I knew Rosie was going to kill me.*)

The cat – *Lauren* – was sitting on a beanbag next to me, broadcasting to a rapt audience. Daryl kept on looking from the cat – *Lauren Lauren Lauren Lauren* – to me and back again and shaking his head.

(*I just knew it was coming. She'd weakened me too much to fight back, I couldn't do it. I thought it was over. All I wanted to do was to get out of there, to get away, to be away, anywhere but there. And then I felt ... this lightness. In my head. Just for a second, like my head became completely weightless. And then ... this rush, like some insane drug, and I was looking at myself, at the room, at Walker and Rosie, and it was like I was just essence, like a gas. A coloured gas ... except invisible. Which I know makes no sense, but it's the only way I can describe it. Then I just sort of ... leapt through the wall, went up through the ground and came out on the street. Honestly, for a second I thought that I'd discovered that there was an afterlife ... and then there was this cat. I think it could sense me, it started to run, but without even really realising I just ... went into it. Into its head. And suddenly I could see from behind its eyes. It was still trying to run, it took me a while to get control, to really realise what had happened.*)

I looked at Alex. 'Is that what it's like for you?'

He nodded. 'Pretty much exactly.'

'Sorry, Lauren,' said Sharon, 'but . . . can you still feel it? The cat?'

(*Yes. It's calmed down, it was pretty freaked out before. It's almost . . . placid, now. It's actually helping me quite a lot.*) The cat – LAUREN LAUREN LAUREN – started washing its paws, like it was a cat, like stuff was all normal and stuff. (*Its whole attitude is so casual, so confident, like it owns the place. I think it's helping me to not go mad.*)

'Oh God, Lauren,' I said, 'I totally forgot, I tried to get hold of Sally earlier but I couldn't. I was worried that she—'

(*It's fine. I packed her off to some friends in Scotland. She didn't want to go, but I had a feeling things were going to get hairy. No pun intended.*) Everybody laughed hysterically at that, even Lauren. In our heads, her laughter had a musical, twinkling edge to it. Kind of like a shimmer. (*She's safe. Hopefully I'll have time to get back in my body before I see her. If I can, now.*)

Oh no. 'Lauren,' I said. 'I . . . shit. I can't believe I . . . there's no . . .' I took a deep breath, trying to collect myself. 'I don't know how to say this. They . . . Walker . . .'

'Oh no,' Sharon whispered.

(*She destroyed it?*)

'Yes,' I said. 'I'm so sorry, I tried to find out where she'd put it, I went into her brain, I was going to find you and bring you back, but—'

(*It's all right. I'm doing better than I might have been doing, under the circumstances.*)

'We'll work something out, I swear. I—'

(*Stanly, it's fine. I'll be all right.*)

This was ridiculous. My friend had been brutally murdered, her body incinerated to hide the evidence, her consciousness trapped in the body of a cat . . . and she was reassuring *me*.

I thought towards her. *But it's my fault. You're . . . what's happened to you. It's my fault.*

(*Actually, it isn't. It's not all about you.*) She said it with total kindness. (*I chose to go against Angelcorp, against Walker and Freeman, because I couldn't just carry on, knowing the truth. Because I didn't want to be a puppet, a pawn, of people whose actions I find despicable. I did it for myself. The consequences are mine to bear. Not yours.*)

'Daryl,' said Connor, suddenly. 'Sorry if this is a personal question, but . . . this isn't . . . I mean . . . did you . . .'

'Do you mean, did this happen to me?' asked Daryl. 'What's happened to Lauren? Is that how I became me?'

'Um . . . yeah.'

'Can't remember.'

'Not to state the obvious or anything,' said Nailah, 'except I'm totally about to, but Lauren . . . this is blowing my mind.'

(*I sympathise.*)

'Particularly the fact that you can do telepathic talking,' said Nailah. 'Like . . . how?'

'That's a good point,' I said. 'Alex, you've never been able to do that, have you?'

'I don't really know,' said Alex. 'I've never tried to. I've never . . . I don't know . . . been aware that I could? I've only ever been in the driving seat of the animal.'

'And telepathy is part of the powers, isn't it?' said Nailah. 'It's a symptom of the powers. And I always thought that the powers came from the human brain. But . . . and sorry Lauren, there's no way of saying this delicately . . . you don't have a human brain any more.'

(*Angelcorp's best scientists have always thought that there was more to the powers.*) Lauren's ears twitched thoughtfully. (*Perhaps they're tied to consciousness, rather than to the physical brain. Honestly, I have no idea.*)

Consciousness . . .

Maybe that was how I'd saved the others? Their consciousnesses had just been floating around, patiently waiting to be re-installed . . .

'Christ on a bike,' said Daryl, wearily. 'This is all a bit too much for my primitive dog brain.'

'It's a bit too much for my primitive *human* brain,' said Connor.

We moved swiftly on. Lauren wanted to know how things had gone down and we each told our own bits of the story. Everyone was more than happy to swap tales – it made it feel like the world wasn't crumbling around us. Connor and Daryl described how they'd busted into the private Angelcorp staff apartments where Smith resided, running rings around the empowered security guards.

'Connor was such a badass,' said Daryl, immediately perking up. 'Running along ceilings and shit. He punched this one guy and I swear he flew about twenty feet down the hall.'

'You made a pretty good living battering ram yourself,' said Connor. 'I don't understand how you can jump so high, your legs are so short.'

'Seriously, Stanly,' said Daryl. 'Did you see *The Raid*?'

'No,' I said.

'Really? Did it come out while you were away?'

'No, I just didn't see it.'

'I did,' said Faisal. 'Such a sick film.'

'Damn right,' said Daryl. 'Anyway, it was like that. Floor by floor, total ownage. No killing though, obvz. I actually wanted us to do it like the lobby scene in *The Matrix*, Connor walks in with a big bag and then the alarm goes off and I leap out of the bag and start laying down violence, but Irish said no.'

'There was no lobby,' said Connor.

'Always sweating the details . . .'

They'd found Morter Smith locked in a bare, almost featureless apartment, in a trance-like state. The thought made me shiver. 'He was easy to shift,' said Connor. 'Barely seemed aware of what was going on. So we grabbed him and took him to meet the others.'

The others were Sharon, Faisal, Skank and Nailah, who had been assigned to the shimmer lab. 'Once we'd found it,' said Sharon, 'getting in wasn't as hard as I was expecting.'

'Faisal took out the security team like *that*,' said Nailah, snapping her fingers. 'Pretty slick.'

'Cheers,' said Faisal.

'Don't let it go to your head,' said Tara, with a smile that made me wonder, not for the first time, if there was something between them.

That'd be cool, I guess.

'Also meant that Sylvester didn't have to use his hand cannon,' added Nailah, 'which was gratifying.'

I'd genuinely forgotten that Skank's name was Sylvester. He shrugged. 'Sometimes it's better not to shoot first.'

'It was pretty distressing when we got in there,' said Sharon. 'There were lots of shimmers in these clear cages. The air . . . it was *thick*, with pain, with their cries. I really had to fight to be able to function properly.'

'Can't imagine what it must have been like for you,' said Nailah. 'I'm not even superpowered and even I could feel it. And I kept on thinking I could see things . . . bad memories, dreams. Ugh.' She shuddered.

'I let Mork talk to them,' said Sharon. 'Sort of. I had a message in my head from him.'

'I can't believe y'all called it that,' said Daryl, shaking his head. 'Mork the Shimmer. How undignified.'

'What would you have called him?' I asked, even though the shimmer's nickname was news to me.

'Dunno. Little Blue? Genie? Mr Meeseeks? Neytiri?'

'Yeah, cos those are all *well* dignified.'

'Also,' said Connor, '*little* bit racist.'

'Also,' I said, '*Neytiri?*'

'Like from *Avatar*,' said the beagle, defensively.

'I know it's from *Avatar*, which, by the way, ugh, but Neytiri? That's the *girl* Na'vi.'

'Oh, and you know for certain that *Mork* is a boy, do you? From your extensive study of shimmer gender terminology and relations? Or did you just lift up its back leg and—'

'Boys,' said Sharon. 'My story?'

'Sorry,' we said, in unison.

'Anyway,' said Sharon, trying and failing to fight an affectionate smile, 'I showed them Mork with my thoughts. Let them feel the memories, feel him. Or she, or they, or it. They could tell it was true. They let us rescue them. And then Connor and Daryl arrived with Smith.' She shook her head. 'Freeman really messed with him. He's effectively been hypnotised for most of the last five and a half years, just doing Freeman's bidding. Every now and then Freeman calls him to his office . . .'

'To top him up?' I said. *Knew it.*

'Yes,' said Sharon. 'But first, he'd undo it. Let Smith think clearly, remember everything. See what was being done to him. Gloat. Then he'd hypnotise him again.' She sighed. 'Not pleasant.'

'You helped him, though?'

'I think so.'

I smiled. 'Should have known. The best clinics in London take weeks – Sharon does it in five minutes.'

'Gotta say,' Nailah said to Sharon, 'seeing you in action? I am now nursing a pretty major crush. Just FYI.'

Sharon blushed. 'Um . . . thank you. That's very sweet. Anyway . . . so, yes. I undid some of what Freeman had done to Smith. He was . . . unhappy.'

'Try enraged,' said Daryl. 'Seriously, I half thought he was going to go postal and try and kill us all, just cos we were there.'

'But he didn't,' said Connor, 'to be fair to him. He got it together. I was pretty impressed. I'd have been a basket case after that kind of treatment, but he was straight to business.'

'We gave him a rundown of what was happening,' said Daryl. 'And he demanded we go straight to Angelcorp.'

'So off they went,' said Nailah, 'and me and Faisal came here to get the upload ready, in case we had to put Plan E-for-Everything-Has-Gone-To-Shit into operation.'

'Lucius was already expecting us,' said Daryl. 'And then we were all arrested! Which was mega fun times.'

'Which brings us to you, young man,' said Sharon.

I insisted on more tea first. Then, fresh cup in hand, I started on my bit. Danielle sneaking us in to Angelcorp – no mean feat – and up to Freeman's private floor. Letting the shimmer in via the ventilation shaft so it could attach itself to his head. The utterly, *utterly* bizarre process of joining me and him together, with Alex as the conduit between my mind and the shimmer's and Tara grounding me, strengthening me with her own power, her presence.

Telling the story of tricking Freeman with giant Stanly, the fight and the fake safe house was a huge amount of fun and everyone loved it, especially Daryl. 'That is so *freaking* awesome,' he kept saying. They were also suitably annoyed by the other Stanly's unwanted intervention, while simultaneously being blown away by his very existence, which also necessitated an explanatory flashback to my meeting him earlier on today, because gawd blimey that had only been today . . .

But then we got to the other world and I started to fudge around things. I wasn't totally sure why. After all, they'd seen monsters before . . . but then again, so had I. That thing, whatever it was, wasn't a monster. It was something else. Something much, much worse. And part of me felt that if I spoke of it, I would somehow be connecting them to it, to the deep and primal horror that it had inspired in me, the utter debasement and hopelessness, the awe-inspiring dread of it. And that, in turn, might give it a signal, allow it to turn its terrible head, see through dimensions, through universes . . .

See this world.

And maybe decide it wanted to pay us a visit.

I was *not* going to be responsible for that.

Plus, five of them had died and come back that evening, one as a cat, and we were all currently fugitives on the run from the most powerful organisation on the planet. They didn't need to know about that thing. They just didn't. So I lied and made up some cool stuff and then . . .

And then.

'So . . . what do we *do* now?' said Danielle. 'I mean . . . what's the next move? What's the plan?'

Worryingly, after the requisite awkward silence, heads started turning in my direction. Like I was the leader or something.

'Um,' I said. 'I . . . have no idea.'

More silence. More awkward looking around. Then Daryl put his head on my knee, looked up at me and said, 'Well, kid. No matter what anybody says . . . you'll always be a chosen one to me.'

And we all laughed and it freeze-framed on our laughter and the credits rolled and everyone lived happily ever after.

PART FOUR

Chapter Thirty-Nine

'STANLY. IT'S A pleasure to meet you.'

I nodded and slowly took the woman's outstretched hand, very aware of her armour-clad escorts tightening their grip on their guns as I did so. She was tall, fortyish, possibly of Chinese descent, dressed in a boardroom-ready grey and black outfit, hair in a long black ponytail, and she wore a smile that looked like it was grudgingly filling in for a much more pleasant smile that had gone on a long holiday.

'Ms Reese, I presume,' I said.

'You presume correctly.' She smiled at my companions. 'Miss Dewornu. Miss Stone. Connor. Daryl.'

Lauren looked imperiously up at Reese. To be fair, that was kind of her default expression. (*Ms Reese.*)

We were in a wide, open courtyard at the centre of a ring of anonymous office buildings, all of which had been emptied of people. Out of the corner of my eye, I could see snipers on rooftops.

'Where are the rest of your friends?' asked Reese.

'Yeah, nice try,' said Daryl.

'We said we didn't want trouble,' I said. 'This meeting took long enough to set up, would be a shame for an itchy trigger finger or a careless thought to balls it all up.'

'My thoughts exactly.' Reese eyed us up. 'Well, I must say. You've been leading us all a merry dance these past nine months. Considering the breadth and sophistication of our surveillance apparatus . . . I am legitimately impressed.'

'Cheers,' I said. 'I'll pass that on.'

'And the . . . activities that you have undertaken in order to fill your days . . .'

'That's the thing about being fugitives,' said Daryl. 'Quite a lot of down time.'

Reese laughed. 'I don't doubt it. Said activities have rather helped your case. After you inexplicably vanished from our custody, there were many who would happily have written you off as terrorists. Enemies of the state. But what's this? Helping from the shadows? Coming to the aid of those in need? Risking capture, in order to right wrongs? Even, in some situations, actively helping Angelcorp personnel?'

'We're pretty cool like that,' I said.

I'm not going to lie – it had been nine extremely stressful months. We had nearly been caught and imprisoned on numerous occasions. Once or twice we'd almost been killed. Everybody had fallen out at some point or another. Major sacrifices had been made.

But at the same time, it had been kind of awesome.

'We've been keeping an eye on Miss Daniels,' said Reese. 'I went to see her myself.'

(*I know.*) Lauren's tone gave nothing away, but it didn't need to. I knew how hard things had been for her, and for Sally.

'I must admit that I was surprised to hear from you,' said Reese. 'Why choose to emerge now?'

(*It seems like things are changing. New management. I always got the impression that you were one of the more morally upright potential CEOs-in-waiting. More honourable than Lucius.*)

'Thank you. Mr Hamilton, it turned out, had some unfortunate ties.'

'So we heard,' I said. 'Which I guess explains his hurry to cover everything up.'

'He was not alone in that desire,' said Reese. 'Things have been . . . tumultuous.'

(*For us too. But the fact that Freeman will get a trial seemed like a step in the right direction. Made us think that maybe dialogue was possible.*)

'Yes,' said Reese. 'Well, of course, not everything will be made public . . .'

'It's better than we were expecting,' I said. 'And it made us wonder about the possibility of a truce. We don't want to be on the run. We don't want to be at war. We don't want to exist like this, on the outside, looking in. We want to be part of the world again. We think we can help.'

'It's rather a tall order,' said Reese. 'After everything you've done.'

'We know,' said Danielle. 'But we also thought you'd agree that the circumstances are . . . pretty extraordinary.'

'I would agree,' said Reese. 'But therein lies the rub. It sets something of a precedent, doesn't it? The government, and Angelcorp, allow a group of superpowered vigilantes – criminals, essentially, no matter how noble your motives – to come in from the cold. What's to stop others from following your example? Taking to the streets? Flouting the law? Ignoring the rules, structures, contracts that keep a society cohesive? You can see why many would rather you were sent straight to prison . . . or left out in the cold.'

'Like you said, not everything has been made public,' I said. 'Nobody knows about what we did, not officially. And what we've been up to in the meantime . . . rumours. Hearsay. Whispered stories between stoners and comic book geeks. Not exactly society-destroying.'

'So you're happy for *some* elements to remain a secret,' said Reese. 'But not others. And there I thought that you were crusaders for truth and transparency.'

'Hey, we're not perfect,' I said. 'Maybe we've picked an arbitrary point to draw a line in the sand. But we know that there have been ripples. From what we did. Unrest. We took down the bad guy. We solved some problems. But we also created new problems. We undid some progress. And there's only so much we can do to make up for that, operating the way we have. Like I said, we want to be part of the world again. We want to help. We want to be useful.'

'For the sake of argument,' said Reese, 'how would you define this usefulness?'

'To be discussed. Basically, we want to offer our services. Our power. We also know that our personal testimony would probably come in handy, as far as Walker and Freeman's trials are concerned.'

'We have plenty of star witnesses.'

'Couldn't hurt to have a few more,' said Daryl. 'And trust me – there's stuff that Stanly and I know that would keep you awake at night.'

'I don't doubt it.' Reese put her head on one side. 'I sense that there's more.'

'Yeah,' I said. 'Prometheus.'

That one caught her by surprise. 'Prometheus?'

'The experimental and highly illegal superpower drug that you guys were so desperate to get your hands on before. We can give it to you.'

'I was led to understand that it had all been destroyed.'

'You and me both,' I said. *Luckily Alex is a sneaky bugger.*

Lauren cut in. (*We're willing to provide a small sample for study. To certain specific scientists of my choosing.*)

'Of *your* choosing.' Up until this point, Reese had been fairly casual about talking to a cat, but she suddenly seemed flustered. 'I hardly think that you're in a position to be making demands . . .'

(*Don't let the fur and tail fool you. I have all the knowledge, all the memories that I had as a human. I know which scientists I would trust, and which ones I wouldn't. I know how far you were from anything approaching what Prometheus can do. I know how valuable it is. I also know how valuable I am.*)

'Between Lauren managing to pack her entire consciousness *and* some of her powers into the body of a cat, and me *curing death*, I think we've got enough to keep your scientists occupied,' I said. 'But like Lauren said – specific scientists.'

'As in, *not* the ones who were experimenting on the shimmers,' said Daryl.

'Speaking of,' I said. 'Are they all right? The shimmers?'

'Rehabilitation efforts are ongoing,' said Reese. 'You can rest assured that there will be no repeat of the horrors they endured at George Freeman's hands.'

'Good to know. We have one who's anxious to be reunited with his friends.'

She nodded.

'Anyway,' I said. 'All this stuff. Regime change, government ties being re-evaluated . . . it's all encouraging. Good noises.'

'I've always been in favour of healthy separation between the public and private sectors,' said Reese.

'Cool,' I said. '*But if we're going to work with you, offer* our knowledge, our power . . . there are caveats. Conditions.'

Reese stared. It felt very much as though she was looking straight into my brain.

'We know you'll have them too,' I said. 'We're not expecting for things to just go back to the way they were, for us to go back to our homes, our normal lives, carry on like nothing happened, no price to be paid. We're willing to discuss, to negotiate. If you guys are into that, then brilliant. If not . . . then we'll disappear. Far away.'

'Our reach extends pretty far,' smiled Reese.

I copied her smile. 'We can run further.'

She stood silently for a moment, taking us in. Me, the human cat, the talking beagle, Thor Blimey, the anti-gravity Irishman. Finally, she nodded. 'I will take it into consideration. I can't promise that it will be a popular proposition. But I will discuss it with the relevant parties. How can we contact you?'

'There's an old post box hidden in the weeds on the east side of the river about one hundred metres north of Tower Bridge,' said Daryl. 'Post any communications – handwritten, please – in a blank brown envelope – white will be ignored – on a Wednesday afternoon. Expect a reply no later than Friday morning.'

Danielle sniggered. Reese raised an eyebrow.

'We'll contact you,' I said.

'Well. It was worth a try.' She held out her hand. 'It was a genuine pleasure to meet you.'

I took the hand and shook it. 'You too. Laters.'

'You're a pain in the ass, dog,' said Danielle, as we walked away. 'I kept a straight face for that whole meeting until you made that damn post box comment.'

'Couldn't not say it once it was in my head,' said Daryl.

'OK,' I said. 'Time to split. Keep an eye out for tails.'

'I can't seem to get rid of mine,' said Daryl.

Danielle giggled. I still wasn't quite used to such sounds coming out of her. 'If you weren't literally a dog, I would be punching you for that pun.'

'If I wasn't literally a dog, it wouldn't even have made sense.'

'Yeah, touché.'

Lauren twitched her nose at us. (*Be careful.*) She and Danielle headed off to the right, and ten or so seconds later Connor clapped me manfully on the back and peeled off to the left. Daryl and I carried on walking, along the designated route.

We're so the best at planning these days.

'So,' said Daryl. 'What do you reckon? Think she'll go for the plan?'

'In its current form? I doubt it. But like we said, asking for too much means more room for negotiation.'

'Cool. But if they change their minds and betray us, are we actually going to up sticks to another dimension? Cos that seems like overkill.'

'What would you suggest instead?'

'Stand together, side-by-side, and rip 'em a new one.'

I glanced down at the beagle. Nothing about his expression suggested that he was joking.

'Yeah, I guess so,' I said. 'If there's nothing good on telly.'

Daryl nodded. 'Damn straight, my young apprentice.' Somehow, he managed to turn his walk into a swagger. 'Oh yeah, Stanly and Daryl. Stanly and Daryl forever, hundred years. Hundred days. Stanly and Daryl dot com. Come and have a go, if you think you've got the midichlorians.'

I looked at him disgustedly. 'That started really well, but . . . *midichlorians*? Are you having a *laugh*, dog?'

'Sorry. Got carried away.'

I sped up, shaking my head. 'I can't *believe* you said that.'

'It was a joke!' he said, running after me. 'I was being *ironic*!'

'Oh yeah, like Lucas was being ironic when he unleashed Jar Jar on an unsuspecting public.'

'Oh come on, I hate Jar Jar as much as the next beagle—'

'Whatever, you *love* Jar Jar.'

'Do not.'

'You want to marry Jar Jar and have a massive Gungan wedding in their underwater city.'

'Leave me alone.'

'Boss Nass officiating.'

'Stop it.'

'Then drive away in a bongo with Just Married written on it. A *bongo*. That's what they call their submarines. *Bongos*. That's the society you want to be a part of.'

'Stanly? I think this is the end of a beautiful friendship.'

The red cave stank. The boy who was not really a boy stood on the sand and tried not to breathe. 'Still can't get used to this smell,' he said, for no-one's benefit but his own.

He walked to the shore of the black, fetid lake, knelt down and trailed a finger in the dead water. It was like oil, like blood, like neither. He stood up, stepped back and closed his eyes. Anybody watching would have seen very little, unless they had been able to perceive thought, because now the cave was full of it. Hundreds of thoughts, all representations of the same word.

Alive.

Slowly, the water began to bubble. Then it started to change colour. At first it stayed mostly black, although there was a subtle pattern in it, as though it were marbled with blue paint, but as it began to bubble more intensely the blue started to spread, eating away at the black, and areas became briefly white and then blue again, first a dark navy and then gradually brightening until the lake was a glowing, ethereal baby blue. At this moment, anyone could have felt the life fill the place, whether they were psychic or not. It made the atmosphere thick, as if the air were solid life that could be gripped and hugged to one's chest like a blanket.

And it wasn't just life: it was dreams. The air was heady with them, and beyond the walls of the cave vast, booming footfalls could be heard, flesh dreams, patrolling benignly.

The boy opened his eyes and smiled as the shimmers chattered to themselves. He waited for a few moments before speaking. He did not speak with his mouth but with his thoughts, with the full force of a mind far too big to fit inside such a small head.

The shimmers fell silent and listened to him.

'I am the shadow,' he said. 'I am the one who destroyed you . . . and I've brought you back.'

The living lake pulsated with emotions. They hated him. They feared him. Yet they also respected him and were willing to listen.

'I have a warning,' said the boy. 'And a gift. You will remain here. You don't mean it, but you bring destruction. Outside of this world, you are dangerous . . . and it is dangerous for you. You almost destroyed one world. I know you don't mean to destroy, but you can't help it. You want to survive. I understand that. But my warning is this – I will stop you if you bring your nightmares beyond this world.'

The lake, for want of a better word, shimmered.

'Some of your number are trapped in another world,' said the boy. 'They may yet return. If they do, they will need to create doorways between there and here. Nothing must come through from here. No monsters, no dreams. None of you. This world is yours, but attempt no landing there.' He doubted they would get that reference, but it amused him. Once again, the lake shimmered. He felt their understanding.

They very nearly agreed with him.

'My gift,' said the boy, 'your price, is this.' He closed his eyes and once again nothing visible passed between him and the lake, but the lake reacted. It glowed, filling the cave with a whispered, chiming song.

'That,' said the boy, 'is enough power to feed you for a year. And when the time comes, I will come back and give you some more. Until then, you can stay and dream and sing to yourselves. But until you learn to contain the monsters you create, come no further.'

The lake, in its own, inscrutable way, agreed to his terms.

The boy smiled. 'Good. Sorry for . . . like . . . killing your whole species. Won't happen again.'

And he turned and disappeared.

Chapter Forty

'THANKS, MUM,' I said. 'It was really good.' I'd forgotten quite how mean my mother's shepherd's pie was.

Mum smiled. 'Good.' She sat back in her chair, sipping a glass of wine. It was one in the afternoon, but it was a Sunday, so what the hell. My dad started collecting the plates and I got up to start washing them.

'So,' said Dad, casual as you like. 'You never did tell us what happened to our car.'

I looked at him, a completely alien - yet totally familiar - 'oh shit I'm in trouble with Dad' feeling rising inside me. 'Um,' I said. 'I kind of . . . I had to psychically throw it at a monster. Trashed it. Sorry.'

Dad blinked, and exchanged a bemused look with my mother. 'Well. There goes the no-claims bonus.' He chuckled.

Wow, he really is mellowing with age.

'How's Tara?' asked Mum, efficiently drying the plates as I washed them.

'She's good,' I said. 'Loving college. Amazing she managed to get a place, after everything. Stuff with her foster parents was obviously pretty bad for a long time.'

'Understandably.' Mum shook her head. 'If you had ever done anything like that to us . . .'

My dad frowned. '*Have* you?'

I chose to smile mischievously and say nothing.

'Stupid boy,' said Mum, flicking me affectionately with a tea towel.

'Anyway,' I said. 'Yeah, Tara's good. She's working on some power-assisted art project at the moment, symbolising the volatile political environment through live psychic sculpting.'

'Wow. How about Daryl, how's he?'

'Fine, but very much not busy symbolising anything. Getting a bit fat, actually. Doesn't get enough exercise. Spends too much time sitting around watching films.'

'Sounds familiar.'

Dad shook his head. 'That bloody dog.'

'He's actually saved my life multiple times,' I said.

'Oh.' He nodded approvingly. 'Good for him. Always knew he was worth keeping around.'

We finished cleaning up and Mum made coffee and we talked. Dad was helping to re-paint one of the pubs in town. He and Mum didn't actually live together any more, but they got on well enough to eat together regularly. Mum was tutoring kids, mostly boys, who had been excluded from my old secondary school. Several of them were the younger siblings of the Neanderthals who had bullied me when I was at school, which was actually kind of sad.

'Do you ever speak to Kloe?' Mum asked.

'Not for a while. She came to London once, a few months ago. It was . . . very intense. And I've spoken to her a few times since then. It's all mega weird.' I shrugged. 'But she's happy. Studying. Think she's going to do a PhD. Then she'll be Doctor Kloe.'

'Blimey,' said my dad.

'Oh, that reminds me, actually,' said Mum. 'I bumped into Mark Topp the other day.'

'Mark . . .' *Oh man. Blast from the past.* 'Wow! My very own Tybalt. How's he doing?'

'Very well. He studied acting somewhere up north and he's been doing theatre work ever since. Apparently he's on the shortlist for a pretty meaty role in a BBC drama.'

'Cool.'

'He said you should look him up sometime.'

'I should.' *He might find it a bit weird that I haven't aged as much as I should have . . .*

He didn't find it weird when I showed him my talking dog.

Although nobody seems to find that particularly weird, to be fair.

We drank coffee and ate biscuits and caught up, and around mid-afternoon I said I really had to be heading off. I had quite a way to go.

'You still haven't really told us where you're going,' said Mum.

'Just . . . travelling,' I said. 'Getting away for a few weeks.'

'But you haven't packed anything . . .'

'Mum,' I said. 'I've got superpowers. Stop worrying.'

Maybe I should have told them. But I felt as though I'd already blown their minds enough, telling them what had gone down over the last year and a half. Our time on the lam, hiding from Angelcorp, trying our best to help from the shadows, wherever we could. Tense, complex negotiations. Eventually being allowed back into the world, back to our lives . . . sort of. Everyone had had to wear electronic power-reducing tags for a while. But we had assured Angelcorp and the government that our motives were genuine. That we wanted to help, take responsibility.

For Alex, that meant handing himself in. He'd volunteered and I'd tried to talk him out of it, if you can believe that. It would be months, maybe years before they worked out exactly how the hell to punish him. For the moment, seeing as he was the only one with remotely relevant experience, he was helping Angelcorp's scientists to work out exactly how the hell to help Lauren. She had taken on a pretty senior role at the company – after all, as she'd said, if they'd been willing to employ a talking beagle, it seemed discriminatory not to employ a telepathic cat, especially one with her experience. She was working closely with Danielle, who would probably have Lauren's old job before too long, and one of their main projects was closing the Undercells and securing proper trials for all those confined there.

Faisal, unsurprisingly, had chosen to disappear. For one thing, he knew of plenty of empowered criminals still operating under Angelcorp's radar. Plus, he wanted to search for the fourth Chavenger, Iron Brew. Part of me wished I was going with him. I predicted awesomeness.

After he'd left, I'd asked Tara if she was upset, whether there had been something between them, and she'd given me a look so sardonic that my face nearly melted.

'Jesus, no,' she'd said. 'He's totally gay. Like, the gayest.'

Apparently my face had been 'literally the funniest thing ever'.

Apart from our roles in the trial of George Freeman – which some people were projecting could drag on for a decade, once it actually got started properly – Connor, Sharon, Skank, Daryl and I were working with Angelcorp. Connor had a pretty major role in rebuilding efforts, as London was far from healed. Sharon helped troubled empowered, people whose memories had been tampered with, stuff like that. She was also involved with plans to incorporate superpowers into medical practice. Skank and Daryl were involved in 'dispute resolution', and every time I asked them to explain exactly what that meant, they exchanged conspiratorial looks and said I wouldn't understand.

As for me . . . I did what I was asked, went where I was needed. Building work here. Group therapy there. Even some writing for Nailah. I already had sacks of respect for Ms Editor, but seeing her in action was humbling. No injustice too big or small to be furious about, no dodginess too scary to investigate, no voice too unimportant to be heard. She breathed new life into the previously fractured and ineffectual Drone-Free Skies campaign, spoke out against surveillance and corruption, and basically never seemed to sleep. I often wondered if she had superpowers and didn't realise it.

Every now and then she'd suggest we finally did that interview . . . and I'd seamlessly change the subject. *A Boy And His Dog* was enough exposure for me, for the foreseeable future.

I was also on the list for a new initiative using superpowers to help dementia patients, which I would be starting in a few weeks. It was starting to feel like making amends for my multifarious screw-ups was a very real possibility.

Well. Sometimes it felt like that. Things certainly hadn't got less crazy. There had been repercussions from taking Freeman down. Alliances had shattered, new ones were rising, some good, some bad. There was tension. Some days I felt as though we'd definitely made a huge mistake . . . other days, I felt sure that we'd done the right thing.

And then, of course, there were the nights when I woke

up in a terrified sweat, stalked through claustrophobic dreams by a great, implacable black presence. That wasn't the most restful thing in the world. But I figured I'd get used to it.

I hadn't seen any other Stanlys for a while. Something told me I'd see that particular one again . . . but for now, it seemed that he'd finally seen fit to leave me alone. I'd opted not to tell Mum and Dad about him. Or the abomination that haunted my dreams. Or curing death.

Or where I was heading after dinner.

Some stuff was just a bit too bizarre to explain to your parents.

I hugged them both on the doorstep. 'Keep in touch,' said my dad.

'Will do,' I said. 'Take care, both of you.' It was only now, in full daylight, that I realised how much greyer their hair was now. It made me a little sad. Not because there was anything wrong with getting old, of course . . . just because it meant that the past was even further away than I'd thought it was. The time when I used to stumble around. Fall asleep in the back of the car. The time before trouble. Before apocalypse and compromise, fighting and terrible, unknowable entities. Before responsibility and decisions. That brief, glowing time when an afternoon spent on the lawn with only a cardboard box and a stick for company was an afternoon well spent. That time which, like all times, you didn't truly appreciate until you realised it had long passed.

But then there's new times. And you do those.

I walked up the path and along the road, waving goodbye. When they were out of sight I nipped up into the woods and breathed it in. It had been a criminally long time since I'd been up here and the place was at its absolute best in summer, every leaf proud and green, chests puffed out, the sunlight dripping an odd, vaguely mystical green-gold shine through the canopy onto the dirt and bracken and mossy, broken stumps. I walked up through the wood, touching every other tree, listening. I was starting to think I could feel things when I touched trees and plants. As though they had a power of their own, something I couldn't quite understand. Maybe one of these days I'd try to climb inside one with my mind. See what they had to say.

You bloody hippie.

I reached a spot I'd always liked right at the top of an ivy-webbed cliff and sat cross-legged on the leaves. As I sat, remembering times in these woods, smiling to myself, it felt as though the forest grew around me, painting and re-painting its cryptic patterns. I remembered all the time I'd spent alone up here. Sitting up trees, reading, spying on people who walked by. Practising my powers for the first time with Daryl, back when I could barely lift a pebble, when I could just about stay in the air for five seconds. That thought, and the gulf between then and now, made my stomach feel like it was falling away, but I took a deep breath, settling myself. I needed to be calm now.

I remembered meeting Ben King up here.

Wonder what he's been up to since the last time I punched him in the face.

Also, how long has it been since I punched anyone in the face? Ages!

I must be growing as a person.

Another deep breath, and I closed my eyes. I'd done a few

test drives, with varying degrees of success. Breaking through was the easy bit. You just had to think your way through the ineffable fabric of reality, whatever the hell reality was. No, the hard bit was once you were through. Trying to get your bearings with every single moment in every single universe happening on top of you at the same time. Trying not to throw up all your internal organs and then vomit up your brain, only for your brain to then throw up, and for its psychic throw-up to throw up, with the sheer infinite nausea of it all, past and present and future colliding and rolling over one another, currents so complex that actually thinking about them would hurt too much, so you just had to try and ignore them.

All that was pretty damn hard. And then pinpointing the world you wanted, using its smell, although it's not really a smell, it's sort of a colour and sort of a flavour and sort of an essence, all happening at once, but not really – that was hard. *Really* bloody hard. And then grabbing hold of it with your mind as it reared and bucked like an unwilling cosmic horse, that was pretty challenging, civilisations rising and falling and people being born and dying and species appearing and seizing the day and losing it again, all of that, and all the tiny intricacies within, all swirling and swirling and swirling, shifting and never changing but constantly changing, trying to keep hold of that so you could focus, so you could try and hear yourself think just a little bit, although of course you didn't really want to think all that much because thinking was dangerous . . .

Again, tricky. And then finding the moment you wanted . . . sifting through billions of years, and the billions and trillions of months, hours, minutes, seconds and milliseconds and so on and so forth *ad infinitum* of which those years were composed . . .

Grasping it with all your hands, physical and mental . . .
Thinking yourself *in* . . .

I opened my eyes and I was sitting in the clearing. It was warm and smelled of recent rain. There was nobody here and I looked around anxiously.

What if I—

Ah!

There she was, walking towards me with her bag across her shoulders. I hadn't seen her in so long. It made her look that much shinier.

'Hi,' I smiled.

She wasn't smiling. She just looked reproachfully at me.

My own smile fell. 'What's wrong?'

Still, she just looked at me. 'Same time, next day?' I attempted, with that goofy trying-too-hard grin I knew I should never do, but which I often seemed to do.

Senia shook her head. 'No,' she said. 'You missed a day.' And then she smiled and her face glowed and my brain breathed a sigh of relief.

'Just the one?'

'Just the one. But I was worried.'

'Damn,' I said. 'Sorry. I'll try harder next time.'

'You'd better. How long has it been for you?'

'A . . . bit longer,' I said. 'Really sorry about last time. I'd had a pretty long day. Cheers for shooting Freeman, that was much appreciated.'

'It's all right. Did you bring my arrow back?'

'Shit. Sorry. I'll get it next time.'

She laughed and passed me a bottle of water. I couldn't stop looking at her as I drank, and I wondered if it was making her uncomfortable, because she was blushing. But she was also smiling. *Oh gawd.*

I'd forgotten how all this stuff worked.

'Sorry,' I said, clumsily, which probably made things even weirder.

'For what?' She didn't flutter her eyelashes, but the way she looked at me had pretty much the same effect and now I was going red.

Oh God, this is ludicrous.

I am a superpowered individual. I cured death. I could be a deity if I tried hard enough!

Yeah, said my talking-to-morons voice. *But she's a girl.*

'Fancy a fly?' I said, pointing at the sky. I imagined grabbing her hand and taking off, flying her across this new world, showing it to her from a whole new angle and—

'I think I'd rather have a walk.' Senia smiled.

'Oh,' I said, surprised but not disappointed. 'OK, then. Yeah. *Pfft.*' I waved my hand dismissively, as if flying was the lamest of the lame things. 'Walking's good. Walking's *great.* I can fly any time.'

So we walked off together and I didn't take her hand, but I felt as though if I had, it would have been all right.

THE END

Acknowledgements

I T'S HARD TO believe we're at this point. Book three. The final chapter. It sort of feels like a straight time cut from first hearing news of the publishing deal to suddenly composing the acknowledgements for the last book. As though there was no time in between.

But there was time in between. And time before. Lots of it. And throughout all that time, there have been people, essential people, without whom I might still be composing these acknowledgements, except as a futile mental exercise in self-torture, lying awake in the middle of the night, miserably chewing on my total lack of a publishing deal.

To my agent Ben Illis, as per the dedication, thanks for the faith. Thanks for taking a chance on me, and for sticking with me, even when literally every single person on the face of planet Earth had passed on the first book (including me). Thanks for taking my work seriously, but also not taking me as seriously as I (sometimes) take myself. Just thanks, y'know.

To Chris and Jen, thanks for publishing the books. Thanks for the collaboration, the support, the ideas. Thanks for the home.

To my fellow Team BIA-ers. Thanks for the encouragement, the tips, the nonsense. Thanks for making an often lonely pursuit feel much less lonely.

To the friends and friends of friends and family members and friends of family members who bought the first two books for themselves, bought them for other people, shared the synopsis over coffee, reviewed them online, and – perhaps most importantly – told me (convincingly) that I hadn't totally wasted my time and should carry on. Thanks especially to those who generally don't get on with all this superhero nonsense.

To Mum and Dad, as always, for everything.

To Cath, for enthusiastically taking that picture when it felt like I was days away from literary superstardom, and then being just as enthusiastic when it took like five more years. Also for everything.

To the readers, for reading.

This book has been typeset by
SALT PUBLISHING LIMITED
using Neacademia, a font designed by Sergei Egorov
for the Rosetta Type Foundry in the Czech Republic.
It is manufactured using Creamy 70gsm, a Forest
Stewardship Council™ certified paper from Stora Enso's
Anjala Mill in Finland. It was printed and bound by
Clays Limited in Bungay, Suffolk, Great Britain.

LONDON
GREAT BRITAIN
MMXVII